Aetheric InFusion

Magical Fusion
Book 3

Jonathan Brooks

Cover Design: Yvonne Less, Art 4 Artists
Edited by: Ellen Klowden

Copyright ©2024 Jonathan Brooks

All rights reserved. No part of this publication may be reproduced, distributed, or transmitted in any form or by any means, including photocopying, recording, or other electronic or mechanical methods, without the prior written permission of the publisher.

The following is a work of fiction. Any names, characters, businesses, corporations, places, and events are products of the author's imagination or used in a fictitious manner. Any resemblance to any actual persons, places, or events is purely coincidental.

Cover Design Copyright ©2024 Yvonne Less, Art 4 Artists

Acknowledgements

I would like to thank all my Patrons on Patreon who are supporting me through my writing endeavors, while also giving me valuable feedback on my works-in-progress!

In addition, I want to thank all my beta-readers for their feedback!

Aaron Wiley
Brett Siegel
Grant Harrell
James Boyles
Kelly Linzey
Nicole Widrig
Zack Devney

Table of Contents

Acknowledgements..3
Recap...6
Chapter 1..9
Chapter 2..17
Chapter 3..24
Chapter 4..32
Chapter 5..39
Chapter 6..47
Chapter 7..54
Chapter 8..61
Chapter 9..68
Chapter 10..77
Chapter 11..84
Chapter 12..91
Chapter 13..100
Chapter 14..107
Chapter 15..114
Chapter 16..122
Chapter 17..129
Chapter 18..135
Chapter 19..142
Chapter 20..150
Chapter 21..156
Chapter 22..163
Chapter 23..171
Chapter 24..180
Chapter 25..189
Chapter 26..197
Chapter 27..203
Chapter 28..210
Chapter 29..217
Chapter 30..225
Chapter 31..232
Chapter 32..239
Chapter 33..248
Chapter 34..255
Chapter 35..264
Chapter 36..272
Chapter 37..279
Chapter 38..287

Chapter 39	294
Chapter 40	301
Chapter 41	307
Chapter 42	313
Chapter 43	320
Chapter 44	327
Chapter 45	333
Chapter 46	340
Chapter 47	347
Chapter 48	354
Chapter 49	360
Chapter 50	367
Chapter 51	375
Epilogue	382
Final Stats	388
Author's Note	392
Books by Jonathan Brooks	394

Recap

Larek Holsten had his entire world turned upside-down when he was accused of trying to kill the Headman's daughter, but that was only the start of his new life. After witnessing a Scission attack on a nearby town, the former Logger was discovered to have the potential to wield a magic he never wanted; as a result of this discovery, he was ordered to attend Crystalview Academy upon the threat of death if he didn't comply.

Along his journey to the Academy, the sheltered teenager learned more about the world than he ever knew existed – though not all of it was good. The prejudice that the common people held toward his height weighed upon him, even though he knew it wasn't something he could do anything about. This prejudice continued after he arrived at Crystalview, though it wasn't quite as intense as he feared; it helped that he learned a little about *why* everyone born in the Kingdom reacted to him the way they did – even if it wasn't fair. Unfortunately, that was the least of his problems.

What he had to worry about instead was his own inability to cast a spell, thanks to his initial efforts that literally blew up in his face. On the other hand, he also discovered that the accidental permanence to his spell patterns was actually beneficial when it came to creating Fusions. Not only that, some strange fluke gave Larek incredibly high starting stats that far outstripped anything a normal Fusionist – even a Grandmaster – could apply toward the formation of Fusions, and his instinctual understanding of their creation put him head-and-shoulders above everyone else.

But Larek also had a secret that he didn't dare to share with anyone. In a world where those with magical potential only became Mages or Martials, who were those with ability to manipulate Stama internally, the former Logger had the ability to become *both*. This came to a head when the Academy was attacked from inside the city and Larek was forced to unlock a Martial Battle Art in the heat of the fight, though he had no control over the process.

Unfortunately, after the battle against the Scissions, his *Fusions* Professor was found to have been killed, and Larek was jointly blamed for the explosion of hundreds of *Healing Surge* Fusions on the roof of the Academy along with the now-deceased Professor, as well as the temporary comas that many of the Mages suffered as a result of using these healing Fusions that Larek created. As a punishment, the Dean of Crystalview decided to send him away to Copperleaf Academy far to the south, along with his friends and a group of first-years that were left without a place to stay as a result of the explosion.

Escorted south by a caravan run by Merchants, Larek and the other transfer students were attacked by Bog Goblins, which eventually led to the Fusionist revealing some of his abilities and even his Status to multiple people – his friends included. After finally hitching a ride on the SIC Transportation Network, which was comprised of giant carriages pulled by equally large Canniks, Larek was able to experiment a little more with his Fusions by creating some physical stat boosts for the Martial trainee graduates that were accompanying them on their journey.

Overall, traveling south was largely uneventful besides allowing Larek to expand his capabilities as a Fusionist, but his introduction to Copperleaf Academy certainly was not. To his good fortune, his studies included an *Advanced Fusions* class with Grandmaster Fusionist Shinpai, who agreed to teach him after learning about Larek's obscenely high Pattern Cohesion and Mana regeneration rates, as well as his ability to make extremely strong and near-permanent Fusions.

Unfortunately, the ecstatic student Fusionist had caught the eye of multiple parties due to completely different reasons. First, his height was noticed by a particular Noble named Ricardo, who ended up capturing and torturing him in order to discover if something catastrophic called "The Culmination" was occurring. During that interrogation, Larek also learned that he was likely something called a half-breed, which was a half-human and half-Gergasi or half-"Great One" – the race of giants that used Dominion magic to enslave the people of the Kingdom, and were still enslaving the Nobles to that day.

Healing and then freeing himself through the use of Fusions, Larek ensured Ricardo and his two Martial trainee helpers couldn't spread the news about his origins and also protected his family from harm by eliminating all three of them and hiding the bodies. That wasn't the only complication to his existence at Copperleaf Academy, however.

Through helping an injured Martial trainee one day, Larek accidentally revealed that he had a Fusion that could heal people – and those in charge of Fort Pinevalley wanted it. Unfortunately, sharing that kind of thing would also likely reveal his dual nature as both a Mage and a Martial, but the choice was taken out of his hands as he was essentially forced to compete in the upcoming Skirmish.

To prepare for the set of competitions that pitted teams of Mages and Martials against each other, Larek created some powerful defensive Fusions for his team to use. Penelope, the blue-haired

Martial trainee that had caused the Fort to start looking into Larek more than he cared for, was their team leader. Other members were two other Martials named Bartholomew and Vivienne, as well as a fifth-year Mage student, Kimble. Nedira joined the team that was expected to fail spectacularly because they barely had any time to practice together, but they managed to pull off wins through the competition because of Larek's powerful contributions.

After his team was accused of cheating with Larek's Fusions, it was revealed by Dean Lorraine to the entirety of the Academy and Fort that Larek was a Fusion prodigy, a person who was able to create Fusions better than anyone else in the world. While that was certainly the opposite of what Larek wanted known about him, it was done because of something a lot more important than what he wanted.

After all, Dean Lorraine and Grandmaster Fusionist Shinpai knew about his status as a half-breed, and desired for him to take down the Gergasi by closing the breach they had created that led into another plane of existence, letting magic leak into the world.

The former Logger wanted absolutely no part in this, of course, because he didn't want to get anywhere near the Gergasi or this apparent breach in the world. But would his wishes even count for anything when the Dean of Copperleaf Academy and his *Fusions* Professor desired more of him? There was only one way to find out….

Chapter 1

"No. I've already told you this before, Larek; you can't just go out by yourself anymore."

Larek Holsten wanted to ignore what the blue-haired young woman was telling him, but when he saw Nedira nodding in agreement, he sighed and put his head in his hands. The loud conversations going on around the Dining Hall washed over him, which only seemed to reinforce the headache that seemed to be growing behind his eyes.

"I *know* that, Penelope; but I'm just going to the bathrooms to get washed up," he responded irritably. "It feels like I haven't bathed in weeks." That was far from the truth, of course, as he had bathed yesterday, but with all the attention being paid to him, he couldn't help but feel, well, *dirty* by the end of the day.

"That doesn't matter," the stubborn Striker responded, taking her bodyguarding duties seriously. "It's the perfect place for an ambush, as you'll be unprepared for an attack."

He shook his head wearily, tired of this whole thing already, despite it only being a few weeks since the Skirmish, where he had assisted in his team's victory even though he was only a first-year student at Copperleaf Academy. While he had helped pull out the win at the end, he still didn't feel like all the attention that had been paid to him by nearly the entire Academy – as well as those from Fort Pinevalley – was justified.

Granted, it wasn't *that* he had helped them win the Skirmish that garnered all the attention; it was *how* he had helped them do it that was the problem: Fusions. The Fusions he had created, most notably the *Repelling Barrier* that deflected most physical attacks away using powerful gusts of air, were so far above and beyond the strength and complexity of anything that had been seen before that they captured the attention of both the faculty and the student body. If that had been all, that would still have been enough to raise the curiosity of those who were interested in Fusions – but then Dean Lorraine had to go and announce, during the award ceremony, that he was some sort of "prodigy" in Fusions. As a consequence, Larek had become the most important person in the Academy for right now – or at least that was what it felt like.

While some people might be excited to be in the spotlight and have everyone want to talk to or get to know them, the former Logger didn't like it at all. Especially when such notoriety brought with it the need for people to watch his back, as the danger of his celebrity status included those who wanted something from him... or wanted to see him dead for a number of reasons.

"Look, I know you're just doing what the Dean asked of you, but it's just a bath," Larek pleaded. "I just can't relax or feel comfortable when Bartholomew is in the room watching me bathe – it's creepy, to say the least." He looked at the young Martial trainee who normally accompanied him into the bathing rooms. "No offense, Bartholomew," he added.

"No offense taken," the Shieldguard quickly responded. "However, I can't say I understand why it bothers you so much; I grew up with servants bathing and dressing me until I came here, and I soon forgot that they were even there most of the time." For a moment, Larek had forgotten that the young Martial was a Noble – a Duke's son, if he remembered correctly.

"Yes, well, I wasn't born into the same sort of situation that you were, so having someone *watching* me feels wrong somehow. It would be different if you were also bathing, as that is what the room is for, but that's not the case."

Naturally, when Bartholomew accompanied him to the baths, the young Martial didn't stand nearby and *stare* at Larek when he bathed, but he was nevertheless in the room and kept an eye on him – as well as on everyone else that was in the room at the time. In fact, most of the time the Shieldguard wasn't actually watching him but was instead focused on the dangers that might suddenly appear, but that distinction didn't really help Larek become comfortable with the situation.

There was a silent communication that was passed between Penelope and Bartholomew that he was unable to translate; fortunately, he didn't have to, as it wasn't long before they came to a decision. The athletically fit, blue-haired woman slumped in place, dramatically sighing as she looked at Larek. "Fine. As there haven't been any attacks, Barty here can wait *outside* of the bathrooms, but he's going to check on you every few minutes to make sure you're safe."

That wasn't exactly what Larek wanted, but he supposed it was the best he was going to get for the moment. "Thank you. I appreciate all you've done to protect me, but sometimes I just need some privacy."

"I know, I know; I just don't want anything to happen to you, and I know that Nedira feels the same way. If they allowed women in there, I'd have your girlfriend join you in the bath to protect you," she added with a suggestive wiggle of her eyebrows and more than a hint of a smirk on her lips, "but alas, even with the protection detail you've been given, there are some rules that we can't break."

Larek blushed a little as he glanced at Nedira, whose face was practically on fire from what Penelope had said, but she also didn't say anything to refute Penelope's suggestion that the Naturalist join him in his bath. The Logger-turned-Fusionist now knew that Nedira was interested in him on a level that was more than just as friends, given the confrontation in the healer's ward a few weeks before. He was relatively ignorant when it came to those types of things, but even he wasn't dense enough to miss how she had accused the Martial trainee of having romantic designs on Larek – and how that had bothered her because it was in direct competition with her own feelings.

Unfortunately, his life had been turned upside down once again after the Skirmish, giving neither of them the chance to really discuss their feelings for each other. It was probably for the best, at least coming from Larek's point of view, because he wasn't even sure if he felt the same way. Sure, he cared for her as a friend, and possibly as more than a friend, but the unfamiliar feelings he experienced when he thought about her or even simply glanced in her direction were difficult to evaluate. Even if he did decide that he felt the same way as she seemed to feel toward him, there was one major problem to the whole situation that he wasn't sure how to resolve.

His Dominion magic.

Supposedly, at least according to the Dean and Shinpai, he had inadvertently used a small amount of Dominion magic – thanks to his father's heritage as a Gergasi – on his Skirmish team, including Penelope and Bartholomew, which subtly influenced them to want to protect him... even at the cost of their lives. He had no idea that he had even done it, nor could he replicate the process upon someone else, and he had no idea how to remove it; the magic wasn't something that he could control – and that was what worried him the most.

It was bad enough that his inadvertent use of Dominion magic may have ended up convincing his roommate, Verne, and Nedira's brother, Norde, to like him; but what if it had also made Nedira care for him as something that was more than friends? Or perhaps even convinced her that she was in love with him? He wasn't sure if it was true or not, but he *was* sure that he didn't want to take advantage of their potentially influenced feelings more than he already had. There was nothing he could do to change the past, and it seemed like they all genuinely cared for him; but to use Nedira's feelings to press for something more felt like a violation of her freedom.

Based on what he knew about his father's people and their propensity for enslaving those of the Kingdom, he knew he didn't want to be anything like them; using his Dominion magic to convince Nedira to love him felt a little too close to the same kind of thing for comfort. Until he found a way to control or negate what little Dominion magic he possessed, he could never be sure that what she felt was real. Therefore, the incredibly crazy schedule after the Skirmish was actually a blessing in disguise, as it prevented him from having a conversation with Nedira about their relationship and what the future might hold.

Larek chose not to respond to Penelope's comment as they left the Dining Hall for his room, with Bartholomew leading the way, Nedira coming next, followed by Larek, and then Penelope bringing up the rear. Verne and Norde had eaten earlier and were already in the shared room when he arrived, as Larek's schedule had been a bit abnormal as of late.

"There you are!" the tree-looking boy shouted as soon as Larek walked through the door after Bartholomew led the way, the former Logger on a mission to drop a few things off before he headed to the baths. "Did they keep you working late again?"

The Fusionist nodded, sighing heavily. "Yes. Just like they have the last few weeks," he said. It was sadly true, because it was now almost 9pm, a few hours after he would normally eat dinner after his last class. "It's... *rewarding* work, but it doesn't leave much room for anything else." He'd even spent most of his days off working with the Dean and Shinpai, so he didn't have much chance to do anything but that work and attending classes.

"They can't keep working you to the bone like this, Larek," Nedira said, trailing her fingers across his arm as she passed, before plopping herself down on the edge of his bed. He felt a tingle pass through his body at her touch, but forcefully ignored it; now that he knew those types of touches indicated an intention that was anything but innocent, he was having trouble seeing them any other way. As much as it might disappoint her if he didn't respond to such things, he was convinced it was for the best that he didn't let anything go further.

"As you know, there's a good reason for it," he said softly, taking a few things out of his robe's pockets and placing them on his desk. The flat pieces of thin, rectangular steel clinked together as he set them down, followed by a pair of wooden circles and a scrap of leather. He had taken to carrying them around with him wherever he went in case inspiration hit him, so that he wouldn't have to wait long before making another Fusion. It had actually been Shinpai's suggestion, and it was a good one; already, he had created a few Fusions using these materials in the Dining Hall or even in a different class, though the latter was frowned upon – prodigy or not.

"Of course, I know that! But it won't help if you work so hard that you can't think straight."

He had to agree, but the reason he had been working so hard was to get some of the unwelcome scrutiny off of him. The Dean and Shinpai had concocted a plan to expose what he could do with Fusions during the Skirmish, all in the effort to cover up the fact that his *Healing Surge* Fusion was based upon the *Minor Mending* spell he knew, combined with the effects from his *Body Regeneration* Martial Skill. The reason this was a problem was because if anyone learned that he had access to Martial Skills, let alone Martial stats, then that could lead to questions about his ancestry, namely the Gergasi – or as the enslaved Nobles called them, the Great Ones. At that point, it would only be a matter of time before he was discovered to be a half-breed, and as his experience with Ricardo had shown him, the Nobles weren't afraid of hurting Larek as some sort of retaliatory measure against those they were forced to serve.

Therefore, because he had to hide the fact that *Healing Surge* integrated the Martial Skill, his first task after the Skirmish was to develop another healing Fusion that wasn't as dangerous – for himself as far as exposure went, as well as for those who used it to heal themselves. He didn't want anyone else to fall into a coma after its use, after all, even if it healed them in the process.

Unfortunately, he wasn't having as much luck as he had hoped he would, but he thought he was on the right track. In fact, he was planning on trying something the next day that *might* work, but he'd already exhausted himself too much that day to start on it right then and there.

"True, but if I can put together all that I've learned tomorrow, I think I can start relaxing a little more," he assured her.

"You've figured it out?"

He shrugged, as he wasn't entirely sure; he was fairly confident it would work, but he'd already had a few failures that hadn't been the solution he had been looking for. "Maybe? I won't know until I create it tomorrow; for now, I just want a bath."

"Fair enough. I'll see you tomorrow, then," Nedira said, hopping off the bed. As she passed by him, she trailed her fingers down his back and he froze in what he was doing; the next thing he knew, she was out the door.

"She's growing bold, that one," Penelope chuckled. "I'm glad we got over our little spat, because I don't fancy my chances against someone like her."

"What do you mean by that?" Larek asked, slightly perplexed.

"Just that she's a bit possessive, if you know what I mean?"

He didn't, but he decided to let it go; it was probably better than he didn't know, he figured.

"Hey! That's my sister that you're talking about!" Norde shouted angrily, his fists up and in front of him like he wanted to punch the blue-haired woman. They hadn't exactly gotten along all that well ever since Nedira was hurt during the Skirmish, and he blamed the Martial trainee for all that had happened.

Penelope chuckled at the young Academy student's outburst. "Well, then you'd know better than I would. Tell me, is she one to—"

"Alright, enough of this," Larek said, cutting her off. He'd rather stop a confrontation before it started, and Penelope seemed to enjoy needling Nedira's little brother. "Bartholomew, are you ready?"

"Absolutely."

"Then let's go." Turning to the blue-haired Martial, he said, "I'll see you tomorrow, Penelope. Have a good night."

"Good night, Larek," she responded, before looking at Bartholomew. "You take care of him, you hear?"

"Of course."

A minute or so later, Larek was in the boys' bathroom, which was thankfully completely empty – a sight that gave his bodyguard an obvious sense of relief as he looked around and let out a grunt. "I'll be outside," he said, before leaving out the door they had entered a moment before.

I'm alone... finally.

Larek hadn't realized how much he treasured the solitude of the Rushwood Forest until he'd been forced to attend first Crystalview and now Copperleaf; it had been a bit of an adjustment, of course, but he thought that he had managed it fairly well. Yet even when attending both Academies, there had been plenty of time that he had been able to just be alone for a while – but that hadn't been possible over the last few weeks. He couldn't remember a single minute when there hadn't been someone around him, and it was slowly becoming more than he could handle.

As he filled up the bath and stripped down, he unstrapped his axe from where it had been positioned along his right leg. The super-sharp edge was secured by a steel cap. While it was not entirely immune to the sharpness of the blade, he had placed a *Strengthen Steel +5* Fusion on it to prevent it from being sliced apart; so, it was more than enough to protect him from accidentally cutting himself. As he placed it on the floor, he looked around again at the empty bathing room and made a decision: Taking off the wooden armlets and anklets that adorned his upper arms and both legs, he slipped them over the handle of the axe and balanced the tool against the edge of the tub, in easy reach.

Gratefully lowering himself into the hot water of the bathing tub, he sighed in relief as he scrubbed himself all over, making sure to get to the areas that were the hardest to clean – which were where his accessories normally covered his skin. He was done within minutes, and he was just finishing up when Bartholomew stuck his head in the door, nodded to Larek as he checked around the room, and then closed it immediately afterward.

When he was clean, he scrunched himself in the tub so that he could sort of lay down, with his knees sticking out of the water and his head lying on the edge. As he closed his eyes and relaxed for what felt like the first time since before he had been abducted by Ricardo and his accomplices, he thought all about his current situation.

While he didn't exactly agree with the plan that Dean Lorraine and Shinpai had concocted concerning sharing his abilities with the Academy and the Fort, he had to admit that being out in the open – with most of his secrets – had been advantageous. The Dean and Professors could be a lot more open in their help when it came to giving him the necessary information to advance his Fusion-making processes, and though he had only learned a few specific spells and techniques based around healing to help with his current project, it was much more than any assistance he'd been given before.

Being able to freely create Fusions and not have to hide it was also beneficial, as he could technically do it right out in the middle of the yard without any repercussions – other than gaining the attention of anyone who could see or sense him working with such large amounts of Mana. It was at those points where he was actually glad of his bodyguards, as they helped to keep people away from him while he worked, because disturbing him during the Fusion process could be dangerous to Larek and any bystanders.

He'd also been accosted by *hundreds* of students, many of them Nobles, who had promised him great numbers of coins if he would make them a powerful Fusion or two, but he'd been forced to tell them to contact the Dean or Shinpai if they needed something specific. Although Larek was inclined to simply make Fusions for everyone who came up to him, as he enjoyed creating them and the challenge of doing something new, the head of the Academy and his Advanced Fusions Professor were prioritizing which ones he could make while also giving him enough time to devote to his healing Fusion project. Every day after classes – and during his Fusions class – he was given a list of Fusions to create, typically no more than 5 or 6 for the entire day.

Unfortunately, they were all ones that he'd made before, with most of them being stat boosts of one kind or another, so they weren't much of a challenge. The rest of the time, he was experimenting with different healing Fusion ideas or learning more about them, which was why he was working late every night.

It wasn't so bad, especially if his idea worked the way he thought it would the next day. Once he developed a viable healing Fusion, he could begin to experiment with other things a little more, including—

His thoughts were interrupted when he heard a noise, but he figured it was just Bartholomew just checking up on him again. Keeping his eyes closed and not looking at his bodyguard, the illusion of being alone was maintained, and he began to go back to his relaxed musings. He didn't get very far before he realized that something was different about the bathing room environment; it was a subtle shift in the air that brought with it the scent of charred wood that caught his attention, which didn't make any sense because there shouldn't have been any burning wood inside of the Academy.

Before he could open his eyes to look around, a gloved hand slapped itself against his mouth, startling him, before he felt a sharp pinch on the side of his neck. His eyes flew open immediately upon feeling the neck pinch, but he couldn't see anything as his head was held backwards so that all he was looking at was the ceiling. He attempted to raise his hands to remove the hand covering his mouth so that he could break free, but after only a quick twitch that showed that he was at least trying, they wouldn't move.

Panicking, his attention was stolen away again as something flashed in front of his eyes, and another gloved hand appeared holding a knife that reflected some of the magical light within the bathroom. As he saw it move out of sight, all he could think about was Penelope looking disappointedly at him, shaking her finger while saying, "I told you so."

I can't believe she was right.

Chapter 2

Larek struggled to move, panic flowing through him as he expected the knife to either stab him in the chest or cut his throat in the next few seconds. He managed to vaguely feel his arms rising slightly out of the water of the bath where they had fallen, but he instantly knew it wasn't going to be enough. His body felt numb and unresponsive, as any sensations were muted and nearly imperceptible. Larek was as helpless as a newborn due to whatever had been pressed against his neck, and he didn't even know who it was that was about to kill him. *Then again, I suppose it doesn't matter because I'll be dead.*

Suddenly, his view of the ceiling was blocked as the shape of a figure looked down at him; he was shocked as he immediately recognized their familiar face. It was hard not to, given that he saw it every day.

It was Vivienne, the Martial trainee and Ranger who had been a part of Team Fusion in the Skirmish and had become a member of Larek's protection detail. She was also supposedly Penelope's lover, though he hadn't dug too far into that, preferring to keep his distance from their private lives.

Has she been planning this the entire time? Why go through with all this—?

"Phew, that's some tough skin, Larek," she said with a creepy smile as she looked down at him. It was only at that point that he realized that the trainee had released his mouth, though he was still finding it impossible to move. "I thought for a moment that my needle wouldn't be able to penetrate your neck, but fortunately I planned ahead and used the heavy duty one because I've seen how durable you are. Hopefully any other assassins in the future won't have that kind of foresight."

What? What is she talking about? What's going on?

He tried to speak in order to ask those questions out loud, but even his vocal cords seemed to be paralyzed, and all that came out was a wheezing groan.

"Oh, sorry about that," she responded to his groan. "The Deepfang Venom is quite potent, but it also doesn't last too long. Some say that it just means that the Deepfangs are weaker monsters because of that, but I think it's because the massive snakes that utilize this venom prefer to feel their prey squirming around after they're ingested." Horror spread through his paralyzed body at her words.

"Fortunately, it only lasts about a minute and there are no long-term side-effects, so you should be able to move—"

As if a huge weight had been lifted off of him, Larek suddenly felt his strength come back. Without hesitation, he whipped his hands up to grab onto the Ranger, intending to prevent her from following through with whatever she had planned, but his hands met empty air as she moved away.

"Whoa! Not only do you have thick skin, but you were able to shrug off the Venom far faster than expected," she said, standing up and stepping out of reach of even his long arms. "However, you're going to need to camouflage your recovery if something like this happens again, because your body practically shouted that you were about to move."

Rage threatened to flood his mind as his victim escaped his clutches, but reason suddenly eclipsed his violent urge to kill the young woman who had nearly killed him. *Or had she?* With her making no move to attack him, and in fact visibly sliding her knife back into a sheath strapped to her arm, she didn't seem like she was intending to follow through on her plans. Even as he shot to his feet inside of the bathtub, sloshing huge waves of water onto the floor, he hesitated as confusion wracked his mind. The only thing he consciously did was wrap his hand around the lower haft of his axe, but he wasn't even sure what he was going to do with it.

Frozen in indecision, he heard the door to the bathing room swing open, before he heard Bartholomew's voice. "Vivienne? What are you doing here?"

Testing out his voice, Larek hoarsely shouted, "She's trying to kill me!"

For some reason, this caused both of them to laugh. "Kill you?" the would-be assassin asked with a chuckle. "Far from it, Larek; I'm here to protect you, after all."

"But you paralyzed me and threatened to cut my throat!" He didn't actually know that his throat was going to be cut, but it made sense with how his head was held back.

"Is that true, Viv?" the other Martial trainee asked, suspicious.

The Ranger *hmphed*, as if she was annoyed at being found out... or was annoyed at someone who just didn't seem to be understanding something she was trying to convey. "Yes and no. I did paralyze you with the Deepfang Venom, as well as flash my knife, but it was only to show you that even when you think you're completely safe, tragedy can strike when you least expect it." She looked past Larek at Bartholomew. "It's also a lesson for you; did you even check to see if anyone was hiding *inside* the bathing tubs? I have to say, it was quite easy to sneak in here and lie in wait for you to arrive, especially considering that it would be simple enough to identify Larek's schedule and plan accordingly. Just like on the walls of a town or city, you have to be looking for a threat to arrive at *any* point; you can't always rely on a glance to tell you that there is no danger – especially with how the Scissions are starting to act up out there now."

Larek understood the last part she mentioned, as rumors of Scissions appearing scattered around the countryside had even penetrated his relatively secluded schedule lately. While there were still a few reports of Scissions appearing relatively close to inhabited areas, most of them were apparently opening up in the middle of nowhere as they released their monsters. These monsters would eventually turn up to attack a town or city suddenly, though with how scattered their numbers were, they weren't typically as much of a threat as a full-scale Scission right outside the walls; the danger came when the SIC members there to protect them weren't prepared for such an attack, especially if it came in the dead of night, as they didn't have the feeling of a Scission opening to warn them. He hadn't heard specifics about how many towns and cities unfortunately realized this was happening too late, but he suspected that it was more than enough to cause the information to spread far and wide.

But everything else she said? "Wait... so you *aren't* trying to kill me?"

She shook her head in obvious exasperation. "Of course not, Larek. I did this to prove two points to you: that you're not invulnerable, and to let us do our jobs. Besides, we've already caught a couple of people trying to sneak in while you were sleeping, and even inside of Grandmaster Fusionist Shinpai's classroom while you were creating Fusions; it was only a matter of time before someone decided to try something here in the bathing room."

"...huh? Really?!" Larek hadn't heard anything about that.

Bartholomew spoke up from the entrance, where he was still hanging onto the door he had pushed open. "Yes. After they were caught, they revealed that they were just trying to speak to you personally about making a Fusion for them, but they just as easily could've been there to cause you harm."

Again, he hadn't known any of that, which made him wonder what else his "bodyguards" were keeping from him. He was actually about to ask that when the Martial trainee by the doorway cleared his throat. "Anyway, I'll leave you both to whatever you're doing, and I'll be right outside," Bartholomew said, his voice sounding a little uncomfortable. "I'll keep in mind what you said, Vivienne; let me know when you've left, and I'll come back and keep my eye on him."

Out of the corner of Larek's eye, he watched the younger Martial trainee exit the bathing room, a blush reddening his cheeks. He was perplexed at why he had a blush for a moment, but fortunately Vivienne cleared it up quite swiftly.

"You know, you may not be *my* type, Larek, but you sure are an impressive specimen," she said, a throaty chuckle escaping in the process. "Why don't you wrap all this up and get some sleep; you've had an eventful night already."

Shocked, Larek looked down, and at the same moment he realized he was naked, having simply stood up out of the bathtub without a thought about his state of undress. He quickly covered himself up, but it didn't really matter all that much since by the time he looked up, Vivienne was already near the entrance. She looked back at him and smirked. "See you tomorrow, Larek." As she exited, Bartholomew came inside no more than two seconds later, standing against the wall in his "normal" position as a bodyguard.

"I don't think I can handle all this," Larek said to the room, shaking his head. As he grabbed a towel he had left on the floor, which was half-soaked from the wave of water he had expelled when he stood up, the young Martial trainee spoke up.

"She's right, you know—as much as you don't want to hear it," he said with a soft, serious voice. "There are some out there who don't want you around or don't want you to succeed, and if one of them had been in here instead of her, they might've killed you."

Larek still had trouble understanding why someone would want to kill him – unless they knew of his real origins, of course – but he knew that his bodyguards were only trying to keep him safe. As much as he was getting tired of constantly being watched, his earlier scare when he was paralyzed and helpless had made the possibility of being killed by some sort of assassin more of a reality than he cared to admit.

For now, he needed their help to ensure his safety, but there was no way he could live like this for multiple months or years, let alone for the rest of his life. There had to be something he could do to protect himself; the Fusions he'd been able to make were powerful, of course, but taking them off at any point made him vulnerable. Then there were some, such as his *Repelling Barrier*, which were powerful but had flaws and were cumbersome to keep active indefinitely. For instance, the slow movement of Vivienne's hand holding a needle filled with Deepfang Venom approaching his neck wouldn't have triggered the Fusion, even if he had been wearing it – which he hadn't, as it was dangerous to use outside of the arena. There was just too much risk of someone accidentally bumping into him and being smashed into the ground with bone-crushing force in response to keep it active all the time.

As he dried off, contemplating Bartholomew's words, he couldn't help but look down at his body again, thinking of ways to protect it. *I wonder if there is another Fusion I could make that would work better than **Repelling Barrier**? But then there's the problem of if I have to take it off, such as in a bath; can it be something that can be shoved under my skin, where it would always be touching me? Or... can I add Fusions to my **skin**?*

He hadn't heard of that being possible for any other Fusionist, mainly because skin was a poor material because it was too soft and flexible to maintain the formation of a Fusion for long. But he had already contemplated using leather for a medium, given that his style of creating Fusions produced a much stronger formation than normal, and leather was like the skin of an animal, right? If he could get one to work, then why not the other?

He wasn't going to experiment on his own skin – or anyone else's – anytime soon, though leather and perhaps even cloth were certainly worth considering. Before he could even think of anything like that, however, he needed to finish his current project with the healing Fusion first.

Dressing quickly and re-equipping his powerful Fusion accessories, he felt almost back to normal. He nodded at Bartholomew as his bodyguard led him out of the bathing room and escorted him to his room. After arriving to see that Verne and Norde were starting to nod off as they studied a few books, Larek thought that was probably a good idea as well. Taking one of his books on Advanced Fusions, he flipped through it for what seemed like the hundredth time, hoping that it would all suddenly make sense. Unfortunately, no matter how many times he read through it, the usual instinctive connection with the knowledge he gained from the books he read on Advanced Fusions just wasn't there. Basic and Intermediate Fusions, when he learned about them from books or from being taught about them directly by Shinpai, seemed to come naturally to him; they were just so simple, even the more complicated ones, that they required very little effort to understand and incorporate into his abilities with Fusions.

But Advanced Fusions were different. It was almost as if there was some sort of transparent veil covering the knowledge he gained. It was seated firmly in his mind to the point where it felt like a part of him, so that wasn't the problem. The issue came about when he tried to access it in relation to creating Fusions; in other words, he could *see* it, but he couldn't *touch* it. It was frustrating to the extreme, but he was trying to be patient because his *Advanced Fusions* Professor told him that he was simply at a threshold in his Skills that he needed to break through in order to handle these types of Fusions. Even with his high Mage stats, he couldn't do what he felt he *should* be able to do, which was highly annoying, to say the least.

Intellect: 70 [133]
Acuity: 104 [198]
Pneuma: 299 [568]
Pattern Cohesion: 5,680/5,680

Mage Skills:
Multi-effect Fusion Focus Level 10
Pattern Recognition Level 18
Magical Detection Level 18
Spellcasting Focus Level 20
Mana Control Level 30
Fusion Level 30
Pattern Formation Level 30

Even after gaining another Skill Level in *Pattern Recognition* and *Magical Detection* over the last few weeks, bringing them both to 18, Larek was no closer to understanding Advanced Fusions than he was when he first started learning about them. Of course, the Skills that really affected his ability to comprehend what he had learned were his *Fusion*, his *Pattern Formation*, and his *Mana Control* – all of which were stuck at Level 30, with no sign of budging. If he was able to break through those thresholds, Grandmaster Fusionist Shinpai indicated that he would finally be able to create Advanced Fusions, but thus far he hadn't been able to discover a way to do that. Most of his advances in Skill Levels had come either through repetition or from gaining some new understanding of the Skill, but neither of those methods seemed to affect these Skills at the threshold.

I'll get there eventually. It'll just take some time, that's all.

Still a little shaken from his near-death experience in the bathing room earlier, he couldn't focus on the book in his lap, so he put it away after a few minutes. As he thought about the next day and his attempt to assemble all he had learned about healing lately into a Fusion, he thought about the paralyzing venom that had completely numbed and immobilized his body, leaving him vulnerable to the knife that his assailant wielded – and he had an epiphany.

Settling down to sleep a little later after spending some time reworking his original plan for the morrow, he couldn't keep the smile off his face as he realized that his chances of success had suddenly increased tenfold.

Chapter 3

Larek impatiently suffered through his morning classes as he waited for the opportunity to experiment later in the day. He spent his limited time in his *Advanced Fusions* class creating stat-boosting Fusions on a pair of staves, all of them +8 in Magnitude for Intellect, Acuity, and Pneuma, as well as a heavy steel shield with +6 stat boosts for Strength, Body, and Acuity. Theoretically, he could create them easily enough to make Fusions with higher Magnitudes, but there was both a limit to the time he had to create them and a limit to the area of ambience that he had to work with. With a staff, it was much easier to spread out the stat boosts along its length; for the steel shield, it was difficult to fit more than the +6 boosts on it without them interfering with each other, even if he doubled up the boosts in a single Fusion. Unfortunately, until he was able to make Advanced Fusions that would allow him to incorporate 3 or more Effects at once, he would not be able to include them all into a single Fusion.

Of course, that didn't mean he hadn't at least tried to get it to work, but unfortunately his Fusions seemed to fall apart when he tried to place 3 different Effects into them. From his studies, he knew it had to do with an Advanced Fusion technique that incorporated his *Multi-effect Fusion Focus* Skill; sadly, with it stuck at Level 10 no matter what he did to try and improve it, accomplishing such a technique was seemingly impossible. While he had accomplished what many people thought impossible in the past, these limitations on his ability didn't seem like something he could brute force his way through without the minimum Skills.

Larek didn't even know who the Fusions he was creating were for, as that was all handled by Grandmaster Fusionist Shinpai and Dean Lorraine, but he honestly didn't care all that much. He figured that they were going to those who needed them the most, as he overheard at one point that at least some of them were going to the SIC members on the walls of the city. He wasn't naïve enough to assume that none of them were being handed out as favors to people in the Academy or Fort, but as long as someone found his Fusions helpful, that didn't bother him.

What came as a surprise to him was the demand for Repelling Barriers, or more accurately, the lack of it. After garnering so much attention during the Skirmish, he had expected to be creating bunches of *Repelling Barriers* for the SIC defenders on the walls; but other than a small handful of them, he had mainly been directed toward creating stat boosts instead. It wasn't exactly groundbreaking work, but the types of boosts that he created were much better than many other Fusionists could make – other than Shinpai, perhaps – and they would also last much longer. He couldn't deny that they would most likely be helpful to those who received them, so he didn't complain.

Following his last class of the day, *The Dangers of Scissions*, of which the curriculum was undergoing some significant changes given the extreme shift in Scission behavior happening throughout the Kingdom, Larek rushed to his *Fusions* workshop to get started with his experimentation regarding a new healing Fusion. All throughout the day, he had fleshed his idea out more and more, up to the point where he was positive that it would work.

"Whoa, you're in a hurry today, aren't you?" Penelope noted, while needing to run to keep up with his long strides.

"Yes. I think I have a solution that will work, thanks to what happened last night."

"Oh? And what happened last night?" the Martial trainee asked innocently.

"I'm almost positive you already know, if you weren't the one who ordered it." He snorted, realizing that it probably *was* Penelope who orchestrated the whole false assassination attempt, even if she hadn't been there herself. She had a lot of clout with his other protectors, after all, and was also Vivienne's lover.

"I have no idea what you're talking about," she replied, though by this point, Larek could tell when she wasn't telling the truth, or at least when she was stretching it more than a bit.

He shook his head as he began to approach the doorway heading into the workshops. "Sure, sure. Anyway, as much as I hated what happened, it was beneficial."

"Ah, so you're going to be more cognizant of the danger you're constantly in?" she asked.

"No. Or, well, I guess, but that's not what I meant by it being beneficial. It was what Vivienne did to me that gave me the last piece of the puzzle I needed."

"Larek, that wasn't the objective of her actions. She was supposed to impress upon you the risks you're at from other people, even in the relative safety of the Academy."

As he reached the doorway, he opened the door and looked back at her, raising an eyebrow. "Oh, really? And how would you know what she was supposed to do, given that you have 'no idea what I'm talking about?'"

She just grunted in response as she followed him inside the hallway that led to the workshops, before slipping past him to take the lead. She took her protection assignment seriously when they were indoors, only allowing him to have a bit more freedom to lead the way while they were outside and threats could be more easily identified.

Nothing and no one accosted them, thankfully, though he received plenty of stares as he rushed by. The biggest difference was that these stares weren't based on his height or anything about his appearance; instead, they were based on the notoriety he had achieved during the Skirmish as he was proclaimed a Fusion prodigy by Copperleaf Academy's Dean. It was annoying, especially when more than a few attempted to talk to him but were rebuffed by his bodyguards. Logically, he knew it was for the best, as otherwise, he would likely be inundated by students – and faculty – who wanted to use him to create a Fusion for them. But he also recognized more than a few of them that had the semi-vacant look that likely meant they were fellow Fusionists. He doubted that they wanted to demand a Fusion from him; he figured they were more likely to be interested in talking about Fusion techniques and advice, but his bodyguards turned them away all the same.

Sometimes, he felt like he was a prisoner and his bodyguards his jailers with the way they kept him isolated, but he supposed it was for the best. Besides, he was already incredibly busy all the time, and stopping often to talk to new people would cut into his work.

When he arrived at the Fusion workshop, Larek noticed that two of the privacy alcoves were occupied by students – which was a fairly common occurrence – while the rest of the room was empty of anyone but Shinpai. On a second glance, however, he realized that there was another person there, standing nearby the Grandmaster Fusionist, though it was hard to make out who it was; whenever he looked in their direction, his eyes wanted to look away – but he was confident there was someone standing there.

He was about to mention it to Penelope, concerned it might be one of the assassins that his bodyguards had so consistently warned him about, but his words died on his lips as Dean Lorraine suddenly appeared where he was previously having trouble looking. Penelope drew her sword in one quick movement, sidestepping to move in front of Larek in a guard position, but she relaxed a moment later once she recognized the Dean.

"Excellent reflexes, Penelope. Also, good eye, Larek; I shouldn't be surprised that you noticed me *despite* my powerful *Redirection* spell, but I just can't get over how incredible it is that you can do things like that seemingly without any effort. Even Shinpai can barely see me when I do that."

"What? I *always* know when you're there, Lorraine," Shinpai said, appearing offended.

The Dean looked at him with a smirk. "Oh? Like the time I caught you creeping through the—"

"Alright, I will admit that sometimes I can be distracted and don't notice you," the *Fusions* Professor cut her off. "Anyway," he continued, ignoring her as he focused on Larek, "I'm glad to see how prompt you are, Larek. I take it by how quickly you got here that you have something you want to try?"

He nodded, moving to one of the privacy alcoves that was open, though Penelope investigated to ensure it was clear and safe before she allowed him to sit down. "I had an... experience last night that gave me an insight into what I was missing," Larek finally responded once he was settled. "Give me a few minutes while I put it all together."

"Take your time. It's better to be safe and fail than to rush ahead and potentially hurt yourself – or others – in the process," Shinpai warned. Larek nodded once again as he pulled out one of the thin, flat, steel plates from underneath his robes and placed it on his lap.

Centering himself as he looked down at where he was going to place the formation, he thought about the healing Fusion that he was going to create. The last few weeks had led up to this, and with one setback after another, he was finally confident that he had the answer he had been looking for.

Originally, the problem was that he couldn't separate the way he applied the channeled spell effect he understood from *Minor Mending* from the Martial-based *Body Regeneration* Skill, so trying to utilize *Minor Mending* in any Fusion simply reproduced the same issues in non-Martials as before. After he realized this, Shinpai and the Dean had him shadow some of the healers in the healers' ward for a day, in order to see if he could learn any additional spells that he might be able to use instead.

His time with them was very informative, even if not all of the information he gained was beneficial. First, he was successful in learning two new healing spells, both of which he gained from watching some of the students who had basic Healer Specializations. This was the most basic of healing-based Specializations, though from what he'd learned from watching all the healers at work and from his *Specializations* class, very few students of the Academy stopped there before they graduated. The reason for that was that the Healer

Specialization was one of the easiest to gain of any Mage-based Specialization, and it was only the first step in their academic journey.

After that, depending on where they focused their studies, they could unlock upgraded Specializations, including ones such as Battle Cleric, Light Soother, Holy Mender, Blood Priest, and more. From what he had learned, Bettra – the healer who had saved his face after it had been torn up by an undead bird, before being killed by a different undead in Barrowford – had been a Light Soother, who was able to utilize light-based attack spells in addition to healing.

In fact, the requirements for obtaining a Healer Specialization were so simple that Larek had unlocked it within a few hours of watching the healers work.

Congratulations!
*You have unlocked the **Healer** Specialization!*

Requirements:
***Mana Control** Skill of 15*
***Spellcasting Focus** Skill of 10*
***Magical Detection** Skill of 10*
Knowledge of these 3 different spells
    Minor Mending
    Lesser Reconstruction
    Localized Anesthesia

*The **Healer** Specialization also provides these benefits:*

5% reduction in Mana Cost for healing-based spells

Do you wish to accept this Specialization? Yes / No

At first, he immediately rejected it because he was a Fusionist, not a Healer. After talking with Shinpai, however, he learned that almost every member of the SIC gained more than one Specialization over time, which was evidenced by the stripes on the sleeves on the Academy's Professors; the more stripes, the more base Specializations they had acquired. By "base", he meant the most basic form of that Specialization, such as Pyromancer, Fusionist, Healer, Naturalist, etc. By delving deeper into a certain field, such as learning additional Fire-based spells as a Pyromancer, they could unlock more advanced Specializations such as a Fire Weaver, a Flamesurger, or Immolator – all of whom applied their knowledge differently.

After learning that it couldn't hurt him to take it, Larek now had a Fusionist *and* a Healer Specialization, even though the latter didn't really do anything for him since he couldn't cast any healing spells. There was also the potential that if he was able to unlock additional Specializations he might be able to acquire hybrid types, which reminded him of the student he had been forced to duel back at Crystalview. Barto had been an Illusionist who had incorporated Air-based effects into his illusions, making them deadly rather than harmless. While Barto apparently hadn't unlocked a hybrid class at that time, Larek had later heard that he was on track to become something called a Cloudshaper – whatever that was.

Even if Larek wasn't able to utilize the spells that went with a Specialization, including hybrids, it didn't hurt to acquire them; not only that, but some of the more "higher-tier" Specializations had bonuses to Skills, so they might actually be beneficial at some point. Knowing that, Larek thought it might be smart to learn as many spells as possible, unlocking as many Specializations as he could get his hands on... except that there was a problem with that.

As much as he tried, he was unable to learn any of the powerful healing spells he saw at work in the healers' ward. What he didn't know before, as it hadn't really come up in any of his classes, was that spells Mages could utilize were slotted into 5 different unofficial categories based on the complexity of the spell formations – identical to the ones used for Intermediate Fusions. **Simple** spell formations were the ones that were taught to almost every Mage, which included *Fireball*, *Ice Spike*, *Stone Fist*, and *Minor Mending* – which were some of the first spells that Larek had learned back at Crystalview. **Lesser** spell formations were ones that he had learned such as *Wall of Thorns*, *Wind Barrier*, and *Static Illusion*. In fact, every single spell that Larek had learned thus far were either a **Simple** or a **Lesser** spell formation, including the two new healing spells he'd learned, which were both **Lesser** in complexity.

But when he attempted to learn **Minor** or **Major** healing spells, his mind couldn't comprehend them, just as his Fusion-making abilities couldn't fully understand Advanced Fusions. There was some sort of block there that he was unable to push through, which meant that acquiring any other Specializations would have to wait. From what he understood, every other Specialization required knowledge of at least one **Minor** spell formation to unlock them; it was only the simplicity of the Healer Specialization that allowed Larek to gain it in addition to Fusionist.

After gaining the two new spells, *Lesser Restoration* and *Localized Anesthesia*, he thought he might be able to figure something out for the healing Fusion, but he was wrong.

New Spell learned!
Lesser Restoration
Base Healing: 7 per second to minor flesh wounds, bone fractures, and organ damage
Base Effective Range: On touch
Base Mana Cost (Initial): 25
Base Mana Cost (Channeling): 10 per second
Base Pattern Cohesion: 5

New Spell learned!
Localized Anesthesia
Base Effect: Blocks bodily pain in a localized area
Base Magnitude: Up to 1 square foot
Base Effective Range: On touch
Base Mana Cost (Initial): 5
Base Mana Cost (Channeling): 1 per second
Base Pattern Cohesion: 3

    The first spell, *Lesser Restoration*, was a step up in healing from *Minor Mending*, as it even worked to fix bone fractures and damage to vital organs – which the weaker spell could not. The problem with the spell, at least for most Healers, was that it attempted to do too much – and the Mana Cost reflected that as it was 25 Mana to initiate the spell and then 10 more every second. For someone who only had 100 Mana, for instance, this meant that they could only heal for a few seconds before they ran out of Mana. More complex spell formations tended to specialize in different types of injuries, thereby lowering the cost, but those weren't yet something that Larek could learn.

    Localized Anesthesia, on the other hand, was similar to his *Pain Immunity* Skill, as it blocked the pain from a wound in a localized area on the body. This was, of course, helpful to ease the pain of any victims of serious injuries, but it also had a secondary effect of slowing down bleeding and helped to stabilize a wound before it could become any worse.

    From the start, *Lesser Restoration* appeared to be absolutely perfect for what he needed for a healing Fusion, but when he attempted to apply it to a formation, the result was less than spectacular. The main issue, when used on an experimental rat that had been seriously injured with broken bones and internal bleeding, was that the healing effect he imparted into the Fusion was *too* strong – as unlikely as that sounded. Even at a Magnitude of 1, the rat essentially exploded as every injury attempted to heal itself at the same time, tearing the poor creature apart.

That inevitably led to him attempting to combine it with *Localized Anesthesia* with the thought of stabilizing the wounded areas, but for some reason it had the opposite effect on yet another injured rat. This time it *imploded*, as the healing was stymied as its body was numbed and unresponsive, therefore being unable to react properly to the healing energy that was pushed into it.

Time and again, he attempted various formations with the help of Shinpai providing advice, but no matter what he did, the result was either horrendously bad or simply didn't provide much in the way of healing for some reason. Larek had briefly thought that it was the spell effects that were the problem, and that he needed a different spell in order to accomplish his healing Fusion.

But he was wrong. What he was missing wasn't a new spell; rather, what he was missing was an *understanding* of the effects the spells created, just like he instinctively understood his *Body Regeneration* Skill he tied into *Minor Mending* to create his *Healing Surge* Fusion.

Thankfully, he gained a new facet of understanding the night before when he was paralyzed by Deepfang Venom. Now it was time to put that understanding to good use.

Chapter 4

The basic structure of the formation was fairly simple, thankfully. Larek had originally thought that it might have to be complicated in order to negate the effects that had been seen in the injured rats, but once his visualization of the Effect he wanted to produce crystalized in his mind, all of the extraneous components of the Fusion didn't really matter to produce the effect he wanted.

But that didn't mean he wasn't going to add some custom elements, anyway.

First, he started with a 3 by 6 grid formation and added a Mana Cost to the bottom left and bottom right sections, with a Splitter settled in between them. Above the Mana Costs were Amplifiers, which would help to boost the amount of ambient Mana being absorbed by the Fusion, depending on certain factors. In between the Amplifiers was a Reactive Activation Method, as he didn't want this to be the same as his *Healing Surge* Fusion, where it could be activated and accidentally left on too long.

To help alleviate that possibility, above the Reactive section was a row of 3 Variables, followed by a row with 2 Variables and a single Input in the center. The Input was focused on evaluating the state of the living being that the Fusion was in physical contact with; in other words, it basically looked at how injured they were. This information was passed to the 5 Variables, which all hit different thresholds.

The first threshold was a state of relative perfect health; basically, if it didn't detect any injuries, nothing would activate. The second was for minor cuts, scrapes, or bruises; the third was for large cuts and serious bruises, as well as minor internal bleeding. The fourth was for bone fractures and minor damage to vital organs. The fifth and final threshold was for any injuries up to what could be considered fatal, including heavy internal bleeding, broken bones, greatly damaged vital organs, and even severe blood loss. What wasn't included in any of the thresholds were injuries that even the best healers in the SIC couldn't fix, which were things such as the destruction of the heart, extensive damage to the brain, or amputation. It couldn't grow back any extremities that were lost or even parts removed from their insides; if they were disemboweled, for instance, and all of their guts spilled out and were lost, the Fusion wouldn't replace them. Until he was able to grasp some more powerful healing spells, it was a limitation that he couldn't get around.

Above the Input and Variables was a row of 3 Magnitudes, as well as a single one in the center of the top row. Each of these 4 Magnitudes was different and corresponded with the different Thresholds. For the first threshold – no injuries – there was no Magnitude associated with it, as it would simply not cause the Reactive Activation Method to activate. For the subsequent thresholds, the Magnitudes were at 1, 3, 5, and 7 – in that order.

Lastly, in the top left and top right corners of the formation were the Effects. The left corner was the actual "healing" Effect based on *Lesser Restoration*, which looked like a series of wavy-looking concentric circles; it was one of the symbols used in the spell's pattern, which he assumed was supposed to represent something growing or being restored. Either way, his focus on the Effect would be the results of seeing it in action while in the ward, as the memories of seeing wounds miraculously sealed up and even minor bone breaks being mended were vivid in his mind. What he saw happened slowly, of course, because he was watching students perform the spells, and the effectiveness of the spell was rather limited in scope; when it was added to his Fusion, however, the Magnitudes would speed up the process considerably.

In the top right corner of the formation was the Effect that he was basing on *Localized Anesthesia*. He'd already tried this previously, of course, but this time there was something different when he focused on the effect he wanted to accomplish. What he had learned the night before, when he was paralyzed by Vivienne in the bathtub, was that he had been thinking about the effect of *Localized Anesthesia* all wrong. He had originally only thought about its ability to block out pain and stabilize a wound, which were naturally excellent effects to have in the Fusion; but it didn't help the main issue with the other Effect, which was that the body couldn't handle the influx of healing energy as it was infused. It responded to the energy violently, mainly because it wasn't directed by a conscious mind like it would be when used in a spell, and therefore it simply tried to do too much – causing severe reactions such as explosions and implosions in the body as a result. While he doubted it would do quite the same thing on a larger person, as it was likely concentrated in the small figure of a rat, none of them wanted to experiment with a volunteer to see what it would really do.

But with his epiphany last night following the fake assassination attempt, his comprehension of both the *Localized Anesthesia* and problems he was having with the healing energies were altered. He now understood that the issue with the healing energy wasn't that it was overloading the body; rather, it was the body's overreaction to it that was causing the problem. But how was he to correct that? Well, by essentially shutting the body down and not allowing it to overreact.

In addition to stabilizing the injury and blocking the pain in a targeted, localized area, he also focused on adding paralysis to the second Effect. It was essentially an extension of what it already did by blocking off the pain, but in this case he wanted it to essentially block *everything* off; that meant no muscle movement, no blood circulation, and no way for the body to react negatively to the energy doing its job. It sounded counterintuitive, and he had to admit that it was, but it also strangely made sense once the thought of it got into his head.

As Larek put all of these different components together into the grid formation he was creating, he locked it into place as he routed the different energy streams through the Fusion. While the Variables essentially activated different Magnitudes depending on the threshold reached, he still had to ensure that the Mana Cost routes were kept separate for each Effect, as he didn't want the same amount of Mana running through paralysis and healing effects. Though he didn't know for sure what might happen if someone was hit with a paralysis using the same amount of energy contained in the healing portion of the Fusion, he had a feeling that it might be counterproductive and potentially harmful; it might even end up killing someone as the localized area expanded enough to include all of their body, which wasn't what the Fusion was designed to do.

When it was all in place, he focused on the different components, ensuring that the Input, Variables, and Effects reflected what he wanted them to do – and then he started to funnel his Mana into the formation.

Hundreds of points of Mana quickly flowed into the two Mana Costs over the next few minutes, regulated by Larek to ensure that everything was dispersing correctly and that he didn't see any instability in the structure. In less than 10 minutes, the flow of Mana reduced to a trickle before it stopped completely.

Looking at the fully infused Fusion, he checked one more time over everything before he let it fully descend into the steel plate, letting it **click** into place without any issues.

As he sat back and looked at it, he was happy to see that he had actually learned and created a new Fusion; the other ones he had made, despite them not falling apart or anything, hadn't actually awarded him with a new Fusion to add to his repertoire. He supposed that meant that it would actually *work*, though the others technically did – even if not in the way he intended.

New Fusion Learned!
Graduated Parahealing +7
Activation Method: Reactive
Effect: Numbs and paralyzes injured areas and sends graduated waves of healing energy through nearby organisms, repairing wounds and non-fatal injuries
Magnitude(s): 10%, 30%, 50%, and 70% of full-strength healing energy
Mana Cost: 36,000
Pattern Cohesion: 600
Fusion Time: 99 hours

    Graduated Parahealing +7 was an odd name, but he supposed it made sense – especially when he described what it did to his Professor.
    "Finished already?" Shinpai asked with a gentle smile.
    Larek nodded before he got up from his comfortable spot in the privacy alcove, nodding to his bodyguard in the process. "Yes. I'm absolutely confident this will finally work. Penelope, if you wouldn't mind?"
    It was a little cruel to watch the Martial trainee reach into the cage sitting on the floor next to the Professor and punch the rat inside, breaking its back and tearing a wound in its side from the force of the punch – but he supposed it was for the best. The pests had been caught attempting to eat through some of the underground storage areas, and it was better to test these types of Fusions on them rather than a person in case something went wrong.
    The rat was screeching piteously in the cage as it couldn't move due to its injuries, but Larek blocked out the sound; if everything went the way he expected it to, the animal wouldn't be suffering for long. Sliding the steel plate through the side of the metal cage so that it ended up gliding under the horribly injured rodent, he stepped back and observed his Fusion come to life.
    Just a few seconds before, the area of ambience around the Fusion was almost nothing, as it hadn't been activated; almost as soon as it touched the rat, however, large funnels appeared above the two Mana Costs, the one hooked up to the paralyzing Effect only about a third of the size of the other. As the Mana was routed through the formation, he began to see a change in the rat's state almost immediately.
    "It's… working? Tell me, what is the Fusion doing, and how did you get it to work?" Shinpai asked.
    Larek briefly explained what he had come up with concerning the paralysis effect, but he also went into more detail on the healing

process itself. "Ideally, I would love to create something that could heal someone within seconds like my *Healing Surge* Fusion, but that was only possible thanks to its reliance on, uh, other factors," he said, not wanting to accidentally be overheard mentioning the *Body Regeneration* Skill. "Therefore, I needed a way to heal a little bit slower without overwhelming the body; the paralysis negates the negative effects of the healing energy, but infusing the entire body with too much energy for long periods of time could still be harmful.

"Which is how I came up with the graduated-healing process, utilizing multiple Variables and Magnitudes with a Reactive Input. For example, as you can see with the rat, the extreme nature of its injuries would be detected by the Input and would trigger a Magnitude 7 healing and paralysis Effect over the affected areas; it nearly looks as though it is dead, but most of its body seems to be paralyzed because of the damage Penelope did to it."

Eventually, there was a hollow *click* that came from inside of the rat as its back seemed to snap into place, and additional movement in the rodent could be seen. "Once the worst of the injuries are healed, the Input would recognize this and a different Variable would trigger, switching the Magnitude to 5, lessening the healing energy flowing through while also reducing the area that is paralyzed and numb to pain." The process was slow compared to his *Healing Surge* Fusion, which only took seconds; in comparison, it took nearly a minute for the first stage to be done, followed by another minute as even more of the internal injuries were repaired at the next threshold. "As the wounds and other damage are gradually healed, the intensity of the healing energy and paralysis is reduced. The entire process is around 4 to 5 minutes, as the slower healing is necessary so that the body isn't overwhelmed, and so that full-strength healing energy isn't forced into a tiny cut or bruise."

Shortly after the rat's back was healed, it moved around the cage slowly, incrementally picking up speed as it rushed around in a panic at what was happening to it. Less than 5 minutes later, it seemed to be fully healed and it eventually calmed down – before practically throwing itself on the small bowl of seeds and cut fruit in the cage.

"While the natural resources of the body are used during the healing process, akin to how most of the healing spells I observed work, most of the work was done by the healing energy passed through the body by the Fusion. Anyone healed by this is going to be hungry afterward, but hopefully not starving; in addition, it shouldn't have any of the coma-inducing side effects that my other Fusion creates in certain people, as it is primarily using Mana over an extended period of time instead of consuming the body from the inside."

"Amazing," Shinpai said, getting up and kneeling by the cage to look at the rat, who had gorged itself a bit with its food, but didn't even empty the bowl before it stopped. "Strong lines in the formation, too. I wish it was something that could be reproduced by other Fusionists, but there would be no way normal formations could handle the rapid influxes of Mana channeled through the Mana Costs."

That was certainly disappointing, but there wasn't really anything Larek could do about that. He'd thought about simpler healing Fusions that didn't use as much Mana and would heal much slower, but while he could make them, anyone else would end up with a Fusion that was only good for one or perhaps two uses before the pattern would break from the channeled Mana running through it.

"That is definitely unfortunate, but at least it works... or at least it should. Should we test it on some other rats?"

The Grandmaster Fusionist shook his head. "No. I think it might be ready for a volunteer; I'm sure we can find someone who would be willing to test it for us."

Larek shrugged. He was confident in his Fusion, now that he'd figured it out, so he didn't see any problems with it. He could even test it on his own body, but he didn't feel like hurting himself if he didn't have to; that, and he wasn't sure if his *Body Regeneration* Skill would skew the results somehow.

"Do you think you can make one a little smaller?" Shinpai asked. "Lugging this large plate around isn't the most convenient, after all."

"Absolutely. Give me a few minutes and I'll have that right up for you."

As he sat down again to create another *Graduated Parahealing* Fusion on a much smaller, round, steel medallion attached to a leather thong, his mind was already moving past the healing Fusion, now that he had finally solved the issues that had been plaguing him in its formation. He was absolutely certain that tests on actual people would be successful, so that meant that he would be able to start making more of them to distribute to whoever the Dean and Shinpai thought needed them. Not only that, but he could also make *Healing Surge* Fusions specifically made for the Martials, as they would be able to use them even in combat without too many issues, and there wasn't much risk of them succumbing to a coma afterward.

That alone would hopefully allay suspicion of his origins and any other secrets that he didn't want to share with anyone other than those who already knew, but it would also open up a whole new avenue of

Fusions that he could work on without fear of getting in trouble. The Dean's announcement of Larek being a Fusions prodigy might have made his life a bit more socially confined, but he couldn't deny that it was essentially what he wanted as far as being able to create and experiment with Fusions.

If only he could figure out what was holding him back from breaking through certain Skill levels, keeping him from creating using his knowledge of Advanced Fusions, then he would be able to design even more wondrous things. He might even be able to dictate what Fusions he created for others and decide on who would get them, instead of simply settling for what the Dean and Shinpai told him to create. Because, unfortunately, despite all of the opportunities he had been given by the two important faculty members, he was beginning to feel as if he had fallen into the very same trap he had hoped to avoid when he first discovered his ability to create Fusions. It wasn't some deep, dark basement where he was chained to a wall and forced to create Fusion after Fusion or else he wouldn't be fed the bare minimum to keep him alive, of course; but did good food, a pleasant environment, and friends nearby mean that he wasn't shackled in a prison of his own achievements?

He didn't know for sure, but he was starting to suspect that all of this was too good to be true.

Chapter 5

Larek's assumption – that he'd be corralled into producing dozens of his new *Graduated Parahealing* Fusions, on everything from metal medallions that could be worn around someone's neck to Mage staves – turned out to be absolutely true. No longer was he making stat boosts for unknown people; instead, he was creating life-saving Fusions that – while still for unknown people – gave him a proud feeling in his chest, knowing that what he was making was going to help people.

Sure, adding stat boosts, strengthening armor, and sharpening the edges of weapons was beneficial, but creating something that could literally mean the difference between life and death was of far greater impact. He had felt a bit of the same way when he had originally designed his *Healing Surge* Fusion back at Crystalview Academy, but he'd also had to keep it secret; now that his talent was out in the open, and his new healing Fusion was being distributed to people who would use it to heal their wounds when fighting monsters, the satisfaction in his accomplishment was on a whole new level.

Unfortunately, his production of the *Graduated Parahealing* Fusions cut into his time to begin experimenting with anything else.

"It's only for a little while, Larek," Shinpai assured him a few days after his successful creation of the healing Fusion. "These are very important to the SIC defenders in the city, especially as they've been sending out groups to scour the local countryside to locate and kill any monsters from the scattered Scissions that keep opening up without our knowledge. Just one of these Fusions you're creating could spell the difference between success and failure."

When his Professor put it that way, it was difficult for Larek to find a reason to complain. Even in his semi-secluded state, he had heard about multiple SIC groups that had set out from Thanchet and never returned. While he still didn't particularly care about the normal people of the city all that much because of their past treatment of him, the Mages and Martials he'd encountered since he was introduced to the larger world had been, generally, good people and were relatively quick to eschew their prejudices once they got to know him. There were, of course, plenty of those – such as the late Ricardo – who were an exception to the rule, but there weren't enough to want any harm to come to them. He was a member of this community now, for good or ill, and he wanted to do his part to save as many of them as possible.

Only a week after he began creating *Graduated Parahealing* Fusions in all his free time as well in his *Advanced Fusions* class, he received the go-ahead to begin adding *Healing Surge* Fusions to the list of ones he was making. Within a day of that happening, he got into a rhythm where he would make one of the new healing Fusions followed by one of the old healing Fusions, thereby splitting up his time to produce a relatively equal number of them every day. Within a few days, he was creating 50 of each type every single day – and yet, he wasn't instructed to stop or slow down.

In fact, he even overheard the Dean and Shinpai at one point mentioning that they might take him out of his other classes entirely once he reached his second year, so that he would have more time to devote to Fusions. At first, he thought that this was an excellent idea, as it would give him additional time to experiment and learn what he could about other spells; however, contemplating more deeply on the way that possibility was phrased made him think that the idea wasn't designed to expand his repertoire of Fusions, but to turn him into a Fusion-creating maniac that they couldn't allow to stop.

"What changed?" he muttered to himself when an entire month went by without any change to his schedule. As of yet, he was still going to classes, but he could feel an invisible pressure on him coming from his Professor and the Dean; it might have been his imagination, but it almost felt like they were desperate and were *willing* him to work faster. He was tempted to try and speed up his process by ditching classes to create more Fusions, despite using almost all of his free time already, but he hadn't taken that step yet.

Nedira was sitting on the edge of his bed as he laid down to relax from the busy day before getting some sleep, his body tired from the hunched-over position he'd adopted while creating Fusions. A quick burst of his *Healing Surge* Fusion would take care of any soreness from the position, as well as his *Body Regeneration* Skill, but neither of them helped with the weariness he felt. She heard his muttering and answered him, even if he hadn't been meaning to ask her.

"I had a chance to go on an excursion outside the walls earlier today to experiment with a few spells in the forest, along with about 100 other Naturalists from the Academy, and I heard some worrying rumors from the city," she said softly, her voice loud enough that Larek could hear it but Verne and Norde – who were studying together across the room – would have trouble catching her words.

"Like what?" he asked, sitting up.

"Just that the situation throughout the Kingdom is worse than what we've heard here in the Academy," Nedira explained. "Apparently, after the first wave of towns was caught unawares and destroyed by random rampaging monsters, the drop-off of attacks against the walls of prepared towns and cities fell to next to nothing. Instead, travel around the Kingdom, even via the SIC Transportation Network of Canniks and carriages, has been reduced to a minimum as almost everything moving out on the roads is a target. Merchant caravans are having difficulty reaching their destinations unscathed, and the normal caravan guard organizations don't have enough people to handle their needs – not to mention that casualties among the guards they *do* employ have increased significantly."

Larek shrugged, as he really didn't care that the caravans were having difficulty moving around. His experience with them in the past was less than flattering when he thought about them, and while he didn't necessarily want them all to die, he wasn't going to go out of his way to help them. The only ones he sort of felt bad for were the guards, because the ones he had met were either indifferent to his appearance or at least courteous enough not to say anything derogatory toward him; *they* were at least doing a job and protecting the ones that had hired them, making them similar in ways to the SIC.

Nedira looked at him strangely, as if she couldn't figure out why he didn't seem to care. After a few seconds, a look of understanding flowed over her features. "Ah, that's right; I remember what you told me of your experiences with them," she said, nodding slightly. "However, while I know it doesn't excuse their behavior toward you, the caravans that travel around the Kingdom of Androthe are literally the lifeblood of the people. Not only is commerce important to the economy, but how do you think all the food that feeds the people of the Kingdom moves from the farms where it is produced to the towns and cities? Not all of it can be produced nearby major cities; instead, it's produced in the large, open spaces in between, where it has been relatively safe for them to operate without fear of being overrun by monsters.

"But now the safety of being away from the walls of a nearby town or city is disappearing, as monsters are rampaging throughout the countryside. From what I overheard, many of the food-producing farms haven't been affected too much, as there are still too few of them gathered together to be of major interest to the monster hordes roaming around, but it's been said that it's only a matter of time before they are threatened. Meanwhile, even if they are able to produce the food, they can't transport it to the people who need it if the caravans aren't able to travel."

Larek hadn't thought too much about where all the food that he ate in the Academy came from, nor was he ever too curious about the origins of the food he ate back at home; his family had always been provided more food than they could possibly need, as it was supplied by the local Baron. He'd seen plenty of farms as he passed through the Kingdom in his travels to the different Academies that he'd attended, but other than noting that they were there, he didn't think about them all that much.

"Where did you learn about all this stuff?" he asked.

She looked at him strangely again, before shaking her head with exasperation. "It's common knowledge, Larek. For those with their heads in the clouds or with your unique history living in the middle of an information void, there are third and fourth-year classes here at the Academy that go into more detail about how the Kingdom functions. Those classes aren't just to educate the SIC members that most of the people will become after they graduate; with the presence of so many Nobles among the student body, it's necessary knowledge for when most of them retire and rejoin their family holdings."

"They can retire?" Larek thought he heard somewhere that the positions in the SIC were essentially for life.

"*Nobles* can retire, if they choose to. I believe they are required to put in anywhere between 10 and 20 years of service in the SIC, depending on how important they are. Commoners, on the other hand, are required to serve for at least 35 years before they can think of retiring, though I've heard that many simply stay as part of the SIC until they are too old to safely defend the walls, because for most of them it is the only life they've known for the majority of their lives."

35 years? Will I even make it that long? Especially with what the Dean and Shinpai want me to do? He didn't want to think about that, however, as he still needed to live long enough to get to that point. With the way the Scissions and the monsters they expelled were changing, 35 years might be an impossibility; if the SIC couldn't get a handle on things, then there soon might not be anything to defend.

Larek also tried not to think about his family far to the north, helpless if a Scission or two opened nearby – or if food suddenly stopped flowing to them from the Baron. He'd already considered that if he was somehow able to escape the Academy and the SIC, it would still be weeks or months until he could make his way up there. Now, with the state of the roads and countryside being what it was, with roaming monsters everywhere, he wasn't sure if he would even survive the journey. As loathe as he was to say it, even in his mind... they were on their own.

Regardless of his own personal worries, Nedira's information made his contributions to the fight against the roaming monsters even more important. She also mentioned that it was likely that even more of the standing force of SIC defenders in the city would be sent out in an effort to patrol the road to make it safer for travel, but only a small portion of the SIC had experience outside of the walls of a town or city. Those with experience, such as the group they had met who traveled with them in the Network carriage on their way to Thanchet, were still out there, far busier than normal – but they apparently weren't very numerous. Because of their inexperience traveling around and hunting down monsters throughout the Kingdom, the SIC members were going to need all the extra help they could get – which, for Larek at least, meant they would be carrying one or more of his healing Fusions with them.

But at his current speed of making Fusions, it was barely enough to keep up with current demand. Just thinking about groups of SIC defenders running around with one or two of his healing Fusions amongst them made Larek realize that he could do so much more for them to survive. Defensive Fusions like *Repelling Barrier* could minimize the need to heal in the first place, while stat boost Fusions could aid in making the Martials stronger and faster, while the Mages could cast stronger spells for longer. Fusions that made armor stronger or weapons sharper could also aid in killing monsters while keeping Martial defenders alive. Possessing something such as a *Camouflage Sphere* Fusion for Mages could allow them to stay unseen while they attacked from a distance.

Then, apart from defensive or supporting Fusions, there were always offensive Fusions to consider. A reluctance to revisit the memory of Ricardo's death along with the other two Martial trainees who had abducted Larek made him hesitate to even mention the Fusions he had created at that time, but he couldn't deny that they might be useful. Possessing a Fusion that could theoretically cast a spell like *Fireball* over and over without having to worry about running out of Mana could be invaluable, and could even be used by Martials. More than that, they could theoretically be used by *anyone*, even the common people of the Kingdom, giving them a power that could potentially rival an inexperienced Mage.

Needless to say, even though it might be beneficial to the common people to possess something like that, his viewpoint toward them hadn't improved enough for him to want to give them that kind of power. It wasn't that he thought he and the SIC were better than commoners and they didn't deserve it; rather, it was because he still didn't care all that much about them. It was probably wrong to view them all as being horrible people, given what he'd learned about their inherited hatred of tall people, but that didn't change how he felt deep down. His emotional psyche had been battered enough that it would probably be a while until he was ready to forgive them.

Over the next couple of months, his routine became a little more varied as he was eventually asked to split his focus between the two healing Fusions and more stat boosts on various items. Somewhere in the third month, Larek was taken out of his *Scissions* class, as the previous knowledge known about them had changed so much over the last few months that it was no longer as useful to most students. This gave him essentially another hour at the end of the school day to get started on creating Fusions even earlier, which helped with his production numbers.

Also around that time, he began to incorporate *Sharpen* and *Strengthen* Fusions into his rotation, creating a multitude of swords and other edged weapons with the same sort of deadly cutting ability as his own axe, as well as reinforcing a different set of steel armor pieces every day. The addition of these different Fusions meant that he was making fewer that were for healing, but from what he was told, they were still in high demand. There were a few times when he asked what the plan was for all these different Fusions, but was only told by the Dean that it was being handled by the SIC General in charge of Thanchet's defenses. It was an eye-opening explanation, because all this time he had thought it had been the Dean and Shinpai who had dictated what he needed to create, but that turned out not to be the case. After learning that, he put his head down and focused on his work, cognizant that what he was creating was saving lives – even if he didn't see it happening directly.

Fortunately, thanks to his friends and bodyguards keeping him aware of his mental state, he didn't fall into anything similar to what he'd experienced before when he threw himself into a certain project. His hyper-focused state was moderated by a purpose, leaving him to concentrate on that while still trying to enjoy himself outside of his work. It wasn't perfect, because he still wanted to branch out and experiment a little, or learn something else that might help him break through his current limitations. That was because, even after making thousands of Fusions over the months, none of his Skills improved… at all. Not just his Mage Skills, either, but his Martial Skills had stagnated because he wasn't doing anything to improve them, and even his General Skills hadn't budged from where they were before.

After a while, it felt like it wasn't just his body that was a prisoner inside the Academy, but that his Skills were also confined and blocked from any kind of advancement – as unlikely as that sounded. Still, the fact that he hadn't been able to increase the Level of anything in months was a good sign that something was, if not wrong, then at least abnormal for him.

The months passed in a blur, and Larek was barely even aware of how much time had gone by when he heard Verne and Norde mentioning something to each other in their room that surprised him.

"Of course! It won't be quite as exciting without Larek participating, naturally, but I'm still going," the tree-like boy said.

Norde countered with, "Yes, but Larek was kind of a cheat—no offense, Larek—so it'll be good to see a Skirmish that is a bit more balanced."

Larek spoke up at that. "Skirmish?"

Verne nodded. "Yep! It's the end-of-the-year Skirmish!"

"End of the year?"

Verne and Norde both looked at him and chuckled. "You're not even aware that our first year is almost finished, are you?" Verne asked with amusement in his voice.

Larek thought hard about it, but he had to admit in the end that he wasn't. "I... didn't even know that much time had passed."

"Well, it did, and in a week we'll officially be second-year students at the Academy!"

Wow. Really? It's been a whole year already?

He doubted that his roommates would be trying to trick him, so he had to take their word for it.

The next day, Verne, Norde, and Nedira went to watch the Skirmish since classes were canceled for the duration – to Larek's additional surprise – but instead of watching the competition himself, he used that time to make more Fusions. He had no desire to watch them all fighting against each other in an arena when there was so much danger lurking outside the walls; his work was too important to interrupt, after all.

After the Skirmish was over, there were two more days of classes, each of which had some sort of end-of-year test that every first-year had to take to demonstrate the knowledge that they had learned. Thankfully, there were no requirements for him to cast a spell, which meant that most of the tests were knowledge-based. While not the smartest student when it came to memorizing all of the information he had gained over the year, he thought he did fairly well being able to demonstrate his manipulation of Mana, along with his knowledge of Specializations, geography, and monsters that could be found coming out of Scissions.

Finally, classes ended for the year, freeing him up for two weeks before the next year began. As he threw himself into the Fusions he was repeatedly making, he wished he could clone himself so that it wasn't just him creating everything; the more he made, the more he realized that what he had made was just a small portion of what was needed to outfit all the SIC members heading out to kill monsters. There was only so much that he, personally, could create, and he feared that it wouldn't be enough.

Chapter 6

Larek was met by Grandmaster Fusionist Shinpai as soon as he arrived inside the *Advanced Fusions* workshop about a week into the break, which wasn't really much different from every other day. What *was* different, however, was that his Professor was standing up and barred him from entering the room any further with his body halfway blocking the doorway.

"No, not today, Larek. You've been going full-speed for months now, and you need a break. I want you to take two days off before you come back, and I don't want you to make a single Fusion during that time."

The confused Fusionist shook his head. "But I'm fine. There's too much to do to take a break now."

"I'm not going to deny that what you've been able to accomplish is one of the most amazing things I've ever seen and is consistently saving lives, but even you need to let your body rest every once in a while. If you don't, your Pattern Cohesion will begin to *permanently* suffer."

Opening his Status, Larek looked at his Pattern Cohesion, but he couldn't see anything different. "What do you mean? It looks just fine to me."

"The numbers on your Status are one thing, but they also reflect *you*; that might seem nonsensical, but each of those stats is dependent upon your body in some way. For Martials, this is easily seen in the strength of their muscles or their speed, but for Mages there is very little physical manifestation of their stats. While Intellect and Acuity affect the mind and how well we are able to manipulate Mana, Pneuma and Pattern Cohesion are directly tied to your pattern, or some might say your very soul. You're imparting a portion of your pattern into every Fusion you create, and while you possess incredible amounts of Pattern Cohesion and are able to regenerate it much faster than anyone I've ever met, you're eventually going to overuse it to the point where it can hurt you if you continue what you're doing."

Penelope had accompanied him as a bodyguard that day, and when she saw Larek's confused expression, she spoke up. "I believe I know what he's trying to say," she interrupted. "It's like when we train too hard and end up straining our bodies past the point where *Body Regeneration* can keep up," she explained. "There have been examples in the past where lingering injuries were sustained after a trainee pushed a little too far; weakened muscles and brittle joints that can last for weeks are the typical side-effects, though I've heard that there have been a few that have suffered *permanent* disabilities from extreme cases. Thankfully, it's rather rare, and our Instructors keep an eye on the trainees to ensure that no one accidentally pushes too far."

Larek listened to her explanation, but shook his head after she was done. "I guess I can understand that, but I don't think it's the same thing for me. I haven't had any sign of—" He trailed off as something occurred to him.

Over the last week or so, as Larek spent most of his days making Fusions rather than having classes to break it up, he had noticed that it seemed to take a little longer than it should have in between creating Fusions. Originally annoyed that his Pattern Cohesion wasn't regenerating as fast as he wanted it to, he had ignored it, assuming it simply reflected him being tired and impatient, and he had kept creating Fusions, only stopping when he had no other choice. Looking back at it now, Larek had to consider whether the reason his Pattern Cohesion seemed to be regenerating slower than usual was because *it actually was*.

Shinpai peered into his face after he stopped talking. "Ah, you see it, don't you?"

Larek reluctantly nodded.

"Given your stats, it shouldn't take your Pattern Cohesion long to recover from the abuse you've been putting it through," his Professor went on. "It might even be better within a day, but I want you to take at least two days off before you attempt another Fusion. Besides, you need a break every once in a while, just like everyone else."

He nodded again without saying anything, as his mind was working overtime to assess all that he had been told. Leaving without a word, he barely recalled the walk back to his room; if Penelope had tried to talk to him on the way, he didn't remember.

As soon as he sat down on his bed, Larek immediately felt extremely tired despite getting up shortly before. Laying himself down, his mind suddenly released all of the furious thoughts roaming through him as they drained away, as though a stopper in a bathtub had been removed. The worry about what he was doing to his pattern from his constant Fusion creation, the pressure he felt from not being able to make enough Fusions for the groups of SIC members going out into the countryside, and the concern over not being able to improve his Skills and access Advanced Fusions flowed out of him until he felt deflated and empty.

He was also exhausted; more exhausted than he'd ever been in his life. Not even the creation of hundreds of *Healing Surge* Fusions back at Crystalview left him feeling like he did at that point. As the debilitating fatigue crashed into him, it only took a few seconds before he fell into a dreamless sleep.

"Larek? Are you alright?"

The Fusionist twitched as he was startled awake, Nedira's voice near his ear causing him to wake up in a flash. It was so sudden that he nearly bonked into her head as he abruptly sat up, confused about what had happened.

After a quick glance around the room showed Kimble the Pyromancer – who was another member of his bodyguard squad – near the doorway leaning up against the wall, he looked at Nedira's concerned expression as she gazed at him. He was about to answer her when his stomach rumbled loudly, interrupting anything he was about to say.

"How—" Larek coughed a few times as his throat felt inordinately dry. "How long was I asleep?" He tried to remember what had happened before he passed out, but it was all a jumble of mixed-up memories.

"It's been about 46 hours," she responded after a few seconds, sitting down next to him on the bed. "We didn't want to wake you up because Penelope said you were exhausted and that your Professor told you to stop making Fusions for at least two days, but I figured you'd had enough time to rest. How are you feeling?"

Larek almost automatically replied with, "Fine," but he stopped himself as he performed an honest evaluation on himself. Closing his eyes, he looked inward, immediately sensing that the large ball of energy in his chest that held his Stama appeared perfectly fine. When he looked at the rest of his body, he immediately identified something different in his internal pattern and the Mana that infused it.

The only way to describe what he saw was that it appeared worn down and frayed – or at least it had been that way a short time ago. What he saw now was the result of it being repaired and healed over time, though there were subtle hints of scarring and lingering damage that were incrementally disappearing even as he looked at them.

I guess Shinpai was right; I was messing myself up without even knowing I was doing it.

Larek couldn't understand how he had missed seeing what was happening to his pattern. From the traces of damage that had been done to it, he could tell that it hadn't been something that happened overnight, so it must have been like that for weeks, if not longer. He'd been slightly angry at first after having been told to stop creating

Fusions for a couple of days, but now that he saw what could happen if he kept pushing himself like had been doing, he was especially thankful that this had been caught before any permanent damage had been done.

"I'm... getting there. Apparently, I was pushing my pattern too much for my body to handle, so once Shinpai told me to stop, my body and mind had had enough and shut down for nearly two days. I'll probably take another whole day off while my pattern finishes healing—" He was interrupted again by his stomach growling at him, causing both Larek and Nedira to chuckle. "But first, I need to eat. I'm starving."

An hour later, after gorging himself on food from the Dining Hall – which had thankfully not been rationed yet like food in some parts of the city supposedly was, as less of it was being safely transported inside – he nearly passed out again when he got back to his room. However, having slept for nearly two days, he didn't feel like wasting any more time, especially as his body and his pattern seemed to increase its rejuvenation after ingesting large quantities of food.

Instead, he chatted with Nedira for a while before Verne and Norde arrived to drag them all outside to the arena. As opposed to Skirmishes, which were put on twice a year, during the break between academic years there was a constant stream of duels held in the arena using shadow-casted spells and blunt weaponry. These duels weren't usually large affairs, as they typically only consisted of one-on-one or two-on-two matches, but this year they were altering it to include larger five-on-five and ten-on-ten matches because it better reflected the environment outside of the walls.

The SIC defenders were going out as groups now, instead of being relegated to being in large defensive formations, and teamwork among smaller parties was very important to staying alive.

"I've even heard that they're changing a lot of the team coordination classes that Academy students take in their fourth and fifth years to adjust to the new way of fighting the monsters coming from the Scissions!" Verne said excitedly as soon as they sat down in the arena stands. Larek noticed that it wasn't nearly as filled as it typically was during the Skirmish, but then again, these duels were more for "fun" rather than for prizes like the larger tournament.

"That is correct," Nedira agreed a second later, nodding at the boy. "There were some alterations to everyone's upcoming schedules, which is the reason we haven't received them yet. Apparently, every student – not just those incoming – will be required to attend classes in the different behaviors that the Scissions have been exhibiting. In addition, survival courses are supposed to be a new addition this year, as learning how to survive outside the walls of a city or town will be important going forward," she explained, a worried tone to her voice.

Larek thought he knew why. "I'm sure that everything will be fine; once the SIC adapts to the change in the Scissions, they'll get a handle on it," he attempted to assure her, though he wasn't sure if he even believed it. After learning some things about The Culmination from Ricardo, he had a feeling things would get worse before they got better.

"I sure hope you're right, Larek, because with all of these dangers cropping up, it's only a matter of time before our parents hear of it and call us back home," she said.

Call them back home? What—? Oh. He had forgotten for a moment that Nedira and her brother – and Verne, for that matter – weren't actually from the Kingdom, so they weren't technically duty-bound to join the SIC. To pay for their instruction in the Academy, many of them did end up joining, teaching, or doing something to contribute to the Kingdom, but he was sure that there were ways for them to get out of that obligation – especially when it came to staying in such a hostile environment. Of course, leaving the Academy and traveling through the lands to get back home was probably not the best idea when there were monsters roaming around, but that didn't mean there weren't any ways to pass through safely if absolutely necessary.

Nothing more was said on the subject at the moment, either because it was something no one wanted to think about or because worrying about something they couldn't do much to affect wasn't productive, so they instead turned their attention to the arena floor. In the center, in between the fortifications that he remembered vividly from the Skirmish he participated in a little over a half-year ago, there were two groups of 10 facing off against each other. Each team held 5 Mages and 5 Martials, and they worked together to score points against their opponents using their blunt weapons and shadow-casted spells. Unlike the Skirmish, blows by weapons were greatly reduced in severity, and it was rare that anyone would receive a broken bone or any serious injuries. Instead, it was more of a test to see what kinds of strategies of working together functioned for the participants, both in terms of defense and offense.

Larek watched with the others, but his interest in it all was quite low. He was never really attracted to the conflicts that took place in the arena, even back at Crystalview Academy, though he dutifully observed them with his friends because it was something to do outside of studying and making Fusions. Since there were no classes at the moment and he was still recovering from what he had done to his pattern, he took a little more interest in it this time, as there wasn't really anything else to do.

For once, he wasn't impatient to get back to work. He knew that he needed to get back to it eventually, but for now, he was reveling in this opportunity to relax.

But even though he tried to relax, some part of his mind always seemed to be thinking about Fusions, even if it wasn't actively holding his attention at the moment. His focus was pulled to the arena floor as he watched one team absolutely dominate the other, which was mainly thanks to the powerful Martials they possessed, all of whom held large wooden swords that reminded him of the one that Penelope used. They moved their weapons so quickly that they were able to block not only strikes by the opposing Martials, but also many of the spells that either attempted to hit them or push past them to hit the more vulnerable Mages behind their line.

Four of the five Martials on the losing side had already "fallen" as they were hit too many times and were considered "out", and three of the Mages had also been overwhelmed by shadow-casted spells coming from their opponents that hadn't been blocked or avoided otherwise. The final two Mages were actually both Geomancers, wielding a specialty in Earth-based spells, and as they moved behind their remaining Martial teammate, they began casting the same spell at the same time.

Normally, this wasn't that big of a deal, as he'd seen hundreds of Mages cast spells next to each other and there were many times when they were similar or the same. This time was different, however, as the spell they cast was apparently a lot stronger and more complicated than simple spells like *Stone Fist*; as a result, it took them nearly 5 seconds to complete the spell pattern and then infuse it with their Mana. As soon as the spell was cast, the two Geomancers visibly slumped as a barrage of shadow-casted rocks the size of an average torso rained down on the entire enemy team. Two of the Martials were unable to block the boulders as they fell upon them, and one of the Mages got bonked pretty solidly on the head, taking them out of the fight, but the last-ditch spells coming from the team with the Geomancers weren't enough to win the day as they were eliminated shortly thereafter.

So why was that significant to Larek?

Because as they were casting their spells, the two Geomancers had – either through chance or planning – been completely in sync, from the start of the spell pattern to the end. Watching the patterns being perfectly completed together gave Larek an idea of something he wanted to try out the next day. If it worked, then it could speed up his Fusion-creating process significantly. If it didn't, then there really wouldn't be anything lost from his experiment, and he would go back to doing things like normal.

But he hoped it worked. He had already shown that he could create a single, powerful Fusion using his abilities... but what if he could create two at the same time?

Chapter 7

The next morning, Larek felt better than he had in months.

"You were right, Professor," he admitted soon after he arrived in the *Advanced Fusions* workshop. "I was wearing down my pattern and I didn't even realize it."

Shinpai reached up and patted him on the shoulder while nodding his head. "I'm glad you were able to see it and stop it before it got any worse. To be honest, I wasn't even sure if you were doing any harm to it at first, given your circumstances, but I can sometimes get a sense of someone else's internal pattern when I've been working with them for a while. I had a feeling that you'd have been fine for another few weeks, but there's no point letting it get to that point if there's no need. I especially don't want you to do anything to hinder your advancement in the future; sometimes I forget that you're still a teenager with how you're able to create such powerful Fusions."

Larek was silent as he considered his Professor's words. He had to admit that he sometimes forgot that he was only 16—*actually, I turned 17 a few months ago. I was so busy that I forgot my own birthday.*

The Grandmaster Fusionist sighed as he dropped his hand from Larek's shoulder. "But now we really need your help with more Fusions, I'm sorry to say."

"About that," he said, holding up a finger. "I have an idea I want to try."

"An idea? What is this all about? Is this something that might let you break through to a higher Skill Level?"

Sadly, he shook his head. Shinpai already knew about his difficulties in advancing any further than he had, and from what he understood, his Professor was looking into various methods that might help him push through. Unfortunately, nothing had come of it quite yet.

"No; at least I don't think so," he answered. "But have you ever heard of anyone creating two Fusions at the same time?"

"Two Fusions? Like an Intermediate Fusion with dual Effects?"

Again, Larek shook his head. "No. I'm talking about creating two *separate* Fusions at the same time. I *think* I might be able to do it; if I can, then I can effectively *double* the number of Fusions I can produce every day. I think that I'll have to take a day off every week to ensure that I don't run my pattern ragged like it had been, but this should make up for that day, and then some."

"Larek, that's imposs—" his Professor began to say, before stopping himself. "Well, I was going to say that it's impossible to create more than one Fusion at a time, but you've already shown me that what I thought impossible is completely wrong. All I'll say is that it's highly improbable that you'll be able to do it, but I'd like to see you try."

Larek was curious. "Why do you think it is either impossible or highly improbable?"

Instead of answering right away, Shinpai walked over to his customary spot on his cushions and waved for Larek to sit down as well. Once they were settled, the Grandmaster Fusionist explained. "Let me ask you a question instead. What are the three fundamentals that a Fusionist *needs* in order to create a Fusion?"

It took him a moment to understand what his Professor was asking. "Pattern Cohesion, Mana, and… knowledge?"

"Correct on the first two, but knowledge isn't absolutely necessary. Remember what I told you before; the symbols inside of a Fusion are only a representation of an idea, so having knowledge of what they are supposed to look like can be superseded by something else."

It only took Larek a moment. "Ah. *Focus.*"

"Exactly!" Shinpai said, nodding. "Now, which of those three is the most important? Or, in other words, which one is the most impactful?"

Larek was going to say Pattern Cohesion, because it was necessary to even construct a grid formation, but he realized at the last moment that it wasn't that. "Focus?"

"Precisely! For Fusionists, their focus is the most important because they need to instill their intent into the different parts of the Fusion while keeping the entire thing together. You've seen the trance-like state that I and most of the other Fusionists at this level adopt in order to ensure we can keep our focus properly during creation; it is necessary for us because our Fusion Time is typically measured in *hours*, not *minutes* like you.

"Now, despite your ability to work much faster than other Fusionists, you still need to keep the same level of focus on your Fusion. Even if you are able to assemble two grid formations with your Pattern Cohesion and have the Mana to feed into both Fusions, you'll still have to split your focus between two separate creations, something that even the greatest Fusionists in history would have difficulty even attempting, so much so that it is doubtful that anyone has even tried.

"But you," he continued with a chuckle, "well, are unique in that aspect, given that you don't seem to have a problem keeping your focus even without a trance. So, while it might be impossible for anyone else, you *might* be able to do it – but I can't help but think that it will still be highly improbable, as I said. All I can say is that you should be careful, as it might be dangerous to attempt creating two at once, especially if they collapsed."

Larek considered what his Professor was cautioning him against, but he honestly thought he could handle it. Sure, it would take a little more concentration and focus, but he had gotten to the point over the last few months that it felt like he barely had to focus now to create the Fusions he did. It wasn't quantified anywhere, unfortunately, as his Skills didn't reflect what he considered to be his increased focus for Fusions; *Spellcasting Focus* was probably the closest, but he didn't think that matched up perfectly with what he was thinking. Acuity might be a better stat to compare with the clarity of his focus, but even that fell flat when he thought about it for long. It was almost as if something was missing from his Skills that reflected his growth, but he had no idea what it was. As far as he knew, there weren't any other Skills available to Mages that he didn't already possess.

"I'm going to try it with something small and simple first: a Basic Fusion. If I can't even hold it together before I start inserting Mana into it, I'll stop before I hurt myself," he said, and Shinpai shrugged.

"Feel free to try. Just be careful… and don't be afraid to hear, 'I told you so,' if you fail," the Grandmaster Fusionist added with a smirk… before scooting backward from where Larek was pulling out two steel plates and resting them side-by-side on his crossed legs.

"Thanks for the vote of confidence, Professor," Larek remarked with a smirk of his own before turning his attention to the two steel plates. With a deep breath, he began by creating a 2-by-2 grid formation on the left plate, before adding the necessary components for an *Illuminate Steel +1* Activatable Fusion; it was one of the simplest and lowest-cost Fusions he knew of, and it was also something he would be able to test immediately by activating it to make it glow. That entire process only took a few seconds, as it was again quite basic, so he shifted his attention to the other steel plate.

As soon as he took his focus off the one he had just finished, the formation began to fall apart to the point where he couldn't recover it. *If I had infused Mana into that Fusion, it might have exploded.* Fortunately, all it did was fall apart harmlessly.

He rebuilt the formation quickly and, while keeping enough focus on the first, he started to construct the second formation. Or at least he *tried* to construct it, but it was as if something was preventing him from placing the necessary lines for the grid to form; instead, it was just a mess of random lines of Pattern Cohesion jumbled together without rhyme or reason. When he saw this, he let everything fall apart before trying again.

A few minutes later, he grunted in frustration as he couldn't seem to hold the focus of one Fusion while constructing the second. He *knew* he had enough concentration to make it work, but for some reason that escaped him, it just wouldn't come together. It wasn't until he sat back, closed his eyes, and took a deep breath that he remembered where this seemingly crazy idea came from. It only took him a few seconds to picture the two Geomancers forming the same spell pattern simultaneously before he knew what he needed to do.

Again, at least he thought he knew what he needed to do, but the end result was just as unfortunate. Forming two separate Fusions simultaneously was difficult at first, because he had to split his concentration between two different grid formations, but after the first few lines it became much easier. Within 30 seconds, which was far longer than it would normally take him to create a single Fusion grid formation, he got the hang of it and finished both Fusions at the same time, something that he previously hadn't been able to do.

The problem came when he attempted to infuse both Fusions at the same time. He was able to keep his focus on both formations just fine once they were constructed, but attempting to split his focus once again to direct two streams of Mana into the appropriate places in the separate Fusions seemed to be impossible. It wasn't necessarily a problem with his focus, he found, but that he was incapable of forming two separate Mana funnels that weren't included in the same Fusion. It was as if there was some sort of mental block that prevented it from happening, or he simply didn't have the ability or Mana Control. Regardless of the reason, it didn't work.

He could fill them one at a time, he found, but that wasn't exactly what he was looking to accomplish. Once he finished both, he immediately eliminated them from the steel plates by starving them of ambient Mana, causing their formations to collapse, before trying again. He wasn't going to give up when he felt he was so close.

Another 15 minutes and numerous failures later, he was beginning to think it wasn't possible. It was in between attempts that Shinpai spoke up, startling Larek a little because he had been so engrossed in his project that he had forgotten where he was. "I can see that you're not having any problems with the formations, which shouldn't surprise me; as for the Mana you're feeding into them, why don't you try moving the plates and the formations you're creating closer together, so that their Mana Costs are near enough that you might be able to fill both with same funnel of Mana you tend to like using?"

Such a simple solution hadn't even occurred to Larek, as he was so intent on trying to split his Mana. As he began to move the plates around, close enough that one was practically stacked on top of the other, he suddenly had an epiphany.

Wait a minute. Why don't I just stack the Fusions and then direct them where I want them afterwards? He already partly did that when creating normal Fusions, after all. When he created the original grid formation, it sort of hovered over the material where he wanted to place his Fusion, and once it was filled he would direct it to fuse into the structure of the material with a *click*. He hadn't ever attempted to move it more than the slight adjustment required for the final push into the material, but he didn't see why he couldn't move it more. At that point in the process, with the Mana infusing it and acting as a sort of glue that held it together, it should be easy enough to shift it to where he wanted it.

With a thoughtful nod in Shinpai's direction, he attempted something else new that he'd never done before: Instead of creating the Fusion directly above the material he was using, he formed the grid formation approximately a foot away from the steel plate in the middle of the air. There was a slight inhalation of air that came from his Professor, but the Grandmaster Fusionist was experienced enough to know not to interrupt another Fusionist while they were in the process of making a Fusion, so he said nothing.

Since he was just making a single Fusion, it only took a few seconds for him to form the pattern and then infuse it with Mana. At that point, when it was completely saturated, he felt a connection with it as it attempted to fully form, but as it was in the air with no material nearby, he was fairly certain it would collapse if he simply let it go right there. This would probably elicit a slight explosion, which sounded like it could be useful as a weapon in the future; at the same time, his instincts were telling him that an unfinished Fusion like this could wind up harming his Pattern Cohesion if he simply let it collapse while he was still working with it.

Instead, he mentally directed it toward the steel plate underneath it, which was more difficult than if it had been directly underneath it, but not overly so. As it clicked into place, he let out the breath he was holding as he tested the illumination on the steel plate and checked over his work, seeing absolutely nothing out of the ordinary. In other words, *it had worked*. More than that, while he was controlling the Mana-infused grid formation, there was something else he intuited that was going to make all the difference.

"That was… odd, Larek. Why did you do that?" his Professor asked.

"Because of this. Watch."

Suddenly confident that his intuition was correct, he quickly eliminated the Fusion from the steel plate, leaving it empty for another one, before concentrating on the air above the two plates in his lap. With a few thoughts, he assembled the same Fusion once again, but this time he made the lines thicker, or more accurately, *deeper*; typically, the lines were fairly two-dimensional, as they were relatively flat with very little thickness because they didn't need it when attaching to a material. But now he pictured the lines becoming more three-dimensional, with a deepness that doubled its thickness, which he could easily see since it was suspended in the air in front of him.

Filling it up with Mana took exactly the same amount as it did when it was thinner, which he figured was because it was still doing the same exact thing no matter its depth. A general feel for how much Pattern Cohesion was used in the Fusion led him to believe that it might have used perhaps 20% more than normal, which was actually quite good considering that it essentially doubled in size.

As he held it in place, now infused with Mana, Larek did something he wasn't entirely sure would work, but his previous experience with moving the nearly completed Fusion led him to believe that it would. Now that the Fusion was largely held together because of the Mana, it also made the formation a little more pliable and able to be manipulated; it was this malleability that allowed it to conform precisely to different-shaped materials, such as rings and armbands that had rounded contours. Larek, however, was using it for a different reason entirely.

With a focused mental *slice* into the formation, he cut it in half like a loaf of bread. The two halves didn't want to detach at first, as if the Mana "glue" was holding it together, but with a slight twist and an inaudible snap, the two halves separated and he was able to control them independently of each other. Without hesitating any further, he directed them onto the two steel plates in his lap, allowing them to click into place simultaneously. As soon as they were fully fused into the material, he checked them over and didn't see any issues that had come from separating them from the original whole. A mental activation turned the illumination on both on, and he smiled in satisfaction before looking up to see Grandmaster Fusionist Shinpai's absolutely flabbergasted face.

"I—"

Larek's explanation was interrupted as a barrage of notifications slammed into him the next second, knocking him flat on his back.

Chapter 8

Focused Division Skill has been unlocked!
Focused Division has reached Level 1!
.....
Focused Division has reached Level 7!

Pattern Recognition has reached Level 19!
Pattern Recognition has reached Level 20!

Magical Detection has reached Level 19!
Magical Detection has reached Level 20!

  The sudden onslaught of notifications caught him off-guard, making Larek temporarily black out for a moment. When he came to a few seconds later, the tingling through his body and his mind slowly disappeared as he made sense of what had just happened.
  Groaning as he sat up, he waved off Shinpai who was up and coming to check on him. "I'll be fine; it was just a bunch of notifications all at once."
  "Notifications? Did you break through past Level 30 in a Skill finally?"
  Looking closer at what he received, he was originally disappointed when neither *Mana Control*, *Fusion*, or *Pattern Formation* increased in Level. He was happy to see that *Pattern Recognition* and *Magical Detection* finally budged past 18 where they had been stuck for months, reaching Level 20, even though he didn't really understand what those had to do with what he just did.
  His disappointment at not breaking through changed to confusion as he saw that he had just unlocked a new Skill – and it wasn't familiar in the slightest. "Have you ever heard of a Skill called *Focused Division*?" he asked after almost a minute. His body and head were quickly adjusting to the sudden increase in Skill Levels, so he was able to think a little better.
  "*Focused Division*? No, never heard of it. Did you... just unlock an entirely unknown Skill?!"
  His Professor's astonished face nearly made Larek chuckle as it was comical-looking, but he kept a straight face as he shrugged. "Uh... I guess so? I have no idea what it means—"
  But that wasn't entirely true, as he concentrated on the Skill to see if it would provide him with any information. While he normally

didn't receive much in the way of information when it came to Skills, he found that there was usually a hint of what the Skills did when he concentrated on them in his Status. It was more of a *feeling* than anything else, and when he directed his insight toward *Focused Division*, what he got back was startling as it was much more than normal.

"It's... well, it's not a Skill that is directly tied to Fusions," he said to Shinpai, the older man's expression a combination of stunned and confused that was even more amusing than before. Thankfully, his concentration was on the Skill he was feeling out, so he didn't laugh at his Professor, which he thought would be quite rude.

"What is it, then?"

"It's a Skill that is related to *patterns*, actually. It allows for the division of patterns once they have been infused with Mana... and, apparently, the higher Level the Skill, the more a pattern can be divided. I received an additional 6 Levels in it immediately after unlocking it, and I believe I might be able to divide a single Fusion pattern into 3, maybe 4, separate Fusions at the same time. I get the impression that the Pattern Cohesion cost increases incrementally for each additional Fusion, but it is relatively stable in growth cost, with each one only requiring approximately 20% per division. In addition, the Mana Cost is only paid once as the Skill transfers the Mana into each Fusion."

"That's... incredible! But how did you gain so many Levels all at once?"

He rubbed the back of his neck in embarrassment, even if what he was embarrassed about wasn't intentional. "Well, see, this Skill isn't intended to be used for Fusions at Level 1 because it is normally quite difficult to manipulate the Fusion pattern like I did. As a result, it was like creating a powerful Intermediate Fusion without even having the Fusion Skill, resulting in quite a few additional Levels."

Shinpai's confusion was back in full force. "But that doesn't make sense. If it wasn't designed for Fusions, then what...?" Larek watched as comprehension dawned on his Professor's face.

He nodded in confirmation of what Shinpai had figured out. "Exactly. This Skill was originally meant to be learned and utilized by spell patterns. It would only be later, as the Skill becomes high enough in Level, that it should be possible to be used in Fusions. Unless, of course, you've already had practice at it like I have..." He trailed off, shrugging once again.

"B-But how has this never been discovered before?! I've never heard of anything like this being used in spellcasting, and I've been around quite a long time."

"I have no idea. I can't even cast a spell without nearly blowing myself up; then again, I haven't really tried again since that first disastrous accident, but my instincts are telling me it would be a mistake to try again even with a better understanding of what I'm doing. If anything, my practice with creating Fusions and their innate strength might even make it worse, so I'm hesitant to even attempt it."

Larek's body and mind, after recovering from the barrage of notifications, felt energized, and he realized he was slightly rambling as he spoke to his Professor. Thankfully, the Grandmaster Fusionist was so preoccupied with the whole concept of the new Skill that he didn't even notice.

"I wonder if it's because it originally seems like a waste of time?" Shinpai mused to himself. "I mean, if I can create the spell pattern for a *Fireball* in less than a second, launch it at a monster, and then create another one the next second, why would I want to spend the time trying to divide a spell pattern, especially in the heat of battle? I could just cast another spell, after all.

"But if this works for *any* spell, then powerful skills such as *Heaven's Wrath*, *Icy Deluge*, and *Fiery Cataclysm* could be used two or more times simultaneously for an additional cost of Pattern Cohesion – which could spell the difference between life and death. That's not even taking into account that this could be used in Fusions like our young prodigy just demonstrated, meaning that a Fusionist's precious time and Pattern Cohesion could be stretched even further out in the field, while also equipping more SIC members with valuable Fusions. This could be incredible... as long as others can learn it." Done with his muttered monologue, Larek's Professor looked at him and asked, "Do you think you can teach me how to do it?"

"Me... teach *you*?" Larek knew that the Dean and Shinpai had originally spoken of him teaching other Fusionists how to create the same sort of Fusions he could make, but that had fallen through when it was obvious that no one else could manage the sheer solidity of his Fusion formations. While he was easily able to instruct others on his methods and the composition of his relatively new *Graduated Parahealing* Fusion, for instance, without the solidity of the formation and the heightened Pattern Cohesion necessary for it to work, no one else could create it.

But perhaps this was something he *could* teach. He'd never seriously tried before, but he guessed that it was at least worth an attempt.

"I can try. I wouldn't advise attempting to do it with a Fusion, even with how comfortable you are with them," he warned, wincing as he realized he was talking to a Grandmaster Fusionist with many decades of experience and knowledge. Again, his Professor didn't seem to be offended by his warning, and only gestured for him to continue. "I can't show you how to do this with a spell pattern, unfortunately, because it needs to be infused with Mana, but perhaps you can adapt the Fusion patterns to your spellcasting technique."

Larek knew that, while spells and Fusions were similar in their construction, they were two entirely different methods of using the Mana inherent in their bodies. He just hoped that Shinpai would be able to consider the differences and figure it out.

"Not a problem," his Professor said, settling himself down to watch Larek work like an extremely attentive student. There was a seriousness and enthusiasm on the older man's face that Larek had never seen before, and it made him a little nervous to have his methods so closely scrutinized.

Thankfully, once he eliminated the Fusions on the two steel plates and got started once again, the distraction of having Shinpai sitting so close and watching the lines of his thick Fusion formation construct in the middle of the air disappeared as he focused on his work. At first, his explanation of what he was doing was slightly disjointed and hesitant, but as he poured the Mana into the formation, he became more confident. Utilizing his newly unlocked Skill, it was almost effortless as he split the Fusion into two halves, before locking them into place on the plates once again.

"...and this is where I would assume the spell would be cast as you release the spell pattern, but I can't speak to that," he finished, having successfully created yet another two Fusions after dividing them from a single one.

***Focused Division** has reached Level 8!*
.....
***Focused Division** has reached Level 10!*

Another notification startled him as he was so intent on showing his Professor how he accomplished the feat that he had blocked out everything else. Fortunately, the influx of additional Levels was only slightly impactful instead of knocking him flat on his back, so he was able to recover quite quickly.

"Amazing. Simply amazing. I'll give it a try."

The next moment, a spell pattern appeared in front of Shinpai as his Professor raised his hands, one that looked familiar in context but was unknown to Larek. At first, it looked like any other spell he'd seen and could learn, as it was obviously a fairly simple spell based on its pattern. After a few seconds, as it hovered in the air, the lines of which it was constructed seemed to thicken as his Professor used his fingers to add more Pattern Cohesion to the structure of the pattern. Unfortunately, after a few seconds, the pattern seemed to collapse as it became lopsided from varying thicknesses throughout the whole thing.

"I believe you need to start with thicker lines from the beginning," Larek suggested, forgetting for a moment that he was lecturing someone who was many times older and wiser than he was.

Shinpai just nodded and started again, and this time the pattern formed much slower than before, as the lines his Professor drew were thicker to start with. However, it became quite obvious that such manipulation of the normal process of spell pattern formation was difficult for the Grandmaster Fusionist, as it wobbled and fell apart after nearly 15 seconds of work, with only about half of it completed.

But just like Larek when he *knew* he should be able to do something, his Professor was stubborn and determined to try again. The next few minutes showed remarkable progress in Shinpai's creation of the spell pattern, but it wasn't until about 15 minutes later that the older man was able to complete the pattern – though the visible strain in his Professor's ability was obvious on his face. He was able to infuse it quickly with Mana, but was unable to prevent it from activating, preventing him from being able to divide the pattern into two separate spells.

A flash of light blinded him momentarily as the spell activated, and he blinked back the spots in his eyes as an orb of light hovered in the air in between the two Fusionists.

New Spell learned!
Light Orb
Duration: 30 seconds
Base Elemental Damage: 0
Base Elemental Effect (Illumination): Creates a hovering orb of light
Restrictions: Anything passing through the Light Orb will cancel the effect
Base Mana Cost: 10
Base Pattern Cohesion: 2

"Well, halfway there, I suppose," Shinpai said, frustration evident in his voice. With a wave of his hand through the *Light Orb*, the spell that Larek had just learned which he recognized as the base source of his *Illuminate* Fusions, the hovering light disappeared. "I'm trying again."

So he did. With Larek giving what pointers he could, he could see Shinpai continuously progress as the next few hours wore on. The biggest problem he discovered with his Professor understanding what he needed to do was that the experienced Grandmaster Fusionist was so set in his ways, when it came to casting spells, that the process of holding the spell stable after it was infused with Mana was *extremely* difficult. Shinpai was so accustomed to simply letting the temporary spell pattern go so that it could be activated that it was as if he was trying to go against his instincts. It made sense, in a way, as it was similar to his own disastrous spellcasting accident, as keeping a spell pattern around for too long was dangerous – because it would want to absorb additional Pattern Cohesion to stay stable. He thought that the Grandmaster Fusionist would be used to it after creating so many Fusions over the years, but apparently the basic training that he was taught when he first learned to cast spells was almost impossible to override.

Almost impossible wasn't the same as impossible, however. Both Larek and Shinpai freely recognized that this was likely the reason why no one had ever bothered to attempt something like this in the past, leaving the *Focused Division* Skill undiscovered until now, because it was just so difficult and against natural instincts that no one would want to try.

After nearly 6 hours of constantly creating the spell pattern for *Light Orb* over and over while attempting to divide it after it was infused with Mana, his Professor finally succeeded. Shinpai only managed to split the spell pattern in half and move the halves away from each other a few inches before he lost control of them, causing them both to activate for a split second before winking out as they touched each other, but it worked.

The smile of pure giddiness on his Professor's face as he unlocked the new Skill was more than worth the hours of unfamiliar teaching to Larek. As he congratulated the Grandmaster Fusionist for gaining the new Skill and turned to his own work, intending to see if *Focused Division* would work for the same sort of powerful Fusions he had been making constantly for the last few months, his Professor said something that at first was heartwarming, but then sent a spike of dread through his entire body.

"Thank you, thank you! You don't know how long it's been since I was able to increase *any* of my Skills – and I even reached another personal Level! This is life-changing in more ways than one, as it will give an avenue of advancement to even us old folks who have hit a wall in our personal development after being unable to progress our Skills past a certain point. I don't think you fully understand what this means for every single Mage in the Kingdom and beyond; this, as strange as it sounds, might be even more impactful than some of your Fusions, though I don't want to downplay their importance by even a little bit.

"Which is why I want you to teach the Dean and the rest of the faculty here at the Academy how to acquire this Skill. The Dean might even have you teach higher-year students this upcoming year, as well."

"Uh... what? No. I'm not really good at teaching and—"

"Nonsense! You taught *me*, and there is just something about the way your words instill a sense of meaning that I don't think anyone else could match. Even though I unlocked the Skill, I am positive that I wouldn't be able to describe the process as easily to anyone else. I don't know if it is due to, uh, *you know*, but it obviously works."

What his Professor didn't outright say was that the Dominion magic that he seemed to possess might have had an impact on his teaching, which was just another reason why he didn't want to try to instruct anyone else. How many people would be affected by this magic he couldn't control? Granted, it could be something else entirely that allowed the Grandmaster Fusionist to learn the Skill, but could he really take that chance?

Unfortunately, it didn't seem as though Shinpai was going to take a no for an answer, though ultimately it would be up to the Dean to dictate who he taught. Just the thought of instructing the powerful figure in charge of Copperleaf Academy was way more intimidating than teaching his *Fusions* Professor, and he dreaded how long it might take being in close quarters with the woman.

"Come. We'll go see her right now."

His new Skill was powerful and could drastically improve his speed in creating Fusions, but he was beginning to suspect that his success was going to be much more trouble than it was worth. Sighing in resignation, he stood up and followed his Professor out of the workshop and up to the Dean's office, Vivienne silently trailing after as Larek's bodyguard for the day.

Chapter 9

Teaching Dean Lorraine was indeed a chore, especially as, for some reason, he had to spend a few hours explaining exactly how he had discovered it and the reasoning behind his experiments. She and his *Fusions* Professor spent another hour or so expounding on the incredible gift that this Skill would bestow upon spellcasters. Larek could see the appeal, of course, though he couldn't necessarily partake in the same sort of excitement since he couldn't cast any spells. He already knew it was an important discovery for his own purposes with Fusions, but the Dean was extremely ecstatic over and above what he expected.

That excitement dimmed over the next *12 hours* as she slowly learned how to direct her spell patterns in a suitable way to unlock the Skill, which ended up lasting until the early hours of the next morning. Larek nearly fell asleep a few times while he was teaching her, though her insistence that he repeat the steps over and over again helped to keep him from nodding off; he forced himself to stay awake by running laps around her office every once in a while because he didn't want to end up hurting himself or someone else if he made a mistake.

While she required twice the amount of time to learn this particular Skill in comparison to Shinpai, her giddiness once it happened was almost identical. His *Fusions* Professor even managed to raise his new Skill up to Level 2 by practicing the method while Dean Lorraine was being taught, though he was still having difficulty moving the spell patterns far enough away from each other once he split them so that they didn't cause any interference – though he was at least able to divide the patterns every single time now.

"I feel like I've been transported back to the days when I was a student at this very Academy, learning how to unlock each of my new Skills and discovering ways to improve them," the Dean said with a nostalgic smile, not even a trace of the tiredness that *he* felt through his entire being showing in her expression. Even though *he* hadn't been struggling to perform the feat in order to unlock the skill, it turned out that teaching someone else how to do something was so much harder and more exhausting than nearly anything he'd done before.

"I know; it was like I felt a wave of youthful exuberance flow through my limbs as all I wanted to do was run around and jump for joy when I managed to Level *Focused Division* up to Level 2. I mean, Level 2! I haven't been this excited about Level 2 in any Skill in… well, so long that I can't even remember," Shinpai agreed with a smile. He, too, didn't seem to have suffered from the lack of sleep as the pre-dawn light started to illuminate the world outside the Academy.

It was a bit annoying, if Larek was being honest, but he was happy that they had managed to unlock the Skill, at least. Now all he wanted was to go to bed and get some sleep. As he stood up to leave, the Dean turned her attention away from what he assumed was her Status she was looking at. "Thank you again, Larek. Seriously. I'll find some way to reward you for this; you have my word." Her words were heavy and filled with meaning, though whatever that meaning was eluded Larek in his current fatigued state.

He nodded and turned to leave.

"Before you go and get some obviously much-needed rest, I'd like to see you later today shortly after lunch. I'm going to have you start teaching some of the other Academy faculty; I'd love to have every Professor possess this new Skill before the new year starts. We're going to put your Fusions on hold for a short time while this information is spread through the Academy."

If he wasn't already thoroughly wrung-out, that statement would've made him even more exhausted. He wanted to protest, but couldn't figure out an appropriate reason why it shouldn't be him teaching this new Skill at all, since the Dean and Shinpai now possessed it. During the entire process, the Dean had stated more than once that she just needed *one* more example and she would be able to get it, and he was convinced that if it hadn't been for him showing her, she never would've succeeded. As it was, he was the only one who could reliably demonstrate the division of patterns, even if it was in Fusion form, as trying to learn from the brief separation of Shinpai's spell pattern likely wouldn't help anyone understand it. Perhaps when he was much better at it with a lot of practice that might change, but certainly not at the moment.

Resigned to teaching the entire staff, all he could do was nod in acknowledgement.

"Oh, don't look so down, Larek. This is a good thing, as it will ingratiate you to the faculty even more than you already are. It's nice to have powerful friends, after all." The Dean smirked at his dubious expression. "Besides, haven't you heard that no good deed goes unpunished? However, while you might think this is a punishment, in reality, it's an opportunity."

Larek didn't really think that was true, but he nodded anyway. He walked out the door to the Dean's lighthearted laughter; it wasn't directed toward him, though, as she seemed to just be laughing for the fun of it. Her giddiness upon unlocking another Skill after so many years had obviously not faded yet.

Outside of the Dean's office, he was surprised to see Nedira waiting near the doors. He was confused for a moment as he thought he remembered Vivienne having accompanied him earlier, but then he realized it was a new day.

"Are you alright, Larek? You look as if the Dean was yelling at you all night. What happened?" she asked, putting her hand on his arm as they walked through the Academy. He wanted to go straight to bed, but his stomach was grumbling because the last thing he ate was a quick lunch the day before. He would visit the Dining Hall, which would open in a short while, before he headed to bed – only to get up and teach even more people about the new Skill.

"I discovered a new Mage Skill no one had ever heard of and taught how to unlock it to both Shinpai and the Dean," he answered. "I'm terribly worn out, but I'll be fine."

"You *what?* A new Skill? Vivienne mentioned that you had discovered something when I took over, but that is so far above what I expected. How did you do it—you know what? Tell me later. I can hear your stomach from halfway across the Academy, and you appear as if you need to sleep for a few days."

He smiled tiredly at her, but he didn't refute that what she said was true. "Unfortunately, I can't sleep nearly that long. I have to get up and teach even more of the faculty sometime after lunch."

She scoffed and shook her head. "She can't keep running you ragged like this. First, it was the Fusions, and now you're supposed to teach the entire Academy staff? When will the Dean stop all this?"

"Probably when she gets what she wants and I end up closing the—" Larek clapped his mouth shut as the words coming out finally registered to his tired mind. A quick look around at the immediate area showed no one within at least 100 feet, so he didn't think anyone heard him...

...other than Nedira, of course.

"Closing the what? What are you talking about? What does she want you to do?"

"Nothing. Never mind. I'm just exhausted and don't know what I'm saying," he replied, hating to lie to her, but it was for her own good. It was too dangerous for her to know that kind of information; in fact, it felt dangerous even for *Larek* to know that information, but unfortunately both the now-dead Ricardo and the Dean had sort of forced the issue.

"I know when you're not telling the truth, Larek. You get this little twitch in your face that gives you away every single time, so I know when you're lying – or at least concealing something for some reason. Tell me, what are you hiding?"

He sighed, disappointed that he wasn't going to get off that easily. "Look, just know that it is something that would be dangerous if you knew about it, and I don't want to see you hurt. I apologize for keeping this from you, but I'm doing it to keep you safe."

She was silent as she walked along with him, and he could practically feel the anger building within her as she considered his words. He couldn't look at her as he feared he would spill all his secrets in order to diffuse the situation and make her happy again, so he kept his eyes straight ahead.

"Fine. Keep your secrets. I know that you aren't deliberately trying to shut me out, and based on everything else I know about you, this secret *must* be quite important if you haven't shared it yet." She sounded hurt, but most of the anger seemed to drain away from her as she continued to walk by his side.

It felt like a large gulf just expanded between him and Nedira, a chasm that hadn't been there before, and he wasn't sure if there was anything he could do to close the distance with her again. Telling her about his origins as a half-breed and his potential for Dominion magic would be dangerous for her if she knew about it, as any hint that she knew could cause her to be a target to get to him. That, and he was selfish because he didn't want her to pull away even further because she feared that he had somehow ensnared her with a magic he couldn't control.

*Maybe this is for the best? I don't want her to get hurt because of who I am, and I also don't want to know if I actually **did** influence her somehow with my magic. I still want her as my friend, but perhaps keeping a distance from her is the best idea. For now, at least.*

Neither of them said any more as they eventually arrived at the Dining Hall; because it was so early, breakfast hadn't been served yet, but Nedira was able to snag some already prepared biscuits and sausages for him, which he consumed so quickly that he barely tasted them. It wasn't long after that he found himself in his room just as the sun was starting to peek over the horizon, finally getting to bed even as Verne and Norde were still sleeping from the night before. He softly said goodnight to Nedira, who sat on the empty bed, staring off into nothing as she refused to respond.

Apologizing again for not being able to tell her what she wanted to know didn't feel like the right thing to do, so he instead just slipped into bed, getting comfortable within seconds. He was out before he let his nightmares about teaching even more people about the new Skill invade his thoughts.

He woke up sometime later to a room empty of his roommates, though Bartholomew was sitting on the empty bed now instead of Nedira. "Boy, what did you say to her? She's a bit peeved at you for some reason."

"What? Who? Peeved?" He was still waking up, instantly knowing that he hadn't gotten nearly enough sleep; at the same time, he realized that he wouldn't be able to sleep that night if he slept too long, so he might as well get up.

"Nedira," the Martial trainee explained. "She seemed angry at you, muttering under her breath as she left. A little lovers' quarrel?" he asked, smirking.

"Huh? Uh, no; we're not—anyway, I don't really want to talk about it." He really didn't, because then he would have to think about the whole situation with Nedira, and not knowing how to fix it properly, it wouldn't do any good to dwell on it.

"No problem. Just know that if you ever need to talk, I'm always willing to listen."

He nodded at the young man. Over the last few months, Bartholomew had filled out quite a bit and grown a bit taller, making him look more like a man than the boy he appeared when Larek had first met him. "Thanks. I'll let you know."

"So, what's on the agenda today? And why are you sleeping so late? You're usually up disgustingly early."

As he got ready for the day, Larek told the armored trainee the basics of what had happened with a warning not to spread the information around quite yet, as he just realized that a thing such as what he had done was liable to attract *even more* attention from the students than he probably wanted right now. "And now I'm going out to instruct some more Professors on how to gain this Skill, which I'm dreading; teaching really isn't my thing, as it wore me out yesterday faster than a full day chopping down trees in the Rushwood Forest."

"Rushwood Forest? That's far to the north, isn't it?"

"It is. Have you ever been there?"

Bartholomew shook his head. "No, not directly, but I believe my father visited the area years ago. It's part of our Duchy, after all."

"Ah." He nodded, not knowing what to say. He still didn't know a lot about Nobility as a whole and what each type of Noble controlled as part of their territory, though there was some passing mention in his *Geography* class the previous year. Political climates weren't discussed as much as other things, however, so his knowledge was fairly poor when it came to things like that.

Perhaps I'll ask him more about that later. It would probably be good to learn some of that stuff sometime, and Bartholomew's a pleasant sort for a Noble.

At lunch, which they caught the tail end of, Larek spent a minute looking over his Status, as he never really got a chance to study it much over the last day. In fact, he hadn't really looked at the entire thing in months, as not much had changed up until he had gotten the new Skill.

Larek Holsten
Fusionist
Healer
Level 19
Advancement Points (AP) : 12/17
Available AP to Distribute: 16

Stama: 590/590
Mana: 1330/1330

Strength: 59 (+)
Body: 59 (+)
Agility: 59 (+)
Intellect: 70 [133] (+)
Acuity: 104 [198] (+)
Pneuma: 299 [568] (+)
Pattern Cohesion: 5,680/5,680

Mage Abilities:
Spell – Bark Skin
Spell – Binding Roots
Spell – Fireball
Spell – Ice Spike
Spell – Lesser Restoration
Spell – Light Bending
Spell – Light Orb
Spell – Localized Anesthesia
Spell – Minor Mending
Spell – Rapid Plant Growth
Spell – Repelling Gust
Spell – Static Illusion

- Spell – Stone Fist
- Spell – Wall of Thorns
- Spell – Water Jet
- Spell – Wind Barrier
- Fusion – Acuity Boost
- Fusion – Agility Boost +7
- Fusion – Area Chill
- Fusion – Body Boost +5
- Fusion – Camouflage Sphere +2
- Fusion – Camouflage Sphere +5
- Fusion – Extreme Heat +5
- Fusion – Flaming Ball +5
- Fusion – Flying Stone +5
- Fusion – Graduated Parahealing +7
- Fusion – Healing Surge +1
- Fusion – Healing Surge +3
- Fusion – Healing Surge +5
- Fusion – Icy Spike +5
- Fusion – Illuminate Iron
- Fusion – Illuminate Steel
- Fusion – Illuminate Stone
- Fusion – Illuminate Wood
- Fusion – Illusionary Image +3
- Fusion – Intellect Boost
- Fusion – Muffle Sound +3
- Fusion – Muffling Air Deflection Barrier +6
- Fusion – Personal Air Deflection Barrier +4
- Fusion – Pneuma Boost
- Fusion – Repelling Barrier +1
- Fusion – Repelling Barrier +4
- Fusion – Repelling Barrier +7
- Fusion – Repelling Barrier +10
- Fusion – Repelling Gust of Air +5
- Fusion – Sharpen Iron Edge
- Fusion – Sharpen Steel Edge
- Fusion – Sharpen Stone Edge
- Fusion – Sharpen Wood Edge
- Fusion – Space Heater +2
- Fusion – Spellcasting Focus Boost +4
- Fusion – Strength Boost +1
- Fusion – Strength Boost +5
- Fusion – Strengthen and Sharpen Steel Edge +1

Fusion – Strengthen Iron
Fusion – Strengthen Steel
Fusion – Strengthen Stone
Fusion – Strengthen Wood
Fusion – Temperature Regulator +3
Fusion – Tree Skin +2
Fusion – Tree Skin +8
Fusion – Water Stream +5

Martial Abilities:
Battle Art – Furious Rampage

Mage Skills:
Focused Division Level 10
Multi-effect Fusion Focus Level 10
Pattern Recognition Level 20
Magical Detection Level 20
Spellcasting Focus Level 20
Mana Control Level 30
Fusion Level 30
Pattern Formation Level 30

Martial Skills:
Blunt Weapon Expertise Level 1
Bladed Weapon Expertise Level 2
Throwing Level 5
Dodge Level 7
Pain Immunity Level 20
Body Regeneration Level 25

General Skills:
Cooking Level 1
Bargaining Level 5
Beast Control Level 9
Leadership Level 10
Writing Level 11
Long-Distance Running Level 10
Speaking Level 15
Saw Handling Level 15
Reading Level 17
Listening Level 42
Axe Handling Level 81

Other than a few increases in his *Speaking*, *Reading*, and *Listening* General Skills, the rest of his Skills hadn't budged from where they had been right around the Skirmish he participated in. With the addition of his new Skill and increases in *Pattern Recognition* and *Magical Detection* to Level 20, he had also gained a personal Level to bring him to 19. It also came with 16 AP to spend on his stats, but he left them where they were for the moment since he wasn't sure where to put them.

Unfortunately, despite repeatedly performing the *Focused Division* Skill for the Dean so she could learn it, his Skill Level didn't increase past 10 in all that time. He had a feeling that it would require either dividing a larger quantity of Fusions at the same time or simply dividing a more complicated pattern, but he hadn't really had the opportunity. He hoped he might have the chance to experiment when he started teaching other Professors about the Skill, but he doubted it.

With resignation, he got up from the table in the Dining Room and said to Bartholomew, "Alright, let's get this over with. Hopefully they get it faster than the Dean, because I really don't want to be up all night like I was with her again."

The Martial trainee guffawed loudly at that, which confused Larek, but his mind was already on the task ahead of him.

Well, this should be fun.

Chapter 10

It was, in fact, far from the definition of *fun*.

Larek found himself directed by the Dean to a classroom he'd never been in before after he stopped by her office. From a few descriptions he'd overheard from Nedira and Kimble, he recognized that the section in which the classroom was located was for fourth- and fifth-year Academy students, but as for what was taught in these classrooms, he didn't have a clue.

"Thank you all for attending on such short notice," Dean Lorraine said to the 10 Professors sitting along the first bench in the otherwise large and empty classroom. All of them appeared slightly annoyed at having been called together in between school years, as the few weeks when classes weren't in session normally provided a bit of a break for most of them. For some Professors, such as Shinpai, they continued working hard even when they weren't involved in teaching classes; these individuals, however, weren't of that sort as they weren't dressed in their normal black Professor's robes, appearing in casual clothing and looking as if they wanted to get back to whatever had been interrupted when the Dean called for them. Larek recognized not a single one of them, but then again, he didn't really know many other faculty at the Academy other than his direct Professors from his first year and the Dean. That, and even if he *had* known them, with them not wearing their Professor robes, they appeared so... odd, he supposed... that he might not have recognized them, anyway.

"What are we doing here? I thought we already had people working on the updated schedules for next year," an older man with long, shockingly white hair abruptly asked. As Larek looked closer at the Professor, he had to reevaluate his assumption that he was old based on his hair color, as the youthful face didn't show even the slightest hint of a wrinkle. *Definitely not from the Kingdom, at least.* That wasn't very surprising, of course, as almost all of the Professors in the Academy came from beyond the Kingdom, and that was certainly true for those sitting casually on the benches in front of him.

"We do, but that's not why you're here. Larek," the Dean went on, gesturing to the young man by her side, who immediately wanted to shrink back and hide to avoid the intense gazes of the Professors, "discovered something new that he has graciously volunteered to teach us."

Graciously volunteered? Not exactly the words I'd use to describe what happened. He kept his mouth shut, though, because he felt more than a little intimidated by the people staring at him. While he had a vague sense that they weren't necessarily as powerful as the Dean was, to have gained a position at Copperleaf Academy likely meant that they were experienced with and knowledgeable about things that he couldn't even imagine.

"The Fusion prodigy?" the same white-haired Professor asked dismissively. "While I can't deny that the Fusions I've seen produced by him are incredible, that's not really my expertise. I barely passed my *Fusions* class at the Academy back in the day as it is, and I wouldn't trust myself to make even the most basic of Fusions today." The annoyance in the man's gruff voice, which was completely at odds with his appearance in Larek's mind, was obvious as he glanced at his fellow Professors. "Moreover, *none of us* are particularly skilled in creating Fusions. Why isn't Shinpai here joining us, as the Head Fusionist Mentor along with the rest of us?"

It took Larek a moment to understand what the man was asking, as "Head Fusionist Mentor" wasn't familiar, but he eventually worked it out. He remembered hearing that there were Specialization Mentors who acted as guides for those who chose a Specialization in later years; for instance, Nedira had a Mentor who focused on the Naturalist Specialization, and it was this Mentor who assisted his friend on the path she was taking in the last stage of her academic journey. He could only assume that Shinpai, being a Grandmaster Fusionist and in charge of teaching *Advanced Fusions*, was not only a Mentor, but the *Head* Mentor. If that assumption carried further, then by the gruff Professor's words, that most likely meant that these others were *also* Head Mentors of their chosen Specialization.

They might not match the Dean in terms of power, but these individuals were strong in their own right.

And I'm supposed to teach them? Talk about intimidating.

The Dean shook her head. "That's because it has nothing to do with Fusions, as unlikely as that sounds. Instead, what young Larek has discovered is…" she continued, pausing dramatically, "…a new, never-before-seen Mage Skill."

There was silence as everyone stared first at the Dean before turning their attention back to Larek. Professor "white-hair" scoffed in disbelief. "What? That's impossible."

Before anyone else could say anything to discount the possibility, the Dean immediately displayed her new *Focused Division* Skill to everyone as it hovered in front of her. Larek was shocked to see that it was already Level 4; he could only assume that she hadn't taken any time to rest after he left her office earlier that morning and had been frantically practicing with it. He had already learned during his first year that his own speedy progression with his Mage Skills was highly abnormal, so for the Dean to have progressed so quickly was amazing. Then again, with how powerful she was and the fact that the first few Skill Levels were typically easy to increase, it shouldn't have been a surprise.

The revelation elicited a response way out of proportion – at least in Larek's opinion – to what it warranted, as there was shocked silence from some, wildly enthusiastic exclamations from others, and there was even one woman who actually had tears leaving tracks down her face as she smiled so widely that it appeared as though her head was going to split in half. Needless to say, it made Larek extremely uncomfortable, especially as they tore their gazes away from the Skill that the Dean was displaying on her Status and focused on the burgeoning Fusionist once again. He suddenly felt like defenseless prey in the sights of some vicious predator as he could practically sense the desire and hunger for this new Skill emanating from their bodies.

Dean Lorraine went on to explain the basics of what the *Focused Division* Skill did and its beneficial uses, which Larek largely ignored because it wasn't anything new to him. She even demonstrated her newfound "expertise" with the Skill by utilizing a training hoop that was near the edge of the classroom, launching two simple *Fireballs* that had their spell patterns just barely separate enough not to interfere with each other. He could tell that the head of the Academy visibly struggled to accomplish even that much, but the triumphant smile on her face belied her efforts in the face of the observers' astonished expressions.

Larek briefly wondered why he was even there teaching these other Professors if she could do it, but when he thought back at how she accomplished the successful *Focused Division* of the *Fireball* spell pattern, he had to acknowledge that she probably wouldn't be very successful at teaching others – at least not right now. Her execution of the division was extremely poor, and lopsided, to boot; and the struggle she had with it caused her to draw the spell pattern, fill it with Mana, and then split it in the blink of an eye – which wasn't exactly a great visual aid. Unfortunately, for her to successfully cast the spells, she had to do it that quickly or risk the patterns falling apart; he could only assume as her Skill Level reached much higher, she would be able to slow down as she could control the patterns better, but for now, that was impossible. Unfortunately, that meant that his demonstrations with a Fusion, which was much more visible and easier to follow, were needed for the moment.

Then the Dean, as if taking perverse pleasure in leaving him to the figurative wolves, claimed she had other matters to attend to and left him there alone with the starving predators. With a sigh and a refusal to look at any of the Professors as they desperately pleaded with their eyes to impart the knowledge of this new Skill unto them, he began to demonstrate the process of creating a thicker pattern, infusing it with Mana, and then dividing it into two separate Fusion formations.

"Can't you show it as a spell pattern?" This came from another of the Professors, a woman with short, spiky, pitch-black hair on top of her head, with a relatively pale complexion compared to those from the Kingdom. "As Professor Purdy mentioned earlier, none of us are as familiar with Fusions as we are with spells."

Larek shook his head. "No, I can't cast any spells, unfortunately."

She appeared shocked. "What? How is it you're so well-versed in Fusions, but you can't make a spell pattern? How did you even discover this new Skill, anyway?"

He hesitated on what to say, but he eventually decided to tell at least some of the truth. "Oh, I can make spell patterns, but I can't infuse them with Mana or they'll blow up and destroy half of this classroom in the process. I discovered this Skill because I wanted to be able to make more than one Fusion simultaneously to save time."

"Are you saying that you cannot cast spells… *at all*? Explain that, if you would."

Larek went on to describe what had happened to him when he first tried casting a spell; it wasn't really a secret, especially now that everyone knew about his ability with Fusions. In addition, he thought that if they knew he couldn't cast spells, they would leave off in asking him to make spell patterns.

He was wrong.

Against his protestations, they had him demonstrate creating spell patterns for some of the most basic spells he knew strictly for the purpose of demonstration. At first, he was extremely wary of doing so, as he flinched at the memory of what happened previously, but he quickly discovered that he had nothing to fear from the spell patterns he created for the others to look at. As long as he didn't infuse even a tiny drop of Mana into it, each pattern was completely inert – and it was strong and stable enough that he could keep it visible for the others to learn from, as they initially had trouble translating what he told them to do regarding the thickness of their pattern lines without a visual aid not in the form of a Fusion.

It was only after the majority of the Professors were able to reliably construct a thick enough spell pattern that he had to switch over to his Fusions once again, as he could then demonstrate the infusion of Mana and subsequent division of the pattern. This method got plenty of annoyed protestations and actual *whining* from a few of the Professors, which further exhausted his already depleted social energy.

Despite Larek wanting nothing more to do with teaching them, after 5 hours of trying to appease them all by thinking of different ways to explain the same thing, he kept on encouraging them to keep trying. As his stomach rumbled, a pair of Academy staff members appeared and delivered dinner so as not to interrupt the training. Larek was thankful – not necessarily for the non-interruption, as he wouldn't have minded a break, but for the food. His teaching methods finally bore fruit as the first of the Professors had a breakthrough and succeeded in gaining the *Focused Division* Skill. The success of the spiky black-haired woman, who had spoken up earlier for him to demonstrate spell patterns, seemed to spur the others on, and 15 minutes later the next one accomplished the same feat. As they practiced with their new Skill, the remaining 8 Professors doubled their efforts and began to follow their success every 10 to 30 minutes.

It was already dark outside before the white-haired man, Professor Purdy, became the last one to unlock the new Skill. As if that was some sort of signal, the Dean swept into the classroom, smiling at the ecstatic expressions on everyone's faces. Well, on every face but Larek's, as he was once again absolutely exhausted, even more so than when he had taught the Dean.

"Thank you so much, Larek!" Dean Lorraine said, actually coming up to him and giving him a brief hug before turning to the Professors, all of whom were still practicing their new Skill. The personal contact would've normally left Larek feeling a bit flustered, but he was so tired after the day of teaching and short amount of sleep the night before that he barely even acknowledged it.

"As you can see, this new Skill is extraordinary, not only for its uses, but for its help in the development of all Mages. I know that most of you have been stuck at your current Level for years, unable to advance any of your Skills despite a lot of effort, but this is a way to get it moving once again.

"But this isn't just for *us*, those who have hit a wall in our development. On the contrary, I want to have this new Skill available to as many as possible, given the current situation with the Scissions throughout the Kingdom. I don't have to explain to you how even a few extra Skill Levels for a Mage can spell the difference between life and death, as an increase in a personal Level can mean enough AP allocated to different stats to help one survive against impossible odds. Not only will Mages be inherently stronger, but this new way of casting a spell and dividing it into two *or more* can change the tide of battle in an instant.

"Because of this, I'm going to be implementing a slight change in our curriculum, centered around our young prodigy here. I will be taking him out of some of his classes to help teach our fourth- and fifth-year students how to gain this Skill this year, before moving on to teaching the SIC stationed in Thanchet. All of this will be in between his own studies and creating needed Fusions, so Larek will be a busy man for the next few months!"

Hearing that, Larek's exhaustion finally caught up with him, and the next thing he knew he was on the floor looking up at the ceiling with no memory of how he got there. Dean Lorraine came into focus above him, her face appearing extraordinarily worried as she gazed down at him. Out of the corner of his eye, he saw Bartholomew hovering at the edge of his vision, shuffling from foot to foot as he looked at Larek with worry. He had forgotten that the Martial trainee had even been there at the door, patiently acting as a bodyguard for him throughout the training.

"Larek? What happened? How are you feeling?"

He wasn't sure how to respond to the questions, as he really didn't know the answer. All he knew was that he was extremely exhausted for some reason, more so than he really thought he should be. When he told her that, she looked confused for a moment before an expression of comprehension seemed to pass over her face.

"Ah. I see. I believe you've been inadvertently using your unique... *trait*... to assist with your teaching more than I considered," she said softly, too low in volume for anyone else to easily overhear. "I think with a few days of rest you'll be better, and we'll see if we can figure something else out for the training for the time being. I had no idea that this would happen, and I apologize for putting you in this situation." She looked up at Bartholomew, gesturing for him to come over. "Let's get him to bed; he's worn out and needs to rest." Staring back at Larek, the Dean said, "We'll talk again tomorrow; I'm going to reschedule or outright cancel some of the other Skill trainings until we can get to the bottom of this."

He felt himself nod, before the Martial trainee was there to help him to his feet. Glancing around the room, he noticed that all of the other Professors were still consumed with practicing their new Skill, as if they were small children who had just gained a new toy. Nevertheless, they all looked at him with gratitude and worry when they saw he was up and around, but none of them said anything.

That was fine with Larek, as he didn't want to talk to anyone else at the moment. The next few minutes were a blur as he was led back to his room, where he collapsed on his bed. He was asleep seconds later, still fully clothed, and descended into a dreamless sleep that felt vaguely like falling into an abyss.

Chapter 11

Larek struggled to wake, his mind and body feeling pained and sluggish to the point where he felt like he was on death's door. Memories of teaching the Academy Professors flowed through his thoughts, drowning out any attempts to reach up past the point of unconsciousness, but he persevered by figuratively swimming out of the flood of the nightmarish onslaught.

Opening eyelids that felt gummy and full of lead, he finally glimpsed a brightness that blinded him momentarily before his vision adjusted to the sudden light on sensitive eyeballs. The first thing Larek noticed was that the ceiling he was looking at was only vaguely familiar, with a half-stone and half-wooden pattern that reminded him of the healer's ward in the Academy. But that wasn't possible, because he specifically remembered going to sleep in his own bed just a short time ago, so the entire ceiling should be wooden beams.

The next thing that he became aware of was a sharp pain in his stomach, a stabbing emptiness that spread a weakness through his limbs to the point where he felt as if he was dying. He attempted to sit up, only to fall back down after lifting his back up off the soft surface beneath him an inch or two, as a debilitating exhaustion sapped all of his strength.

"He's awake! Go tell the Dean!"

The voice coming from somewhere off to his right startled him as it was both loud and sudden, and he lethargically turned his head to see the blurry sight of Vivienne approaching his bedside. *Did she... Did she poison me again?*

His thoughts were a mess of confusing questions, as he had no idea what was going on. The exhaustion he was feeling reared its head again as his eyelids closed of their own volition, but just as he was drifting off to sleep again, he heard the indistinct sounds of people talking nearby. Forcing his eyes to open and his head to turn toward the voices, he blinked a few times to clear his vision as he saw Dean Lorraine and Shinpai talking to Vivienne.

"Larek? How are you feeling?"

Seemingly out of nowhere, the Grandmaster Fusionist was by Larek's side, his words strangely echoing the same question that the Dean had asked him shortly after he collapsed in the classroom.

His voice was rough and cracking as he tried to answer. "Tired and... hungry." It was at that time that he realized that the pain in his stomach was actually his body telling him that he was literally starving, which was strange because he had just eaten the night before. Sure, it was a quick meal because he was still teaching the Professors, but it was at least *something*.

"That's not surprising," Shinpai said, sitting down on the edge of his bed as he smiled sadly at him for some reason. "You've been unconscious for over a week. The healers were able to sustain you, but your body needs external sustenance soon."

A... week? What?!

His *Fusions* Professor surreptitiously looked around before he moved his fingers in a quick cast of a spell. There was an audible *pop* as his ears felt assaulted by a vacuum of air, and he could see a spherical bubble of something surrounding himself, Shinpai, and Larek's entire bed.

"We believe you've overextended your Dominion magic, which wasn't something we were even aware you could do, having no real understanding of how it works," Shinpai continued, and the way he was speaking so openly about Larek's secret made the exhausted Fusionist believe that they couldn't be overheard. "For that, we sincerely apologize; both the Dean and I thought you might be using it to help impart the necessary instruction to gain the Skill, but you have to believe me that we had no idea it would do something like that to you."

Larek slowly nodded, finding that the simple act of moving his head took entirely too much energy. His nod was more of an acknowledgment that he understood what his Professor was telling him; it was in no way an absolution. Even if they hadn't expected it, they were deliberately using his connection with Dominion magic to gain something they wanted, even if it was ultimately for a good cause. His dislike of and disgust for the magic he didn't have any control over made him *never* want to use it again after learning of it, and he had mentioned that same thing to both of them at the time. For them to believe that they could use it for their own gain was like a violation of his trust in them, and he felt his faith that they knew what was best for him start to erode as he stared at the contrite expression on the older man's face. The Professor's regret seemed real, prompting a part of Larek to want to forgive and forget it ever happened, but he squashed that feeling as tired anger suffused his body at the thought of what they did to him.

"Now that we know, we can work on regulating how much of your special magic that you're using when you teach—"

"No."

"—the rest of the... what? Did you say something?"

It took him a second to clear his throat since he was parched. "I said *no*. I... don't want to use this... vile magic anymore."

"But think of the good you can do! You would not believe how powerful this Skill is—"

Larek shook his head once. "No. You... teach." He was aware that he sounded like his speech skills were degenerating, but it was getting harder and harder to speak.

Shinpai appeared frustrated. "We've already tried, but for some reason it seems as though anyone new trying to learn the new Skill can't seem to grasp it even after days of trying. The Dean is hopeful that others will eventually pick it up, especially since she was able to unlock it despite not being affected by your Dominion magic, but it's slow going. We *need* your help—"

"No. No more."

It wasn't just that he didn't want to do it, but with how much he felt like he nearly died from the process, it was to ensure that he didn't hurt himself. The slight scare he had with his pattern not that long before discovering the *Focused Division* Skill made him a lot more cognizant of his limits, and whatever this Dominion magic was doing certainly passed those limits without his awareness. If that wasn't reason enough to not want to teach anyone else, then the simple fact that he didn't want to be *used* like that was all he needed.

They could use him to make Fusions all they wanted, as that was something he actually *enjoyed* doing (even if he was starting to tire of creating the same ones over and over), though he was curious whether there was some sort of compensation he could get for his work. He'd learned that some Fusionists were able to earn something for the Fusions they made above and beyond what was required for the SIC; since he was technically part of the SIC (or would be once he graduated), didn't that mean he should be earning something? Not necessarily for him, but perhaps for his family so that they could eventually move to somewhere safe? He still had his winnings from the Skirmish, but would that even be enough? While he'd picked up a little bit about how much food and other things cost on his brief travels through the Kingdom, he didn't really know how much it would cost to completely pick up and move somewhere else.

So, Fusions he didn't exactly mind being asked to make, but manipulating him to utilize his mysterious Dominion magic? *No.* He wasn't having it. There were a lot of things that he could and would put up with, but that wasn't one of them.

Grandmaster Fusionist Shinpai patted him on the leg and got up, his expression seeming a bit patronizing to the exhausted Larek.

"We'll talk more when you've recovered. Rest up and enjoy the vacation from classes, because your second year just started." Before Larek could say anything else, his Professor turned around and walked away, the spell that had prevented anyone from listening disappearing as soon as he passed through its edge. Larek turned his head to watch him stop near the Dean, where they spoke in voices too low for him to hear. The head of Copperleaf Academy just looked inside the room and nodded in what he took to be an apology, before the two of them left.

Almost immediately upon them leaving, Vivienne walked inside with a wooden tray filled with something that smelled good. Larek was disappointed not to see anything hearty and delicious, as the only thing on the tray was a huge bowl of soup and a cup of water.

"You're going to need to start slow to get your energy back, and so that you don't hurt yourself with solid food. You gave us a little scare there, Larek, and we don't want you to have a relapse," the Ranger said, placing the tray down on the bedside table that he hadn't even noticed until now.

And then she began to spoon-feed him soup, which made him feel like an invalid. *I suppose I am right now.* He couldn't sit up or even lift his arms, so he unfortunately needed the help, as embarrassing as it was. Still, he didn't refuse to accept the assistance, and even thanked her after he was surprisingly quickly full, only to pass out minutes later.

The following days were more of the same, but after the second time he woke up Larek was propped up and was able to lift his arms by that point as his energy started to return. He still felt inordinately weak, as if something not only negated every single Martial stat point in his Status but took away his natural strength as well; that feeling wasn't actually reflected on his Status, which he looked at the second time he woke up to see if anything had changed. He even added another AP to Strength, Body, and Agility to bring them all to 60 just to see if that would have any effect on his recovery... but nothing happened.

Nothing else was different and nothing appeared on his Status that indicated what might be wrong with him. There wasn't much he could do other than wait for his body to recover, which happened slowly at first; a little over 4 days after waking up in the healer's ward, his strength seemed to return overnight, and he felt revitalized and raring to get up and out of bed the next morning. Once he finally got up and moved around, the lingering traces of weakness worked themselves out within minutes, and he felt better than he had in a long, long time.

Through all that time in the healer's ward, he didn't see Nedira a single time, though Verne and Norde mentioned that she had briefly visited while he was asleep. The avoidance bothered him greatly because he still considered her a great friend, which made him thankful that she was waiting in his room by herself as soon as he felt well enough to leave the healer's ward.

"Nedira! I'm so glad you're here; I've missed you." That was the truth, too, as he felt like he was missing a part of his life when she didn't show up to visit or act as a bodyguard while he was awake.

There was a guilty look on her face as she turned away, mumbling something that he didn't catch. Sitting heavily down on the extra bed next to where she was sitting, he reached out his finger to turn her head so that she was facing him. "What was that?"

She turned her head away again, but he brought it right back with a gentle finger. "I... I'm sorry."

"What do you have to be sorry for?" he asked, generally confused. *Is she sorry that she didn't visit? Or is it something else.*

"I shouldn't have been mad at you for keeping secrets from me," she reluctantly said with a sigh. Tears suddenly threatened to spill out of the corners of her eyes, as she blurted out, "And I was so afraid that you pushed yourself too far because of me that I couldn't face you while you were in the healer's ward." At that, she burst into tears for real, before burying her face in the front of his robe, tightly gripping onto it as it quickly became soaked.

Awkwardly putting his arms around her, he held her close while she sobbed, unsure what to do or say. There was unfortunately some truth to his secret being the cause of his collapse and stay in the healer's ward, though it wasn't due to anything that Nedira had done to him. Larek softly said as much to the top of her head, since that was all he could really see of her when he looked down at her clutched to his chest. He wasn't even sure if she heard him, but after a few minutes she started to pull herself together.

Sniffling and wiping at her eyes as she pulled away, she looked at him and asked, "Is that true? It wasn't anything that I did?"

He nodded. "It's true. It was purely a situation that was caused by something no one could've accounted for," he explained. "Regardless, I'm determined not to let it happen again."

"You know what caused it?"

Again, he nodded. "Yes, but you don't have to worry about it. I won't let the Dean or Shinpai force me into that situation again."

Sucking in her breath, she asked in surprise, "*They* did this?"

"They caused the situation, but it wasn't necessarily their fault that it happened because no one could've guessed this would occur once I was pushed too far. Again, I won't let it happen a second time."

Nedira pulled back slightly at his tone. "All this secrecy, huh?" Sighing, she seemed to come to a decision. "I'm not going to let it bother me like I did before. I don't know what it was; it was like some part of my mind was angry that there was something you didn't share with me, like you were deliberately shutting me out. I was in turns angry and close to tears, and there was nothing I could do to control it." She suddenly smiled, placing her hand on his knee. "But that's all in the past. We can move forward now and pick up where we left off."

Uh, oh. Is this my Dominion magic at work? Is she being affected by it right now, or was her reaction before caused by it? Her wildly fluctuating emotional state was obvious even to Larek, who was far from an expert on such things, and he couldn't help but think that he was the cause.

As she leaned forward, her eyes locked onto his lips, the door to the room suddenly burst open with a bang. Flinching as he remembered the last time that happened, he was relieved to see that it was only Verne and Norde rushing inside.

"Larek! We heard you were released and figured we'd find you here—oh!" Verne shouted, before his roommate spotted Nedira sitting close to Larek. "Are we interrupting something? Have you two made up?"

Feeling the blood rushing to his cheeks as he realized what Verne was trying to insinuate, he shook his head. "No, we were just talking. And yes, I think we've worked past our issues. Anyway, tell me what's going on with you? How's second year?"

His two roommates were very excited to tell him all about the new year at the Academy, including all the "advanced" classes they were attending now that they weren't lowly first-years. Larek briefly wondered when he would get his own class schedule, as he hadn't thought to ask about it until now, but apparently Nedira could read his mind.

"I'll bring it by tomorrow morning. I was told that you're still off for another full day to recover, so you don't have to worry about it until then. As for me, I need to be getting to a late class right now; as a fifth-year, I have a lot more self-instruction time to do what I want, but there are still some required courses." She scooted over and kissed Larek on the cheek, causing him to blush once again, before rushing out the door.

His two roommates smirked at him before they left as well, as they still had one more class that they were already going to be late to, but they wanted to take the time to check on him to see how he was doing. As soon as they left, Penelope entered and checked up on him before taking up a position outside of the door, giving him some privacy.

What am I going to do about Nedira? This all feels extraordinarily wrong, but I don't want to push her away because now I think that will hurt her more than anything else I could do. Seeing how affected she was when she thought I was shutting her out, I have a feeling that if I try to keep my distance, it will cause even more problems.

    He didn't know what the correct answer was in this situation, but he eventually decided to wait a few days to see how things were going with his second year of the Academy. It was entirely possible that he would be too busy to worry about spending too much time with her, especially if he returned to creating more Fusions.

    No matter what, though, he was not going to be teaching any more people about the new Skill he had discovered. That tree had already been felled, as his father used to say; there was no going back once he made the decision. It might get him in trouble, but what could they do? Kill him?

    He'd rather die than be forced to knowingly use his Dominion magic again.

Chapter 12

The next morning, when Larek and his two roommates went to breakfast, Nedira was waiting for them inside of the Dining Hall.

"There you are! I've been waiting for *hours*—"

Her brother snorted, interrupting her. "Yeah, right. You probably only got here a few seconds ago based on the way you look all frazzled," Norde said with a smirk before sitting down. "Besides, you don't usually get up early like Larek, so it's doubtful that you've been awake for more than a few minutes."

Larek sat down next to Nedira, smiling at the interaction between the siblings, remembering his own family and how they would rib each other after a long day of working in the Rushwood Forest. While *he* didn't participate in such antics very often, as his attention was usually focused elsewhere, it was still familiar enough that it brought forth thoughts of their current situation. Having been gone more than a full year, he hoped he would've heard word if something had happened to them, but he knew that was unlikely. For one, the basic communication system set up throughout the Kingdom was essentially based on the SIC Transportation Network, which could pass along messages at the speed of their carriages. Since those carriages didn't necessarily reach all the way up to Rushwood, it was unlikely that any information on the area would ever reach him unless someone went out of their way to inform the wider world.

Secondly, while he had learned about some sort of magical long-distance communication that was in use, it was apparently only available to Nobility and was expensive to set up and use. All he knew was that it relied on complicated Fusions, which made him want to eventually learn how it worked once he was able to make Advanced Fusions, but its rarity meant that any communications passed through these means were unlikely to contain any information on his family.

Lastly, he still didn't know the situation there with the headman and if knowledge of Larek's continued survival after being dragged away was commonly known. Trying to communicate with his family – or the opposite, them trying to communicate with Larek – might put them in danger, which was the last thing he wanted.

Regardless, he pushed thoughts of his family out of his mind as he looked at Nedira questioningly, as she typically didn't join them for breakfast since her classes last year had been on the opposite side of the Academy. He wasn't sure what her schedule was this year, as he hadn't had a chance to question her about it the day before, so he could only assume she had some free time in the morning.

"I brought your schedule. It's…" Nedira started to say, but then she hesitated.

"It's what?"

Instead of answering right away, she slid a piece of paper toward him. As he picked it up, she continued – still with a hesitant lilt to her speech. "Your schedule is a bit different from what, well, it should be. I'm not sure if this is better or worse," she stated with a shrug.

Larek looked at his schedule on the paper and had to agree.

Advanced Fusions 1 – 9am to 9:50am
Workshop 405
Advanced Fusions 1 – 10am – 10:50am
Workshop 405
Advanced Fusions 1 – 11am – 11:50am
Workshop 405
Lunch – 12pm – 12:50pm
Dining Hall 3
Intermediate Mana Manipulation – 1pm – 1:50pm
Workshop 315
The Changing Environment of Scissions – 2pm – 2:50pm
Classroom 240
Skill Training – 3pm – 3:50pm
Classroom 510
Skill Training – 4pm – 4:50pm
Classroom 510
Skill Training – 5pm – 5:50pm
Classroom 510

The first three classes he had every day were *Advanced Fusions 1*, which he supposed made sense because of his Specialization. He remembered the Dean and Shinpai mentioning something about him spending more time working on creating vital Fusions for the efforts against the changing situation with the Scissions throughout the Kingdom, and having a larger chunk of time devoted to this purpose could be beneficial. He also hoped that it would allow him to have some time to try out some different Fusions and attempt to advance his Skills, something that he hadn't had much time for lately.

After that came lunch, followed by something called *Intermediate Mana Manipulation*. From what he could tell based on it being in Workshop 315, this was a third-year class, just like Advanced Fusions was technically a fourth-year class, though the ones in it last year had mostly been fifth-year students. He wasn't sure what this class was, though he had to assume that because of his Mana Control that they wanted to see how well he manipulated it in other ways – and he was looking forward to finding out.

Following *Intermediate Mana Manipulation* was what he assumed was the restructured class on Scissions. *The Changing Environment of Scissions* sounded exactly like what he needed to know about the sudden change of Scissions appearing away from towns and cities, where they had primarily appeared for nearly 1,000 years. It was definitely a beneficial class to take considering that it was important to know what the Scissions were doing outside of the towns and cities, because he expected that, at some point, he would leave the Academy for one reason or another.

Whether it was because he graduated and was stuck creating Fusions for the SIC, or on a secret mission given to him by the Dean to close the rift-like access point to a magical world that the Gergasi opened up a millennium ago, all depended on a number of factors in the future. However, he had absolutely no desire to get anywhere near the Gergasi or this hole in the world that spewed out magical energy and monsters, even if the Dean thought he could do something about it.

Looking at his schedule and the last three classes – all of which were identical – he noticed that there weren't any classes on spellcasting, Specializations, geography, or monster knowledge like the ones he had taken in his first year.

As for those last three classes, they didn't appear to be classes at all, despite the fact that *Skill Training* took place in a workshop.

"What is 'Skill Training'?" he asked, but before she could respond, he suddenly knew.

They want me to train more people in Focused Division, don't they? I already told them no, but they went and did this anyway. I'm not doing it.

"I'm not completely sure, but I assume it has to do with—"

He nodded, causing her to cut her own statement off. "Yeah, I believe so. Too bad I won't be doing it."

"What? Why?" Verne suddenly asked, having listened to the conversation. While his roommate was aware of the special attention that had been paid to him just before he collapsed, he didn't know the full story – or as much of the full story as he wanted to share. Larek softly shared a few more details with him and Norde, explaining that it was the teaching of the new skill that caused him to nearly perish. They seemed skeptical at first but eventually took his word for it, considering that Larek had just recovered from his obvious convalescence.

"What are you going to do?" Nedira asked, concern in her voice. Larek could well understand why she might be worried, because he was essentially telling the Dean "No".

"I already told Shinpai that I wasn't going to do it, and I'll tell the Dean just the same. They could put me in some other classes, because there won't be any more 'Skill Training' from me."

Verne looked excited. "That's great! There are so many classes that it doesn't appear that you have, including *Spell Pattern Construction*, *Magical Theory Applications*, and *Balancing Your Stats: Proper AP Management*! I know, they don't sound all that fun, but if we can get into some of the same classes, that would be great!"

Larek wasn't sure if any of those classes would be beneficial to him, given his inability to cast spells, but he would rather attend those classes than do any more teaching. "I'll see what they can do, especially since I'll have three periods free when I tell them I'm not going to be teaching any others."

After they ate, Larek made his way toward the Dean's office with Vivienne as his shadow for the morning while the others headed off to classes. Thankfully, no one stopped him on the way there and he discovered that the Dean was, in fact, in her office, so there was nothing hindering him from confronting her about this whole *Skill Training* thing on his schedule. Yet, as he stood outside her office door, he froze while lifting his hand to knock. The simple fact was that he wasn't accustomed to saying no when someone asked him to do something, as he was usually more than willing to help out wherever he could. Unfortunately, he'd found that it was much easier to act as a doormat and let people walk all over him rather than stick up for himself when it came to conflict. Of course, in matters of life-and-death, he was more inclined to defend himself by all means necessary, such as what happened with Ricardo and the two Martial trainees, but this was different.

It *shouldn't* be different, as it *was* technically a matter of life and death if he pushed himself too hard… but he couldn't help but think that it was. There was something in him that wanted to pursue some sort of compromise, such as limiting the amount of teaching he did to ensure he didn't end up straining his Dominion magic too greatly; however, just the thought of his Dominion magic being used in the act of teaching others a new Mage Skill was enough to put those thoughts to rest.

"You need to do this, Larek," Vivienne spoke up from where she was positioned near the doorway leading to the Dean's office. "I can't say that I understand what is happening, but if this has anything to do with why you collapsed and were unconscious for days on end, then it's my job to ensure you stay away from anything that could cause that to happen again. *Is* this related to what happened to you?" she asked.

There was no point in Larek pretending not to know what she was asking, so he just nodded. He wasn't going to tell her any more details than that, as even his friends didn't know everything. It was bad enough that the Dean and Shinpai knew, but there wasn't anything he could do about that.

"Then get in there and tell her that you're not doing it," Vivienne said shortly, gesturing to the door as if it was the most obvious thing in the world.

Taking a deep breath and giving her an almost imperceptible nod, Larek knocked on the door.

"Come in, Larek."

He'd given up on learning how the Dean always seemed to know who it was outside of her door, so he entered and saw the head of Copperleaf Academy sitting behind her desk, a few random papers scattered along its surface. Sitting across from her was Shinpai, the last person he wanted to see at the moment considering his visit. *Shouldn't he be in one of his classes?*

"Larek! It's so good to see you, my boy! Come and sit down," Shinpai said as he got up at his entrance, before gesturing to one of the super-comfortable chairs nearby. As much as he didn't want to follow his instructions out of spite, Larek refused to give in to such pettiness and instead sat down where indicated. As soon as he sat down, his *Advanced Fusions* Professor asked, "So, what can we do for you?"

As of yet, the Dean hadn't said a single word, as she only observed him coming in with folded hands sitting steady on top of her desk. Regardless of her lack of interaction, he addressed her instead of Shinpai, as she was the one that should have final authority over his schedule.

"It shouldn't be a surprise why I'm here, especially after I received my schedule," he started. "As I told Professor Shinpai, I will not teach *Focused Division* to anyone else, so if that is what 'Skill Training' is all about, then—"

"Shinpai?" the Dean finally spoke, cutting Larek off as her attention snapped to the Grandmaster Fusionist. "Tell me you didn't put that on his schedule."

"I sure did," the older man said, seemingly proud of it. "Larek just doesn't know what's going on out there, but we both have heard the reports. The Mages in the SIC need this Skill to get stronger so they can take back control of the Kingdom, because otherwise it is only a matter of time before complete chaos overruns everything," he continued seriously, looking between Dean Lorraine and Larek. "Besides, the Skill Training isn't just for teaching other people about the new Skill, but for practice in controlling his output of Dominion magic. It should be like a Skill, anyway, and with enough practice, he won't collapse after using it."

Larek was already shaking his head before his *Fusions* Professor stopped talking. "No. I already told you that I don't want anything to do with—"

"But you may need it when you go against the Gergasi!" Shinpai shouted him down, practically spluttering. "With you unable to make Advanced Fusions, you're going to need any advantage you can get."

"You said it yourself that it was only a matter of time before I figured out what was holding me back, and—"

Larek was getting really tired of being interrupted, as his Professor did it once again. "But not everyone breaks through the blockages in their Skill. I don't want to see you stall in your development, and your Dominion magic might be exactly what you need to keep improving!"

"No."

Both Larek and Shinpai were surprised when *the Dean* spoke the single word. "What?" the Grandmaster Fusionist abruptly asked.

"I said, 'No.' We've already asked so much of our young Fusionist here without forcing him to do something that could harm or *kill* him if he overdoes it – not to mention that it is something that he clearly despises, which is somehow worse." She turned away from Shinpai, who appeared furious, and addressed Larek directly. "The *Skill Training* class is one that you can use for whatever purpose you like; with everything else you're doing, I believe you need some time to experiment and further your development in other ways. While it won't be what Shinpai wanted it used for, I believe it will be beneficial for you, nonetheless."

"All three of them?"

Larek saw her eyes open a fraction wider as she turned them toward the *Advanced Fusions* Professor. "Three? Really?"

"What of it? The process takes a long time for others to learn the new Skill, so I wanted to ensure he had enough time," he said unapologetically. Thankfully, he also sounded resigned that he wasn't going to get what he wanted, leaving Larek feeling slightly relieved; he didn't really want to see the Grandmaster Fusionist every single morning for three class periods if he was going to hold a grudge.

"Fair enough," the Dean said, looking back at Larek. "Yes, all three of those class periods. I imagine that he took out most of the classes that won't benefit you much, given your limitations on spellcasting, but you can always attend them if you so desire; I'll let the Professors in your year group know that you have permission to attend, but aren't required to go."

Larek suddenly sagged in his seat as he heard the gift he was being presented: free time to experiment. "Thank you. That's all I wanted."

As he made to get up to leave, the Dean stopped him. "One more thing. If you ever do want to try teaching again, let me know; while the use of your Dominion magic is detestable to you, it is also extremely beneficial in teaching others *Focused Division*. We've attempted to duplicate the same sort of learning method with poor results, though we think it might work over a prolonged period of time."

"I will let you know," he said politely, though he already knew that such a thing was highly unlikely.

"Good. Now, rest up and continue with your recovery for the rest of the day, and we'll see you later," she finished, a clear dismissal in her voice. Seconds later, Larek was up and out the door. A strange giddiness flowed through his body as he realized he had succeeded, despite his reluctance to stand up for himself. A new confidence infused his step as he smiled, thinking of all the time he'd have coming up to do what he'd been wanting to do for a long time now.

"It worked. I'm free from all of that, so I should be safe now," he told Vivienne as soon as the office door closed behind him. "Let's go celebrate with an early lunch; for some reason, I'm starving." He couldn't help but hum under his breath as they left the area around the Dean's office, his prospects for the future looking much better than they did earlier that morning.

*   *   *

"Risky, but it seems to have worked," Lorraine said, slumping back in her chair as she blew out a deep breath.

Shinpai chuckled. "I told you; the kid just doesn't think the way the Nobles do, let alone how *we* do."

She had to acknowledge that her old friend was right. "True. Any Noble would've seen through the obvious schedule fixing for some deeper meaning, especially as he told you in no uncertain terms that he didn't want to do it anymore. I agree, though it's not necessarily for the same reason as you." Lorraine was worried that Larek might permanently damage his burgeoning Dominion magic if he knowingly pushed it like they had just done; while she had suspected that was what was going on during the teaching, what happened with his collapse was a complete accident. It was an accident she didn't want to have happen again.

Shinpai was more concerned about the Skill being spread around too far, eventually catching the attention of the Great Ones. It was a valid concern, though she wasn't sure how much it would matter right now, especially with the recent news they'd heard the night before.

"It was all necessary for the next step," the Grandmaster Fusionist said seriously, looking at her with meaning. He didn't have to explain, of course, because she was well aware of the next step that Larek needed to take if he was ever going to accomplish what she wished of him.

"I know, I just wish we had more time."

After decades that just seemed to drag on and on with very little changing within the Kingdom and the SIC, the differences that less than a year could make upon just about every facet of their lives was scarily incredible. Now, sooner than anyone would like, things were about to come to a head.

And, unfortunately, it was all her fault. *While that's not entirely true, it's true enough that it doesn't make a difference.*

She had held off as long as she could, but the slave bond she possessed with the Great Ones finally triggered enough that she was forced to vaguely communicate the presence of someone that may or may not be related to them. It wasn't one single thing that prompted the bond to trigger, but a culmination of everything she'd seen Larek do over the last 7 months; it was his use of Dominion magic during his teaching and his subsequent collapse that simply tipped the scales for the worse.

Thankfully, she'd kept most of the details regarding Larek a secret in the communication, though that wouldn't stop one of the Great Ones if they happened to arrive and start snooping around. The likelihood of that happening was slim, fortunately, as she couldn't remember hearing about any Great One leaving their Enclave for as long as she'd been alive – which was a distressingly long time when she thought about it.

Regardless, it was only a matter of time before someone came to investigate, and she needed Larek to be as prepared as possible for that eventuality. It wasn't fair to him what they were forcing him to do, of course, but they didn't have the luxury of fairness right now.

She just hoped that he was ready for it when that time came, because otherwise all this effort would've been for nothing.

Chapter 13

The next day was relatively quiet as far as Larek was concerned – which was exactly how he liked it. In the morning after breakfast, he went to the *Advanced Fusions* workshop and spent 3 hours creating Fusions that he was instructed were needed for the SIC – something that he had no problem doing now that he was fully recovered from his overuse of his Pattern Cohesion as well as straining his Dominion magic. He kept in mind that he wanted to ask about some sort of compensation for what he was creating, but held off for the moment because of one reason, and one reason only: He wasn't asked to spend any more than those three hours creating Fusions for other people.

His thought was that he was in his class, and anything in there was considered part of the curriculum, so it was just normal classwork. While that was a very flimsy justification for all the work he was putting into the Fusions he created, he chose not to pursue any extra remuneration for his efforts right now. In the future, that might change, but he was more than happy to make these Fusions if it meant he didn't have to teach anyone else the new Skill he had discovered.

After lunch, his *Intermediate Mana Manipulation* class was in the third-year workshop section of the Academy, where his Professor reminded him of Nedira and Gharina – the SIC member in charge of Garventon – but to her long, reddish-gold hair and relatively similar features. The biggest difference between Professor Norreen and the other two female representatives from Tyrendel was one of height; whereas Nedira and Gharina were just over 4 feet in height, Professor Norreen was just over 6 feet tall – one of the tallest people that Larek had ever seen, other than himself. Her height didn't seem to cause any of the students to treat her any differently than any other Professor, which was a refreshing experience to observe.

Since he had started this class later than everyone else, he was at first a little lost when it came to what he would be learning, but he soon caught on when the other 39 students in the workshop began manipulating their Mana outside of their bodies with intricate movements and a much finer touch than anything that had been accomplished back in his first year. Given that every student was in their third year, he supposed that made sense; most – if not all – of them had been able to cast spells in their second year, and there were even two that had obtained a Specialization already. From what he had learned, that wasn't necessarily common, but some Mage students tended to catch onto casting spells faster than others and were able to understand spell patterns in a certain field much quicker than others. Granted, both of the Specializations were Healers, as it was one of the easiest to obtain, but that didn't lessen their achievements.

"Again, this year we'll continue to hone your *Mana Control* Skill to better manipulate the Mana as it is withdrawn from your body," Professor Norreen stated a few minutes after class started, walking through the workshop as the students silently manipulated their Mana. The workshop was nearly twice the size of the *Advanced Fusions* workshop that Larek was familiar with, though with many more people needing to occupy the space, it was necessary. Similar to the *Fusions* workshop, there were large pillows set up around the floor, spaced equally apart from each other, where the students could sit and practice their Mana manipulation in comfort. Instead of privacy alcoves, it was simply a large, open space where the young Mages were only separated by a few feet, creating a 5-by-8 grid-like pattern to the pillows and their placement. The Professor was traversing the walkways between the students, watching them as they worked.

Or at least where most of the students worked; Larek wasn't exactly sure what he was supposed to do, even after watching the others for a few minutes.

"Remember, the finer control you have of your Mana, the better your spellcasting will be. Not only will you be able to create your spell patterns much faster and with smaller chances of making a mistake, but you'll also be able to infuse that spell pattern with your Mana almost instantaneously," the Professor continued, before stopping and leaning down to gently correct something one of the students was doing wrong. She was finished in only a few seconds before she moved on, picking up where she left off. "The closer you can form your Mana into the same shape as your spell pattern, the faster that spell pattern will be able to absorb it and activate. When it comes to a life-and-death situation against a monster spawned by a Scission, every second you can save in battle could mean the difference between success and failure. By improving the manipulation of your Mana, you'll be one step closer to success out there in the real world."

Larek was starting to understand the purpose behind the class now. Every time he had observed and learned a new spell, it had typically been either performed slowly enough that he could see every single step in the process, or was used so many times in succession that he couldn't help but pick it up. What he hadn't realized until that point was that most Mages, at least those who had graduated from the Academy, cast their spells much faster than what he'd observed. The speed at which they did this varied, but it was usually so fast that he could barely even see that a spell pattern was even being created, let alone the subsequent infusion of Mana that necessitated its activation.

How was it they were able to cast it so quickly? Mana manipulation – which was exactly what they were all learning in this class.

There were two parts to casting a spell, but there were multiple ways of completing those parts. The first was the spell pattern, which was formed by essentially drawing with the Mage's Pattern Cohesion the necessary components used to accomplish the spell's effect. In the first and second year of the Academy, this was taught to be done by drawing the pattern with a finger, giving them practice in meticulously forming it without any mistakes.

Later on, as they became more adept at manipulating their Pattern Cohesion in the form of a spell pattern, they didn't necessarily need to *draw* it anymore; instead, they would manipulate their Pattern Cohesion into the shape of the spell pattern with a flexing of their mind – similar to how Larek was able to alter his Fusion grid formations without having to draw every single line to perfection. He still used his hands for the most part, as it was easier for him to do it that way, but he thought that – with some practice – he might be able to construct an entire Fusion without moving his body at all. Thanks to his experience using *Focused Division* and manipulating multiple Fusion formations with his mind, he didn't even think that it would be all that hard.

The second part of casting a spell was infusing the spell pattern with Mana. At first, a bunch of Mana coming from the Mage was shoved into the pattern in order to fill it up and activate it. This sometimes took a bit of time and was wasteful if too much Mana was removed from the body, especially if any leftover Mana wasn't reabsorbed afterwards. After the students began to learn to better control their Mana, thanks to classes such as the one Larek was attending, they would be able to pull out exactly the amount they needed for the spell, as well as shaping it so that it matched the spell pattern. Once the Mana was formed into the same shape, it could be sent into the spell pattern like a key into a lock, powering and activating it immediately.

It was this kind of thing that allowed those such as Kimble to cast his Fireballs so quickly, as he had mastered forming the spell pattern immediately with his mind, and then filling it with a quick burst of Mana shaped exactly as he needed.

Unfortunately, Larek couldn't see how this would help him with his Fusions, but he had to admit that it was probably a good idea to learn what he could. He still manipulated his Mana, after all, even if it wasn't necessarily used as the basis of a spell; if he was being honest, his Mana funnels were a bit crude when it came to the delicate work being done by the students he saw inside the workshop.

"Ah, the new student," Larek suddenly heard, broken out of his reverie by the voice nearby. He looked up to see Professor Norreen looking down at him, which was a change for once; typically, even if he was sitting on the floor, he was tall enough that he was normally around eye-height with most other students and Professors in his classes. "Larek, correct?"

He nodded.

"You weren't here for the preliminary classes, so you likely have no idea what you're supposed to do, right?" Again, he nodded. "Not a problem. Since you're only now a second year, you likely haven't had much experience casting a spell, which also means you likely haven't had much reason to practice with controlling your Mana. Now, I know that you're some sort of Fusion prodigy, but that doesn't count. I'll get you started on the path where you'll be casting spells in no time."

Shaking his head, Larek said, "I can't cast any spells. My Pattern Cohesion is too strong." In the past, he had wanted to keep such information hidden so as to not stand out, but enough about his circumstances was known that he thought it prudent to put that knowledge out in the open. Of course, he wasn't exactly planning on sharing *how high* his Pattern Cohesion was, as that wasn't necessary for his Professor to know.

"Really? I'd love to hear the story I can sense behind that sometime," she said as she smiled back at him. It didn't seem as though the revelation was a surprise or that she didn't believe him, which was a relief. "Well, I assume you use your Mana to fill your Fusions, so let me see what we're working with so that we can determine where you can start."

At her encouragement, Larek pulled out a small, square, steel plate from his pocket and put it on his lap. Without really thinking about what he was doing, he created a Fusion formation for a basic *Intellect Boost +7*, something that he had been making frequently for the SIC. Having formed the grid so often, he had it finished within 15 seconds even after triple checking it for flaws, before he began to create his Mana funnel and started shoving the energy into the Mana Cost section of the *Boost*. Since this Fusion only required about 30,000 Mana and his current Mana pool was around 1,300, it only took a few minutes for him to fill it completely after letting it regenerate in stages. Once it clicked into place, he looked up from what he was doing to see his Professor staring at him in what appeared to be shock; worse than that, the rest of the students in the workshop had stopped what they were doing and were watching.

It took Larek a few seconds to realize that this was probably the first time that someone other than those close to him for one reason or another had seen him creating a Fusion. He forgot for a moment that his process was highly unusual and prone to catching the attention of others.

Then the whispers started, though they were loud enough that he heard most of them.

"...you see that?"

"...didn't think anyone could handle that much Mana all at once!"

"...how much Mana does he have?!"

"...isn't that the Fusion guy from last year's Skirmish?"

"...hadn't seen it for myself, I wouldn't have believed it!"

He ignored it all as he absently handed the steel plate to his Professor. He didn't need it, after all, and he figured she might be able to find a use for it.

"Alright, back to work! The show's over!" His Professor had suddenly discovered her students weren't working anymore, and so she shouted over her shoulder at them. A few snapped back to their work immediately, but most of the others reluctantly turned away – though Larek could tell they were just going through the motions rather than concentrating on their Mana manipulation.

"Larek? What was that?"

Kneeling down by his side, Professor Norreen kept her voice low as she composed her shocked expression, though it was obvious that she was still affected by what she saw. He shrugged and explained that it was how he filled his Fusions with Mana.

"How are you able to handle that much Mana? I would warn you that constantly passing that amount of Mana through your body is dangerous, but you seem... fine? How?"

Again, he shrugged. He was going to leave it at that, but he decided to explain a little bit more. "First, I have an extraordinary Mana regeneration rate, which allows me to supply large amounts of Mana in a short period of time. Second, my Mana doesn't exactly pass through my body."

"What? What does that mean?"

He hadn't really told anyone about how he had discovered his Mana and his ability to control it, as it had been part of the secrets he had been trying to keep. Later on, it hadn't exactly seemed important to share it, but if his Professor was going to help him improve his *Mana*

Control and manipulation, then she probably needed to know. "I was taught that there is a source of Mana inside of every Mage's body that they can access and pull from, directing it to pass through and out of their bodies so that they can control it. That never worked for me, as I didn't have a pool of Mana," which was true because he had a pool of Stama, instead, "but I eventually discovered where the Mana was located. It was spread throughout my entire body, like the blood that runs through my veins."

"That's imposs—sorry," the Professor began to say before apologizing. "You're obviously telling the truth, as hard as it is for me to believe something like that. Based on what I just saw, though, it's probably the only thing that makes sense. I wonder how that came about...?" she asked, her eyes looking past him as if she was trying to figure it out.

Rather than let her have the time to wonder about it more than was probably prudent, he asked, "Is there anything you think I can do to improve my Mana manipulation? I honestly don't have any reference points regarding this kind of thing, and I would appreciate any advice about how to make it better."

Her eyes refocused on him and she smiled at his question. "Of course!" She thought for a moment before saying, "First, I noticed that your, uh, *funnel* was a bit oversized for the purpose you were putting it to; I can think of a number of ways that you can improve its efficiency and speed of transfer. Second, have you thought of trying to infuse the *entire* Fusion with Mana, rather than just the Mana Cost?"

"What? I thought you had to use the Mana Cost section so that it could spread it through the rest of the Fusion; are you saying there is another way?"

She shrugged. "Possibly? I'm not an expert on Fusions, as I only took the required classes in the Academy, but I don't see why you can't try. It would be similar to infusing a spell pattern all at once, though I'm not sure how it would work with Fusions requiring an amount of Mana exceeding your current pool. It's something to try, at least." Looking around at the rest of the class, the Professor sighed. "It'll have to wait for next class, it looks like, because this has already been enough of a distraction for the other students. I'll see if I can design some exercises that you can perform to improve your Mana flow; I'll also talk to some of my colleagues and ask about filling an entire Fusion all at once."

He thanked her as she got up and moved through the workshop again, directing the students back to their work – though more than half of them surreptitiously stole curious glances back at Larek, who simply looked around and watched the others.

After class was done, he retreated quickly and moved to the second-year section of the Academy, to Classroom 240, which turned out to be a large lecture hall that seated hundreds of students. While the class wasn't as enlightening as *Intermediate Mana Manipulation* had been, the Drome Professor teaching the class constantly expressed that the current environment outside of the city was ever-changing, and that everything they were going to cover was subject to being altered as more information was gained. This first class he attended covered most of what he'd already learned from multiple sources, in that the Scissions seemed to be leaving towns and cities alone, and instead were opening all over the countryside. Subsequent classes would cover what was being done to locate and fight the monsters that spilled out of the Scissions, which was something that not everyone knew about; Larek only knew some of it because he was actively supplying Fusions to the SIC groups that were going out to fight those monsters.

It was only when that was done that Larek experienced his first opportunity of having free time to pursue whatever he wanted. With his last three hours now no longer dedicated to teaching others about the *Focused Division* Skill, he could finally experiment and explore what he could do now with that same Skill, as well as moving on to different Fusions that he'd been thinking about for some time.

The hardest decision was where he wanted to start first.

Chapter 14

Sitting inside a closed privacy alcove in the *Advanced Fusions* workshop, the first thing that Larek decided to work on was to see how far he could push his new *Focused Division* Skill. He'd used it a few times during his creation session earlier in the day on some Basic 2-by-2 Boost Fusions, but he hadn't had the opportunity to try an Intermediate Fusion yet. Given that his Skill hadn't increased past Level 10 even though he'd made hundreds of Fusions using *Focused Division*, he knew that it was likely that he would need to experiment to see if he could increase it a few Levels.

Starting with a Simple Intermediate Fusion, one that he had created the year before to demonstrate to Shinpai that he was capable, he set up the 2-by-3 grid for the *Spellcasting Focus Boost +4* Fusion. Thickening the lines in the formation was easy enough to do, as well as filling it with Mana; the biggest difference was when he divided the Fusion in half once it was full. There was a slight strain on his mind as he forcibly separated the pair of identical Fusions, something that hadn't been an issue on Basic 2-by-2 Fusions since he had originally unlocked the Skill, but it wasn't anything too strenuous.

Focused Division *has reached Level 11!*

After he directed the Fusions onto a pair of circular wooden disks, provided by his roommate, the notification he was hoping for flashed into his mind. Pleased, he choked off the flow of ambient Mana into the Fusions he just created and eliminated the Formations, before reconstructing the thick *Spellcasting Focus Boost +4* once again. This time, when he divided the filled formation into two separate Fusions it was much easier, with only a hint of strain.

Focused Division *has reached Level 12!*

Another pair of Fusions after that was completed with absolutely no sense of strain, similar to how the Basic Fusions were, though there also wasn't an increase in his Skill Level. After eliminating and recreating the Fusions another half-dozen times without another increase, Larek was convinced that it would likely take something more than that to raise his Skill Level.

The next obvious step was to move onto a Lesser Intermediate Fusion, followed by a Minor, Major, and Supreme Intermediate Fusion in quick succession. By the time he finished the last Supreme Intermediate Fusion, he was pleased with his progress.

***Focused Division** has reached Level 20!*

He had even been able to divide one of his newer *Graduated Parahealing* Fusions, meaning that he would be able to create even more of the healing Fusions for the SIC once he was back to making them in his morning classes. While each of the higher difficulty Fusions had strained his focus slightly as he progressed through them, by the time he hit Level 20 in the Skill the strain had essentially disappeared. That also meant that he wasn't able to push past Level 20, as his progress seemed to stall at that point – but he wasn't quite done yet.

It was time to see how many times he could divide a formation.

He'd experimented a few times when he was training the Professors by creating three of the Fusions he was using as a demonstration, with no real strain to speak of even at Level 10 – but he thought he could do more. Recreating the *Illuminate Steel +1* Fusion that he had made many, many times over the course of his teaching, he thickened the lines even further, giving them a depth that was 4 times larger than normal. He absently noticed that he was originally correct in his assumption that each "layer" only required another 20% more Pattern Cohesion to create, so as he was attempting to create 4 Fusions at once, it was essentially 160% of its original cost.

Regardless of the cost increase in Pattern Cohesion, it was still a *huge* savings in terms of time and his personal resources if he was able to make 4 Fusions at the same time.

Contrary to Larek's expectations, slicing up the Mana-filled Fusion wasn't a strain on his mind at all. He thought that it was likely because he was already Level 20 in the Skill, meaning that this was something he probably could've been doing a while ago without any trouble.

So, logically, he increased the number of Fusions he was dividing for his next test. Creating 5 filled formations from the Basic Fusion he was working with was equally as easy, as was 6... then 7... and then 8. Excited and slightly astonished, as he hadn't expected it to go this well, 9 separated Fusions came next – only for his attempt at 10 Fusions to show the first sign of a strain on his mind, as keeping the different Fusions from falling apart was a bit difficult. When he attempted 11 right after that, he failed to divide them all for the first time ever, as he couldn't focus on each of them simultaneously. The formation fell apart in front of him, creating a tiny explosion that scared him more than hurt him, and he took a breather afterwards to order his thoughts.

I'm so glad that Fusion only had a small amount of Mana in it; otherwise, that could've been disastrous. It thankfully didn't do anything serious to me, as I seem fine, but that definitely could've been different with a more-powerful Fusion. I wonder if 10 is the absolute limit, or just my limit at the moment?

Regardless of the scare, his failed attempt was successful in another way.

Focused Division has reached Level 21!

The *Focused Division* Skill increased to 21 despite it not working the way he intended. He began to attempt to try for 11 Fusions at the same time again, but as he was constructing the formation once again, he stopped before he filled it with Mana. Some internal instinct was telling him that it still wouldn't work, so he listened to that instinct and let the formation fade away once he let go of his control.

Encouraged that his efforts were working, he moved on to a Simple Intermediate Fusion yet again. This time, he only managed to create 9 separate Fusions before he started encountering the same sort of strain he'd experienced before. Rather than risk it falling apart and exploding again if he attempted to do 10, he instead created 9 Simple Intermediate Fusions a second time, which netted him another increase in his *Focused Division* Skill.

Moving on to a Lesser Intermediate Fusion, Larek's efforts gained him another two Levels in his new Skill, bringing it to 24 – while at the same time, he was only able to simultaneously create 8 of them before the strain became too much for him. The trend continued for a Minor Intermediate Fusion where he was only able to create 7 Fusions at one time, gaining 2 more Skill Levels; a Major Intermediate Fusion only produced 6 copies of the same formation, along with an additional pair of Skill Levels. When he came to a Supreme Intermediate Fusion, he wasn't surprised to discover that he could only simultaneously create 5 of them – though he did manage to bump up his *Focused Division* Skill to Level 30, where it seemed to stall just like his other Skills.

Once he hit Level 30 in the Skill, he went back and attempted 11 Basic Fusions again, where he discovered that it was, indeed, now possible. In fact, he was able to make a total of 14 Fusions before he felt the strain again, meaning that an additional 10 Levels converted to an additional 4 Basic Fusions he could separate from a single formation. Experiencing the difference that more Skill Levels could make, he went through all the different Intermediate Fusions again, finding that he could now create an additional 2 Simple Intermediate Fusions, as well as another Lesser and Minor Intermediate Fusion. There was no change in the number of Major or Supreme Intermediate Fusions that he could create simultaneously, but he felt like an additional Level would see to another Major Intermediate Fusion being possible.

If he was being honest with himself, being able to create 14 Basic Fusions at the same time was incredible, especially as all his Boosts fell into that category. His *Graduated Parahealing* Fusion was classified as a Major Intermediate Fusion, which meant that he was only able to create 6 of them – but that was far more than he'd been able to do previously.

With all of the advancements to his Skill Levels, that also brought with it an increase in his personal Level. Bringing up his Status, he was astonished to see that he had already made it to Level 20 – which was apparently twice the required Level a student needed to achieve before they were allowed to graduate from the Academy.

Larek Holsten
Fusionist
Healer
Level 20
Advancement Points (AP) : 15/17
Available AP to Distribute: 30

Mage Skills:
Multi-effect Fusion Focus Level 10
Pattern Recognition Level 20
Magical Detection Level 20
Spellcasting Focus Level 20
Focused Division Level 30
Mana Control Level 30
Fusion Level 30
Pattern Formation Level 30

He also now had 4 different Mage Skills seemingly stuck at Level 30, as his continued experiments with his *Focused Division* Skill hadn't gained him any more advancement. There were also 3 Mage Skills – *Pattern Recognition*, *Magical Detection*, and *Spellcasting Focus* – stuck at Level 20, while *Multi-effect Fusion Focus* was seemingly stuck at Level 10.

I really wish I knew what it takes to break through these thresholds; if even discovering an entirely new Skill didn't do it, then I have no idea what it would take.

Fortunately, he now had the opportunity to experiment and explore different avenues of learning thanks to the free time he now had each day. He was actually about to start looking into that after he finished playing around with *Focused Division*, but his internal clock – and the grumbling in his stomach – was telling him that it was about time for dinner.

Getting up off the comfortable pillows he had been sitting on, he stretched and opened the door to his privacy alcove. Grandmaster Fusionist Shinpai was waiting for him with a smile across the room. "Just in time, Larek. I was going to take a chance and interrupt you soon, as it's already past your last class period. It figures that your body wouldn't want to miss a meal, as you're at that age where your stomachs just seem bottomless – or so I've observed," he added with a smirk.

"That's quite accurate, actually." While Larek wasn't *always* hungry, he found that he could eat quite a bit at every meal and it took a while for him to feel full.

"What was that explosion I heard earlier? Are you alright?"

Slightly embarrassed, as he'd never had one of his Fusions explode on him while he was working on it – the *Healing Surges* back on the roof of Crystalview didn't count – Larek felt the heat in his cheeks as he ducked his head and mumbled, "I'm fine. I was pushing my *Focused Division* Skill a little too hard and it blew up in my face."

"Oh? How did that go, by the way?" his Professor asked, his tone indicating that he was interested more than usual. Since Shinpai had the Skill as well, Larek suspected that he was searching for any more tips to help increase his Level.

"It went amazingly well... until it didn't. I'm stuck at Level 30 similar to some of my other Mage Skills," he admitted.

The Grandmaster Fusionist's eyes looked like they were going to pop out of his head. "Goodness! You're Level 30 *already*?!"

Rubbing the back of his neck, the embarrassment came back at his Professor's shocked exclamation. "Uh... yes?"

"How—no, never mind. I already know how you accomplished that, but I still can't believe it. Did you know that it normally takes Mages – even those who are blessed with extraordinary abilities – *years* to get any of their Skills up to Level 30? And here you've done it in just barely over a year – and you have what? A total of five Skills at Level 30?"

"Four, actually," he corrected his Professor. "The others are stuck at 20, while *Multi-effect Fusion Focus* is stuck at 10."

"Oh, only *four* Skills at Level 30, my apologies. That's still ridiculous, especially considering that you barely knew anything about Mages or spells a year ago." Shinpai sighed and shook his head. "Anyway, enough of this old man complaining about the unfairness of a prodigy. A more important question: Did anything change with your increased Level? Is there something to look forward to when I finally reach Level 30 – in a decade or so?" he added with a snort.

"Well, I discovered my division limits for now."

His Professor raised one of his eyebrows and tilted his head to the side. "What do you mean?"

"Oh, you know, the limit on how many Fusions I could create simultaneously. For Basic Fusions, my limit is 14; Simple Intermediate is 11; Lesser Intermediate is 9; Minor, 8; Major, 6; and finally, I can only create 5 Supreme Intermediate Fusions at the same time. I noticed that the maximum limit increased as the Skill Level went up, so if I'm able to find a way past 30, I should be able to do even more. Do you have any other ideas on how I can break through my Skill bottlenecks?" he asked, hoping that Shinpai or the Dean had come up with more things that he could try.

But the Grandmaster Fusionist was still stuck on what Larek had said before. "Wait—*14 Fusions?!* How is that even possible?" There was a pause as a thought apparently occurred to him, before he seemingly began talking to himself. "If Fusions are actually more difficult to divide, then that means spells are technically easier – obviously. But does that also affect the maximum limit? At Level 30, would I be able to create 30 *Fireballs* simultaneously, or would I be limited to 14 like Larek?"

It didn't seem like his Professor was actually asking him the question, so he kept quiet – and his stomach loudly grumbled in response. After apologizing for interrupting their conversation, Larek was waved off by Shinpai as his Professor said, "Don't worry about it. Go get some dinner, and I'll see you tomorrow morning. Now that I know you can easily make multiple Fusions, that will help immensely with supplying those who need them in the SIC." As soon as he was done speaking, the Grandmaster Fusionist's focus seemed to wander as he was likely processing what he had learned from his student, so Larek just nodded and waved, finding himself outside the workshop seconds later and heading toward the Dining Hall.

"Was that a good study session?"

Larek, distracted with reviewing his efforts with his *Focused Division* Skill, jumped slightly as Kimble spoke up next to him. The sixth-year Mage was technically due to graduate last year before officially joining the SIC, but the Dean kept him around so that he could help to guard the Fusionist prodigy.

"Yes; yes, it was. Very productive – and I even gained a few Skill Levels." He didn't necessarily want to announce that he had gained *20 Levels* during the three hours he had dedicated to his studies, though of course that wasn't something that was easily repeatable right now. As it seemed his advancement was stuck once again, such a productive session of experimentation wasn't likely to happen for a while.

"A few? That's quite impressive!" the Pyromancer said, seemingly genuine in his praise. Of all his bodyguards, Larek wasn't as familiar with the sixth-year Mage, which meant that he didn't really know him enough to tell if he was just saying something like that or if he meant it.

"Thanks. It was a lot of work, but quite worth it."

He just hoped that the rest of his experimentation sessions were equally as beneficial and productive.

Chapter 15

The next few weeks were more of the same – though that wasn't a bad thing at all. Larek continued to create more Fusions in his morning *Fusions* classes, though his production ramped up significantly; it got to the point where he could tell that Shinpai and – in the few times she visited – Dean Lorraine were astonished at the rate he was pushing them out. While he didn't necessarily notice it when it was there, there was a distinct lessening of tension in their whole demeanor once he began producing higher quantities of Fusions. Neither of them pestered him about teaching other Professors about the *Focused Division* Skill, for which he was grateful, and things seemed to be running a lot more smoothly as a result.

His *Intermediate Mana Manipulation* class was a bit less productive – but that didn't mean it didn't provide any value to his magical education. Professor Norreen had him working on specific exercises that condensed his Mana funnels into a tighter spiral, which was a lot more difficult than he expected. The problem was that he was used to his previous method of simply shoving the Mana into his Fusions by the easiest and simplest means, and changing it up was something he had to actively concentrate on – which distracted him from holding together the formation. He never lost control of it entirely, but he came close a couple of times.

Still, despite the difficulty, he was making some progress in tightening the spiral in his Mana funnels, which he could immediately tell was making a difference in the speed at which he could fill his Fusion. In comparison to his normal method, he could think of it like trying to fill an empty pool with a waterfall pouring on the Mana Cost section of the Fusion, with extra Mana going everywhere, wasting time as he had to gather it back up and force it in; but a tighter spiral to the funnel focused the stream of Mana to flow within a more consistent pathway, meaning that less of it splashed outside of the pool, and that what did land in the pool was contained much faster. It wasn't the best analogy, but he thought it explained what was happening fairly well.

That was all he had a chance to practice with in his *Mana Manipulation* class, however, as the Professor was still trying to determine if infusing the entire Fusion all at once was even possible. His method of filling a Fusion was already out of the norm, as the Mana that a Fusionist typically fed into a Fusion was more like a steady trickle rather than a waterfall like what Larek provided, so she was a bit out of her element. Regardless, it was still useful, and he figured that once he got the knack of tightening his Mana funnel, his speed would increase significantly.

His *Scissions* class was more of the same as his first day, meaning that it was more descriptions of what they might face outside the walls of the city. Toward the end of the few weeks, however, the curriculum was getting more into group formations and tactics used against different types of monsters, most of which were still in the experimental stages because these circumstances were so new.

Larek could well understand that almost everything *had* to be experimental, as most of the SIC was used to defending towns and cities, standing on the wall or just outside of it in a defensive formation – and not wandering around hunting down roaming monsters throughout the Kingdom.

He listened to the lectures about tactics and other strategies being employed, but he didn't really pay attention to them all that much. Larek wasn't planning on being in a situation where he would have to utilize them, after all. Dean Lorraine might have some lofty plans for him in the future, but all that Larek ultimately wanted to do was stay safe behind sturdy walls and create Fusions to help protect his friends. That might change in the future, but that still didn't mean he was planning on joining one of these "Hunting Parties" that were quickly becoming a popular strategy to combat the monsters threatening the Kingdom.

As for his free time, after increasing his new *Focused Division* Skill to its current maximum Level of 30 and exploring its limits, he turned to something that he'd been thinking about for a while. Namely, it was whether or not he could apply Fusions to more pliable materials, such as cloth and leather, or even something thinner and more flexible, such as paper.

His first experiment was with a scrap of cured leather approximately a foot square in size. He figured that if the firmer material of the leather wasn't able to maintain the Fusion on it, then anything softer or thinner wouldn't be able to, either.

Using a *Strengthen* Fusion, he changed the Effect so that it applied to leather rather than iron, steel, stone, or wood like the Fusions he knew already. With the Magnitude at just 1 rather than anything stronger, he was hoping that if the formation fell apart, the aftereffects wouldn't be as dangerous as something with a lot more Mana invested in it.

New Fusion Learned!
Strengthen Leather +1

Activation Method: Permanent
Effect: Strengthens leather
Magnitude: 100% increased durability
Mana Cost: 22
Pattern Cohesion: 1
Fusion Time: 21 minutes

Creating the Fusion and placing it on the scrap of leather was amazingly easy. The material took the formation easily enough, and it settled into the leather without any problems at all.

The problem with it immediately became apparent when he started to manipulate the scrap. First, the 100% increased durability that the Fusion imparted upon the leather simply made it, for lack of a better description, more stiff. Whereas before it was fairly flexible, the scrap of leather was now harder to bend; that meant that it was also harder to pierce, which was exactly what he was intending with the Fusion.

Now, all of that might sound good, but the benefit of leather armor over something like full-scale plate armor was its flexibility. At Magnitude 1, many of the Martial members of the SIC would likely still be able to maintain a decent range of movement in some armor with this Fusion applied to it, but anything more would result in them being hindered in one way or another. Still, it was something that could be added to be beneficial – if it wasn't for its glaring weakness.

When he bent the scrap of leather in the area where the Fusion's formation was located, the pattern snapped apart, and the Mana infused in its construction was released. Thankfully, there was no sudden explosion that he had to contend with, though the leather was slightly scorched where the rapidly disappearing Fusion used to be. The sudden release of so much Mana from a structured formation caused a bit of heat, it appeared, which should have been obvious with how one of his failed Fusions exploded in his face. In this case, there was no explosion because the Mana wasn't released all at once, but instead was forced out of the pattern through multiple breakages in the formation that snapped in succession.

With those glaring weaknesses, it didn't seem as if his experiment to strengthen softer materials would work.

...Or would it?

Perhaps I'm looking at this the wrong way.

In actuality, he was looking at the problem in a couple of wrong ways. The first, and most obvious, was that he didn't necessarily need to "strengthen" the leather; harder materials needed that strengthening to ensure they couldn't be broken or deformed, which would also prevent the Fusion from snapping like it had done with the leather. But softer materials needed something else to make them more effective, more resistant—

That was it. Leather and cloth didn't need *strength*; they needed *resistance*. They just needed to be able to resist being cut through by a monster's claw, weapon, or any other cutting implement. He briefly thought about trying to find a way to stop even blunt damage, but couldn't think of a way; even the *Strengthen* Fusions didn't stop something like that, as they only prevented the material from bending, cracking, or breaking.

But why stop there? Why make it only resistant to cutting, when I could make it resistant to many other types of damage?

If he stopped thinking about the specific leather he was working with, which might be used in an armor piece used to protect someone, and instead thought of the material alone, then what would he want his Fusion to do? Just thinking of the fighting he'd seen in the past, whether it was person-on-person or person-on-monster, and then taking into account the information he'd gained in his first year at the Academy in his *Monster Knowledge* class, he knew that simple cutting and blunt damage were the least of the attacks most SIC members would face. Elemental effects from natural elements associated with a monster, such as a **Lava Salamander** or a **Windblade Hawk** (which used lava and projectile blades made from wind to attack), were more common than not. But actual magical attacks, such as a *Fireball* or a *Water Jet* could be resisted as well. While they weren't commonly utilized by monsters, the effects that these types of spells produced were still something that was copied, one way or another, by some monsters.

Therefore, if there was a way to resist being affected by these attacks, it would serve exactly the purpose the material needed to fulfill. Ideally, he would love to be able to completely negate the attacks, which might even help to reduce impact damage for whatever was underneath the material, but that seemed like it was beyond him at this time. What he thought he *could* do was increase the resistance of the material so it could withstand just about anything without being damaged in the process.

That just left the biggest – and less obvious – problem with this type of Fusion. Even If he was able to work out a resistance effect that maintained the material's flexibility, then it would still leave the issue of the formation bending and ultimately snapping apart. He could certainly increase the resistance of leather, for instance, but as soon as the Fusion was bent past a certain point, all that protection would go away.

At first, he thought about a way to simply attach something made from a stronger material – such as steel – to the other material and use his Multi-effect Fusion Focus to ultimately affect both materials – just like he did with Rheina's earrings on the Network carriage months ago. The problem with that was that he wouldn't be able to strengthen the steel where the Fusion was placed at the same time; if he was able to incorporate the strengthening Effect into the resistance Fusion, then he would end up with a stiff leather or cloth as well. If the steel wasn't strengthened, then a hard enough hit to it would deform the metal and cause the Fusion to break. What he needed was to figure out a way to make his *Fusion* flexible so that it was nearly impossible to break apart when it was bent out of shape.

It took him 2 weeks of constantly trying different techniques to figure it out.

In the end, through attempting more and more elaborate ideas, the answer was – as seemed to be the norm for him once he made a discovery – quite simple, yet was also something that he wouldn't have even considered trying if he hadn't been looking for this particular solution. The answer?

Plants.

He actually got the idea from Nedira and her Naturalist Specialization, after watching her practice with her *Rapid Plant Growth* spell. At one point, she had used the spell to grow a small fern into something that was 12 feet tall and just as wide, with its multitude of long, thin leaves forming massive fans. Using a higher-tier spell that Larek was unable to learn, she was able to strengthen the plant to the point where it could withstand the blows of Penelope, who was using a blunted sword in their practice bout to get to the Naturalist hiding behind the fern.

Instead of the plant being ripped apart by the powerful sword blows, it instead bent out of the way with the attacks, bouncing back after the initial blow and appearing seemingly unharmed. The resiliency of the fern was amazing, as it was able to stand up to the attacks, and Nedira explained that it was simply a part of its nature to bend without breaking. It, of course, couldn't stand up to being seriously cut apart or any massive blunt damage that might crush the entire plant, even with the extra strength she infused into it, but it could still stand up to a lot.

That was exactly what Larek needed for his Fusion. Once he figured out what he wanted, it took him a couple of days to incorporate it into his Fusion. All it took was a change in his perception of the Pattern Cohesion from which he was constructing the formation.

Normally, the lines of his Fusions were a pure white color, something that he hadn't really thought about before that point. But when he applied the idea of growth and natural resiliency to the lines he used to construct the formation, they slowly changed into a bright green color that reflected the thought of nature and the flexibility of the fern he had observed.

Miraculously, it worked. Once his Fusion was on a scrap of leather, he was able to bend the material in half without it breaking, and he could even see the lines of the Fusion stretch and warp slightly, while still maintaining its overall formation. There was a limit, he found, because as soon as he began poking holes in the leather, it would collapse as it began missing key parts that were keeping it intact. He also found that if he were to stretch and squish and ball up the leather scrap to the point where the Fusion was pushed and pulled in different directions, even the strength of his normally strong Fusions couldn't handle the strain.

Overall, though, it was exactly what he needed, and it would work more than well enough for his purposes.

As opposed to the weeks used to discover a way to make his Fusions flexible, it only took a few days to design an Effect that would work for the softer materials. In essence, he started with the idea behind *Strengthen* as a base, but then used the principles behind the *Localized Anesthesia* spell he learned earlier to enhance it to the point he required. By the end, he wound up with a 3-by-3 Lesser Intermediate Fusion that had a Reactive Activation Method, an Input that detected the severity of the incoming damage, two Variables that led to different levels of Activation depending on what needed to be resisted, an Amplifier to help provide enough Mana to resist the most serious damage, and an Effect that essentially increased the resistance of the material to the point where it wouldn't be negatively affected by the incoming damage.

In other words, using the idea of *Localized Anesthesia* and *Strengthen* Fusions, he made the material numb to anything trying to affect it while strengthening it to the point where it could shrug off that attack. The blend of ideas was unique, he had to admit... but it worked.

New Fusion Learned!
Multi-Resistance Leather +2
Activation Method: Reactive
Effect: Causes leather to resist most forms of damage

Magnitude: 100%/200% increased resistance
Mana Cost: 500
Pattern Cohesion: 25
Fusion Time: 100 minutes

His initial Fusion only used a Magnitude of 1 and 2, resulting in a 100% or 200% increased resistance – which wasn't too bad all on its own. When he experimented with it, the leather was certainly much harder to punch any holes through with a sharp implement, and he even had Kimble try one of his *Fireballs* against it. The leather still burned up after a while, but it took three times as long before it did, compared to a scrap of leather with no Fusion on it. When he tried a higher Magnitude of 7 and 5 inside the Fusion, the leather got to the point where it was able to resist a cut from his axe!

New Fusion Learned!
Multi-Resistance Leather +7
Activation Method: Reactive
Effect: Causes leather to resist most forms of damage
Magnitude: 500%/700% increased resistance
Mana Cost: 60,000
Pattern Cohesion: 1,000
Fusion Time: 113 hours

"Why the different Magnitudes? Why not just a single one that blocks everything?" Nedira asked when he described to her later in his room what he had created.

"Well, for one, it's to cut down on the Mana and Pattern Cohesion cost. Using the Amplifier to pump more Mana into the Magnitude 7 threshold enhances the resistance Effect rather than simply making a higher Magnitude Fusion, which costs more. Second, the area of ambience is much higher in the Magnitude 7 Effect, meaning that it can end up interfering with other Fusions nearby – especially once the Amplifier goes into effect. To reduce the strain on other Fusions, less-damaging attacks can be resisted with the smaller Magnitude, thereby lessening the amount of ambient Mana that is absorbed to do so.

"Thirdly… I needed to balance out the Fusion, and it looked more aesthetically pleasing to me," he added with a smirk.

She sighed in mock exasperation before playfully smacking him on the arm. "Only you would make a Fusion more complicated because it 'looked better'."

Shrugging, he couldn't keep the smile off his face. "It works, at least. Now I need to try it on cloth and—"

"Larek!" Verne shouted as he ran inside their room, Norde hot on his heels. Larek immediately noticed the panicked expression on his face and became concerned.

"What is it? What's wrong?"

He barely got the words out before he felt something outside the Academy, like a pressure in the air that was trying to envelop him with a persistent force. In some ways, it was similar to what he felt when a Scission appeared nearby, but it was also vastly different; it was as if a Scission was more general pressure that promised danger, while this was something more... *personal*. Regardless, it was something he'd never felt before, and by the looks on the faces of the others, he could tell that it was new to them, as well.

But if I've never felt something like this before, why does it feel so familiar?

Chapter 16

"I don't know what it is, but there's something coming," Verne said in a rush, nearly out of breath as he came to a stop in front of Larek and Nedira. "Something powerful enough that everyone can feel it; even the Professors we passed on the way here are freaking out!"

Larek quickly slid off his bed and snatched up the axe which was always propped up nearby in easy reach in case he needed it. This seemed like a time when he was going to need it.

"Has the Dean announced anything?" he asked, even as he felt the incoming pressure mounting. Now that he was focused upon it, he realized that he had been sensing it for a while now, but had been ignoring it while talking to Nedira. Thankfully, it didn't seem to be harmful or debilitating; instead, it was more like an irritating presence just out of sight.

"We've heard nothing," Verne answered even as he grabbed a wooden amulet from his desk and slipped it over his neck, followed quickly by Norde as he did the same. Larek recognized the *Repelling Barrier* Fusions he had made for them months ago, a defensive precaution he was happy enough to provide for them in case something like this happened. Ideally, keeping it on all the time like the one Larek wore would be safer, but the possibility of something inadvertently triggering it as they moved around the Academy was too high to risk hurting someone else. Rambunctious boys will be boys, after all.

The same went for Nedira, who had a *Repelling Barrier* amulet in her own room instead of on her person, so Larek opened one of his own desk drawers and pulled out one of his identical copies of the Fusion he had lying around and handed it to her. "Just in case," he said, and she slipped it over her head without another word.

"Let's go see what this is all about."

Larek led everyone out of the room and down the hallway to the exit, joined by dozens of others as they also departed their domiciles. He recognized many of the students that had departed Crystalview with him and his friends among the crowd, as they were still living in the same rooms that they were given upon their arrival. Their frightened faces reminded him of the attack at the Academy that led to the deaths of students and Professors – including Fusionist Annika.

Soon enough, the much-larger group streamed out of the exit doors and into the interior yard of the Academy and Fort – only to be nearly bowled over by the cacophony of loud, scared, and questioning voices of thousands of people wondering what was going on. Unlike the

Scission attack that occurred in his first year at Copperleaf, a time that Larek didn't like to think about often because that was when Ricardo had imprisoned him below the Academy, the panic was heightened because this was a complete unknown. The pressure everyone was feeling was vaguely similar to a Scission opening, yet altogether different in a way that confused the people milling about the yard, and they didn't seem to know what to do with themselves.

In short, it was utter chaos as Larek and his friends joined the panicked crowd. With those in authority – otherwise known as the Professors – all seemingly as shocked and scatter-witted as the students, there was no real place to turn to for answers.

"What is going on?" Nedira shouted at Larek, the only way to be heard despite them standing next to each other.

He shook his head in answer, not wanting to speculate or even say anything out loud at that point, even though he was beginning to suspect he knew. As the pressure he was feeling grew, it started to resonate with something buried within his mind and body; he attempted to pinpoint where it was coming from, but was unable to track it to its source. The only thing he was fairly certain of, however, was *what* it was that was resonating within him.

His Dominion magic.

If he was correct, then whatever was coming closer to them also possessed Dominion magic, though in a much greater quantity and strength than anything Larek could produce. If his Dominion magic was like a candle's flame, then what he felt was like a raging wildfire.

Based on what he'd been told, and he didn't have any good reason to doubt it, then there was only one thing that possessed Dominion magic in such massive quantities that it could be felt from a distance.

The Gergasi. Or the "Great Ones," depending on who he talked to.

Larek could think of only one reason why one of them might be making an appearance there.

"Settle down! Be silent! Answers will be forthcoming soon, as long as you don't panic!" Dean Lorraine's voice rang out over the entire central yard of the Academy and Fort, enhanced by a spell that he was able to see traces of wisping through the air. It took nearly a minute for everyone to stop running around and talking, though it helped when a column of stone approximately 10 feet across suddenly shot up from near the arena, extending 50 feet upwards so that everyone could see it no matter where they were. On top of the stone column were two people, whom Larek immediately recognized as Dean Lorraine and Vice General Whittaker, the head of Fort Pinevalley.

"There is no cause for alarm," the Dean continued once the majority of the noise settled down. "We are determining the cause of this disturbance, but there should be very little danger—"

The Dean's speech was interrupted as something suddenly shot across the sky above, with burning trails of flames coming off of it, and moving so quickly that it was almost impossible to make out any details. That changed as it seemed to bank abruptly in the air, making a turn that brought it down toward the Academy and Fort building. Panicked screams rang out as it seemed as though whatever was coming toward them would crash into the walls, causing incredible damage to the structure, but the object narrowly missed the tops of the walls and instead shot toward the center of the yard where the stone column the Dean had constructed was located.

As the object closed in on the column, its speed slowed down to the point where it could be made out a lot more clearly than before.

It turned out that it wasn't some sort of flaming projectile, which he and many of those around him had thought it might be, but a figure. This figure was unlike anyone he'd seen before, though there was a familiarity to it that resonated similarly to the Dominion magic he sensed emanating from it. Completely bald, the powerful figure was clothed in a simple dark purple tunic with bright white trim, belted at the waist by a golden rope; black leather pants covered their legs down to their shins, but there were no shoes upon the feet, giving the person a deliberately unfinished look. It was almost as if it didn't need any shoes, or disdained them, to complete its outfit – and Larek had to admit that it worked.

That would probably be because he and everyone else was distracted by the giant sword the figure was firmly wielding in its hand, which he estimated had to be at least 10 feet long and a foot wide, larger than any sword he'd ever seen before. It was a dark black color that seemed to suck in the light around it, reflecting not a single thing from the sun overhead, and while Larek couldn't see its edges, he could only assume that they were very sharp.

If everyone wasn't looking at the massive sword the figure wielded, then they were probably staring at its wings.

Yes, wings.

They emerged from the figure's back and extended at least a dozen feet outward, shining with a transparent, prismatic glow that outlined their otherwise delicate-looking construction. If he had to describe them, they were more akin to a butterfly's wings than the leathery kind employed by dragons, and they barely seemed able to lift the figure by themselves.

As the sword-wielding person delicately alighted upon the stone column, the wings on its back suddenly disappeared into a rain of sparkles that evaporated within seconds, which told Larek that they weren't *real* – they were likely some sort of spell. While he hadn't been a Mage for long, and was quite ignorant of the types of spells available to learn, he hadn't heard of anything remotely like these wings before. It was just further proof that this was one of the Gergasi, and its strength was obvious even if it wasn't for the pressure pounding down on everyone in the yard.

While the figure was a bit of distance away from him, he could tell that it was *much* taller than the Dean and Vice General standing next to it. If he had to guess, it was at least 8 feet tall, possibly nearing 9 feet; so, even taller than Larek, himself. It was also completely devoid of any features that – at a distance – indicated whether it was male or female, as its bald and lithe form could be either.

It was only when it started talking with a deep voice that he had a hint that it was male; of course, it was the subject of the speech that made him certain.

"WHERE IS MY CHILD? YOUR REPORT INDICATED TO ME THAT THEY ARE HERE."

Oh, no. Is that... my father?

He was distracted by staring at the figure that towered over the Dean and Vice General, but he tore his gaze away when he noticed something out of the corner of his eye. Not understanding what it was at first, he quickly realized that hundreds of students that had been nervously milling around the yard had suddenly frozen in place, their gazes locked on the Gergasi on top of the column. It didn't take him long to realize that these were Nobles, or at least Nobles with a higher station, who had been directly influenced by one of their "Great Ones" and were now reacting to the Dominion magic that already bound them as slaves.

The shock of what could potentially be his biological father being there nearly made Larek want to speak up and meet him; the desire to announce his presence and meet his long-lost parent was almost physical in nature, and he found himself *just* about to take a step forward. However, before Larek could move, the sight of the enslaved Nobles reacting to the presence of this stranger snapped him out of that ridiculous thought, and he held himself still and silent. The way the students seemed to have their free will taken from them in an instant further reinforced his desire not to have anything to do with Dominion magic – even if it came from his father.

This is wrong.

"Your child? What do you mean?" the Dean asked, audible even over the murmuring crowd despite her not enhancing her voice with a spell.

"DO NOT PLAY WITH ME, SLAVE. BRING THIS STUDENT TO ME NOW!"

Even Larek felt the command fall upon him as his father spoke, but he easily shrugged it off. Looking at his companions, they seemed to struggle with it a little bit, but he could see them visibly relax after a few seconds. *I wonder if it has to do with their proximity to me and my Dominion magic. Have I influenced them enough to help defend against my father's magic?* He didn't like the fact that his despised magic had led to them resisting the command Larek felt in the words just spoken upon the stone column, but he would deal with that later. At the moment, all he could think of was fleeing.

Of course, that was easier said than done, given that everyone around the four friends seemed to have been caught by the commanding Dominion magic the powerful Gergasi had used upon not just the students and trainees of both the Academy and Fort, but the Professors and Instructors, as well. Eyeing the closest ones around him, he could see that they physically struggled to resist the command, but none of them were strong enough to break free from it.

Larek's mind rapidly evaluated the strength of the Dominion magic that was acting upon them, his instinctual use of the hated power coming to some use as he made some determinations. While it was undoubtedly stronger than anything that he could produce, he could also tell that the command wasn't as powerful as a slave bond. Larek suddenly remembered something he learned from Ricardo during his interrogation, about each Gergasi being unable to enslave more than a certain number of people. He could only assume that this enslavement was something *permanent*, while what he was witnessing here was only *temporary*. It was more than likely that anyone without a slave bond – such as what he saw with the hundreds of Nobles among the students – would be freed from the Dominion magic after his father left the area.

He also determined that there was absolutely no way for him to break someone out of that magic while his father was nearby, unless they were already freed for another reason. That reason was likely because *Larek* had already affected them with conflicting Dominion magic, for good or ill.

That meant that escaping was going to be difficult, because while no one was looking at him right now, as no one but the Dean and Shinpai knew he was likely the "son" that the Gergasi was talking about, those caught in the Dominion magic would likely see him running as a target of interest. Glancing at Nedira, Verne, and Norde, all of whom looked around with wide eyes and appeared on the verge of bolting, he shook his head slightly and then demonstrated looking up at the scene playing out on the stone column. Thankfully, the abnormality of the situation was enough for them to understand, and they mostly stopped fidgeting as they stared up at the Gergasi making demands of the two most important people at the Academy and the Fort.

"I am sorry, Lord Vilnesh; I was unaware that you had any of your children here with us, or I would have ensured that they would've had all the courtesy demanded by a Great One—"

"LIES! YOU KNOW EXACTLY WHO IT IS. PRODUCE THEM NOW, OR I WILL FIND THEM MYSELF!"

The Dean was on her knees now, joined by the Vice General, bowing to the Gergasi. *Lord Vilnesh? Is that my father's name?* Ultimately, it wasn't important, but Larek found he was distracted by the smallest things as he fought against the Dominion magic he could feel emanating from the Gergasi with invisible waves of force.

It was at this moment that his mind reviewed all the words that the Gergasi and the Dean had exchanged, and he felt a surge of rage bubble up as he realized that the Dean had given him up to his father in some sort of report she had sent. But that rage was stymied by confusion as it seemed as though the Dean was fighting against the slave bond to protect his identity for some reason. *Whose side is she on?*

The question was still unanswered when she spoke up again. "I swear, oh Great One, that I don't know—"

The attack was so quick and sudden that he missed it entirely. It was only when Dean Lorraine's head went sailing off into the air to land among the students below, that Larek realized the Gergasi had decapitated the head of Copperleaf Academy with his sword, too fast to follow. Even as her kneeling form collapsed on top of the stone column, blood fountaining out from her headless body, Larek's father turned to the Vice General.

"I HOPE YOU HAVE A BETTER ANSWER THAN THIS ONE, SLAVE. WHERE IS MY CHILD?"

Larek's vision was locked onto the horrific scene, so he was able to see the visible gulp that Vice General Whittaker took before he answered.

"I believe that the one you're looking for is—"

The head of Fort Pinevalley was abruptly cut off, in more ways than one, as a massive Scission suddenly emerged in the middle of the yard, slicing not only through the neck of the kneeling Vice General but entirely through the stone column they were standing on. The column abruptly split in half, both halves inexorably falling toward the gathered students below, who began to scatter upon the appearance of the Scission, the Dominion magic controlling most of them overridden by their innate sense of self-preservation.

As for the Gergasi, his wings suddenly appeared again on his back as he lifted off the falling stone column, the Scission just missing bisecting him as well. He roared in frustration even as he stared at the rapidly strengthening portal that would spew out monsters soon, his sword out in front of him defensively.

"THIS IS ALL *YOUR* FAULT, YOU FOOLS! IF YOU HADN'T DELAYED ME, THE AETHERIC CORRUPTION WOULDN'T HAVE LOCKED ONTO MY SIGNATURE OUTSIDE OF THE ENCLAVE!"

Aetheric corruption? What is that? Larek was plagued by a hundred questions from that one statement, but now wasn't the time to pursue them further. Instead, it was time to run, because the yard had been thrown into chaos by the appearance of the Scission, so their movement wouldn't be noted now.

As he began to move, intent on gathering his friends so that they could start running, a hand closed over his arm, stopping him in place.

Chapter 17

Startled, he looked down to see Grandmaster Fusionist Shinpai at his side. "Larek. I need you all to come with me."

Ripping his arm away from his Professor's hand, he was instantly suspicious. "Why? The Dean—"

"Did what she *had* to do," Shinpai said quickly, his emphasis telling Larek what he meant by that. He was insinuating that the Dean's slave bond forced her to communicate his presence in a report to her Great Ones. "She also wanted you to live, and live *free*, but if you don't come with me right now, that won't happen. Please, just trust me on this."

The pressure of Dominion magic coming off of his father, who was hovering in the air in front of the Scission, had been overshadowed by what he was feeling from the Scission itself. Larek wasn't an expert quite yet on such things, despite being near a few of them, but he was quite convinced that the Scission was just about to start spewing out monsters within the next few minutes, if not the next few seconds. He didn't have a lot of time to consider what to do; all he knew was that he had to get out of there before the Gergasi turned its sights on the child it was trying to find among the students.

But do I trust Shinpai? Or should we just make a run for it on our own.

In the end, it came down to a sudden change in the Scission that made the decision for him. Out of the corner of his eye, he watched the gigantic portal begin to rapidly change colors, heralding the beginning of the next phase. Having no idea where he would even go in the Academy to escape not only the monsters that were about to emerge but also his father, he decided to trust Shinpai to help them. If it turned out that he was being double-crossed, he would deal with it when the time came.

"Fine. Everyone, let's follow Shinpai."

The others didn't have any objection, as they didn't experience the same sort of indecision about the Professor as he had, and they quickly took off after the surprisingly agile Grandmaster Fusionist as he raced through the panicked crowd of not only students but Professors. Looking back toward the Scission, Larek watched as the colors finally stabilized, ending up with a bright red color that – according to his studies the previous year in his *Scissions* class, indicated that what would come out was likely to be something that had to do with heat or fire.

As soon as it settled on the color, the pressure it was giving off disappeared, and Larek saw the first ranks of the monsters coming through. Dozens of 4-foot-tall blobs of moving lava rolled out of the Scission, which Larek recognized as **Lava Oozes** from his *Monster Knowledge* class. They were difficult to kill only because most normal weapons couldn't hurt them; only weapons enhanced with some sort of Martial Battle Art or with a Fusion designed to combat these types of monsters would work against them. Of course, there were plenty of spells that Mages could use to defeat them, as there was a heart or core of obsidian inside of them that – once cracked – would destroy them completely. Even a simple Ice Spike could punch through the lava and reach it, though the caster would have to be very lucky to hit it on the first shot because it tended to move around inside of its oozy form.

What he also knew about these **Lava Oozes** was that they were only seen in Category 3 Scissions and above in differing numbers. Based on the size of the Scission, he estimated that this was *at least* Category 5, if not larger; his perspective on the whole thing was a little skewed because he was so close to it and he was currently running for his life.

The Oozes were still emerging from the front of the Scission by the time Shinpai reached the main administrative offices of the Academy, and he disappeared inside after beckoning them to follow. Larek told the others to go through the door first to get to safety; as for himself, he stopped at the door and looked back at what was happening at the Scission, and was surprised to see the Gergasi attacking the Lava Oozes as they emerged. At first, he expected the powerful figure to simply lay waste to the monsters by slicing through them with his sword, which seemed more than capable of destroying the obsidian hearts inside of them, but he instead cast a frighteningly effective spell.

Storm clouds billowed out from his upraised hands, the sword he was carrying somehow attached to the golden rope at his waist, and they spread out until they were covering nearly half of the yard. At some point, another gesture by his potential father produced a torrential deluge of icicles, each of them at least a foot long and the thickness of Larek's thumb. They pounded down upon the Lava Oozes as they rolled toward the retreating students and faculty, and their internal obsidian cores cracked when they were struck by dozens of these icicles within seconds. Wave after wave of Oozes fell under the onslaught of icicles, but they kept emerging from the Scission with no signs of stopping. At least a hundred of the Oozes were killed by the time he heard Nedira shouting for him.

"Larek! Hurry up!"

As he turned away from the Gergasi and the battle ensuing outside, for a moment he thought he saw the powerful figure start to turn toward him, as if sensing that Larek was looking at him, but the Fusionist retreated inside before he could tell for sure. Slamming the door behind him, as if that would somehow prevent his father from breaking into the building, he raced after Nedira and his friends as they turned the corner up ahead. At full speed, he caught up to them in seconds, tapping into his Agility stat for a moment to speed through the hallway, though he made sure to slow down when he got near them to prevent his Repelling Barrier from activating when he got too close. He was moving much faster than 10 miles per hour, after all, and barreling into them might cause all of their protective Fusions to activate at the same time.

Yet another flaw in its formation that he wanted to fix when he had the time, as well as the ability; he suspected that he would need to master Advanced Fusions to upgrade it with the necessary fixes. Unfortunately, now was not the time to do any of that, as he rushed up the stairs after Shinpai.

It didn't take Larek long to realize where they were going, and he began to slow down when they approached the Dean's office. *Is this some sort of elaborate trap?* He didn't know for sure, as he was still conflicted over what the head of the Academy had done, and he was still unsure when he saw a group of people huddled around the doors leading into the Dean's office.

"There you are! What took you so long?"

Strangely enough, Penelope, Bartholomew, Vivienne, and Kimble were apparently waiting for them, though how they knew Larek and his friends were coming aroused his suspicions once again. Either Penelope was a spectacular actor, as her question seemed completely genuine and concerned, or she was actually worried over their late appearance.

I didn't even know we were on a schedule.

"What is going on? What are they doing here?" Larek asked, now thoroughly confused.

"Get inside and I'll explain. We don't have much time," Shinpai instructed, before pushing the doors open and ushering them inside. As soon as he closed the doors behind them, he brought something out from a pocket and placed it on the door. Larek immediately recognized that it was a Fusion of some kind on a wooden disk, but that was all he saw before the wood of the doors suddenly fused together, creating a single piece of wood that appeared inseparable. The effect also spread to the hinges and the doorframe, enveloping them so that the doorway looked less like a door and more like a solid wall.

"What was that—?"

His Professor cut him off. "There's no time. There's a few things I have to give you and then you have to run. Don't stop and don't look back; get as far away from here as you can."

"Professor Shinpai, what is going on?" Bartholomew asked. "We were told to meet at the Dean's office if something catastrophic ever happened, but I never thought that one of the Great Ones would appear. I've never heard of them leaving their Enclave, precisely because of what just happened out there."

Everyone stopped and stared at the young Martial trainee. "You already have the slave bond, don't you?"

"I... do." Bartholomew looked confused. "But it's like it's muted for some reason. I still feel it there, but I get the sense that I don't have to obey it anymore." His eyes widened as he looked around the room. "Wait; I wasn't supposed to tell anyone about that. How is this possible?"

Shinpai was moving toward the Dean's desk, and as he arrived and started opening up one of the drawers and pulling it out completely, he said, "We don't have time for a full explanation, but suffice it to say that it's because of your charge right there." He waved toward Larek, before reaching inside the desk to the spot that was left after the drawer was removed.

"What? What's going on, Larek?" Nedira asked, and everyone else looked at him expectantly, as if he had all the answers. While he had *some* answers, he didn't want to get into it right now.

"I don't know; why don't we ask Shinpai, as he's the one who brought us here," he responded.

The Grandmaster Fusionist started pulling out leather bag after leather bag, each of them small enough to fit easily in his large hands. They clunked on top of the desk with the sound of metallic jingling, hinting that they were coins of some sort or other. As soon as he was done putting approximately two dozen of these bags, as well as what appeared to be four canvas backpacks, on the desk, Shinpai looked up at Larek with a resigned look upon his face.

"I'm sorry, Larek, but they need to know," he started to say, before a massive explosion coming from somewhere outside rocked the entire building. "Never mind, we're running out of time. Long story short, the Dean was forced to report your presence because of the slave bond, but kept your name and description out of it." Shinpai tossed a bag toward him and Larek deftly caught it. "Inside that bag are a few things you'll need; I created a *Perceptive Misdirection* Fusion on a ring in there which will make people believe you are shorter than you actually are. It won't hold up to physical contact, but I'm sure you can see where it might be useful. It's an Advanced Fusion, so if you are able to break through your Skills, try and copy it or improve it so you can keep it for where you're going.

"As for where that is, you're all heading to Silverledge Academy and Fort Ironwall. There are transfer papers for everyone here, signed by the Dean herself a few days ago when she suspected something like this might happen. You, specifically," Larek's Professor said, staring right at him, "are going to Fort Ironwall. They are the premier Fort for Martials, and if they can't teach you what you need, no one can."

"What? Why is he—?" Penelope began to ask, but Shinpai cut her off.

"Later, Penelope. These bags are also filled with gold and platinum coins so that you can make your way to Silverledge and Ironwall by any means necessary. You can thank Larek for it all, as it's what the Dean has been keeping safe for him for all the Fusions he's been making lately." Turning once again to Larek, he asked, "You didn't think we were just giving them all away for free, did you?"

"Well, I—"

"Regardless, this is only a fraction of what you made from your work; there was too much to store here safely. If you're ever able to get back here in the future when it's safe, I'll get you the rest..." he said, before adding in a softer voice, "If I'm still around, of course. I imagine the fallout from this is going to be, to put it lightly, extraordinary."

There was another explosion that shook the building even more, and everyone looked at each other in shock and worry, wondering what was going on outside. Well, all but Larek, because he absolutely, positively did not want to know in the slightest.

Directing Larek's bodyguards to begin packing up all the bags into the backpacks, Shinpai moved to the wall to the left of the office entrance before pushing a few specific pieces of the wooden paneling, which depressed under his touch. A moment later, there was a soft click and a portion of the wall slid aside, revealing a dark passageway leading down a spiraling stone staircase.

"Wow; I didn't even detect that that was there," Kimble noted with some wonder.

"You wouldn't; it was made by entirely mundane means, no Fusions or magic whatsoever," the Grandmaster Fusionist explained in a rush. "Now, get moving before it's too late. This will bring you to a very long passageway that leads under the city, and it emerges in the nearby forest approximately 5 miles to the west of Thanchet. Unfortunately, you're going to have to backtrack a little once you're out of the tunnel and head northeast, making your way to Silverledge and Ironwall. It'll be dangerous, especially with the current environment and the SIC Transportation Network only running sporadically, but I have faith that you'll make it. Just like the Dean had faith in you, Larek, to see this through to the end."

There was another, closer-sounding explosion, and Larek realized that it was coming from *inside* the building.

"Run! I'll close this after you, buying you some time. Go!" Shinpai shouted, pushing the young students and trainees into the passageway. Larek came last, and his Professor stopped him momentarily. "No pressure or anything, but with the way things are going, both the Dean and I believe that you're our only hope of anyone surviving what is coming. We were hoping that you would have more time to learn everything you needed to, but everything escalated faster than we expected. Stay safe and—"

Another crash outside the room was followed by a banging against the door. Without another word, Shinpai pushed Larek inside the dark passageway before closing the wall again, leaving him in complete darkness. A sudden illumination coming from a spell cast by Kimble lit the short passageway and the spiral stone staircase ahead, and Larek could see the frightened faces of his friends and the shocked-but-determined expressions of his bodyguards.

"About what he said—"

"I'll explain later," he cut off Penelope's question. "We need to move and get out of here as quickly as we can. We'll have plenty of time to talk soon enough." With a nod, she turned around and led the way down, with Kimble right behind her with the light.

Leadership *has increased to Level 11!*

With a final glance back at the closed portion of the wall behind him, where he could hear what sounded like the office door being absolutely demolished, Larek followed the group down the stone steps into the darkness below.

Chapter 18

Absolutely devastating the **Lava Oozes** that streamed out of the Scission, Vilnesh swiped his Ebonblade across the weak monsters as he fumed. Not even bothering to activate any of his Battle Arts after his *Ice Storm* spell had devastated most of them, his newest attacks were created solely by the qualities of the sword he wielded, crafted from a piece of an Ebonlord, a frighteningly powerful monster that came through the Source in the Enclave over a hundred years ago. Vilnesh still remembered the battle against the enormous dark construct, which had nearly killed a dozen of his people before it was taken down.

The material his Ebonblade was made from was only a portion of the spoils they had gained from its corpse. It had been a great boon to their ongoing advancement, even if it was dangerous in the process. Nothing came easy for them, after all, which just made them appreciate it all the more when forced into a challenge.

This Scission, however, was not a challenge in the least. For Vilnesh, it was more an annoyance than anything.

If only that blasted slave had given up the whereabouts of my child, this would never have happened!

That wasn't entirely true, of course, but after he had obtained the information passed along the slaves' communication network concerning the presence of some sort of prodigy, their sources – which, he begrudgingly admitted, were much more widespread and comprehensive than his people's own – investigated further. When knowledge about some sort of half-breed had potentially been sighted around the Kingdom, it didn't take long for Vilnesh to put it all together.

There had been only one impregnated slave that escaped from their clutches over the last few centuries, and *his* spawn was the likely result of that pregnancy. It was the only thing that fit the timeline, after all, and it was his duty to see it was returned to the Enclave. Success in reproducing viable progeny was only a matter of time, given all the work they had gone through toward that end. After their own females had become sterile after the Transition, it was up to Vilnesh and his fellow males to expand their numbers using the slaves as breeding stock.

Unfortunately, even after nearly 1,000 years of trying, every single half-breed born in the Enclave had been a failure. Sickly and deformed, many of them didn't live past age 20, especially after it was discovered that their magical talent was either nonexistent or simply dysfunctional. They'd made progress through magical infusions into their impregnated breeding stock over the years, slowly eliminating one malady after another from which the half-breeds suffered, until the first semi-successful attempts occurred a few decades ago. While still sickly and deformed, for the first time their magical abilities were finally available in both forms, Mage and Martial – or so the slaves called them.

In reality, they stemmed from the same thing: Aetheric Force.

After breaching the veil between their world and another, which was filled with this Aetheric Force that his people took for their own, everything seemed to go wrong. After the majority of the Gergasi, his people, were extinguished attempting to tame this incredible Force, Aetheric Corruption began to spew out from the breach, forming what the world now knew as Scissions that released transformed Aetheric Force in the form of monsters that ravaged the land.

Vilnesh still remembered those chaotic days when it was all his people could do to keep their empire together, finally resorting to forcing their much-diminished slaves to obtain a portion of the Aetheric Force in order to defend the land. Reduced in numbers, it was all that his people could do to keep the breach from becoming worse, while running their empire – or as the slaves called it, their Kingdom – from their Enclave. It wasn't by choice, having to hide away, but due to the fact that the Aetheric Corruption was somehow able to trace his people whenever they ventured away from the breach. Originally, it wasn't that big of a problem unless they stayed in one place for more than a few days; but over the centuries, if they were someplace stationary for a few *hours*, then a Scission would appear and attempt to destroy them, ignoring everything else.

Some of his people ventured that there was a consciousness behind the Corruption, targeting its gatekeepers.

Vilnesh didn't necessarily believe that, though, as he just thought the Corruption was a mindless pest that continued to become more and more annoying as time went on. Now that the Culmination was upon them, with the Aetheric Corruption increasing its flow and haphazard appearances around the Kingdom, causing a Scission to appear only minutes after he stopped moving, it was downright maddening how it was preventing him from finding his child.

A child that, to all intents and purposes, seemed to be their most successful half-breed of all. *If only Keandra, that worthless daughter of some Duke I don't even remember the name of, hadn't escaped from the Enclave, then we would've already had my child within my grasp.*

Unfortunately, their Dominion magic had some flaws to it, as powerful as it was. The biggest one, and the one most important to the woman's escape, was that all Dominion magic upon her person was neutralized while she had his spawn in her belly. A slave to his magic no longer, the impregnated woman had somehow found a way to escape and avoid the search teams sent out to look for her. Until a short time ago, most considered that she had simply died after she escaped, her body unable to be found, as there had been absolutely no trace of her until now.

That trace was his child, whoever it might be. The reports leaned toward it being a son, though there were a few that mentioned a daughter; it didn't really matter, of course, as either would suit their purposes as evidence that successful reproduction was possible. If this child was healthy, unlike their other recent half-breeds that had a full complement of Aetheric Force and yet their bodies couldn't handle the energy coursing through them, leading to their untimely deaths more often than not, then they needed to know. If, as they also hoped, this child also gained a measure of Dominion magic, then that could start a new wave of control as they birthed thousands of these offspring, sending them out to take control of the rest of the Kingdom, putting every single person under their rule.

From there, they could finally expand to encompass the entire world.

As Vilnesh swept the Ebonblade through yet another score of Lava Oozes emerging through the Scission, he felt a hint of something pushing against his senses. At first, he wasn't sure what it was that had gently poked against his mind, because it felt familiar and yet foreign at the same time. It was only when he realized *why* it felt familiar that he swung his head around behind him, seeing a flash of something disappear into one of the Academy's doorways.

That's my child! It has Dominion magic!

That revelation was so momentous that he was distracted, as he turned toward the main offices of the Academy with the intent to go after his spawn. Unfortunately, it was at that time that the next wave of monsters arrived – and they weren't going to let him go that easily. A score of **Fire Graspers** raced out of the Scission, their spheroid bodies comprised of flames approximately 15 feet long and just as wide. They used their multitude of 50-foot-long jointed arms made of stone and fire to move swiftly toward him, the ends of which were tipped with grasping hands that latched onto Vilnesh.

The burning pain in his upper arms and his left knee were ignored as the closest Grasper clamped fiery extremities along his body, and he roared out in anger as he used his prodigious strength to rip himself away from it. Another grasping hand attempted to snatch him back up, but he simply caught it with his left hand as he separated its leg from the rest of its body with a slice of his sword. Gathering himself for another spell, he quickly threw the detached Grasper arm away and formed the pattern for *Frost Nova*, which he empowered with a quick flick of his Mana.

Detonating with an explosion of icy cold, the spell impacted everything within 100 feet of his location, excepting only himself. The trio of Graspers close to him were frozen entirely solid, while those a little further away were slowed. With a leap, he brought his Ebonblade down in a downward chop that shattered the frozen monster that had dared to touch him, that had dared to delay him, and thousands of frozen Grasper shards went flying everywhere. With a grunt as he landed on the ground again, he began to run toward the door he saw his child escape through, but was caught yet again by a fiery stone hand and prevented from moving.

Thoroughly enraged at this, he roared in displeasure and grabbed the grasping arm, pulling at it as he activated *Titan's Strength*, a Battle Art that enhanced his Strength by 200%. With an easy yank, he lifted the Fire Grasper into the air above his head, again ignoring the burning coming from the exterior of the monster, as he slammed it back down on a trio of nearby monsters. His abrupt attack not only absolutely destroyed those three Graspers, but also shattered the other pair of frozen ones formed by his *Frost Nova*, as well as sending the others skittering backwards from the shockwave.

Letting go of his impromptu weapon, he once again ran toward the interior wall of the Academy, intending to find his child, but the remaining Graspers chose that moment to leap after him using their long legs to cover the distance. He was incredibly fast and made it there before they did, but with them just outside the offices, he couldn't take the chance that they would kill his offspring before he could discover what made it work when all of their other experiments had ultimately failed.

Stopping right in front of the doorway to the offices, he turned around and waited for the remaining Graspers to arrive after their jump. As soon as they landed, he activated yet another Battle Art, *Shockwave*. With his *Titan's Strength* still active, he channeled his Stama through his hands and into the Ebonblade, which further amplified the effect, and then slammed the weapon down to the ground. An enormous shockwave spread out from the point of impact, rising in a wide semi-circle of force that lifted from the ground and slammed through every single Grasper around him. The *Shockwave* was powerful enough that it literally snuffed out every spot of flame on their bodies and limbs before sending them flying away, their broken forms dead before they hit the ground.

Panting from the exertion, as it was more Stama than he was expecting to use at the moment, he saw that no other monsters were coming out of the Scission – but it was only a matter of a minute or two before the next wave arrived.

Vilnesh turned around and ripped the door out of its frame as he rushed inside, heading up the staircase he saw a short distance away. As he was taking the steps four at a time, practically flying up them, his *Titan's Strength* Battle Art finally subsided, leaving him feeling weak as its debuffs hit him, reducing his Body and Strength stats by 50% for a short time. He didn't have time for weakness as he reached the top, looking around for a brief second before deciding on a direction. His decision turned out to be correct as he discovered what appeared to be a room with its door sealed up, completely preventing anyone from opening it. Vilnesh immediately recognized what had caused it to seal up, and he couldn't help a sneer from alighting on his face.

"Filthy Fusions; they're worthless and a waste of time. As soon as I find my child, that'll be the first thing I beat out of them." To say that it was a disappointment to hear that his child had taken it upon themselves to study Fusions, which was a slave adaptation of Aetheric Force that the Gergasi didn't dabble in because it was virtually useless in their eyes, was putting it lightly. While it had uses in the slaves' Kingdom, especially for the commoners, Vilnesh had never seen the potential for it other than as a curiosity; that curiosity had lasted all of a decade before he never studied it again.

After all, why put in so much work for something that didn't last *and* could be copied in better form with a spell?

He ran full speed at the closed doorway, expecting to burst right through it, but his reduced stats apparently betrayed him as he bounced off, only causing a few cracks to form. Grunting in anger, he whipped up the Ebonblade by his side and impacted the wooden doorway, cutting through it easily. Over the next 10 seconds, he carved his way through the surprisingly sturdy portal, emerging on the other side as he frantically looked around.

"WHERE IS MY CHILD? BRING THEM TO ME!"

Using his Dominion magic on the older slave he found inside, he was momentarily taken aback when it didn't work, at least not entirely. Normally, he could immediately sense that his magic had taken hold, but just like the Dean had done shortly before, he was able to fight it somehow. *Did my child do this?* That was the only explanation he could come up with for why his Dominion magic didn't work the way he expected.

The old man dropped to his knees, a shaking through his body, evidence that he was fighting the command Vilnesh dropped onto him. With a little bit more pressure on the slave, he forced his magic to cut through whatever was preventing him from taking control.

Gasping, the man abruptly said, "No. You'll never find him—"

A sudden crash echoed through the building, before a giant fist of magma slammed down from above, smashing through the ceiling and falling upon Vilnesh. Even though he was weaker than he had been a minute or so ago, thanks to the debuff from his Battle Art, he was still fast enough to dive out of the way of the fist. The old man, however, was caught unaware while he was battling for control of himself, and he was crushed under the fist, along with half of the floor.

*A **Magma Behemoth**? The Corruption really wants to kill me. Too bad for it that I'm a lot harder than that to kill.*

He picked himself up from where he had dove out of the way of the fist, looking back to see that the old man was literally just a smear on the broken floor. He wasn't getting any other information from him, obviously, though he did have it confirmed that he was looking for his son, and not a daughter. Unfortunately, he didn't have time to look for where this son of his went, as another fist slammed to the side of where the last one landed, and he was forced to dodge yet again.

Enough. I'll take care of this Behemoth and then track him down. He couldn't have gotten far.

Pulling out every trick he had in his repertoire, he launched himself out of the broken ceiling and took the fight to the 100-foot-tall Magma Behemoth, noticing that the Scission had closed after the Behemoth had emerged. Spells and Battle Arts flew through the air as he battled the giant monster made of pure magma, but their confrontation wasn't without even more destruction heaped upon the Academy. When the Behemoth finally fell, Vilnesh knelt in exhaustion as he stared at the completely destroyed main offices, along with half of the building along the wall where it was located.

My son. I just need to dig through the rubble and—

Before he could get started on searching for his son, or at least the remains of him, Vilnesh could feel a subtle buildup of Aetheric Corruption coming from all around him. Cursing in annoyance, he knew that it would probably take another 10 minutes or so before another Scission opened in his location, but that wasn't nearly enough time for his search.

He's probably dead, but I'll have the staff here locate the body and send it to the Enclave.

On a time limit, Vilnesh quickly Dominated the nearby staff he could see cowering in the entrances around the Academy, imprinting commands upon a few of them with instructions to carry out his will. Another flex of his Dominion magic caused another wave of his power to flow through every living person within a mile of the city, forcibly suppressing their memories of the last 24 hours. Knowledge of his presence was more dangerous than a Scission appearing within the walls of the Academy and Fort, and it was important to eliminate it as soon as possible.

With reluctance and not a little bit of annoyance at the corpse of the Magma Behemoth, which was setting fire to sections of the wooden half of the building, Vilnesh left and headed back to the Enclave, where he would await any information from the body that was recovered after the mess was cleaned up. He *would* get answers...

...one way or another.

Chapter 19

Larek followed his friends and bodyguards down the spiral stone staircase, the only light for now coming from Kimble's *Light Orb* spell a ways ahead, but it was more than enough for him to see even further back in the group. A moment later, the former Logger passed Bartholomew on the narrow stairway, and he looked at the Martial trainee with confusion.

"Just guarding our back end," the armored young man whispered in answer to his unspoken question. Larek nodded as he passed him, indicating that he understood.

Everyone was quiet as they descended, not wanting to draw any attention to themselves, though with how much the entire building seemed to shake less than 30 seconds after they started their descent, he didn't think anyone would hear them. Cracks in the walls and ceiling suddenly echoed through the stairway, followed by puffs of dirt and streams of pulverized stone as everything seemed to shift slightly.

"Faster! It feels like the entire building is going to come down!" Nedira shouted to be heard over the reverberating emanations coming from the walls, and those ahead immediately raced down the stairs. Another enormous pounding against the building nearly caused Larek to fall, but he managed to catch himself with a hand against the wall; at the same time, he reached out and caught Verne, who was just about to tumble down the stairs in what would've been a very painful experience. Up ahead, he heard Kimble let out an "oof," and he heard Penelope asking if he was alright, but that seemed to be the only injury, as slight as it was.

With Larek now convinced that Nedira was correct, he began urging everyone on, even picking up Verne and Norde and having them hang off of him as he descended; Nedira gave out a startled squeal as he picked her up and carried her in his arms. "Sorry," he apologized quickly. "Faster this way."

"I'm not complaining." She said a little breathlessly, which was probably because she was nearly hyperventilating. "Whatever it takes to get to safety quicker, I'm all for it."

Catching up to the others ahead of them, Kimble looked back to see Larek carrying three people without any difficulty, and he looked at Penelope. "Can I catch a ride?"

"Jump on and we'll go!" The Pyromancer immediately jumped on her back and wrapped his arms and legs around the blue-haired

Martial trainee; other than a grunt when his weight settled on her, the young woman didn't seem to notice.

With an unspoken command, Penelope (with Kimble catching a ride), Vivienne, Larek (with his passengers), and Bartholomew began moving much faster down the stairway. It was approaching breakneck pace when Kimble turned his head and shouted behind him, "I see the—"

Whatever he was going to say was cut off by the shaking of the entire stairway, as something impacted the building above them with such force that Larek stumbled and crashed against the wall, nearly falling once again as he crashed into the back of Vivienne. The Ranger was fortunately able to stabilize both herself and Larek, but Penelope took a tumble with the weight on her back. Kimble and the Striker fell another half-dozen steps before they hit what turned out to be the bottom of the staircase; neither of them appeared terribly hurt, though the Pyromancer had dropped his staff on the stairs.

It was then that Larek heard something that caused him to shout, "Run!"

Even as Kimble scrambled to his feet and started heading back for his staff, Larek blocked him as he came down. "Leave it! The stairway is collapsing!"

The red-robed Mage hesitated for a half-second before he turned around, jumping on Penelope's back once she got up from her own fall. She didn't complain but instead took off with him on her back, followed by the others. A second later, a tremendous crashing sound behind them shook the stone-lined tunnel they were moving down. Unfortunately, the tunnel was only about 6 feet tall, causing Larek to have to duck while he ran, but he had no reason to complain as it was getting them away from the collapsing stairway. A sudden cloud of dust and debris wafted past them from the chaos happening behind, and everyone started coughing as it filled the tunnel to the point where it was hard to breathe. Larek had to put Nedira down because he needed to wipe his eyes, which were now filled with grit, and Verne also hopped down with Norde to do the same thing for themselves.

Despite not being able to see or breathe very well, the group didn't stop moving down the tunnel. After about 5 minutes, the tunnel cleared up enough that they weren't coughing every few seconds, and the dust that had filled the corridor had settled enough and was only kicked up as they passed.

Again, no one spoke as they trudged along, not because they thought someone might hear them, but because the tunnel was dark and oppressive. At least, that was why Larek didn't speak; he could only guess that the others were a bit hoarse from coughing out all that dust.

They walked for what felt like hours, as the tunnel curved slightly to the right before heading back to the left, but the corridor seemed almost endless. Larek was getting a crick in his back as he walked hunched over, but he was reluctant to ease it with his *Healing Surge* Fusion because it would make him hungry after a while. Given that they had to leave so abruptly, it was entirely possible that no one had any food on them. Unless it was in one of their bags, of course, but Shinpai hadn't mentioned it before they were forced to flee.

As much as I don't like how both the Dean and Shinpai manipulated me, I hope the old Fusionist is alright.

Thinking about the potential death of his Professor, in the dark confines of the seemingly endless tunnel, made him a bit morose about his situation. First, it seemed as though everyone with some authority who was trying to help him, regardless of whether they had a selfish reason for it, ended up dead. Fusionist Annika wasn't even the first if he considered the SIC group that had taken him from Rushwood; they were, of course, followed by Dean Lorraine and potentially Grandmaster Fusionist Shinpai – though he still held out hope that he had survived.

Am I putting my friends in danger just by being around them? It was a question that was easily answered by the evidence that they were currently fleeing for their lives through a dark tunnel that led to who knew where, after a Gergasi killed the Dean and somehow caused a Scission to open up in the middle of the Academy yard. If that wasn't being put into danger, then he didn't know what would qualify.

Second, he was somewhat dreading telling his friends and bodyguards the truth about himself, as he wasn't sure how they would react. They might even be quite angry and blame him for their current circumstances; that was something he wouldn't blame them for, however, as that was unfortunately 100% true.

Last, he was trying to decide if he was going to do as Shinpai said the Dean wanted and go to Fort Ironwall while Nedira and his roommates went to Silverledge Academy – if they could even make it there in one piece. While he thought that learning more about his Stama and Battle Arts might be beneficial, he still didn't have any desire to actually fight in a battle where such "Arts" would be needed. Every confrontation he'd been involved in had been completely circumstantial; there had been no conscious thought to go looking for a fight, as he was only defending himself and his friends from attack. He had no desire to go save the Kingdom by eliminating this hole into another world or whatever that the Gergasi had opened 1,000 years ago; he wasn't a hero in some tale, nor did he wish to get involved with any relatives of his. He was frightened enough by the figure that was likely his father to never want to meet another one.

But he had to admit that, with the way Scissions were opening up all over the Kingdom and releasing monsters everywhere, that defending himself with something other than just Fusions would make sense. Since he couldn't cast a spell, and had already gained one Battle Art (accidentally, but it still counted in his mind), then any advantage he could find that would allow him to survive longer in the crazy environment that the Kingdom was turning into would be helpful. Therefore, heading to the Fort and seeing if they could help him figure out his whole Stama problem seemed like the sensible choice.

Then again, it was what the Dean wanted, and while she was unfortunately deceased, it was almost like she was still trying to manipulate him from the grave. He wasn't sure what to do, if he was being honest with himself, but he resolved to put that decision off until he was forced to make it. Regardless of what he eventually chose to do, he would at least see to it that Nedira and his roommates made it to Silverledge Academy, as they still needed to finish their magical education, and at least Bartholomew still needed to finish his at the Fort; he was fairly certain that Penelope, Vivienne, and Kimble were all sixth-years that only stayed on because they were guarding Larek, so they were technically free to go and join the SIC or do whatever else they had planned for after they graduated.

Larek could see that Verne and Norde were dragging their feet after a while, as well as Nedira, but none of them asked to hitch a ride on the Larek carriage again. The rest of the Martial trainees were perfectly fine, likely used to the physical exercise that walking gave them, if not a lot more than this; if there was one detrimental thing he could say about both Academies he'd attended, it was that they didn't seem to have a comprehensive exercise program. Granted, it wasn't as if there were a bunch of extremely out-of-shape and overweight students that went to each Academy, but most of them certainly weren't able to walk for hours before becoming extremely exhausted. Now, if *Larek* was in charge, he would combine the curriculum of both the Academy and the Fort so that the Mages obtained a better exercise and even defensive weaponry program than they did at the moment, while the Martials would get a better education about the spells and Fusions that Mages created. His experience with the two graduates from Pinevalley hinted that they were relatively unfamiliar with both spells and Fusions, other than in a general sense, but if they attended the same place of learning, then they might pick up a lot more and therefore be more effective in a team.

There must be a reason they kept them separate—

His musings were interrupted when Kimble and Penelope abruptly stopped ahead of the group, and Larek was so deep in his own mind that he bumped into Verne, who had halted ahead of him. Thankfully, the Fusionist was fast enough to grab the boy before he could fall, and he apologized to his roommate quickly before he looked to see why they had stopped.

It didn't take long to realize they had come to a dead end.

"What is this? Are we trapped down here?" Kimble asked, running his empty hands over the dirt wall that had stopped them.

Penelope looked back at Larek, a questioning expression on her face, but he just responded with a shrug. She knew just as much as he did, after all.

"Maybe there was a turn-off somewhere that we missed? Did anyone see any hidden passageways?" Nedira asked, leaning tiredly against the stone-lined wall. When no one spoke up, she slumped to the ground, soon joined by Verne and Norde as they got off their feet.

"Anyone have any ideas, then?" Penelope asked, looking around the dead end.

Larek didn't, but Bartholomew spoke up. "Uh, well, we have an escape tunnel on my father's estate, though I haven't personally seen it," he admitted, seemingly embarrassed.

"You have an escape tunnel? Why?" Verne asked.

"Because, see," he began, but then forged on, ignoring the question entirely. "Anyway, we have an escape tunnel that comes out away from the city like this one is supposed to, but the exit was hidden somehow. Ours was hidden in the back of a cave in the Worthskill Mountains, covered by a large boulder that would take a strong Martial to shift – or a powerful Mage. It's possible that this is similar, but instead of a boulder, it's a wall of dirt."

Glancing at the walls and ceiling around the dirt wall, Larek thought that might be a good assumption. The stone blocks continued *into* the dirt, meaning that they didn't necessarily stop there, so it was possible that this tunnel kept going.

"I'm not the best at Earth-based spells, but I can certainly try and move some of this dirt away," Kimble said, approaching the wall, but Nedira stopped him.

"My second focus was on Earth spells after my Natural bent, so I probably have a better chance of getting through," she explained. "Alright, everyone get back."

There was no argument as everyone got behind the fifth-year Naturalist, and Larek watched her cast a spell that he could sense was literally designed to move dirt. Surprisingly, he was able to learn it as she cast it multiple times over the next few minutes, each cast of which pulled dirt from the center and pushed it to the sides of the tunnel, gradually making a hole.

New Spell learned!
Furrow
Magnitude: 3 cubic feet of dirt
Base Elemental Damage: 0
Base Elemental Effect (Dirt Manipulation): Gently moves a certain amount of dirt in a desired direction
Restrictions: Rocks greater than 3 cubic inches cannot be shifted
Base Mana Cost: 15
Base Pattern Cohesion: 2

It took him a moment to understand why she would even want something like that, considering that it just moved dirt. When he remembered that she was also a Naturalist that dealt with plants a lot, he figured a spell like this would be useful in farming; he had seen farms and the people working on them on his travels, and being able to turn the dirt with a spell seemed like it would save a lot of time.

As he began to wonder if this was what Nedira had in mind after she graduated from the Kingdom's Academies, as she had never mentioned actually joining the SIC for a time, his friend's efforts to move the dirt bore fruit. One moment, there was still a relatively solid dirt wall in front of them, and the next there was a small hole leading into a void. That small hole was widened extensively over the next minute as Nedira cleared even more dirt and moved it to the sides of the tunnel.

"Well, I guess that answers that. Shall we?" Penelope asked, before heading through the hole that was created. Kimble followed quickly after her, his recast Light Orb illuminating what appeared to be some sort of cramped natural cave – or at least that was what it looked like to Larek from his position near the back.

"Looks clear," Penelope whispered back toward the others, and the Fusionist realized that just because they were out of the city where the Gergasi and the Scission threatened their lives, that didn't mean that they were out of danger. His father could still be looking for him, or there could be enslaved people searching for their exit, or there might even be monsters roaming around from a random Scission. Therefore, it was probably for the best to be as silent as possible.

The others caught on to this quickly as they spoke in hushed whispers, just loud enough to barely hear each other, as Penelope led the way out of the dark, jagged stone cave they found themselves in. When she had Kimble get rid of his light, the way was even darker, but thankfully it didn't take long to squeeze themselves out of a slight twisting of cave walls that barely let Larek through because of his size. The smell of fresh air and forest, as well as the sight of trees ahead made the former Logger feel nostalgic for Rushwood, though these trees were nothing like the magical wood where he grew up. These were pine trees, whose leaves were actually thin and needle-like, and which didn't shed in the winter. They also didn't grow quite as tall as his familiar Rushwood trees, though these ones were relatively impressive as they were around 60 feet tall, the majority of their branches far above their heads.

As they moved out from the cave, Larek realized that they had gone further than he expected, as they had journeyed nearly to the mountain range that ringed the majority of the valley where Thanchet was situated. It was approaching dusk, meaning that the light was failing, but when he turned toward where he knew the city should be, a break in the trees allowed him to see Thanchet in all its glory. Or, to be more accurate, its lack of glory, as he could see what was left of the Academy, which seemed to have been halfway destroyed, with the fiery glow of burning wood lighting up the ruins in scattered places.

"Wh-what happened?" Verne asked, as shocked as everyone else was as they stared in silence at the devastated Academy.

Penelope broke the silence as she cleared her throat. "I have no idea what happened, but there's nothing we can do right now. We've got our orders, so we need to get moving. I'd like to put as much distance between us and the city as possible before we're forced to stop for the night."

As much as he knew that it was dangerous to travel when the light was fading, let alone at full night, Larek couldn't help but agree. He wanted—no, *needed*—to put as much distance between himself and his father as possible, because being discovered by the Gergasi was just too much of a likelihood if he stuck around for long. While he still didn't know if he would be fulfilling the Dean's last request of him by going to Fort Ironwall, there was no denying that he couldn't go back to Copperleaf Academy at this point.

"Let's go," Larek agreed, turning away from the damaged Academy. "Lead on if you would, Penelope."

"Oh, don't worry, I will. We'll keep all you squishy Mages safe while we travel," she said, flashing a smile back at him as she marched on ahead, leading the way in the fading light.

I hope so, Penelope. For all our sakes, I desperately hope so.

Chapter 20

Darkness fell upon the group of Mage students and Martial trainees faster than Larek anticipated, but that should have been expected considering they were near a mountain range and traveling through a pine forest – both of which blocked the light fairly quickly once the sun fully descended behind the horizon. Located on the western side of the valley, Larek knew that they would have to eventually head to the northeast to make it to Silverledge Academy and Fort Ironwall, but for now they were simply trying to put some distance between them and Thanchet before true night fell.

The direction Penelope led them was more west than north, leading further up the ringing mountain range, but Larek assumed she had a purpose for it. That was discovered shortly after the light was nearly completely gone from the area, meaning that they had to pick their way carefully through the darkened forest or risk another *Light Orb* to help illuminate their way. By unspoken agreement, they decided to forgo any source of light unless absolutely necessary, as even though it would largely be blocked by the trees covering the side of the range, anyone looking out from the walls of the city could likely spot it with ease. If the Gergasi was still looking for him, it wouldn't take long before that information was relayed to the powerful giant.

Fortunately, just as their footing was becoming dangerous from the lack of light, Penelope stumbled upon what she had apparently been looking for.

"Vivienne," the blue-haired Martial whispered to the Ranger, "scout it out for us, would you?"

There was an even deeper darkness in the side of a hill they approached, which Larek immediately identified as being some sort of entrance to another cave. The leather-clad Ranger immediately slipped inside the hole in the hill, disappearing immediately from his vision, as she somehow navigated her way through the darkness inside the cave. No light shone out from inside, meaning that she didn't have any artificial light to see by, and he was wondering how she was able to scout it out if she couldn't see anything. It was only when she emerged less than a minute later, a pair of knives clutched easily in her hands, that he saw her eyes glowing slightly with what he could only assume was Stama. *A Battle Art that allows her to see in the dark? That could definitely be handy.* It was another reason for Larek to attend Fort Ironwall as the Dean wanted, because being able to see in the dark using Stama would be beneficial, even life-saving in certain situations.

"It's clear," Vivienne whispered, loud enough that everyone could hear. Without another word, everyone moved toward the cave entrance, and Larek followed the others inside, only to nearly run into a wall as the passageway not only narrowed, but curved abruptly to the left. Some shuffling blindly into the complete darkness of the cave eventually led him back to the right, until the echoes around him picked up enough to tell him that he was in a much larger space.

"It's safe," Penelope said, and before Larek could ask who she was talking to, a *Light Orb* cast by Kimble suddenly appeared, blinding him for a few seconds until he was able to blink the spots away.

Looking around, he discovered that they were in a cavern at least 50 feet wide at its widest point, though it was only about 20 feet in depth. Scattered around the dirt-covered stone floor were the bones of small animals, with no trace of all the flesh and fur that had been covering them at one point. He could only assume that this was originally the den of some sort of predator, and while he wasn't necessarily a Hunter or a tracker of some sort, he had the impression that it hadn't been used in a while.

"These caves randomly cover the entire range, so I was hoping that I'd find one before it got too dark to see," Penelope explained. She gestured to the entrance, which was hard to see as it blended in with the wall as it switched back on itself. "We're fortunate that the layout of the entrance is the way it is, as it will block most – if not all – of the light from escaping. I believe we'll be safe for the night... or as safe as we can be, considering what we just left."

At that, everyone turned to stare at Larek. A second later, the *Light Orb* that Kimble had cast ran out of its duration and he had to cast it again as everything descended into darkness, and Nedira copied him a moment later, staggering her own *Light Orb* so that they wouldn't be left in darkness.

"I can understand that everyone wants an explanation, but let me take care of our lighting problem first," he said as he looked around the cave, searching for something to create a Fusion upon. Surprisingly, there weren't any rocks other than small pebbles to be found in the cave, so Larek reached under his robe, detached his axe from its holder around his waist, and started delicately carving off small, relatively rectangular slabs of stone from the walls. It reminded him a little of his time on top of Crystalview Academy, when he created hundreds of *Healing Surge* Fusions, but this time he wasn't planning on making quite that many.

Once he had a half-dozen of these stone slabs, he sat down and placed the material in front of him, before beginning the Fusion process.

Using Focused Division to create 6 identical Fusions and splitting them between the half-dozen stone pieces was easy enough, especially as he was only creating Activatable *Illuminate Stone +1* Fusions, as they didn't need to be very bright; in the confines in the dark cave, anything stronger would likely be blinding. If they needed more light, all 6 of them could be activated simultaneously.

Less than a minute after he got started, he managed to transfer the Fusions to the slabs, locking them in place by manipulating the filled formations with practiced ease. Once they were done, he looked up to see everyone staring at him once again, though for a different reason.

"I don't think I'll ever get over how impossibly easy you make that look," Kimble muttered. Larek ducked his head at the words, slightly embarrassed for some reason, even as he handed the slabs out to the others. A few seconds later, all six Fusions were activated and spread around the cave, which helped to light it up without it being too bright, and Kimble and Nedira let their Light Orbs lapse.

"Viv, can you keep an eye and ear out for us? I want to make sure nothing sneaks up on us, and you should still be able to hear even from around the corner." The Ranger simply nodded at Penelope's suggestion, moving back through the entrance, though Larek had the impression she stopped where the passageway switched back instead of moving outside completely.

"Alright, Larek, spill it. What's going on?" Penelope asked, leaning up against the same wall that he had just taken chunks off of to make the Fusions. The sound of metal coins *thunk*ing on the dirt showed that Bartholomew and Penelope had dropped the bags they had been given to take with them by Shinpai, and he suddenly realized that he was still lugging his own along as he slipped it off his back and let it fall to the floor. Looking at the blue-haired Martial, he thought that even though they were relatively safe inside the cave, she still looked ready to act the part of the bodyguard at any moment, as if she couldn't relax.

Larek took a deep breath before releasing it, putting his thoughts into order. A brief thought of continuing to conceal his secrets flitted through his mind before he dismissed it. With all that had happened, as well as what Shinpai hinted at, it wouldn't take them long to work out at least some of it. A glance at Nedira's pale face as she stared at him hinted that she had already likely figured out some – if not all – of it, so there was no reason to hold back now. The original reason for keeping it a secret had been to protect them from something like this, but that reason was no longer valid considering their current situation.

"First, I want to be completely clear on something before I go into this," he began, looking around at everyone with as understanding of an expression as possible. "If any of you choose to leave and go your own way after what I'm about to tell you, I completely understand – and I even encourage you to do so. You've already been in terrible danger because of me, and that danger is only likely to increase as time goes on. I would never think less of you for taking the safe route here and leaving, going back to your lives after graduation," he said, pointedly looking at Kimble and Penelope, as well as speaking to the entrance where Vivienne was located, "or simply continuing your education at an Academy or Fort without being associated with me. The last thing that I want is for anyone else to die because of me, because of who I am." At this, he looked at Nedira, pleading with her to take his words seriously. As much as he would like her to stay with him, as she'd been an absolutely awesome friend – and possibly something more, given some time – he didn't want her to be caught in his nightmare of having a Gergasi as a father.

No one spoke or gave any indication that they were leaving, though Bartholomew shuffled in place a little nervously. Given that he was the son of some important-sounding Noble, he could only assume that the young man was thinking about his own family obligations that he might be abandoning if he continued to act as a bodyguard for Larek.

Taking another deep breath, he began to speak. "I was born far to the north…" He went on to detail where he grew up and the life he led up in the Rushwood forest as a Logger, before moving on to the events that led to his detainment and subsequent transfer to Crystalview Academy. He only left out the personally embarrassing parts of his story, glossing over the treatment he'd experienced from the common people of the Kingdom, as he really didn't want to revisit them.

When he came to his actions during the first Scission beyond Peratin's walls, where he described unlocking some Martial Skills for the first time, he heard the intake of breath from both Penelope and Bartholomew. "Yes, I have both Mage *and* Martial stats and Skills, though I'm having trouble accessing my Martial side," he explained after he saw their reactions. "Hence, the reason the Dean wanted me to go to Fort Ironwall."

"But how—"

He held up his hand to forestall the blue-haired trainee's question. "I'm getting to that."

He went on to explain the whole *Healing Surge* Fusion fiasco on top of the Academy's roof, and then followed it up with the story of his angry reaction to seeing the deceased form of his *Fusions* Professor and subsequent unlocking of a Battle Art during the second Scission attack at Crystalview. Widened eyes greeted that revelation, but he wasn't done yet.

Some of them knew of the events afterwards, with his journey to Copperleaf Academy to the south, but he went over everything again for them. It was the capture by Ricardo and the two Martial trainees that caught Penelope's attention, as she was both shocked and vindicated at the same time.

"See, I told you that you needed guarding."

Then he described, in basic detail, what he did to them after he escaped, excluding only the gory details and disposal of the bodies – as they didn't need to know that. "I was wondering what happened to them," Bartholomew muttered, seeming to know who the Martial trainees were, if not Ricardo.

"Ah. They were all Nobles, right?" Larek asked.

He nodded. "I didn't know them very well, but I knew *of* them."

"Anyway, that whole thing led to gaining attention from the Dean, which turned out to be a blessing and a curse at the same time," he continued. "For the first time, Dean Lorraine – along with Shinpai – were able to tell me why I was *different*, which was something I'd been wondering about since my height suddenly shot up when I was younger. Of course, it was what I turned out to be that is concerning, and is currently why we're likely being hunted even now."

"Y-you're a Great One!" Bartholomew suddenly blurted out, pointing at him. "That's the only explanation I can see for how my slave bond didn't activate back at the Fort."

He shook his head at the frightened expressions of his companions. "Not exactly. According to the Dean, I'm a half-breed. My mother is from the Kingdom, while my father... was, most likely, that Gergasi – or 'Great One', as Bartholomew mentioned – back at the Academy. And the reason why that slave bond wasn't activated back there was because of me, or at least that's my assumption. I, too, have a form of Dominion magic, though I have no idea how it works or even how to consciously use it."

Silence and horror met his revelation, as the implications suddenly occurred to them all. "You've... been using it on us?" Nedira asked, her eyes showing the hurt and betrayal he had been expecting, but hoped never to see.

"I suppose so? I have no control over it, nor can I even determine what it does, but it is most likely why none of you were directly affected by my father when he attempted to dominate all our minds back at the Academy." He bowed his head. "I sincerely apologize for what I've done, even though I had no control over it. It is wrong for it to be used on *anybody*, let alone those whom I truly consider to be my friends. I told the same thing to the Dean and Shinpai, which was why I refused to teach any more people how to unlock the new Skill I discovered; it was using my Dominion magic to make the process easier, and was what also caused me to collapse after instructing the Specialization heads. I *hate* that I have this magic, and I am going to do whatever I can to ensure that I don't use it again."

His proclamation was met with suspicious stares, but that was only understandable. Larek would be rightly suspicious of anyone who proclaimed to have a magic like his, too. Nedira pulled away from him, sitting at the other end of the cave while he went on to explain what he had learned about the Gergasi, the Transition, and the potential Culmination to Penelope, Verne, and Norde – all of whom had heard bits and pieces of the information, but not the inside information that only Nobles seemed to possess.

"I have a question for you, Larek," Bartholomew said seriously when he was finished. He had apparently heard all about the Gergasi before, given that he'd had to accept a slave bond from one of them. "What does the Dean have to do with all of this? Why was she helping you, if you are a half-breed, as you say? Didn't she have a bond, as well?"

He nodded, answering the last question. "She did. I believe it is because of that slave bond that she was helping me."

"Why?"

Here is where he hesitated for the first time, as he wasn't sure if he wanted to reveal that woman's plans for him. In the end, he mentally shrugged and decided to tell them all. "Because she thinks I may be the only one that can shut this hole in the world, which would ultimately take power away from the Gergasi as well as stop the Scissions from appearing," he said simply. "In other words, she wants me to save the world....

"Unfortunately for her, I have absolutely no desire to actually do that."

Chapter 21

***Speaking** has reached Level 16!*

Larek ignored the notification and didn't look away from the silent stares of his friends and bodyguards, as much as he wanted to escape from the current uncomfortableness he was feeling. Their judgment weighed upon him like a physical force, but he felt it was better to face it rather than try and slink away like he would have a year ago. Having been introduced to the wider world had opened him up to a bevy of different awkward situations, but if he'd learned anything from his handling of them over that time, it was to see them through and suffer the consequences for things that were – and weren't – under his control.

Suddenly, Verne shrugged and grinned at him. "I don't blame you, Larek. Who wants that kind of responsibility, anyway?" he asked. "Regardless, you're my roommate and my friend, and it doesn't matter who your parents may or may not be. Nor do I care about this magic of yours, because having something that you can't control isn't your fault. It's like having excessive flatulence, similar to Nor—"

The boy by his side spoke up quickly. "I'm with you, too, Larek. I don't care about all that stuff."

Despite the seriousness of the situation, Larek couldn't help but chuckle at the antics of his roommates. He hadn't noticed that Norde had "excessive flatulence" in their shared room, so it was likely that Verne was just messing with him. Either that, or Larek had been in his own head for so long that he just didn't see it. Or hear it. Or smell it.

"Sure, I'm here for the ride, as well," Penelope suddenly stated. "It's not like I have a lot to look forward to going home, and I believe that sticking by you – even if you're not planning on 'saving the world' – is important. Whether it's this Dominion Magic working on me or not, I don't really care. I've had more interesting things happen to me over the last year than in my whole life before, and I'm eager for more."

Vivienne poked her head out of the entrance. "I go where *she* goes, so I suppose that means with you." That was all she said before she disappeared again.

There were a few seconds of silence before Kimble cleared his throat. "You know, I always wondered what it was that shifted my attitude toward you to one of protectiveness rather than the envy that I remember having when I found out about your ability with Fusions," he mused, putting his hand to his chin in apparent contemplation. "Even now, I think I can *feel* this Dominion magic working on me in a subtle way, though it isn't insidious in the least. If anything, it's only amplifying what was already there; I can only believe that there was something inside of me that recognized what a difference you could make to the Kingdom with what you can do with Fusions and wanted to protect it. I thought that just meant against potential assassins or students with a grudge after the Skirmish, and I was starting to rethink my position as one of your protectors over the last few weeks.

"But all this," he continued, waving in the general direction of Thanchet and the ruined Copperleaf Academy, "changes things. Being only minor Nobility and just barely able to secure my spot at Copperleaf, I'd heard whispers about the Great Ones, as Bartholomew mentioned, but I was never forced into a slave bond – nor did I ever hear of it before now. Now I wonder if my parents know about it, and whether they have this bond."

"Is your father a Baron?" Bartholomew suddenly asked.

"Uh, well, yes?"

The Martial trainee nodded. "Then they were bonded. The Great Ones aren't able to enslave *every* Noble, as there are too many of us, so with minor Nobility such as Barons, they only enslave the heads of their houses. When your parents pass on their title to you, which will hopefully be a long time from now, you'll be required to visit the Enclave of the Great Ones and will be forced to take the bond."

Kimble's face turned pale as he listened to Bartholomew. Turning to Larek, he asked, "Will killing these Great Ones remove the slave bond?"

The former Logger shrugged. "Probably? I don't know enough about it to say for certain, but I would think if they were gone, there would be nothing to enforce the Dominion magic forced upon them." He paused for a second. "If you're thinking that by staying with me, you'll see me go up against them and tear down their entire Enclave, thereby freeing your parents, I already told you that I have no intention of doing that. If I have one wish, it would be to stay as far away from them as possible."

"Nevertheless, there's a chance that you might be up against them in the future. If I can do something to free my parents, as well as helping the Kingdom at the same time, then I'm willing to stick with you on that possibility alone."

Larek shook his head. "But I told you, confronting the Gergasi is the last thing I want to do."

"You never know what the future will hold. Whether you do, indeed, confront these Great Ones or not, I have to agree with Penelope here," he smirked. "Sticking close to you is bound to be interesting, no matter what happens."

The Fusionist really hoped Kimble was wrong, but he had a bad feeling the red-robed Pyromancer was speaking the truth.

"On that note, I'm staying with you, too," Bartholomew declared. "If there is a chance, however slim, that you can yank the Nobility out from under the yoke of the Great Ones, then I'm going to take it. The fact that I can even *think* that, let alone *say* it, means that you've made a difference already."

Larek wasn't really comfortable with this misplaced confidence in him, but he didn't really know what else he could say to dissuade them from continuing with him. Then again, did he really want them to leave? For their own sakes, and for the relative safety of staying away from the trouble he would inevitably cause in the future? Yes, of course. But he selfishly hoped that they wouldn't leave, if only because it was going to be hard enough to survive throughout the Kingdom on his own.

That only left Nedira, who hadn't spoken yet. When he looked her way, she just shook her head and said, "I don't know. I—" She cut herself off and didn't say any more, and instead looked away from him and stared at the far wall of the cave.

Truthfully, he expected something like this, especially since she admitted that she had feelings for him – if not necessarily stating that explicitly. While he thought he could see himself returning those kinds of feelings she had toward him, his Dominion magic really complicated matters. From her perspective, Larek had manipulated her feelings toward him, even if Kimble was correct and Larek had only amplified what was already there. That really didn't change the fact that he had done something to her to make her at least begin to become infatuated with him, which was a violation of trust.

Or something like that. Larek had been trying to learn as much as he could about social situations ever since leaving home, and while he still had a long way to go before he got a good handle on them, he thought this was fairly accurate.

"That's alright, Nedira. Take all the time you need to make a decision," Larek said softly in the silence that was thick amongst the people in the cave.

"I have so many more questions," Penelope said after nearly a minute, "but we all need to get what sleep we can. We're going to push hard tomorrow to travel as far away from here as we can, and with the day we've all had, I'm sure we're all tired. Vivienne will take first watch and I'll take second, since it's the most difficult. Barty, would you take third?"

The young Martial trainee had evidently given up trying to get the blue-haired Striker to stop calling him by that shortened nickname because he didn't even complain when she used it. Instead, he just nodded wearily and began to make himself comfortable on the floor – or as comfortable as it could be on the dirt floor of a cave, while still fully armored.

"Do you want me to take a watch?" Larek asked, but Penelope shook her head.

"No. You need sleep just as much as everyone else, and this is what we do. We'll be fine."

Shrugging, he copied Bartholomew and laid himself down on the dirt floor, finding it thoroughly uncomfortable. Fortunately (or unfortunately, depending on how he looked at it), his body was more tired than he thought, as he found himself drifting off within a minute of closing his eyes.

It felt like no time had passed when he was shaken awake by Bartholomew at some point. Immediately on guard, he looked at the young man questioningly, but the Noble trainee didn't seem worried.

"It's almost dawn," he whispered to Larek. "Penelope wanted us to be on the move as soon as it's bright enough to see."

Larek nodded, agreeing with the idea. Stretching to wake himself up, he felt multiple sore spots all around his body from his awkward and uncomfortable sleeping position, but they quickly faded as his *Body Regeneration* kicked in and soothed them away. As he looked around, he saw that he was the first one up other than Penelope, who was already standing near the entrance, keeping an ear out for any danger, he supposed.

Before too long, everyone was awake and looking at each other as if wondering what they should do. Verne and Norde were looking at Larek, but the rest – including Nedira – were staring at Penelope as if she had all the answers. The Fusionist thought that was a good assumption, because *he* surely had no idea what they were doing.

"Unfortunately, we have no food, no water, and no other supplies that would be necessary for those crossing the Kingdom without the aid of a caravan or the Transportation Network Carriages," the blue-haired woman stated, ticking off each thing they were missing as she spoke. "We can hunt, of course, and there are numerous streams and rivers that we'll cross as we head northeast toward Fort Ironwall and Silverledge Academy, but I doubt that will be sustainable for long. With the number of monsters that I've heard are roaming around the Kingdom, game has been scarce outside of a few protected areas; unfortunately, those areas are precisely where we *will not* be passing through. Our best bet is to hit up the villages, towns, and cities along the route to secure supplies on the journey, and possibly see if there are any caravans that we can tag along with. Better yet, if the Network is running any carriages, we can see if we can hitch a ride."

"Is that the best idea, though?" Nedira asked, her voice sounding strained and tired. She also didn't appear to have gotten much sleep, as far as he could tell. "If they're looking for Larek, and by extension, *us*, then wouldn't they head to the closest towns and cities first?"

Penelope nodded. "That is true, which is why we won't be following the roads, to at least lessen the likelihood that we're found along those routes. Unfortunately, we're going to have to visit someplace with people before too long, because we'll never make it without supplies."

"I have to agree," Verne spoke up, nodding at the blue-haired Martial trainee. "Just talking about food and supplies is making me even hungrier than I already am. Besides, it's not like we don't have the money for it," he chuckled as he gestured to the bags that were piled together in the middle of the cave. "I couldn't sleep much last night, so I spent some time looking through them all. Did you know that you're rich, Larek? Shinpai wasn't lying about there being more than just gold coinage in there."

The former Logger was curious now, as he'd never really had much need of money when he lived with his parents. Of course, he received his winnings from the Skirmish a while ago, but he hadn't spent any of it; even now, it was stashed back in his room at the Academy – if that portion of the building was still intact, of course.

"How much is there?"

"Enough that, if it weren't for the SIC and your obligation to enlist, you could retire and never have to make another Fusion for as long as you lived. And you would live very comfortably, indeed."

"Yes, but how much is in there?" Bartholomew asked impatiently, echoing Larek's thoughts. Being a Noble, the young man probably had a better idea of how much this kind of money was actually worth.

"I counted 43 platinum and around 200 gold coins, though I may have been off in my count by a few since I was tired and it was *very* early in the morning."

That still didn't give Larek a very good idea of what it was worth, but by the widened eyes of everyone else, they seemed to think it was worth *a lot*. Bartholomew, seeing the blank expression on his face, attempted to help. "This is more than my father's entire Dukedom earns in a year from collected taxes," he began, but changed tactics when that still didn't mean anything to Larek. "A good-sized house inside of a decent town would cost someone anywhere between 50 and 100 gold; a similar house in the capital city might cost 500 gold. Most commoners take home between 5 and 10 gold *a year* for basic jobs; merchants and specialized positions can earn anywhere between 50 and 500 gold a year, though the latter is rare except for the larger merchant conglomerates."

That helped a little bit, but other than telling him that there was enough to buy a bunch of houses, its value was lost on him. Regardless, he nodded in understanding, as it didn't really matter if he didn't comprehend it all. It was a means to an end, and if it helped them obtain supplies, then that was all the better.

"Well, we'll use whatever we need for our journey and then save the rest for an emergency," Larek told them all. "I agree that we need to visit at least someplace that might have supplies for us, and that we also need to stay off the roads as much as possible."

Penelope nodded. "Fair enough. We can evaluate the danger at our first stop and see if it would be prudent to avoid any settlements from thereon out. Either way, we need to start moving if we're going to get anywhere today." Without another word, she picked up one of the bags, slung it onto her back, and then led the way out of the cave. Vivienne and Bartholomew did the same, the latter handing the fourth bag to Larek, as he was the only other one that could easily lug it around due to its weight. Before they left, he gathered up the stones that he had used for his Fusions the night before, deactivating them as he slid them into the bag as well, and then followed everyone else out of the winding entrance.

Outside, the pre-dawn air held a chill to it that was absent inside their cave, but it was also invigorating after being cooped up in their confined quarters. It also reminded him a little of back home and getting up before dawn, and the surrounding forest only emphasized his previous occupation. He patted the axe underneath his robe, mentally promising his long-time friend that they would again fell some trees together, but his action also reminded him that he was wearing a very distinctive article of clothing. Thankfully, he continued to wear his comfortable overalls and shirt underneath the robe, and he stopped the others just after exiting as he stripped it off and shoved it into his bag.

Whether or not he ended up going to Fort Ironwall, there was no need to wear the robe right now. Freed of the extra cloth that had covered him, he stretched with his new range of movement, glad to have the itchy article of clothing off of him. It wasn't that it bothered him overly much, but it had never been something he considered overly comfortable.

"That's a good idea. We'll have to get Verne and my brother different outfits, as well, so that no one questions why some young Academy students are wandering around," Nedira said, though the entire time she didn't look at Larek once. It seemed as though she was still having difficulty coming to terms with the former Logger and his half-breed status, along with his inadvertent use of Dominion magic. That was fine with Larek, as he wanted her to have as much time as she needed to adjust to the situation.

Thankfully, everyone else was either already in clear Mage attire or were outfitted as a Martial, though they might question Bartholomew's age as he was technically only a third-year trainee if Larek remembered correctly. Regardless, it was something they would deal with in the future, and if they kept to their plan, they wouldn't be around too many people until they reached Fort Ironwall and Silverledge Academy.

"Alright, everyone. We're going to be traveling a long way today, so keep the noise down to a minimum and watch out for danger. This close to the city, it's unlikely that we'll encounter any wandering monsters, but it's still possible. If you see any *people*, then try to hide in case they are looking for us, and don't approach them. Viv, if you would scout for us? And if you see anything we can bag for lunch, don't hesitate to take it down." With Penelope's little speech marking the official start of their journey across the Kingdom, they set out toward the north until they were out of the valley that contained the city of Thanchet, where they would begin heading toward the northeast and their eventual destination.

Whether that would be Larek's ultimate destination was still to be determined.

Chapter 22

The relative quiet of the early morning didn't last long as Larek's group made their way down the gentle slope of the forested mountain. Unlike what he thought might disturb the silence in the group, which was some of the other people asking him questions that he really didn't feel like answering while they were on the move, it was something entirely different and inherently more dangerous.

Monsters.

As if mocking Penelope's supposition that there wouldn't be any this close to the city, which was less than 10 miles behind them at that point, Vivienne suddenly came back from her scouting ahead of the group to report that they had a problem.

"It's a **Jumping Squirrel** swarm. It appears as though they've made a home in the trees ahead," she told them.

"A home? They're not moving toward the city?" Nedira asked. Larek was wondering the same thing, given that they were so close to Thanchet.

The Ranger shook her head. "No. It's… odd behavior for Scission monsters. This was probably something that would've been covered in classes this year, but they hadn't gotten to it yet."

It certainly was odd to Larek, based on what he'd learned about Scissions and the monsters that appeared from them. From what he previously knew, monsters would invariably head toward the largest concentration of people, be it a town or city – even if the Scission opened further away than normal. That appeared not to be the case anymore, however; the latest reports he'd overheard from the Dean and Shinpai were that attacks on towns and cities had tapered off, and not just because Scissions weren't appearing near them. Instead, it was almost as if the monsters were only concentrating on everything in between the population centers, as if they were staking out their own territories and attacking anyone who got too close to them.

The SIC, of course, were leaving their walled defenses and venturing out into the Kingdom to wipe out these concentrations of monsters before they could become a problem, but even Larek was aware that they were getting a late start. After the abnormal appearances of stronger-than-normal and multiple Scissions near towns and cities stopped, it had taken them months of isolated reports of monsters roaming around the Kingdom before they started to act. Adding to that the fact that the majority of those that were part of the SIC were inexperienced in *hunting* monsters, as they were used to defending a fixed position where the monsters would come to *them*, the progress they had made finding the monsters all over the land had been minimal.

At least, that was the impression he'd received when he'd heard about how everything was going. Having witnessed it personally, when not just one but two separate caravans he was traveling with were attacked first by **Night Wolves** and then **Bog Goblins**, he could only extrapolate from the information that things in the Kingdom were much worse than anyone would admit in front of him. Given that there were monsters so close to Thanchet, when he had heard that the area around the city was clear for at least 50 miles in every direction due to the SIC's efforts, Larek could only assume that the SIC from the city was actually being overwhelmed.

*No wonder the Dean and Shinpai were so adamant about me helping to provide them with Fusions. If they're already behind on eliminating the influx of monsters in this area, then they would need all the extra boosts they could get. And if it's this bad **here**, I can't imagine how it is everywhere else.*

"Can we go around?" Penelope asked the Ranger.

Unfortunately, she shook her head. "Not really. They're spread out for at least a mile from the east to the west near the valley's outlet, though they stop before they reach the road out from Thanchet leading north. We can either cross the road and take our chances on the eastern side of the valley, or we can head further up the mountains and take a much rougher route – if there even is one."

Larek tried to picture what he was being told in his mind. Remembering a map of the area he'd seen during his *Geography of the SIC* class, he knew that the valley that housed the city and the Academy was essentially ringed by mountains, other than to the north, where it narrowed into the outlet that Vivienne was describing. If these Jumping Squirrels were blocking off access to a portion of their way out, it would take a bit of travel to get around them. The easiest solution was to take the road, as the Ranger had mentioned that the Squirrels stayed away from it, but that came with its own problems; avoiding some monsters just to be found by the Gergasi and the people looking for them wasn't exactly the smartest trade.

"How many do you suspect there are?" Larek asked, surprising the others with his abrupt question. He didn't know why it should be surprising, because it was obvious to him what they needed to do at that point, given that they couldn't afford to waste any time getting as far away from the source of their troubles as possible.

"Too many to easily count. I suspect there are nearly a thousand of them spread throughout their territory, but it could be a bit more or less."

"Is it normal for a single Scission to let out that many?"

Penelope answered for Vivienne. "If it was a particularly high-Category Scission, perhaps. Otherwise, this could be the result of multiple Scissions of similar design coming together – which is an altogether frightening supposition if it's true."

It was impossible to tell what the answer was at that point, of course, but what mattered now was getting through them.

"They're not particularly strong, if I remember correctly," Verne noted, seeing where this was going. "But with those numbers... it might still be better if we went around them somehow."

The blue-haired Martial trainee shook her head. "It might be safer in the short run, but it puts us at too much risk of being found by others. We should be able to push through them if we're careful."

"But we're just students," Norde warned them as he spoke up. "Verne and I have no way to defend ourselves since we can't even cast a spell yet, though we're both close to success after all our practice." Larek was surprised that they had gotten that far already, though he knew they had been diligently working on putting everything together to cast their first spell. Or at least they *had* been working on it, but with their need to flee the Academy, the former Logger was sure their free time to practice was going to be severely curtailed.

"That's true; I don't feel comfortable letting my little brother knowingly walk into danger, and leaving them behind isn't an option," Nedira stated with finality. "I know that we're all equipped with those *Repelling Barrier* Fusions that Larek created, but we all know that they aren't perfect."

The mention of the *Repelling Barrier* caused Larek to think for a moment before making a decision.

"I can help with that. Give me a few minutes."

Ignoring their looks of confusion, Larek looked around and gathered up four branches that had fallen off one of the nearby trees at one point. Taking his axe out, he quickly trimmed them so that they were relatively straight shafts of wood, approximately 3 feet in length. Without another word, he sat on the ground and placed the four trimmed branches in front of him within easy reach, and then began to create a Fusion.

This was one that he had designed in a hurry back when he was intent on ending the threat that Ricardo and his Martial trainee helpers were to him, but its overall effect was exactly what he needed. *Icy Spike*

+7 was a bit stronger than the one he had attached to a staff underneath the Academy, of course; ensuring that whatever it was aimed at was killed or at least hurt severely was important to ensuring that his roommates would be able to defend themselves. The one thing he changed – other than the Magnitude – was that it was now Activatable by a simple mental command when it was held in their hand, rather than being Reactive and requiring the word, "Activate."

Icy Spike +7
Activation Method(s): Activatable
Effect: Creates a large ice spike that is propelled swiftly in the oriented direction
Input(s): Physical touch
Variable(s): Directional orientation
Magnitude: 700% of base ice spike strength, propels up to 70 feet
Mana Cost: 84,000
Pattern Cohesion: 600
Fusion Time: 99 hours

Instead of the 99 hours that the Fusion Time of this new Fusion dictated, it only took Larek about 10 minutes to infuse it with enough Mana to fill the overly thick formation, before he used *Focused Division* to transfer it to all four of the trimmed branches. As the Fusion delicately wrapped around the 1-inch-thick lengths of wood, his focus strained a little as he curved them enough that they would lay flat along the base of the sticks. When they were in place, he let them finish and he sat back and evaluated his handiwork.

Looking at his new creations, he realized he probably should've added a *Strengthen Wood* component to it, because the wood was liable to break if it was forced to be used in close-quarters to defend themselves. Deciding not to redo his work, he quickly created another Fusion and added it to the other end, which he delicately shaved to a point so that they would know which way to point forward, as well as to provide something to stab into a monster if it was necessary. The *Strengthen Wood +3* that he ended up adding was relatively weak compared to what he could do if he wanted, but he didn't want the two areas of ambience attached to the Fusions to conflict with each other.

"What did you create, Larek?" Verne asked hesitantly, staring at what essentially looked like crudely sharpened stakes.

"Let me show you," the Fusionist said as he picked up his new creations when he got to his feet. Taking one of them in his right hand, he aimed it behind him – and out of range of anyone else – and mentally activated the Fusion as he targeted a tree trunk.

Almost instantaneously, a large ice spike approximately the size of his forearm appeared at the tip of the stick; it floated there for approximately a half-second before it shot forward with incredible speed. Larek hadn't aimed it very well, so the sharpened chunk of ice hit the side of the tree and bounced off, though it had a strong-enough impact that it ripped off a small chunk of the bark and inner wood. As for the projectile, it was deflected off to the side and down, where it buried itself in a layer of dried pine needles and the dirt underneath them.

"Whoops. Well, I didn't aim very well, but you get the idea, I assume?" he said, turning back to the others with a smile on his face, only to be surprised by their facial expressions. He had been expecting shock and perhaps excitement over his Fusion, as it would give the two students a way to contribute (as well as himself and perhaps Kimble, as he had lost his staff and using fireballs in a forest wasn't the best idea), but he wasn't expecting the horror he saw on Nedira and Kimble's faces.

"What? What's wrong?" he asked worriedly.

Nedira slowly walked up to him and reluctantly put her hand on his arm; he felt the pressure of it, as if she was trying to reassure herself that he was fine. "Such a Fusion shouldn't work, at least not more than once," she delicately explained. "It's similar to your healing Fusions, but worse; such an influx of ambient Mana should quickly destroy the formation, causing it to rupture. Just like single-use healing Fusions before this, there have been single-use Fusions that have been used for attacking monsters, but they all invariably explode as their formations crack and they start absorbing too much Mana. Kimble and I have been warned against this in our classes, and to see you using something that by all rights should've exploded in your hand was frightening." She took a deep breath. "But I'm sure *your* Fusion won't have that problem, will it?"

Larek swiftly looked at the stick in his hand, the one that he had used to shoot out the spike of ice, and tried to detect any sign of strain or cracking in the formation. Given that he'd only used this Fusion once in the past, and not for very long, he wasn't sure what to expect after prolonged use. However, his perusal of it showed that it appeared just as solid as it had before, with no sign of anything wrong. He would have to check it again after it had been used for a while to see if there were any changes, but for now it seemed fine.

He shrugged. "I don't see any weakening, so it should be fine. I can always activate it a few dozen times and check it again?" he offered, but Nedira shook her head.

"If you think it's fine, then I... I trust you," she choked out, as if it was difficult for her to say that. Remembering that she still wasn't sure she wanted anything to do with him after the whole Dominion magic revelation, he realized how much it took for her to say even that much.

"Thank you," Larek said softly and sincerely, but when he went to put his hand over hers, she reflexively jerked it back. He sighed, but didn't let it show how much it hurt him for her to do that. In the end, he was still of the opinion that it was best that she keep her distance from him, as he wasn't sure if his unconsciously used magic was still in effect even now.

"Are those for us?" Verne asked excitedly, stepping up with Norde close behind him.

Larek nodded, but as he held a pair of the sticks out to them, he warned his two roommates to be careful with them. "Don't point them at anything but a monster, and be careful not to activate it when that sharp end is aimed at you. All it would take is a stray thought to activate them at the wrong moment; they're weapons, so you need to treat them like the dangerous implements they are."

They nodded solemnly at his words, before snatching up the sticks from his hand with enthusiastic smiles. *I just hope they don't hurt themselves or each other. Perhaps I should've made the Fusions weaker?* His musings were cut off when Nedira asked, "What's with the other two?"

Larek looked down at the remaining two sticks in his hand and shook himself from his internal thoughts. "Oh, uh, one of them is for me. The other is for Kimble, as launching *Fireballs* in the forest isn't the best idea, unless that idea is to burn the entire thing down. The amount of dried fuel under our feet is a bit worrisome, after all," he said, stepping on a pile of dried needles near his foot for emphasis.

"Good point," the Pyromancer agreed, before stepping up and taking one of the sticks with a clearly hesitant grab. "So, how does it work?"

At that question, Larek had them all practice for a minute against a few nearby trees to get used to using them, as well as accustoming themselves to the slight delay in the icy projectiles' launch. It didn't take long for the horror and worry on Kimble's face to transform into excitement, especially after he learned that the stick could fire them out rapidly – approximately one every second.

"Hold on, let me look at them again just to make sure they're alright," Larek offered when they were finished. Both Verne and Norde had used their Fusion weapons slowly, getting used to aiming and the way they worked, while Kimble had gone all out – so he wanted to see if there was a difference in the stability of the Fusion.

It only took a quick look to show that there was.

Verne and Norde's appeared perfectly fine; their rate of fire had probably been 1 every 10 seconds or so. Kimble's, on the other hand, was starting to show a little bit of strain in the Mana Cost section of the formation, where the rapid influx of Mana needed to create and launch the sharp ice chunks had begun to warp the containment barriers. It wasn't anything significant quite yet, and it was far from failing, but he also guesstimated that another 5 or 10 minutes of such a rate of fire would cause it to rupture.

It was a humbling reminder that even though his Fusion formations were powerful, they weren't impervious to harm.

He remarked on this to the Pyromancer, who blanched visibly when he was told that his actions began to destabilize the formation. "Don't worry about it; this was a good test to see what would happen," Larek consoled him. "Take this one for now," he went on, giving Kimble the one that he was going to use, while taking Kimble's slightly warped one for himself, "and try not to fire more than one every 10 seconds or so."

"That will prevent it from breaking?" the red-robed Mage asked, holding the stick in his hands away from him, as if he was handling a live snake.

"It should, and it could probably handle something a little faster, but there's no reason to test that theory," he warned. Larek was fairly certain that it could probably handle 1 every 3 or 4 seconds with no strain, but he thought it was better not to force the issue.

"If we're going to do this, let's get a move on," Penelope interrupted, which got everyone moving as she had intended a moment later. "And I want one of those for my own at some point, because being able to attack from range is super useful," she added as she looked at Larek. He just nodded as he followed behind the others, clutching his axe in his right hand and his new Fusion weapon in his left.

It might be just a bunch of oversized squirrels they were going up against, but he was as prepared as he was going to get without wasting any more time. As he glanced at the others, he saw fear on the faces of his roommates, as well as Nedira, but the others looked like they were ready for a battle.

Strangely enough, despite his reluctance to engage in fights against monsters, Larek had to admit that he was looking forward to expending some of the anger that had unconsciously built up over the last day about what had happened at the Academy.

Chapter 23

Despite spending most of his life in a forest, Larek wasn't exactly what anyone would call stealthy. His movements through the trees were loud as he crunched the dried pine needles underneath his large work boots, which seemed to set Vivienne on edge as she kept glancing back at him in irritation. When he stopped for a second to listen to the others, he discovered that all of them – even Verne and Norde – were moving through this forest with a lot less noise than he was, and even Bartholomew with his armor and Noble upbringing only made a little more sound than the others. Compared to them, Larek was practically stomping through everything without any regard to being quiet.

"It's a good thing we weren't trying to sneak by the Squirrels, because they could hear you coming a mile away, Larek," Penelope muttered, just loud enough to be heard over his steps.

"Sorry," he whispered back.

She waved it off. "Not your fault if you haven't learned how to move appropriately through different environments."

"Is this something they taught you at the Fort?"

The blue-haired Martial nodded. "Yes, though it's more about how to move in combat regardless of your environment, because changing situations during the defense of a town or city can lead to needing that kind of knowledge to survive and protect those who can't protect themselves."

That made sense to Larek, giving him yet another reason why attending Fort Ironwall was a good idea, but he still hadn't decided one way or the other.

Vivienne suddenly appeared near them, her face stern as she shook her head. Larek started to apologize for talking, but the Ranger put her finger to her lips in a universal signal to be quiet. "Their territory starts around 200 feet from here," Vivienne whispered as they came to a stop.

"Thanks, Viv," Penelope whispered back, before turning to the others who had come up around them when they came to a halt. "Alright, standard formation; Martials up front with Mages in the back. Larek, you stay in the back, as we can't lose you."

"We can't lose *anyone*, Penelope," he asserted.

"That's not my point, and you know it." She appeared exasperated as she sighed, but she unslung her massive sword that had miraculously made it all the way out from the tunnels underneath the

Academy despite its size. The woman didn't seem to notice its weight, and she moved with it as if it were an extension of her body. "Everyone ready?" she asked.

At their indications of assent, Bartholomew and Penelope led the way, with Vivienne just behind with her bow at the ready, followed by everyone else another dozen feet behind, creating a separation between the two groups. The others were all looking up into the lowest branches of the trees, so Larek did the same, trusting that he wouldn't trip over anything.

It didn't take long to find the Jumping Squirrels, as they were busy scurrying through the boughs of the trees, causing the branches to bounce up and down as they moved. While Larek had learned about these particular monsters in his *Monster Knowledge* class, it wasn't the same as seeing them in person.

Standing nearly 3 feet tall when on their hind legs, the Jumping Squirrels were definitely not the cute woodland creatures he remembered back in the Rushwood Forest. Instead, these Scission monsters had black and dark grey striped fur, they each had a bushy tail that had stiff bristles that could pierce normal skin like little needles when they brushed up against it, and they also possessed 4-inch-long claws on their forepaws that were capable of cutting through basic leather. But what made them more intimidating were their powerful hind legs, which comprised nearly a third of their entire bulk; it was these legs and their ability to jump up to 20 feet vertically and 40 feet horizontally that made them dangerous. This danger was only heightened when the Squirrels were in a tree, as it allowed them to jump even further to attack those down below.

"Mages, knock them out of the trees! Bartholomew, hold and prepare to defend!"

At her shout, chaos ensued. The nearest Squirrels, over 60 feet away and just barely visible to Larek, heard her and immediately turned toward the group on their tree branches. The Fusionist heard the *twang* of a bow string and he saw one of the furry monsters fall out of the tree ahead of them, skewered by an arrow that he barely even saw fired by Vivienne.

The moment he saw a trio of familiar ice spikes shot out courtesy of the sharp sticks Larek had created Fusions on earlier, he raised his own with his left hand and aimed it at yet another Squirrel in the trees. With a quick mental activation, he sent his own projectile shooting toward the monster, but it jumped a split-second before impact. Instead of hitting it square in the chest like he had been hoping, the spike made of ice clipped its left leg as it was in the air, ripping it entirely off. The impact also had the effect of causing the Squirrel to rotate vertically in the air, and it was soon flipping uncontrollably as it was knocked off whatever course it was on, blood flinging out in an arc as it spun in the air on its way down to the ground.

He didn't watch it after that, because he was distracted by the sight of three other furry monsters dropping from the trees, the ice spikes that Verne, Norde, and Kimble sent out hitting their targets well enough that the Squirrels didn't survive the attack. Yet another of the bushy-tailed monsters jumped and was figuratively slapped out of the air by a powerful gust of wind; looking over, he noticed Nedira had her hands out in front of her, and the lingering Mana used in a *Repelling Gust* spell dissipated around her. Larek only recognized it because he had learned the spell from her, after seeing her cast it multiple times on the roof of Crystalview, though this one seemed to have a little more Mana infused into it to give it some extra "oomph".

Those Squirrels, unfortunately, weren't the only ones nearby. Another dozen of them jumped toward the group from the surrounding trees, with one of them actually launching itself far enough to slam into Bartholomew's shield that he had upraised – before being slammed into the ground when the Martial trainee's *Repelling Barrier* activated.

Compared to the other Martials he saw in the Skirmish being flung around by the protective Fusion, the furry monster was much lighter – and therefore was affected all the more by the powerful gusts that sent it crashing into the dirt and pine needles on the forest's floor. The bone-crunching force of the impact was so loud and so quick, in fact, that it was just one big **snap** that startled some of the others from the sheer violence inflicted upon the monster.

The other Squirrels landed ahead of Bartholomew and Penelope, but half of them didn't get a chance to go far as a half-dozen brown roots emerged from the ground and wrapped themselves around their bodies, holding them in place. Nedira's *Binding Roots* effectively kept them out of the fight, at least temporarily despite their attempts to cut through the tough roots with their sharp claws.

The last five hit the ground and jumped again, heading straight toward the awaiting Martials. One was skewered in the air by an arrow that sent it flying backwards from the force of the impact. Two more were bisected by Penelope's sword as she swung at an angle that cut through both of them with one slice; another was impaled by Bartholomew's spear mid-jump, with the last being violently repelled by the Martial trainee's shield, similar to the one before. Once those were dead, Penelope and Vivienne raced toward the other bound monsters and finished them off, one using her sword and the other a pair of knives that had been strapped to her waist.

Looking over the heads of Penelope and Bartholomew, Larek saw that the beast he had partially hit with his icy projectile was still alive somehow, though it was heavily injured. Before he could even aim his sharpened stick, yet another arrow released by Vivienne pierced it through the heart as it struggled to move with only one hind leg, and the final Squirrel was finished off. In a matter of seconds, they managed to kill 18 of the monsters without any problems at all.

"That wasn't so bad—" Larek began to say, but movement out of the corner of his eye made him snap his mouth closed. "I guess I spoke too soon."

Gathering in the surrounding trees just outside of the range of their *Icy Spike* Fusions were *hundreds* of the monsters, all staring at the group and weighing the branches down to the point where Larek thought they might snap at any point. They kept coming, eventually attaching themselves to the trunks of the trees using their sharp claws, and it soon became obvious that hundreds more had circled around them, penning them in from all sides.

"Uh, is this normal?" Norde asked nervously as he moved closer to Larek and the Martials, Verne joining right behind him.

"No, definitely not," Nedira answered.

The more Larek looked at them all gathering as they did, he couldn't help but agree. More than that, he had the distinct feeling that they were all staring at *him* as they congregated in the trees; it might have just been that he was starting to feel the weight of so many monsters gathered around that it might have seemed as though all their attention was on him, but for some reason he didn't think so. There was a malevolence in their gaze that he'd never experienced before, and it was a bit unnerving.

"Uh, guys? What's the plan here?" he asked.

Penelope was visibly shaken. "This... this shouldn't be happening. Those close enough should've simply attacked us, leaving us a hole through their territory that we could slip through," she said, her previous bravado and confidence absent from her tone. "I don't think we can escape this."

Larek knew that was the original plan: Kill a few dozen and then run through the Squirrel's seeming territory before the rest could attack them. That was a tactic that had been discussed in the few new *Scissions* classes he'd attended, as the behavior of the monsters was something that could be predicted – at least for most of the weaker ones. But something like this was definitely not covered in the curriculum, or at least hadn't been yet.

"Larek? Why are they staring at *you*?" Nedira suddenly asked.

He looked at her in surprise. "You think so, too? I had wondered…"

"Yeah, it's fairly obvious," Kimble abruptly confirmed her observation. "Their unblinking eyes are staring right at you and are following your movements. It's as if they aren't even paying attention to *us*."

That's not good… but why?

Before he could even ask that question, the number of Jumping Squirrels must have reached some sort of critical threshold, because it was at that point that they attacked. If it hadn't been obvious by their stares, the trajectory of hundreds of furry monsters as they launched themselves off of their perches made it obvious that Larek was their target.

Even as the others braced themselves for the attack, Larek told the others with the *Icy Spike* Fusions to fire. "Don't stop; the Fusions can handle a few minutes of constant firing, and we're going to need it." As the wave of Squirrels propelled toward them, Larek and the others let loose a barrage of sharp ice spikes toward the furry rain of death coming their way. Kimble also transferred the stick to his left hand and started flinging out *Fireballs* with his right; thankfully, the mass of Squirrels was so thick that he didn't miss with his spells, meaning that he wasn't about to set the entire forest on fire with any stray flaming projectiles.

Nedira, on the other hand, was frantically casting Nature-based spells, as one *Wall of Thorns* after another appeared to help surround the group, though they didn't reach far enough up to stop the majority of the Squirrels if they were determined to jump over. At best, they would help to funnel the furry monsters toward certain spaces where it would be easier to defend against them; at worst, they were obstacles that would actually impair their own sight of the attackers as they made their way toward them.

The group soon found that, even though the deadly Squirrels had their sights set on Larek, that didn't mean they ignored the others. As most of them landed not more than 10 to 15 feet away from the group, they targeted the nearest obstacle in their way – otherwise known as the group of people with him – and sprang toward it without missing a beat. Nedira's thorn walls turned out to help more than he expected, as instead of jumping vertically over them, the furry monsters instead changed their direction to leap in between the barriers, which helped… sort of. The ones that jumped straight at Penelope and Bartholomew, for instance, were immediately cut down or slammed into the ground when their *Repelling Barriers* were activated, and the same went – for the most part – for Vivienne, who quickly pulled out her knives when the enemy was too close to use her bow.

As for the others, including Larek, they were barely able to stem the flow of Squirrels jumping through the gaps in the wall with a barrage of ice spikes killing a few of them every second or so, but there were just too many. Before long, even that wasn't enough as they arrived en masse, the first few dozen slamming into the ground as they ran into the protective wind barriers of the defenders. Before long, though, the press of furry bodies was too great, and Larek watched Kimble get knocked over as two Squirrels managed to push through the *Repelling Barrier* while it was engaged in protecting against other threats. As he fell onto his back with a cry, that left his feet unprotected, as there was no barrier below him; as a result, another three monsters scurried up his legs, tearing into him with their claws even as the two that had knocked him down went to work on his upper body.

"No! Get off of him!" Larek cried, moving toward the downed Pyromancer, but before he could reach him, an inferno arose around the Mage, burning everything around him in a matter of seconds. The fire was so hot that it made Larek take a step back, but it was also deactivated shortly after that, leaving little but the charred bodies of Squirrels behind as a result. As for Kimble, Larek could see that he was unhurt by his own spell, but he was injured enough by the claws that had torn great rents in his body, chest, and legs; the shock was too much for the man as he closed his eyes and was rendered unconscious. Worried that he had died, Larek was relieved that he could still see him breathing shallowly – but his relief was short-lived as the tide of Squirrels kept coming.

Ignoring the unconscious form of Kimble on the ground, now that he was no longer an obstacle, there was now an avenue of attack for the Jumping Squirrels to reach Larek. Even as Verne and Norde launched ice spikes at them, Nedira cast *Binding Roots* on a few, though the number of those caught by the spell was but a drop in the bucket. Changing tactics, the Naturalist instead cast a spell that she had mentioned was called *Poison Fog* – which was too complicated for him to learn, unfortunately – that summoned a greenish-brown cloud of poisonous fog that covered the opening between two of the walls she had created earlier.

The Squirrels jumping through the fog were immediately affected by it, as their jumps fell short and they appeared sickly, but that didn't stop them from continuing to attack. If anything, the fog led to them bunching up together to attack as a larger group.

Seeing the wave of Squirrels coming for him, Larek dropped his pointy stick and grabbed his axe with both hands, setting his feet as if he was just about to start chopping into a tree. *Me and you, Bestie. Let's do this.*

While Larek certainly knew how to swing an axe, his combat awareness left much to be desired. As soon as he swept into the first of the furry monsters coming his way, killing five of them with the tool in no more than a second, he was quickly pushed around as dozens of Squirrels slammed into him from behind and the sides. As many more were smashed into the ground by his protective Fusion, but there were too many of them for his *Barrier* to compensate, which led to him being hit multiple times. The worst part was that, even though the monsters jumping into him didn't knock him down, they were close enough that they were able to attack him once again, tearing through his overalls like they were paper before slicing into his skin. Thankfully, with his Body stat so high, the slices were no worse than cuts on his skin, which would heal in short order with his *Body Regeneration*, but within seconds he was surrounded and was practically covered in small wounds.

A quick activation of his *Healing Surge* anklet was enough to heal his injuries without difficulty, but he was beginning to have trouble moving as the onslaught of Squirrels piled up against him. Now that they weren't moving more than 10 miles per hour being so close to him, his protective Fusion did very little good, and he was instead forced to frantically chop at them with his axe and even smash their heads in with his fist. His Strength stat was high enough that their skulls were no match for his fists, and they crumpled under his strikes, but there were just too many of them.

As their corpses piled up around him, he continued to hear the others fighting but could spare not much more than a glance to check on their condition. Other than Kimble, who was still down on the ground, the others seemed to be fine, as the concentration of furry bodies around them was much less than that around Larek, and most everything that got through their attacks was killed by their *Repelling Barriers*. He saw that Verne had a bloodstain on his right shin where some sharp claws had somehow made it through his protection, but he was still upright and attacking with the makeshift weapon that Larek had created for him to use.

Even if he had wanted to go to their aid, there was no way that the former Logger could move from his defensive position. After nearly a minute of constantly fending off attacks, he estimated that he had killed nearly 100 of them based on the corpses piling up around him; the benefit of that was that the bodies were covering up his lower half, preventing most of the Squirrels from attacking from below, but it was also giving them a ramp to reach his upper body and face better.

Larek attempted to activate his one and only Battle Art, *Furious Rampage*, but nothing he tried seemed to work. He needed to break out of his current predicament, because before too long he would be inundated by so many corpses that he couldn't move, and he thought he might be able to push through the bodies with some extra Strength – but that thought was put on hold when he couldn't activate the Ability.

Thankfully, after another minute and a further 100 or so dead Squirrels created by his handiwork, the onslaught lessened considerably. At that point, Larek was in a highly focused state of defending himself and healing the constant wounds he was accumulating, and it took him a few seconds to realize someone was shouting at him.

"We're coming, Larek! Hold on a little longer!" Penelope screamed at him when he didn't respond, and he snapped out of his focus long enough to nod in her direction.

Over the next few minutes, as the corpses piled up higher and higher around him, nearly reaching to his upper chest and with his arms just barely free enough to swing around, he began to feel extremely tired and nearly ravenous. Realizing that he'd been healing himself on and off for the last few minutes, this didn't surprise him, but he barely had the strength to swing his axe one more time to easily slice yet another Squirrel in half.

Thankfully, that was the last one, as no more assaulted him; after a few seconds of tensely awaiting another attack, he slumped where he stood, finding that he could barely shift around with the furry and bloody corpses pressed up against him.

"Larek? Are you alright?"

Wearily, he struggled to focus his gaze outside of his little sphere of death, seeing Penelope climbing up the virtual mountain of dead Squirrels to reach him. He belatedly recognized that he hadn't killed *all* of them, as there were more than he remembered killing himself; based on their wounds, he could only assume that the others were killed trying to get to him. Further out, he saw hundreds more furry corpses scattered around where his other group members had fought their own battles, and while his bleary eyes were still a little unfocused, other than a few bloody scratches that showed on everyone else, none of them appeared to be seriously hurt. Even Kimble was up on his knees, clearly having woken up, and he was trying to get to his feet, his wounds still bleeding slightly, but he appeared as though he'd live.

The strange thing about gazing around him, however, was the fact that everything looked a little hazy for some reason. It was almost as if there was a cloud of something dark with streaks of grey in it hanging about; though it was largely transparent, he wondered if it was some other version of the *Poison Cloud* that Nedira had cast earlier.

"Um, yes?" he finally answered after a few seconds. "But I'm exhausted and starving—"

He was forcibly cut off as the dark cloud around him suddenly moved and began streaming toward his body. A sharp pain struck him in the stomach and at first he thought it was hunger pains, but it was an altogether different feeling. The pain rapidly faded as it spread throughout his entire body, though he didn't think it was because of his *Pain Immunity* Skill. Instead, it was almost as if his body was reacting to whatever was invading it and somehow spreading it out in an attempt to... tame it, perhaps.

Whatever it was doing, in his exhausted state, he couldn't handle it for more than a few seconds, and the next thing he saw was the back of his eyelids as he lost consciousness.

Chapter 24

Larek came back to awareness abruptly, his eyes snapping open as he went from unconsciousness to absolute wakefulness in a matter of seconds. He automatically sat up and reached for the axe by his side by reflex, as the last thing he vividly remembered was being attacked by vicious, blood-thirsty Jumping Squirrels that were unhesitatingly targeting him for some reason. His fingers only met the rough, familiar cloth of his Academy robe, and he panicked for a moment before he took in his whereabouts.

It became immediately obvious that he was no longer outside in the forest surrounded by hundreds of furry corpses, but was instead inside of yet another cave. This one was more open to the outside, unlike the last, and what he saw past the activated *Illuminate Stone* Fusions around the cramped space showed that daylight was still shining down through the nearby trees.

"Larek! You're awake!" Nedira suddenly shouted behind him, and he immediately felt something impact his back, before he saw a pair of arms attempt to circle around him in a hug. Immediately recognizing Nedira's limbs, he smiled at them in confusion. He wasn't confused at what they were doing around him, because that part was obvious enough; no, it was more of the fact that he wasn't exactly sure what had happened after the Squirrel assault.

A bout of weakness suddenly descended upon him after his initial spurt of energy immediately after waking up, and the smell of cooking meat met him a brief second later, causing his stomach to cramp up in hunger. Thankfully, it wasn't the same sort of pain that he had experienced just before—

Wait. What was all that? I remember a dark cloud of something... and then my stomach seemed to suck it in, causing me pain before it was diffused through my entire body.

"What happ—"

Larek was abruptly rocked by a brief, incredible pain that flooded his entire being; a torturously long few seconds later, the pain disappeared, but the sensations that had accompanied it – but he'd been unable to feel because of the pain – remained. He was reminded of when he had first arrived at the Academy and had his Mage stats and Skills unlocked, because it felt vaguely familiar. For a moment, he thought it might be some sort of unlocking of his Martial side of things in a similar manner, even if he already had Martial stats and Skills; what he didn't have was any sense of control over anything like his Battle Arts or his Stama like he should.

When the sensations evaporated a few seconds later, leaving his body irrevocably changed in the process, a flood of notifications flowed through his mind.

He was wrong. It wasn't some sort of unlocking of his Stama and Martial Abilities.

It was something that he immediately thought of as a blessing... and a curse.

Congratulations, Guardian! You have passed the threshold required for Aetheric Assimilation!

As a Great One, you are responsible for guarding the Aetheric Breach responsible for the introduction of Aetheric Force into this world! To assist with this endeavor, your body is now ready to assimilate the Corrupted Aetheric Force infused into the physical manifestations of the Corruption, which is attempting to widen the breach by either eliminating all Guardians or destroying all sapient life.

Upon Assimilation, Aetheric Force will aid you in breaking through your thresholds, allowing you to advance and become stronger as a result. Because of your enormous potential, unlike those with access to only one aspect of Aetheric Force, the accumulation of assimilated Force is necessary to extend the maximum Levels of all Skills from now on. Actual advancement in Skills will stay the same as it was before, but without additional Aetheric Force invested into a Skill, they will no longer increase in Level.

New Status information has been unlocked!

Axe Handling *has reached Level 82!*

Body Regeneration *has reached Level 26!*

Thankfully, he wasn't knocked flat on his back by the notifications this time, due in part to the fact that he only ended up increasing two Skills a single Level, but the other information left him speechless, nonetheless.

"Larek? Larek?! What's wrong?"

The feeling of someone shaking him broke him out of the trance-like state he was in as he stared at the notification, unable to believe what he was reading. From what he could understand, the Gergasi – labeled as Great Ones, even in the notification for some reason – were labeled as "Guardians" of the breach they had opened, letting what was called Aetheric Force spill out. To make things more complicated, there was a "Corruption" that came from this other world, place, dimension, or whatever it was, which is where the Scissions and their monsters came from. From those monsters was born Corrupted Aetheric Force, which he intuitively understood was the dark cloud of stuff that came from the dead Squirrels and what his body had absorbed, and that this assimilated Force was the only way he would be able to advance his Skills any further. It explained why he was having issues breaking through certain Levels in his Mage Skills, as much as he didn't like knowing the answer.

Because what it meant, as horrific as the thought of it was as it filled his mind, was that in order to increase his Maximum Skill Levels, he would need to obtain more of this Aetheric Force; to get that Force, he would have to kill these physical manifestations of this Corruption and assimilate the Corrupted stuff that they left behind.

In other words, he was going to have to kill monsters.

I'm cursed!

While the solution to his Skill problem was a bit of a blessing, the way he was supposed to go about it was anathema to everything he wanted. Larek had no desire to go hunting for any monsters, after all; he'd rather stay as far away from them as possible. The only reason he had wanted them to make their way through the Squirrels was because of the threat of a *bigger* monster in the form of his father, but that apparently didn't make much difference in the end.

To pile on the horribleness, he was becoming more and more like his distant relatives than he cared to admit, especially if he was now on the same type of path that they were with this whole Aetheric Force thing now a part of his advancement. What would come next? Would improving his Dominion magic be required to develop even further? If so, he wanted nothing to do with it. That was, of course, if he had any other choice – just like what was happening with the Scission monsters he needed to kill in order to advance.

It was either fight and kill monsters and advance or do nothing and stagnate his development. Granted, at the moment, his abilities with Fusions were fairly impressive, he admitted to himself without modesty, but was that enough to survive? Sure, he could probably improve the Intermediate Fusions he'd created in terms of protection and weapons, but he *knew* that he could do so much more than that. That knowledge that he was able to improve and make even better

Fusions in the future just by killing monsters was a driving force that he would be hard-pressed to ignore for long, if at all.

"Can I display notifications to you?" he asked with a tired sigh, speaking for the first time since he just had his life and future advancement opportunities abruptly altered.

"What? Of course you can; you can do it the same way you can display portions of your Status. But what's wrong? What—?"

Larek figured it out quickly, applying the same technique to display part of his Status to do the same thing to his notification. A second later, hovering in the air for her to see – which also included everyone, he noticed a second later as he looked around the cave – was his notification.

"What exactly does this mean, Larek?" Penelope asked. "Is this true about the so-called 'Great Ones' and their role as Guardians? Is Aetheric Force really a thing?"

Larek shrugged. "I have no idea. This is the first time I've heard of either of those things. You probably know more than I do, to be honest. Or at least Bartholomew might, given his... relationship with them."

A quick glance in the young Martial trainee's direction showed that wasn't the case, as Bartholomew appeared just as shocked and confused at the notification as everyone else.

"What did it change?" Nedira asked softly, coming around to look him in the eyes. Her posture was still a little standoffish, but something had either changed in her opinion of him over the last few hours or she wasn't letting her confused emotions regarding him keep her from being concerned about his safety.

For a moment, the secrecy of his stats, abilities, and origin that he had held close to his chest for so long made him balk slightly about sharing his Status with the others. Even when he was telling everyone his life's story the night before, he had only revealed a few things such as his Martial stats and his Battle Art, never the whole thing. It felt like baring his soul to another, something that he didn't take lightly, but he also knew that they had agreed to accompany him despite the danger, so he felt like he could trust them. The fact that none of them seemed as if they were frightened into leaving by the reaction of the Squirrels to his presence only helped to further solidify his feelings toward them.

"I don't know. Let's take a look."

For the first time ever, he bared his entire Status to the others; the entire cave full of people looked at the changes at the same time he did.

Larek Holsten
Fusionist
Healer
Level 20
Advancement Points (AP) : 16/17
Available AP to Distribute: 30
Available Aetheric Force (AF): 312

Stama: 600/600
Mana: 1330/1330

Strength: 60 (+)
Body: 60 (+)
Agility: 60 (+)
Intellect: 70 [133] (+)
Acuity: 104 [198] (+)
Pneuma: 304 [578] (+)
Pattern Cohesion: 5,780/5,780

<u>Mage Abilities:</u>
Spell – Bark Skin
Spell – Binding Roots
Spell – Fireball
Spell – Furrow
Spell – Ice Spike
Spell – Lesser Restoration
Spell – Light Bending
Spell – Light Orb
Spell – Localized Anesthesia
Spell – Minor Mending
Spell – Rapid Plant Growth
Spell – Repelling Gust
Spell – Static Illusion
Spell – Stone Fist
Spell – Wall of Thorns
Spell – Water Jet
Spell – Wind Barrier
Fusion – Acuity Boost
Fusion – Agility Boost +7
Fusion – Area Chill
Fusion – Body Boost +5
Fusion – Camouflage Sphere +2

- Fusion – Camouflage Sphere +5
- Fusion – Extreme Heat +5
- Fusion – Flaming Ball +5
- Fusion – Flying Stone +5
- Fusion – Graduated Parahealing +7
- Fusion – Healing Surge +1
- Fusion – Healing Surge +3
- Fusion – Healing Surge +5
- Fusion – Icy Spike +5
- Fusion – Icy Spike +7
- Fusion – Illuminate Iron
- Fusion – Illuminate Steel
- Fusion – Illuminate Stone
- Fusion – Illuminate Wood
- Fusion – Illusionary Image +3
- Fusion – Intellect Boost
- Fusion – Muffle Sound +3
- Fusion – Muffling Air Deflection Barrier +6
- Fusion – Multi-Resistance Leather +2
- Fusion – Multi-Resistance Leather +7
- Fusion – Personal Air Deflection Barrier +4
- Fusion – Pneuma Boost
- Fusion – Repelling Barrier +1
- Fusion – Repelling Barrier +4
- Fusion – Repelling Barrier +7
- Fusion – Repelling Barrier +10
- Fusion – Repelling Gust of Air +5
- Fusion – Sharpen Iron Edge
- Fusion – Sharpen Steel Edge
- Fusion – Sharpen Stone Edge
- Fusion – Sharpen Wood Edge
- Fusion – Space Heater +2
- Fusion – Spellcasting Focus Boost +4
- Fusion – Strength Boost +1
- Fusion – Strength Boost +5
- Fusion – Strengthen and Sharpen Steel Edge +1
- Fusion – Strengthen Iron
- Fusion – Strengthen Leather +1
- Fusion – Strengthen Steel
- Fusion – Strengthen Stone
- Fusion – Strengthen Wood
- Fusion – Temperature Regulator +3

Fusion – Tree Skin +2
Fusion – Tree Skin +8
Fusion – Water Stream +5

Martial Abilities:
Battle Art – Furious Rampage

Mage Skills:
Multi-effect Fusion Focus Level 10/10 (100 AF)
Pattern Recognition Level 20/20 (200 AF)
Magical Detection Level 20/20 (200 AF)
Spellcasting Focus Level 20/20 (200 AF)
Focused Division Level 30/30 (300 AF)
Mana Control Level 30/30 (300 AF)
Fusion Level 30/30 (300 AF)
Pattern Formation Level 30/30 (300 AF)

Martial Skills:
Blunt Weapon Expertise Level 1/20 (N/A)
Bladed Weapon Expertise Level 2/20 (N/A)
Throwing Level 5/20 (N/A)
Dodge Level 7/20 (N/A)
Pain Immunity Level 20/20 (N/A)
Body Regeneration Level 26/30 (N/A)

General Skills:
Cooking Level 1
Bargaining Level 5
Beast Control Level 9
Leadership Level 11
Writing Level 11
Long-Distance Running Level 10
Saw Handling Level 15
Speaking Level 16
Reading Level 17
Listening Level 42
Axe Handling Level 82

Overall, there weren't that many changes, but the first thing he noticed right away was he now had an entry for what was mentioned in the notification: Aetheric Force or (AF). Right now, he only had a total of 312 AF; he wasn't sure how this was tallied, as there wasn't an explanation. Further down the Stats, where his Skills were listed, he discovered another change.

Where his Level was previously shown, such as **Fusion Level 30**, it was now written as **Fusion Level 30/30 (300 AF)**. When he concentrated on it, he immediately understood that it was saying that his maximum Level for his Fusion Skill was Level 30 and he had maxed it out; furthermore, if he wanted to raise the maximum by *a single Level*, he would have to spend 300 of his accumulated Aetheric Force to make that happen.

"That's crazy, Larek. How did you get so strong, so fast?" Verne asked, but the others just looked at him. "Oh, yeah, half-Gergasi and all that. I guess that makes a difference."

"I think it's more than that," Nedira said, shaking her head. "There's something different enough about Larek that it literally forced his father to come look for him. According to everything you've told us, the Gergasi haven't left the Enclave for centuries, if not longer; when I remember what I heard him say back at the Academy about the Aetheric Corruption tracking him, that might be why. I think that whenever they leave their Enclave, the Corruption follows them and opens up Scissions in order to kill one of the 'Guardians' keeping it from breaking through completely. That's also most likely why those Squirrels targeted you, because they could sense that you're one of them. Not a strong enough one that they might drop a Scission on you at any time, but once they were close enough, they could tell… somehow."

That caused a silence to descend over the cave as everyone considered the implications of her words. It sounded entirely plausible when she said it out loud, which was yet something else that he had to worry about in the long-run. If he became stronger with his advancement, would he then have to worry about attracting Scissions? If so, was there a way to prevent that? Or would it eventually happen even if he didn't get stronger?

There was no way to know the answers to these questions without going to someone with more knowledge of such matters, but that meant going to the Gergasi and his father – something he'd rather avoid for as long as possible. As much as he didn't want to admit it, he was beginning to suspect that the only way to ensure his survival was to get stronger and ensure he was capable of defending himself even if a Scission opened up near him; to do that, it meant killing monsters and assimilating their Aetheric Force.

"Why do you only have 312 Aetheric Force?" Norde suddenly asked. "There were over 1,000 of those Squirrels out there, so shouldn't it be more? Or if you only received a fraction of a point, how does that work?"

Larek was about to say that he had no idea, but it turned out that he did. While there hadn't been any information about it in the notification, he realized that when he focused on the actual 312 number, he received an impression of where it came from.

"It was how many of those furry monsters that *I* personally killed, or assisted in killing," he explained. "Even though you killed many of them near me, for some reason those didn't count. It's almost as if I need some sort of connection to them in order to designate myself as the recipient of the Corrupted Force, however *that* works."

Thoughts of accompanying his group and having them do all the fighting in order to accumulate more Aetheric Force went right out the window with this new knowledge, further driving him down the path of killing monsters. It was as if the world was pushing him down a raging river toward a certain goal in the future, one which he only had the vaguest idea about, and there was no way for him to escape its watery clutches; the only way to survive was to hang onto the safety of a floating log as it made its way down to the sawmill of fate.

It appeared that if he wanted to avoid whatever this "fate" was that was in store for him, he would have to ride that log at least a little ways until he could find an alternative path, or else he'd be swept away by the raging current. Larek just hoped that he was able to find a way to survive without suffering the same end as all the trees he'd felled back in the Rushwood Forest.

He really didn't want to find out what being cut and shaped into uniform planks felt like, after all.

Chapter 25

It was at that point that Larek's stomach tried to eat him from the inside out. The smell of roasting meat overwhelmed his senses, and he looked around the small cave to see where it was coming from. It wasn't until he looked slightly outside the stony entrance that he saw what appeared to be spits made from fallen tree branches set up over a campfire ringed by rocks.

"You sound like you have a monster in that belly of yours, Larek," Nedira chuckled. Patting him on the shoulder, as he was still simply sitting up, she said, "We decided to gather and cook some of the Jumping Squirrels, since we were going to have to wait for you to wake anyway. It should be just about ready—ah, thank you, Norde."

Nedira's brother brought over a steaming hunk of cooked Squirrel meat on top of what appeared to be a flat piece of wood. Recognizing Verne's handiwork in the makeshift plate, he gratefully took the food from Norde and began to shove his face full of the meat, uncaring of the temperature in his effort to get it down. In less than a minute, the plate was empty and he heard chuckling from the others when he came up for air looking for more.

"Give us a few minutes to finish cooking the rest, and I'll get you more," the second-year Mage student informed him. "You healed *a lot* earlier, so you're going to need it."

Larek nodded. That definitely fit with how he was feeling and with what he remembered. While he was waiting, he attempted to get up to assess whether there were any lingering injuries, but the weakness in his body hit him again suddenly, and he was barely able to remain upright and scoot himself over to lean his back against the nearby wall.

"I'm exhausted. I don't think I can leave again today, unless you all carry me," he admitted.

"We were certainly able to get you here," Penelope said, "but it took both myself and Bartholomew to lug your unconscious body around without it flopping all over. I wouldn't feel safe with us having our hands full if we were attacked, so it's probably better if we stay here through the night and leave tomorrow morning. This cave is a bit out of the way, and we're far enough away from Thanchet that they can't see us from there or the road, so it should be *relatively* safe. At least, I hope so."

"That works for me," Larek agreed. "I think I should be better by morning." He wasn't sure of that, of course, but he would be much better than he was at the moment. Especially if he got enough food; from the pile of Squirrel corpses outside, he didn't think that was going to be too much of a problem.

As he – and everyone else – ate roasted Squirrel meat, other than Verne who feasted on a few plants he found nearby in the forest (being a vegetarian), Larek couldn't help but look down at the robe he was wearing. "I thought I took this off. What happened?"

Nedira blushed at his question even as Bartholomew answered. "The Jumping Squirrels happened. They absolutely shredded your overalls and nearly everything else you were wearing. Your boots barely survived, but everything else was either torn off your body entirely or was hanging off you in rags. You were practically naked when we brought you here," he added with a smirk, which caused Nedira's blush to deepen.

"Ah. I see." Larek was extremely disappointed to hear that his clothes had essentially been destroyed, as he'd had those clothes since he left home. Wearing his robe with absolutely nothing else underneath was a bit disconcerting, not to mention the fact that his outfit practically shouted untrained Mage; the same went for his roommates, as they were still in their greyish robes, also. As much as he feared visiting a nearby town or city in the worry that he would be noticed and give their pursuers a lead to his location, they were going to need both supplies *and* clothes now in order to blend in. The others could easily pass for members of the SIC, but a couple of non-Specialized Mages such as Larek, Verne, and Norde? They would certainly stick out.

In the meantime, who knew what was between them and civilization again? From what he understood, based on their conversations earlier when they decided what to do and where to go, he knew that the nearest town to Thanchet was approximately 15 miles to the north of the city, which was situated along the major route leading toward the capital. There was a danger in visiting that one, however, as it would likely be the first one that someone would check if they were looking for Larek and his group. There was another town approximately 25 miles to the northwest which was a bit further but wasn't along the main artery leading north; reaching a little further from there, there was a town almost directly east of Thanchet once you got past the mountain ranges, approximately 40 miles away.

It was this town, situated far enough from the main road leading toward the capital, that they decided upon visiting for supplies despite the distance, as it was the safest of those available to them. The town of Whittleton was a bit of a trek, of course, especially considering their current lack of any supplies; regardless, they also had to think about their safety, and venturing further afield to obtain a measure of that safety was worth it.

They just had to survive getting there, crossing over the dangerous countryside; a countryside that was likely filled with Scission monsters, not unlike the Squirrels they had just fought. As Larek was now a target that they would undoubtedly want to kill if he was seen by them, they needed to be able to defend themselves.

That was where the tired Fusionist came in. After eating his fill, consuming what had to have been at least a couple Squirrels' worth of meat, he felt a lot better as far as exhaustion went – but he was still physically weak. A bit of the tiredness remained, but it wasn't enough to affect his focus, which was something he needed to rely on if he was going to ensure that everyone was properly equipped to survive the next few days on their journey toward Whittleton.

"Since we're going to be here the rest of today and tonight, I might as well prepare us for the trip to come," Larek told everyone once they had settled down to wait. Vivienne was scouting around outside to ensure that they were safe from any monsters or pursuers getting ready to descend upon them, but everyone else was inside or near the cave entrance.

"What do you mean?" Penelope asked. "We already have the Fusions you put on our weapons back at Copperleaf," she added, patting her sword. Larek remembered doing that shortly after the Skirmish on their "permanent" equipment, which was different from the blunted weapons and different gear which was used in the competition. But it was time for an upgrade now that he had a reason to do it and time to work.

"I'd like to overhaul everything, now that I've learned how to apply Fusions to not only leather, but cloth, without it suffering from the potential for breakage as it is bent out of shape. I had just discovered how to accomplish this shortly before... that Gergasi showed up, so no one other than Nedira knows about it yet." Larek didn't want to associate himself with the one that destroyed half of the Academy and was likely on their trail, so he felt better simply calling him "the Gergasi" rather than his father. As far as he was concerned, he wanted nothing to do with his male biological parent.

"You can? That's awesome!" Verne exclaimed a little too loud, but calmed down after he was shushed. Even though they were relatively safe in a cave up in the mountains, shouting could potentially draw danger toward them.

"I can – which brings me to you," he said, pointing at his roommate, before his gaze took in the other Mages. "But not just you – every Mage here. I need your robes so I can put a Fusion on them; it will prevent most anything from cutting through the robes, and they'll be able to resist many types of magical and natural effects, such as fire and extreme cold. What it can't do is prevent impact damage, though I'm still thinking about how I would go about that for the future."

"You... want our robes?" Kimble asked, his gaze darting toward Nedira meaningfully. "I only have the barest covering underneath..." he continued.

Blushing yet again, Nedira abruptly squared her shoulders before she placed her staff to lean up against the wall. Before anyone could say anything, she reached down and pulled the hem of her robe up and over her head, pulling it off completely before throwing it to Larek – who sat there stunned. She wasn't *completely* nude underneath the robe, unlike the Fusionist who even had his underdrawers shredded by Squirrels, but the narrow green bands of fabric covering her chest and lower region contrasted remarkably with her smooth, unblemished, and pale skin.

"Stop staring and get to work," she growled, crossing her arms uncomfortably over her chest.

It took him a few seconds to tear his gaze away, his thoughts racing as he felt a stirring in his body that he stringently ignored. *I never realized how attractive she is—*

No, this wasn't the time.

Distracting himself from those errant thoughts, he belatedly realized that – not to be outdone – Kimble and his roommates also pulled off their robes and tossed them to him; they, too, were wearing undergarments covering up their lower regions, which made Larek a bit envious that they had such when he was now having to go without.

Shaking his head to clear every distraction out of it, Larek arranged all 4 of the robes in front of him along the floor of the cave, with the areas around the lower hem and lower back portions most prominent; he debated pulling off his own and adding it to the grouping, but after turning the robe around his body so that the back was in front, meaning that the same areas were exposed and flat enough for his purposes, he realized that he didn't need to. He could add some Fusions to it even as he continued to wear it. Besides, he really didn't want to sit naked on the cold stone floor of the cave if he could help it.

Before he did anything else, he pulled up his Status again and looked at the 312 AF he had received from the Jumping Squirrels he had killed. With a deep breath and a hope that it worked, he mentally directed 300 of it toward his *Fusions* skill; at first, nothing happened, but after a few seconds he felt something inside of him shift slightly, weakening one portion of him while strengthening something else. He didn't need the notification to tell him that it succeeded, as he intuitively knew that it had worked.

*Maximum Level for **Fusion** Skill increased by 1!*
*Current **Fusion** Skill Level/Maximum: 30/31*

Thankful that it seemed be successful, he followed Nedira's instructions and got to work. Recalling what he did to create the *Multi-Resistance Leather* back at Copperleaf, Larek envisioned the green, plant-based lines of the formation, but this time changed the material to cloth. Thankfully, it didn't matter what kind of cloth it was, as he could tell by feel that the Naturalist and Pyromancer robes were different than the grey robes he and his roommates wore; all that mattered was his intent behind the Effect, which was to attach this Fusion to the material it was being placed upon. This observation made him think that he didn't really need for it to be focused on a particular material at all, as long as he could concentrate enough on what he wanted done; it was something to think about for the future, potentially as a way to make things easier for him. At the moment, it was a distraction that he put aside as he finished building the formation, making it thick enough that he could make multiple Fusions at the same time.

Feeling a major drain on his Pattern Cohesion, he realized he probably should've done this one at a time rather than relying on his *Focused Division* Skill, but it was already too late to change things now that he started to infuse it with Mana. Using the technique of a rotating spiral to funnel the Mana inside of the grid formation with a speed that would've left the other Mages astonished if they hadn't seen him do it before, it only took a little over 10 minutes to finish filling it up. With a mental focus on dividing it into 5 equal sections, he quickly directed them to inhabit the lower back area of each robe – including his own as he sat perfectly still. He'd never actually had to worry about the material he was adding a Fusion to moving before during the process, and wasn't sure what would happen if it was shifted even slightly before it was finalized.

With the accustomed **click** that told him it worked, he let go of the breath he didn't realize he had been holding and sagged in place because of the major drop in his Pattern Cohesion. When he had recovered a few minutes later, to the worried looks from the others as he assured them he was fine, he looked down at his handiwork.

New Fusion Learned!
Multi-Resistance Cloth +9
Activation Method: Reactive
Effect: Causes cloth to resist most forms of damage
Magnitude: 700%/900% increased resistance
Mana Cost: 150,000
Pattern Cohesion: 2,125
Fusion Time: 251 hours

Fusion has reached Level 31!

  His new Fusion was able to increase the resistance of the cloth robes by 900%, which would be able to stop most minor threats; the Jumping Squirrels, for instance, wouldn't be able to pierce through it with their sharp claws. He was sure that many of the much larger and deadlier monsters he'd learned about could probably pierce through it with their naturally sharp appendages, but at that point, the impact of being hit by something like that would probably be worse than any cuts. Regardless, he had wanted to make these robes as strong as possible against magical effects and slicing attacks, and he thought he had succeeded quite well; a quick check with his axe blade showed that it could cut through the material slowly with enough pressure, but his extremely sharp axe was a bit of an extreme case as it was.

  The only thing that he hadn't accounted for was the cost of the Fusion. It wasn't the 150,000 Mana, which was admittedly a lot, but was instead the Pattern Cohesion of 2,125. Alone, that was less than half of his Pattern Cohesion – which was already pushing it – but when he used Focused Division, the cost increased by 20% per additional Fusion. As a result, he had 3,825 Pattern Cohesion suddenly drain from him all at once; he thought that the only reason it hadn't made him pass out and hurt him during the process was because each Fusion was considered separate when it came to the strain his body took from the drain. If he had created a single Fusion with a Pattern Cohesion cost of that size, it was entirely possible that it might have damaged him, or potentially even killed him.

  As he waited for his Pattern Cohesion to recover, he told those waiting on him to finish, "One is done. Give me a few minutes to recover the Cohesion used in that, then I'll complete the rest."

Since he had time to spare, Larek looked at his Status again. While there was very little AF for him to spend now that he used it on his *Fusion* Skill, which he was ecstatic to have finally increased past the threshold he had been stuck at, he had actually increased a personal Level, as well.

Larek Holsten
Fusionist
Healer
Level 21
Advancement Points (AP) : 0/18
Available AP to Distribute: 47
Available Aetheric Force (AF): 12

With 47 AP to spend, he knew exactly where he wanted it. The strain on his body, both from the healing and the use of large amounts of Pattern Cohesion, made him look at his Body stat once again. Through painful trial and error when he was trying to escape from Ricardo, he knew that he needed to keep his Martial stats even lest he become unbalanced, so he started adding another point to Strength, Body, and Agility every few seconds until he reached 75 – an extra 15 in each. That left him with 2 AP to spend, but he kept them in reserve in case he needed them later.

Almost immediately after finishing the AP distribution, Larek felt his body actively recovering from the healing he had done earlier that day and the strain on his Pattern Cohesion. It wasn't a *dramatic* increase in his recovery, but it was noticeable enough that he was sure he'd be just fine the next day to travel along with everyone else.

Strength: 75 (+)
Body: 75 (+)
Agility: 75 (+)
Intellect: 70 [133] (+)
Acuity: 104 [198] (+)
Pneuma: 379 [720] (+)
Pattern Cohesion: 4,578/7,200

With a Pattern Cohesion now over 7,000, Larek felt like he could create just about any Fusion he could think of. There was still a limitation of how much he could spend on a single Fusion without straining his body, but as long as he kept improving his Body stat, he could keep doing more without hurting or killing himself.

Satisfied with his progress, he waited until his Pattern Cohesion completely filled up a few minutes later and added a *Graduated Parahealing +7* Fusion to every robe but his own along the front bottom hem; since he could handle something suited to Martials, he added *Healing Surge +3*, instead.

Since this was something that would be touching their skin most of the time, he thought it made more sense to be on the robe than something that could be easily removed, such as an armlet, anklet, or necklace. Since this didn't take much Pattern Cohesion, at least not nearly as much as the first Fusion, he quickly moved onto the stat boosts. On the upper left sleeve of each robe he added a dual *Intellect and Acuity Boost +10*, a step up from anything they'd had before, and on the upper right sleeve was a *Pneuma Boost +10*; he did it this way because it was more likely that they would be holding a staff or stick of some sort in their right, and he didn't want the area of ambience to interfere with the weapon.

It was the same reason he had directed the *Multi-Resistance Cloth* Fusion to the lower back, because he added a *Repelling Barrier +10* Fusion to the chest, replacing the need for a medallion around their neck. They would still keep the medallions, of course, because they could be slipped on when they needed to take a bath, for instance. It wouldn't stop an assassin slowly creeping up on them, similar to when Vivienne ambushed him in the bath, but it was better than nothing.

When he was all done, less than 45 minutes after he started, he gave them back to the others, who were starting to shiver from the cold. Gratefully, they redressed and grinned enthusiastically when Larek explained what he had done.

"Ouch! What was that for?" Kimble exclaimed, taking a step away from Bartholomew. It turned out that the young Martial trainee had wanted to see if the Pyromancer's robe was indeed more resistant and had poked him in the side with his spear; while it didn't pierce through the cloth or the Mage's skin, the impact was hard enough to leave a bruise.

"Just checking," Bartholomew said cheekily, even while Kimble quickly healed the bruise using the robe's *Graduated Parahealing* Fusion. "It looks like it works. Nice job, Larek," he continued, ignoring the Pyromancer's grumbles.

Tiredness weighed down his eyelids, but Larek pushed through, knowing that it was better if he got this all done now rather than wait until later. *I'll sleep tonight when everyone is safe.*

"Alright, who's next?"

Chapter 26

Larek ended up working straight through for the next few hours, before he nearly passed out after having yet another meal of cooked Squirrel. Thankfully, by the time he was done, he had managed to finish everything he had intended to do – as well as a few things he didn't even think of suggested by the others.

To finish off what was needed for the Mages in the group, Verne went out and gathered a few pieces of wood that he helped to shape into long, straight staves that Larek was able to convert into weapons for each Mage. Because they didn't need to have boosts or healing on them anymore, he added two projectile Effects – one on either end – which included *Icy Spike*, *Water Stream*, *Flying Stone*, or *Flaming Ball* all at Magnitude 7; it all depended upon what they preferred. Since Kimble was already adept at casting fire-based spells, he chose *Water Stream* (to help put out some of his fires if he didn't care to use a spell) and *Flying Stone*, both of which would help to expand his repertoire. Nedira also chose *Water Stream* but went with *Flaming Ball*, while both Verne and Norde chose to add *Icy Spike* and *Flaming Ball*.

Those Fusions were located on the ends of the staves, while approximately two-thirds of the way down the staff was something he placed that would add yet another layer to their protection: *Camouflage Sphere +6*. He would've made both the projectile Effects and the *Sphere* larger in Magnitude, but the three of them were already pushing the limits of their area of ambience when they were in effect – especially when he added a *Strengthen Wood +7* Fusion in between the *Camouflage Sphere* and one of the projectile Effects. It wouldn't do anyone any good if the staves broke easily, so the *Strengthen Wood* Effect was necessary.

Eventually, when he was able to make Advanced Fusions, he would be able to combine more of these types of Effects together into a single Fusion, meaning that he could add more; for now, this was about the limit of his capabilities.

As for Bartholomew, his leather-and-steel-plated armor was fully decked-out in Fusions, as Larek was able to use his *Focused Division* Skill to do multiple pieces at once. The leather portions received a *Multi-Resistance Leather +2* Fusion, which was less than he'd like, but there were so many different unconnected pieces along his chestpiece and helmet (which also received a *Healing Surge +3 Fusion*), as well as being near steel plates, that the areas of ambience would otherwise overlap. The steel plates over his vitals were enhanced with *Strengthen Steel +5*, meaning that they would be able to take *a lot* of damage before they were compromised.

The only exception to his work was the Shieldguard's pants, which were made from two large pieces of leather to which he was able to add a pair of *Multi-Resistance Leather +5* Fusions, a dual *Strength and Body Boost +10* on the left leg, and an *Agility Boost +10* on the right leg, and – because it didn't fit anywhere else – *Repelling Barrier +10* on his buttocks.

His wood and steel shield, an upgrade to what he'd used in the past, contained multiple dual *Strengthen Steel and Wood +7* Fusions that he was able to place where the two intersected in its construction, which would help him block a lot of damage from getting through to him.

Lastly, his spear received something Larek hadn't thought of until the young Martial trainee mentioned it.

"In addition to making the spearhead sharper and stronger, as well as strengthening the shaft, would you be able to add some sort of magical effect to it?" he had asked.

"Like what? Flames?"

Bartholomew shook his head. "What about some sort of ranged attack? The one drawback from my Specialization is that I have nothing to attack monsters from afar; I have to wait for them to come to me, or I have to move to them. If I'm staying back, guarding you for instance, then moving out of position could be dangerous; being able to hit any threats from a distance could be useful."

"I... *think* I can do that."

As a result of that conversation, the Shieldguard now had an *Icy Spike +7* on the butt of his spear. Larek would've liked to have placed it on the pointy end, but that already had a *Strengthen and Sharpen Steel Edge +7* Fusion for the spearhead, so on the butt end was the best compromise he could figure out. Thankfully, Bartholomew was dexterous enough with his fingers that he was able to twirl the staff around in his hand, such that he could quickly switch between the ends without hurting himself, so it wasn't that big of a deal.

Vivienne got the full treatment of *Multi-Resistance Leather +7* on her outfit of leather armor, as well as adding *Repelling Barrier +10*, *Healing Surge +3*, and +10 boosts to her stats where he could fit them in. The knives she possessed received *Strengthen and Sharpen Steel Edge +7* to them, but instead of having them with a Permanent Activation Method, Larek made them Activatable at her insistence. It didn't make sense until he realized where they were held on her body –

her back, around her waist in a pair of sheaths – and that the necessary Fusions for the leather sheaths to ensure she didn't accidentally cut herself would be difficult to juggle with areas of ambience. In addition, she wanted to be able to use them as "normal" knives if she wanted to, which didn't make any sense to him, but he did it anyway. It wasn't that big of a difference, after all, and an easy switch during the Fusion process.

Her bow received a *Multi-Resistance Wood +7* Fusion, another new Fusion for Larek, but having become familiar with the Fusion by that point it wasn't that difficult of a change. *Strengthen Wood* wouldn't work on the bow because that would've made it unable to bend, but the resistance-based Fusion worked well enough to help prevent damage from external sources, as well as to lessen the strain of overuse and pulling too hard – especially since it would take the Ranger a little while to accustom herself to her new, higher-Magnitude *Strength Boost*.

Her *arrows*, on the other hand, received a *Strengthen Wood +5* Fusion on their shafts and *Strengthen and Sharpen Steel Edge +5* Fusions on their arrowheads. Or at least most of them did; Vivienne also had an idea that she wanted to test out with Larek's help.

"In training, most of the time that I've failed to hit my target – typically other trainees – was because they were able to see it coming. With a high enough Agility stat, it was easy enough for them to dodge my arrows when they saw them coming, and even snatch them out of the air if they were paying attention well enough. The same could be done by monsters who are fast enough, and there are plenty of them out there." She paused dramatically for a moment. "But what if they weren't able to see their death coming for them?"

"What do you mean?"

She pointed toward the robes that Larek had finished up earlier. "I saw that invisibility effect that you put on there; do you think that would work on one of my arrows?"

He had to think about it for a moment. He had originally created the Fusion to hide a person, but in reality it simply camouflaged a certain area around the formation's location. Theoretically, it could be used on a smaller object like an arrow, though how well it would work was anybody's guess.

"I can try, but you saw them moving around?" he asked. "It's not exactly invisibility; the *Camouflage Sphere* bends the light around the area and is affected by movement, so they would still see some sort of distortion."

"That's better than nothing," she said, shrugging.

Thankfully, with the area needing to be camouflaged being so small, he only needed a Magnitude 1 *Camouflage Sphere* to cover the entire arrow. Once she had it in hand, the Ranger activated the Fusion and shot it toward a nearby tree; Larek heard it whistle through the air and the *thunk* as it buried itself in the tree trunk, but he only saw the barest of distortions as it flew.

"Not bad. I think I'll take a few of those."

And that's how she got her "invisible" arrows. In fact, she liked them so much that one of her leather boots was downgraded in their *Multi-Resistance Leather* protection and a *Camouflage Sphere +5* Fusion was added to it, allowing her to move around even better without being seen in her scouting forays.

Lastly, Penelope had absolutely no modesty as she stripped down and gave every scrap of clothing and armor to Larek for him to work with. Desperately ignoring the buff, incredibly *naked* blue-haired woman standing in the middle of the cave waiting for him to "work his magic" on her stuff, he got the process done in record time.

"Norde; stop staring," he heard at one point coming from Nedira.

"I-I-I can't! She's just so—"

He vaguely heard an argument coming from the two for a few minutes, while Penelope looked on with amusement written all over her face, but Larek was somehow able to keep his concentration on his work. In the end, her armor and clothing got the usual resistance, boost, healing, and protective barrier Fusions the others did, with nothing extra asked as far as those went. The only special request she had was for her oversized sword in addition to making it stronger and sharper – and it was unusual, to say the least.

"You want what?" he asked, incredulously.

"You know, that, uh, paralysis thing you use in your new healing Fusion."

It took him a second to understand what she was saying. Thankfully, she was fully dressed again by that point, so he could concentrate. "You're talking about *Localized Anesthesia*?"

"Yeah, I guess so. Do you think you can apply *just* that to my sword? Make it so that I can activate it and anything I touch with it is paralyzed?"

He immediately started to shake his head, but then he thought about it. In reality, he thought he might be able to do it, as all he'd have to do would be to eliminate the healing Effect from the Fusion he had created, and then increase the Magnitude of the *Anesthesia* so that it affected the entire body...

"I can do it, but the paralysis effect would only be active when your sword blade is touching their body. In addition, if it was used against someone who knew what was causing the paralysis, they could deactivate it with a thought."

"Not a problem. That would still be incredibly effective against most monsters."

In the end, the Fusion was so simple that it was only a 2-by-2 grid formation, making it a Basic Activatable Fusion that would push the Effect behind the *Localized Anesthesia* spell through an entire body. Or at least as much of the body it could influence with a *+10* Magnitude; he suspected that if it was used against something massive like a dragon, it would only affect a small section of their body temporarily. In addition, it wasn't designed to be used against non-biological monsters, so something like the Treedin he fought back in Crystalview, or the Lava Oozes he saw coming from the Scission that accompanied the Gergasi's arrival would be entirely unaffected.

New Fusion Learned!
Paralytic Touch +10
Activation Method: Activatable
Effect: Sends a paralyzing pulse through a biological body at a touch
Magnitude: Affects target bodies weighing up to 1,000 lbs.
Mana Cost: 75,000
Pattern Cohesion: 1,150
Fusion Time: 157 hours

When she used it against Bartholomew, who volunteered as a test subject despite Larek's objection, the younger Martial immediately started collapsing to the floor of the cave as he lost all control of his body. The moment his hand left the flat of the blade where he touched it, his control came back, but the abrupt loss of any feeling throughout his body – and being unable to manipulate anything – for even a half-second was enough to send him to his knees before he recovered.

"That's just cheating, you know that?" he complained. His complaints were even louder when he realized he had peed a little as he had lost control of his bladder for a half-second, but he was able to recover fast enough that the floodgates didn't fully open.

"Yeah, but I also have to make sure to hit your bare skin – how often is that going to happen in a friendly bout?" Penelope asked, gazing at her newly Fusioned sword as if she was in love with it.

"Stop looking at it like that, or I'm going to get jealous," Vivienne teased, smacking her on the back of the head lightly. The blue-haired Striker ignored the blow and sighed, before abruptly turning around to scoop the Ranger up in her arms, planting a very noisy kiss on her lips.

"Nothing could replace you, babe," she said with a smile, and Larek had to look away, feeling a little uncomfortable as he noticed Nedira staring at him. He wasn't exactly sure why he felt uncomfortable, but he was too tired to mentally investigate it after all the Fusions he'd created.

For now, it was time to sleep; he figured he'd have time to think about it when they were on the move the next day.

Thankfully, the next morning, he felt largely recovered from all of the events with the Squirrels and Fusions he'd created. He was also adjusting to the repurposed wooden armlets, as he had added small Martial stat boosts to them; they weren't needed for their original purpose anymore since those Fusions were now on his robe, but he also needed to work on the physical side of his nature coming up. He started with smaller Magnitudes because he wasn't sure how his body would react to them, and he was glad that he did; even a Magnitude 1 boost to his Strength, Body, and Agility stats was difficult to accustom himself to.

It just felt... *strange*, if he was being honest with himself, as if his physical body was rejecting the set of boosts as if it was a foreign invader. Over time, though, he could feel it adjusting and accepting the boosts, but it was going to take a little longer before he could equip something like the +10 Magnitudes that the other possessed. He could handle them without paralyzing himself, at least; more than a few minutes of contact filled his entire being with pain, however, and he knew such things were a long way off for him. Magnitude 1 was his limit for now.

Despite that, he was feeling better about their journey than he had at the start, as he had done everything he could to protect his friends from the dangers that were sure to confront them along the way. It was with that positive thought process that they left the cave the following morning, packing up as much of the leftover cooked Squirrel meat as they could before they left, and they ventured back into the trees on their way to Whittleton.

Chapter 27

"Watch out! They're coming from—" Whatever else Nedira was going to say was overshadowed by the explosion of dirt erupting from all around the group, accompanied by the cracking of tree roots as they were demolished from underground. Larek threw himself backwards from the rumble he felt under his work boots, and he landed on his backside before he rolled back to his feet.

"I thought you said it was clear!" Penelope shouted, accusing the Ranger, who looked slightly embarrassed as she began unleashing her arrows into the sides of the monsters that emerged from below.

"It was! At least, it was up here!"

Larek couldn't blame anyone for not identifying the threat from below, because it wasn't until there were some slight tremors under their feet as they walked through the forest that anyone realized there was even any danger nearby. It was entirely possible that Vivienne had scouted the area and not drawn the ire of the monsters, given how light on her feet she was; what was *more* likely, however, was that they sensed Larek nearby and *that* was what caused them to attack.

The former Logger held out his left hand with his staff held tightly in it, as he aimed toward the monster that nearly ate his feet. Standing only 5 feet tall, the **Dirt Golem** was virtually indistinguishable from the nearby ground in between the thick trees of the forest they had begun navigating through earlier in the day. Dead pine needles were stuck to its exterior, and small pebbles were interspersed inside of the large clumps of dirt that the Golem was comprised of. The irregular, solidified chunks of earth were arranged and stacked on top of each other in a parody of a person, though it had no "head" to speak of. What it did have, though, was a sharp, stone-toothed mouth on its upper torso that was at least a foot and a half wide, which had nearly snatched Larek's lower limbs up from below. His *Repelling Barrier* wouldn't prevent something like that happening, given its directional location, so he was glad to have rolled out of the way.

"Hit them just below their mouths!" Verne shouted, his roommate's knowledge of monsters overriding Larek's temporary fear at the presence of the Golems that had sprung up all around the group. Out of them all, the young Mage student had been one of the better students when it came to monster knowledge; thankfully, Verne also wasn't one to freeze up at the sight of danger, and was already using his projectile staff to launch an *Icy Spike* at one of the Golems. As Larek watched him out of the corner of his eye, the boy deftly flipped the staff around and sent a *Flaming Ball* out of its end, following up his previous attack. *It looks like he's already become accustomed to using that thing.*

The same couldn't be said for Larek, who refocused his efforts on the Golem nearest him. His own staff was similar to the others' in its Effects, and he had chosen to utilize *Flying Stone* and *Water Stream* as his projectiles. His first attack, which was nearly point-blank range at only 5 feet away, shot a chunk of stone at the Dirt Golem just under the mouth as Verne had directed. Somehow, the Golem ended up turning just enough for its left dirt-clump arm to intersect the projectile, which blasted the earthy appendage apart, but it was otherwise fine.

Rather than strain the Fusion by using another stone, he attempted to twirl the staff in his fingers like he saw Verne do, but all he managed to accomplish was to drop the projectile-slinging weapon as he fumbled the maneuver. While he thought he might have enough time to pick it up, he left it where it fell because he felt the ground tremble slightly behind him, and he jerked himself forward in time to avoid a blow from another Dirt Golem from behind. His *Repelling Barrier* might have blocked and redirected it downward, but when he looked back at the attacking Golem, he realized that the punch wasn't necessarily fast – just strong. With the fact that it might not have even triggered the protective Fusion if it had managed to land the blow, he made sure to keep moving in order to not be surrounded.

Axe in hand, he maintained his forward momentum and chopped downward at the Golem that had blocked his *Stone* projectile a few seconds before. The cutting edge of his tool was incredible, as it didn't care whether it was cutting through dirt or stone, as it cleaved its way through the upper torso and mouth of the monster like it was nothing, before there was a slight resistance just below its bisected orifice. As he yanked his axe out from the wound, he saw a brown glow coming from inside the lower torso that suddenly snuffed out; a second later, the entire Golem seized up and then fell apart, becoming no more than a pile of dirt on the ground.

Ah, so that's what holding them all together. Thanks for the heads-up, Verne.

Conscious of the Golem behind him, Larek swung around after he watched his previous victim fall apart, just in time for his axe to cut entirely through another dirt punch coming for him. As it split in half, a chunk of the dirt slammed into him, the *Barrier* not stopping it because it wasn't moving fast enough; but other than feeling the impact, his robe held up to a few sharp rocks that been inside of the dirt. Unfortunately, the Golem kept coming for him despite its arm being cut in half, and he had to step back in order to get a full swing; he stumbled and nearly fell when his foot encountered the dirt pile that was all that was left of the previous monster, but he managed to keep his feet somehow.

Setting his stance once he regained his balance, Larek swung with a sideways chop at the Golem's torso, his long arms giving him a reach advantage over the dirt monster. Just like he would cut into a tree trunk in an effort to fell it, the blade of his axe entered into the Golem's main body and sheared through it entirely. The cut was so clean and swift that the Golem didn't even have time to separate into two pieces as its internal, glowing core of earth was cut apart; instead, it collapsed where it stood, creating yet another pile of dirt that Larek now had to avoid. Thankfully, he had a brief second to look around and get his bearings before he threw himself back into the fight.

He hadn't really gotten a good look at how many of these Dirt Golems there were because they had attacked so suddenly, but now he could see that there were at least 300 of them that had either surrounded or come up under his group. Thankfully, with all the protections they possessed, the defenders were able to survive long enough to begin to fight back, and already there were dozens of dirt piles that were accumulating amongst the trees as they battled it out with the monsters attacking them.

The Martials were absolutely devastating the attacking Golems, with Bartholomew stabbing them quickly with his spear, Vivienne skewering them with her arrows as she fell back, and Penelope bisecting them just as easily as Larek had his last victim, though with what seemed like even more ease than that with which he had accomplished the deed. That wasn't to say that Kimble and the other Mages were slouching in their efforts, because that was far from the truth. The Pyromancer started casting *Fire Spears* at the Golems with his right hand, which produced a long, thin spear of superheated flames that were able to penetrate the lower torso of the monsters in order to break their earthy cores; he wasn't quite as fast with the *Spears* as he was with *Fireballs*, but he also used his left hand – which was holding his staff – to launch *Flying Stones* and *Water Streams* that cut deeply into the Golems and were able to smash or cut limbs off his targets.

Nedira used *Binding Roots* to trap a half-dozen Golems in place while she worked on dismantling them with other spells and her staff's projectiles. Verne and Norde were standing back to back, taking on all comers as they released another projectile every few seconds, their speed designed to put less strain on the Fusions that provided the attacks. It was a method that would help to prolong the staves for years to come, though if they ever got into real trouble, they had at least a few minutes of rapid-fire projectiles that would hopefully keep them alive until help could come.

Even in the few seconds Larek had to observe all this, he witnessed at least one Golem strike Nedira and Kimble in the back as they were attacked on all sides. The one that attacked Nedira, thankfully, activated her *Repelling Barrier*, and its dirt-clump arm was ripped clean off its body because of the Fusion. Unfortunately, the one that hit Kimble made it through, and the Pyromancer was knocked off his feet, the blow strong enough to both move him and potentially crack a rib. Even as he was getting up, groaning in pain, Larek could see the *Graduated Parahealing* Fusion being consciously activated by Kimble as his body was healed, while at the same time the red-robed Mage used his staff and its *Water Stream* to cut the legs off the Golem that attacked him. That delayed the monster for a few seconds as its upper body reformed with the detached legs, but it was enough of a delay that it allowed Bartholomew to speed over and pierce its torso with his spear before defending against yet another Golem that was trying to attack him.

Speaking of the young Martial Trainee, he was already adapting to the *Icy Spear* on his weapon, adding yet another level of combat that Larek was astonished to see. At one point, the Fusionist watched him stab and kill a Golem, only to sense a second behind him ready to attack; a mental command shot the icy projectile into its lower torso, not quite piercing the core inside, but the attack caused it to stagger backwards. Reaching out to block an attack by a third Golem with his shield, which didn't activate the *Repelling Barrier*, Bartholomew ripped the spear out of the first one he killed, twirled it around in his fingers so that the spearhead was facing backwards, and then shoved it in the hole that had been formed by the *Icy Spear* a few seconds before. After killing that second dirt monster, he angled himself so that the butt of the spear was aimed at the third, and after blocking yet another blow with his shield, he unleashed a second *Icy Spear* at the Golem. A swift yank of the weapon out from the crumbling pile of dirt left behind by the second monster was followed by yet another twirl of the spear, and a quick poke by the spearhead into the knocked-back third Golem was enough to finish it off.

In fact, watching the Martials fight, the speed and grace with which they attacked and defended made Larek feel a bit envious. While he might be strong and have some skills utilizing his axe, he felt like a drunk mule staggering around the battlefield in comparison to the trainees.

Regardless of his "intoxicated" method of attack, he still got the job done, even if it wasn't as pretty. He quickly threw himself back into the fight with his axe rather than stand back and use his staff from range, because he knew that he needed to kill as many of these monsters as possible for his own development. As he struck out at the nearest line of Dirt Golems heading his way, he felt his Agility stat kicking in as he moved faster than he had during the initial fight, and he was able to weave his way through the monsters coming for him, avoiding their strikes using whatever means were available. His quick speed as he ran at them actually helped their blows pass the threshold the *Repelling Barrier* needed in order to activate, and simply charging headlong into a few of them was enough to smash them into the ground with a strong burst of wind.

Unfortunately, the Dirt Golems were quite a bit more resilient than something like the Jumping Squirrels, as even if they were smashed into the ground by his Barrier, they were only lightly damaged. Even that light damage was rapidly fixed as dirt was rearranged around their bodies, as the only way to really "hurt" these monsters was to destroy their core.

Still, it was sufficiently more of a benefit than a detriment for Larek when the *Barrier* activated, even if he was forced to come back and finish them off, because it allowed him to attack the others without having to worry about being surrounded. After a minute or so, he was starting to get the hang of the Golems' speed and attacks, which were all fairly basic and without any major variations; it didn't take long for him to get into a rhythm, treating the Golems like tree trunks that needed to be cut through as he maneuvered his way around the seemingly endless horde.

That latter observation was proven to be a lie less than 10 minutes later as he cut through yet another Golem, leaving behind a dirt pile; he started to move toward the next one, only to realize that there was nothing moving around him. Pulling his hyper-focus of the fight up from where it had been, he looked around, only to see his group standing in a bunch off to the side, chatting amongst themselves as they stared at the loose-dirt-filled forest surrounding them.

"Done?" Penelope half-shouted the question, as he was approximately 50 feet away from the group. He slowly nodded, seeing no more Golems. "Good. You need some serious training, but you did well enough."

"It, uh, got the job done, though... didn't it?"

The blue-haired Martial nodded reluctantly as she walked over. "It did. This time. Thankfully for you, these Dirt Golems are pretty dumb and don't use any speed or tactics to attack. If they had been faster or smarter, you might not have had such an easy time of it."

"Easy?" He had to think about it for a few seconds. "Yeah, I guess it was." After the initial ambush, he hadn't felt all that good about his performance, but he supposed he made up for it once he really got moving. They weren't as easy as the Squirrels to kill individually, though the furry-tailed rodents had speed and numbers on their side.

"Now what—?" he began to ask, before a familiar fog suddenly streamed out of the dirt piles near him. A few seconds later, it shot toward Larek, filling him with Corrupted Aetheric Force, which his body immediately started to process. Looking at his Status, there was no way to see how much he initially absorbed; but every second he watched his available Aetheric Force increase by 2. Meanwhile, he could feel the Corrupted Force inside of his body being... cleansed? Converted? Whatever it was, it felt like a gentle itch underneath his skin that was constantly moving around his body; thankfully, it wasn't horrible, and it was gradually diminishing – even in the first few seconds of the process.

"Are you alright, Larek?" Nedira abruptly asked, startling him out of exploring the sensations he was feeling. This was the first time he'd actually experienced it, given that he passed out during his initial absorption of Aetheric Force, so it made sense that he wanted to explore the process.

"Yes, I believe so. I definitely received more of that Aetheric Force, but it takes a little time to convert into something usable," he explained. "It feels strange, but not debilitating."

"How much did you get from the Dirt Golems? We left the rest for you to kill when it looked like you could handle it, so that you could get as much as possible."

Larek shrugged. "I'm not sure yet. It looks like it'll keep adding up as it is... uncorrupted?"

"Purified, maybe?" she offered as a solution.

"Sure, that sounds about right." Looking around at the mounds of dirt, he asked, "Is there anything worth keeping from these things?" A lot of monsters had valuable parts that could be reused in the construction of armor and weapons, or so he was taught. At the Academy and the Fort, they only used basic issue weapons and armor because those were fairly inexpensive to produce; weapons and armor using monster parts were apparently only seen on the more senior members of the SIC. He wasn't sure why that was, because there were always plenty of monsters to go around, but he suspected that it was because of a lack of those able to make use of the material. The average village or town blacksmith wouldn't normally be able to process tough **Clamp Lizard** scales for use in something defensive, for example, or turning the claw from a **Roc King** into a deadly sword wasn't necessarily common.

He made a mental note to look into what it actually took for someone to work with those materials in the future, but for now he was just concentrating on staying alive.

"Some of them can have small amounts of ore and precious gems," Verne answered helpfully.

Penelope shook her head. "We don't have time to dig through all of these, and it's not like we need money," she said, bouncing slightly as the bag on her back jingled with the coinage inside.

"I had forgotten about that," Larek admitted. With everything else going on, the presence of the coins had slipped his mind; he realized that they could probably afford anything they needed once they got to Whittleton, without needing to scavenge from the monsters they killed. Unless there was something extremely valuable that it would be a waste to leave behind. "If that's the case, let's get moving – as long as everyone is fine?" A quick look at everyone showed that no one was hurt, at least not currently; if they had been injured, their healing Fusions would've taken care of it.

A chorus of agreement answered him, and Vivienne led the way once again. "Don't forget to check *underneath* us, Viv," Penelope jokingly scolded the Ranger. "We don't want to get eaten by any other Dirt Golems, after all."

"Yeah, yeah – whatever. I'm an awesome scout, but I can't see through the ground, you know."

The blue-haired Martial cocked her head and looked at Larek. "Can't see through the ground? Fail. Larek, would you be a darling and get right on making a Fusion that could do that?" she asked, the joking tone still in her voice. The others chuckled, likely still riding the high of a fight that wasn't necessarily easy, but wasn't as dangerous as it could've been.

Larek, on the other hand, now had something to think about to occupy his time as they continued their journey.

Chapter 28

Dodge *has reached Level 8!*
Dodge *has reached Level 9!*

As they walked through the forest, Larek finally took the time to look through his notifications, though not a lot had changed. Only *Dodge* from his Martial Skills had increased in Level throughout the fight, as he had used his speed to avoid the attacks of the Golems quite a bit. Even with all the use of his axe during the battle, he didn't receive another Level in *Axe Handling*, so he assumed it was going to take a while for it to get there.

He also discovered that he had killed 134 of the Dirt Golems himself – if he was correct in his assumption that he had received 2 AF per kill. It wasn't long after the resumption of their trek through the forest that the process of purifying the Corrupted Aetheric Force had finished, giving him an extra 268 AF to add to his previous 12 he had left over from killing the Jumping Squirrels. His new total of 280 AF was enough to raise the maximum Level for some of his Mage Skills that were lower-Level, but he held off for now. As for his Martial Skills, they were stuck where they were; instead of there being a cost to increasing their maximum Level, they just said "N/A".

"Why do you think that is?" he asked Nedira as they walked northeast through the rapidly thinning forest. At first, the trees had been thick in the valley and mountain range that circled most of the area where Thanchet was located, but the further north they traveled, the density of the forest diminished rapidly. From what he remembered of his *Geography* class, as well as the little he saw on his original journey to Copperleaf Academy more than half a year ago, the trees would eventually fade away, revealing gently rolling foothills where miles and miles of farms were placed, with the main north-south road passing directly through them. Depending upon which direction you went, you would eventually hit a vast scattering of lakes and ponds to the west, flatter wild grasslands to the north, or a drier plain to the east.

"I don't know, Larek," the Naturalist answered after a moment of thought. "There's so much we don't know about what this Aetheric Force is that it could be anything."

Penelope, having overheard the question, ventured her own thoughts on the answer. "It could be because your Martial side hasn't been cracked open yet."

It took him a few seconds of pondering her statement before he concluded that he had no idea what she was talking about. "Uh... what?"

"Cracked open," she restated, before she glanced at the incomprehension on his face. "Kicked awake? Forcibly initiated? Activated? Any of these ring a bell?"

"Do you mean like what happened on the first day of classes when my new stats were unlocked?" he asked, beginning to understand what she was trying to say.

"Yes! Exactly!"

Confusion colored his thoughts. "But I have the Martial stats and can unlock and improve Martial Skills; I even have a Battle Art, as I showed you. Shouldn't that have... cracked me open?"

The blue-haired Martial chuckled. "Not cracked *you* open, Larek," she explained. "It refers to the opening of access to your *Stama*. Like cracking open an egg to get to the yolk inside, the same thing happens during this process that every Martial goes through as soon as they arrive at the Fort. However, Stama isn't exactly as docile as the yolk of an egg, as it will begin fighting you as soon as your body has access to it."

Larek had heard that before, but wasn't exactly sure what it meant. With Mana, it was easy enough to manipulate it because it was just *there*, hanging around his entire body ready to be used. He knew his Stama was located in a condensed ball of power in his chest, but he had never figured out how to use it. Unlocking his Battle Art at Crystalview had seemingly been a fluke, as he hadn't been able to activate it or do anything with his Stama that wasn't automatic like his *Body Regeneration* Skill.

"What do you mean?"

Stepping over a dead branch in her path, Penelope looked over at him with a serious expression on her face. "Stama is dangerous if it is allowed to do what it wants, which is why the first and only Skill we unlock after having it cracked open helps with reining it in." A few seconds later, something appeared in front of her that he immediately recognized as a very small portion of her Status.

Stama Subjugation Level 8

"It didn't occur to me until later, but I don't remember seeing this extremely important Martial Skill when you displayed your Status to us before," she explained. "At that point, I thought that you might have simply left it off for some reason, but now it's obvious that you don't even have it. I don't even know how it is possible that you *don't* by this point, but it would explain your inability to use your Battle Art. And why you can't increase your Skill Level maximums, I suppose. It's like your Stama is locked behind a door and you haven't been given a key; some of it leaks out from underneath, supplying you enough to aid in *Body Regeneration*, for example. As for how you utilized it to create a Battle Art, I think that is a result of the danger inherent in Stama in the first place."

"Danger? Is it going to hurt him?" Nedira asked with concern in her voice.

But Penelope just shrugged. "Who's to say? This is all new to me as well, but the danger of letting Stama get away from us was drilled into our minds almost every day of training. At first, with our Stama pools so low, there isn't too much to worry about; as we increase in Levels and apply AP to our stats, our Stama pools grow in relation to them, heightening the danger it poses. Without a proper *Stama Subjugation* Skill Level, it can start to act on its own, sometimes reacting to our subconscious thoughts or simply acting out wildly. This can be as harmless as it flooding your eyes with Stama to temporarily let you see better in low-light situations, or it can become horrifically damaging by sending a flood of wild Stama into your arm when you're trying to hit someone. The rapid influx of energy can literally make your muscles explode if it is uncontrolled, or even kill you if that muscle is your heart.

"It can also, as you discovered, create a Battle Art – but Battle Arts created in this manner are typically worse than anything you could create with your conscious direction, and almost always have a downside. Is that the same with your Battle Art? *Furious Rampage* isn't something I've heard of before."

Larek had to think back at what his Battle Art did, and he had to agree with her. While the ability doubled his Strength, it also reduced his Body stat by 30%. He had thought that it was a worthwhile exchange, but perhaps he was biased because he didn't really know much about Battle Arts in the first place.

He explained what it did to her, and she nodded. "That's not actually as bad as I feared, but it's still worse than if you had consciously formed the Battle Art yourself. That's the importance of *Stama Subjugation*, as it will prevent something like that – or worse – from happening on its own in the future."

That made sense, he supposed, but there was an even more important question to ask. "Could you crack open my Stama to give me the necessary Skill?"

She immediately shook her head. "Nope. It's not something that is taught to trainees, as far as I know. I'll ask the others, but I'm pretty sure it has to be forcibly activated by an Instructor, or at least by someone who knows the correct technique. I'm sure there might be a way to crack it open on your own, but I don't know the way."

Disappointment and worry flooded Larek as soon as she denied being able to help, though he knew it wasn't her fault. She even briefly explained what occurred during the process with her, which Bartholomew quickly confirmed was the same for him; Vivienne was out scouting, so she wasn't there to chime in, but he could only assume it was similar for her, too.

Basically, instead of a spell being cast that affected everyone within range, unlocking their Mage stats and Skills, one of the Instructors held their hand against the new trainee's chest and forced their own Stama out of their bodies and into the trainee's. Whatever this process did effectively "cracked open" the trainee's Stama, giving them Level 1 in *Stama Subjugation* and allowing them to access the energy at will.

When he proposed having one of the Martial trainees do the same thing to him, they all immediately refused. "No way. Especially not now," Penelope said, waving her hands in the air in emphasis to her words. "The only things I know for certain are that the one doing it needs to have incredible control over their Stama, not only in their body, but externally; more than that, they need to be *stronger* than the one they are doing it to, which is the only way their Stama can interact with the foreign Stama. As it is, while the boosts you provided us increased our maximum Stama enough that it tops your own maximum, none of us have enough *Stama Subjugation* to do something like that. I don't even know how I would even transfer my Stama into your body, for instance, even if my Skill Level is relatively high for a trainee."

"Level 8 is high?"

"For *this* Skill, yes," Bartholomew interjected. "I'm only at Level 4. It's also one of the few Skills that can't be improved artificially through the use of a Fusion, so there's no getting around that limitation."

That was exactly what he thought he might be able to do, but to have that hope dashed before it could come to fruition wasn't all bad. Regardless, he wasn't even sure he *could* make a Fusion for it, given that he had never seen a symbol for it in all the books he'd read, and he didn't have it himself to apply the Effect to a Fusion.

"So, what you're saying is that I need to find someone with an exceptional *Stama Subjugation* Skill Level *and* the knowledge of how to use it to crack open my own Stama so I can use it? So... like at the Fort we're going to?"

"In short, yes."

Larek's wavering on whether to go to Fort Ironwall as the Dean wanted was starting to become less of a choice and more of a necessity.

"But you might be able to find some veteran SIC members that could do it, if you were able to convince them somehow to do it."

Now *that* was a good alternative. Whether he'd be able to find someone like that was the largest obstacle, given that they were going to try and avoid towns and cities on their journey to Silverledge Academy and Fort Ironwall.

Regardless, it wasn't something that he could do much about at the moment, given that there was no one but them around and the Fort was many, many miles away on the eastern side of the Kingdom. He still had some time to search for someone that could help him, or barring that, decide to attend the Martial training school at their eventual destination.

Larek just hoped that his Stama behaved and didn't try and influence his body before he was able to get a handle on it; however, with the amount of fighting he was going to have to do, he didn't have a lot of confidence that it wouldn't be trying to do *something*.

The next few hours of their trek through the trees were relatively quiet, with only one other interruption. Shortly after sprinting across the clear road in their bid to head to the northeast, they entered the sparse trees again and were immediately set upon by a swarm of **Snow Spiders**, which were 2-foot-wide and 1-foot-tall 8-legged monsters that only vaguely resembled the spiders they were named after. Rather than thin, spindly limbs, each of the Snow Spiders' legs was thick chunks of ice that squealed when they rubbed against each other, and their bodies were round like a spherical snowball. Instead of webbing, everywhere their legs touched was temporarily flash-frozen in a layer of ice, which could've been a problem for the group if it wasn't for their defenses – and the warning given by Vivienne at their presence, which was easily spotted, since 200 feet into the tree line, the forest was half-frozen.

The Snow Spiders were remarkably fast, which was actually a detriment to them, because the *Repelling Barriers* the group possessed smashed them apart when they tried stabbing their victims – because they were also remarkably fragile. The ice that comprised their legs would shatter like glass when the gusts of air slammed them into the ground, and even a swing by one of the Mages' staves was enough to shatter them. When a few of the snowy monsters managed to make it through the *Barriers*, their robes were resistant enough that the flash-freeze would only make the material stiff for a short time, leaving the bodies beneath the robes unaffected other than being a little chilly from the contact.

Kimble had a blast fighting against the Snow Spiders, given that his Pyromancer Specialization was uniquely suited toward absolutely devastating them. The red-robed Mage ended up killing approximately a third of the attacking monsters, which numbered around 300, while another third was killed by the others, leaving Larek to finish off the rest for their Aetheric Force. These, too, ended up providing 2 AF per kill, netting him just under an additional 200 AF to use in raising his maximum Skill Levels. With 476 AF now available to him once it was done purifying, he used 300 of it to increase his *Pattern Formation* Skill maximum. The Skill didn't automatically increase, of course, as he'd have to use the Skill later to raise it, but if he could continue raising the maximum Level of all his Skills, he thought he could knock out a few Level increases when they stopped for the night.

The sun was beginning to set by the time they passed through the last of the trees, arriving at the edge of the gently rolling hills they had been expecting to see, and the fields of grain that were planted on a nearby farm butted right up to its edge. Instead of pushing it any further that night, they decided to retreat slightly into the trees and find someplace to camp for the night. With no nearby cave to huddle into, their camp was exposed, but Vivienne spent some time checking the nearby area and confirmed that there was nothing dangerous nearby. They still kept a watch throughout the night, but everyone else was so exhausted that they fell into a deep sleep within minutes of flopping themselves down on the ground.

It was with great disappointment that Larek felt someone shaking him awake in what felt like an hour later. He opened his eyes, expecting to see the pre-dawn light of morning, but to his surprise it was almost entirely dark outside. The sliver of the moon in the sky barely illuminated the surrounding area underneath the trees, but Larek was able to spot everyone else up and crouched around each other; a quick glance at who had woken him up revealed it to be Vivienne, who held a finger against her lips for silence.

"*Monsters in the field. Small. Hard to see. Dangerous,*" she whispered, just barely loud enough for him to make out. For her to say that they were dangerous worried him, because to date she hadn't seemed worried about anything they had fought.

As he slowly got up and crept to the others as silently as possible, he met the barely visible eyes of his companions as they looked back at him. He nodded in what he hoped was assurance as he looked toward the north, where the edge of the fields was approximately 150 feet away. Vivienne disappeared from sight into the shadows, and Larek activated his own *Camouflage Sphere* on his staff; seeing him do it, the other Mages did the same, which covered not only them but Penelope and Bartholomew waiting right next to them.

    The wait for something to happen was almost torture, but when he saw the Ranger speeding back to their location with the slightest bit of fear in her eyes, something he'd never witnessed before from the normally taciturn Martial, he knew they were in for a fight.

Chapter 29

For a moment, Larek thought he was wrong about the danger that was heading toward them from the fields, as a small figure appeared as it ran out of the tall stalks of grain. At approximately 2 feet tall, the front of it appeared to be humanoid in appearance, though it had a bulbous, oversized nose and severe features marked by a mouth filled with pointed, serrated teeth. Its dark brown skin was leathery in appearance, making the monster appear old and worn, which was further reinforced by its spindly arms and legs.

Despite the relatively small appendages, the monster's body was wide; from what he could tell, this was because its back was filled with foot-long quills like a porcupine. The entire package made for a strange sight, but it also made him question why Vivienne was running away in fear from it. It didn't look too tough, and even if there were hundreds of them, they would still be easy to kill. Other than the quills on its back and vicious-looking teeth, he couldn't see anything concerning about it; even its hands seemed delicate and not tipped with razor-sharp claws or anything like that.

"A **Pukwudgie**," Verne whispered shakily nearby. Larek was still confused at why he sounded fearful, but could only assume he was missing something.

Within seconds of the first appearing, another five of these Pukwudgies ran out of the field, stopping at the edge of the tree line alongside the first. As they peered through the sparse trees – looking for Vivienne, he assumed – Larek still didn't understand what the issue was about these things. He was tempted to attack them from range and even raised his staff up to point toward them, but he held himself back out of respect for the caution the others were exhibiting.

After the first minute of no one moving, the *Camouflage Spheres* helping to hide them from the Pukwudgies' sight and Vivienne having faded into the forest to who knew where, the monsters began to turn around and head back into the field. Relief surged through Larek as they started to leave, and he shifted slightly where he was crouched and watching them. His movement inadvertently jostled the bag he forgot was attached to his back, and the clink of the coins inside impacting each other rang out in the otherwise silent atmosphere.

Uh-oh.

Upon hearing the sound, each of the half-dozen Pukwudgies turned unerringly toward Larek as if they could *see* him. A sudden growling coming from the small figures reverberated within his chest, the strength of it surprising him; it was then that the monsters began to change.

Growing from their original 2-foot-tall size to towering over 12 feet, the transition took place over no more than 2 seconds; he was left speechless as he watched them grow impossibly large, with their back quills now reaching several feet long by the time they were finished growing.

The *twang* of a bowstring snapping, followed by the impact of an arrow punching through the upper chest of one of the Pukwudgies startled him, but no more than the shout that followed it up. "Fire! It's too late to hide!"

Spurred on to action, Larek launched a *Flying Stone* at the one closest to him, noticing at the same time that the one that Vivienne hit with her arrow had shrunk slightly... but otherwise, there was no visible wound left by the projectile. Just as the first barrage of *Flying Stones, Flaming Balls,* and *Icy Spikes* sent out by the Mages (and Bartholomew) approached the line of Pukwudgies, they all suddenly disappeared. He could tell immediately that they hadn't simply turned invisible where they were standing, because their attacks went *through* the empty space without stopping. Fortunately, they were at the edge of their range so they didn't travel much further than that, as setting the field of grain behind them on fire would be a disaster.

"Where'd they—?"

"Behind us! They can teleport!" Verne shouted, turning around just in time to be smacked by a hand that was half the size of his body. Larek could tell that the *Repelling Barrier* had activated, but the powerful gust of wind seemed to flow through the appendage as if it wasn't even there.

The young Mage student went flying backwards, the blow hard enough that Larek could hear a few hollow cracks coming from his chest that indicated a broken bone or two. He didn't have a chance to see if his roommate was alright after that because there was another of the Pukwudgies behind *him*, and he was barely able to throw himself forwards out of the way of a similar blow.

Rolling to his feet, he fumbled with his staff so that the *Water Stream* was pointed toward the teleporting attacker, and he activated it with a thought. The powerful stream of water cut into the lower legs of the monster as he moved the attack to hit both, but to his surprise it didn't seem to damage the Pukwudgie; instead, it simply seemed to shrink its 12-foot-tall frame by approximately a foot, with no lasting damage left behind.

*What **are** these things?!*

Dropping his staff, he gripped the shaft of his axe with both hands just in time to try and deflect another blow coming straight at him, but despite his strength and the toughness of his body, he was knocked flat on his back when the fist slammed into his raised tool. Hitting his head on the ground, he was momentarily stunned as his vision swam, but a quick application of his *Healing Surge* Fusion helped to clear it up. He got to his feet in a flash, keenly aware that he was in real danger here, and he swung his axe reflexively at another attack. The blade of his best friend cut through the fist coming for him, splitting it in half; but no blood spilled out, and the appendage didn't detach in any way. Instead, he saw in real-time how the bisected fist seemed to stitch itself together while also visibly shrinking the Pukwudgie by another 2 feet, meaning that it only towered over Larek at a slightly smaller height of 9 feet by that point.

    A feminine scream of pain off to his left caused him to miss another attack aimed at him, and he took it on the shoulder as he attempted to dodge at the last second. The blow was slightly weaker than before, which meant it only sent him flying rather than breaking his collarbone and shoulder, and he was already healing himself before he hit the ground. As soon as he landed, he looked around to see Nedira had fallen victim to yet another Pukwudgie, as she was lying on the ground with her left leg bent in a direction it really shouldn't be. Both Verne and Norde had come to her defense and were launching attacks on the monster to try and distract it, joined by the Naturalist as she fought through the pain and used her own staff offensively.

    The Pukwudgie they were fighting shrunk to approximately half of its original transformed size, meaning that it was still 6 feet tall. As soon as it hit that threshold, it disappeared once again, but this time it didn't reappear behind them. Instead, the monster reappeared in a nearby tree, its weight nearly snapping one of the branches, and it was facing the other direction. It wasn't long before they realized what that meant, as a ripple went through its porcupine-like back and a barrage of quills shot out toward the struggling Mages down below. Thankfully, whatever had seemed to negate the *Repelling Barrier* earlier didn't apply to its quills, as they were deflected into the ground as soon as they were near enough, though one nearly impaled Nedira's leg as it slammed into the ground.

    Meanwhile, Kimble cast a *Flame Wall* in front of the Pukwudgie that appeared behind him, and the monster was visibly shrinking as it burned inside of his spell, even as he launched other spells that hastened the process. It, too, disappeared and reappeared with the intent to impale him with quills, but it had just as little luck as the one trying to hit Nedira and the boys.

Out of them all, though, it was the Martials who were the most effective against the monsters. Penelope was a whirlwind of death as she sliced up and even chased after her victim when it escaped into a nearby tree, though she had difficulty reaching it when it was there. Larek saw her arms and sword glow a few times, which meant she was using a Battle Art, and it seemed to make a difference in the "damage" she was inflicting in regards to how much the monster was shrinking.

Bartholomew was able to use his shield to block most of the blows sent his way by his own opponent, before stabbing it multiple times with his spear. Just like Penelope, he also had a glow around him, though it was focused on his shield and shield arm, which apparently allowed him to withstand the attacks coming his way without being knocked over.

Vivienne had abandoned her bow for her knives, and she was quick enough – especially with her new boosts – that she was able to circle around and slice, stab, and nick the exterior of the Pukwudgie with impunity. Each of her attacks didn't do a whole lot to make it shrink by themselves, but there were a lot of them, especially when a glow lit up her left hand and the knife it held, and the strike she performed seemed to do at least 3 or 4 times as much damage.

Distracted by looking at everyone, Larek fell victim to another attack that came his way, but he reacted in time to dodge the attack completely, before deciding he'd had enough of this bizarre monster. Jumping forward, he raised the axe above his head and chopped down with all his strength like he was intending to split a log in half; the Pukwudgie attempted to move out of the way, but was only able to avoid having its head split in twain as the axe blade struck its upper shoulder. Larek's strike cut all the way through its entire body, inflicting incredible amounts of damage… only for it to reform before his eyes, though it was much smaller by that point, having lost at least 4 feet off its frame. As he recovered from his own attack and lifted his axe to strike again, the monster disappeared. It didn't take him long to find that it had teleported on top of a nearby tree branch, where it began to launch quills at him – which he ignored entirely.

"Nedira! Are you alright?" he shouted, moving next to her and lifting her up off the ground; she cried out in pain at the movement, but didn't protest as he moved her broken leg back in place so that it could heal properly as she activated her healing Fusion. Once it was straightened as well as he could, he set her back down.

"Thanks," she said with strain evident in her voice. She flinched when some more quills slammed into her *Repelling Barrier*, before being shunted off to the ground. "Go. We need to finish them off before they do anything worse."

"Right. On it." With a nod at Verne and Norde, the three of them turned to the others, only to find that every single Pukwudgie was up in the trees, each of them at different sizes, and they were bombarding the group with quills to very little effect. Worse than that, unless his eyes were deceiving him, the monsters were starting to grow larger as he watched.

Vivienne took over at that point, as she was their resident expert on long-range attacks. "Focus fire on one at a time!" she shouted, pulling her bow off her shoulder and releasing an arrow in no more than a second. The one she targeted was the largest of the Pukwudgies on the tree branches and nearly looked like it was about to break the tree limb; when the arrow sunk into its body and passed through it completely, the monster shrunk by about 6 inches.

Seeing the logic in her attack, Larek stepped back to where he had been fighting before and grabbed his staff while Kimble, Verne, Norde, and even the injured Nedira launched their staff projectiles at the same monster, reducing its size even further. Larek let his own stone projectile target the same one… only for the now 4-foot-tall Pukwudgie to disappear yet again, reappearing on a different branch in the same tree.

Vivienne targeted the next-largest after the first one fled so easily, and the group was able to whittle it down – only for it to disappear right before the next round of projectiles hit it. Vivienne was fast enough with her bow to hit the teleporting Pukwudgies, but the other projectiles took longer to aim and travel the same distance, which meant hitting the little buggers was extremely difficult.

This is annoying. Enough of this.

Unfortunately for the Pukwudgies, their potential victim was a Logger. A *former* Logger, at least, but he hadn't lost his touch; more than that, Larek now had the speed, strength, and superior tool to get the job done in a small fraction of the time. Rushing toward the nearest tree with a monster hanging out on the branches, he angled his axe to make a deep, diagonal cut into its trunk, the blade slipping through the wood with ease. Ripping it out and chopping again with incredible speed, his *Axe Handling* Skill allowing him to place it exactly where wanted it, the top diagonal cut was done.

Quills rained down on Larek as he worked, the barrage so thick that his *Repelling Barrier* couldn't handle them all; he felt a few impact his back and throw him slightly off balance, but he was in his element right now, and nothing would deter him. Activating his *Healing Surge* Fusion temporarily to ease the large bruises that would likely be dotting his back in a minute or so, he ignored the injuries as he deftly turned his axe so that he would be chopping a straight cut into the tree trunk. One chop followed after another as he finished carving a large wedge out of the trunk, hearing the tell-tale splintering that let him know that he had accomplished what he set out to do, before he planted his left foot and *kicked* the wedge he had cut out of the tree with his right. The large hunk of wood shot out with ease because of his great Strength stat, his kick working even better than expected, and the tree began to fall as it couldn't handle its own weight with a chunk of its base missing.

All told, it had taken him a total of 5 seconds from start to finish – a record to be sure, especially up in the Rushwood Forest. Even as it fell in the exact place he was aiming for, Larek was already on the move, angling his way to the next tree. He was just finishing up his second when the first finally hit the ground, and a quick look at it showed that the Pukwudgie had teleported out of the falling arboreal behemoth into a nearby tree. Unfortunately for it, that tree was the one he was currently finishing up.

The process repeated itself as the monsters continued to teleport from one tree to another as he chopped them down, but they all stayed close by, rather than retreating further into the forest. As a result, when Larek finished chopping his twentieth tree in a circle around the group in just a few minutes, the Pukwudgies teleported out of the trees and attempted to attack the group once again, with 3 of them targeting Larek specifically. As his companions hadn't been idle during his deforestation spree, most of the creatures were relatively small after suffering the attacks of those with ranged ability, so when they finally engaged in close-combat, they were weak and easy prey for the Martials, who quickly engaged and slaughtered them.

Larek, with the joy of once again employing his axe for its original purpose, threw himself into the Pukwudgies who surrounded him, slicing them apart with great swings of his best friend. At first, they continued to shrink until they were reduced to the size they were when he first saw them running out of the field; after they hit a point where they couldn't shrink anymore, they began teleporting around him constantly, making them hard to hit, but Larek was much faster than he used to be. All it took was one point of contact with his axe to finish them off, the blood that spilled from them finally demonstrating that they could be killed.

When all was said and done, all 6 of the Pukwudgies were lying on the ground, any sense of their gigantic size absent in death. Getting his breathing under control, he looked around at the others and saw their wide eyes as they observed the destruction around them.

"Wow, you really were a Logger, weren't you?" Bartholomew mused, seeing the fallen trees laid out in a precise circle rather than falling haphazardly around them.

"Yes; yes, I was." He was proud of his upbringing and his former profession, even if it wasn't as glamorous as some.

"Gather up some of the quills, if you can," Verne said, already bending down to pick some of them up near his feet. "I believe that they are very valuable."

Vivienne nodded, even as she ventured around the battlefield picking up the arrows she had expended during the fight. "They are filled with an essence of... spatial illusion? Or something like that. It's what gave them their ability to shapeshift and teleport."

"Spatial illusion?" Larek asked, curious. "Is that why we couldn't hurt them?"

Verne took over the explanation. "It is. While most illusions are insubstantial, Pukwudgies have the ability to give them physicality through an application of their spatial affinity."

That didn't mean a whole lot to Larek, but he took the boy's word for it. Especially whatever "spatial affinity" was, because it didn't really mean much to the Fusionist.

"You know, we should've died there," Penelope said, looking at Larek even as he felt the Corrupted Aetheric Force enter his body from the corpses of the monsters he had personally slain. From what he could tell as it moved through his body, it was *a lot*; more than he had earned from the Squirrels and the Golems *combined*. Given what the blue-haired Martial had just said, though, he could only assume it was because these Pukwudgies were much more powerful.

He nodded in agreement as his body went to work purifying the Corrupted Force he absorbed. "I... can well imagine. It was a close one."

"Closer than you think," Kimble interjected. "Pukwudgies are dangerous because they are highly resistant to magic, though not invulnerable; when you tack on the fact that they can teleport, including to the top of a town or city's walls from below, and their incredible strength, ranged attacks, and regenerative capabilities, they are very difficult to kill without suffering casualties, even with an experienced group of SIC members." He looked around at the corpses again, waving at them all. "And we just killed *six* of them without anyone dying. Incredible," he added, shaking his head in apparent disbelief.

"It's these Fusions that Larek created," Nedira pointed out. "If not for them, I don't think we would've survived."

"Don't forget that our resident Fusionist also chopped down half the forest," Verne added cheekily.

There was a small chuckle at that. "But there are obviously some flaws to your Fusions, Larek," Penelope cautioned. "You already know what they are, of course, but now you're able to see them even clearer. The *Barriers* didn't stop the melee attacks by the Pukwudgies because they were mostly illusion, for example, even if they had a physical form. Thankfully, it appeared as though the quills were something different; otherwise, most of us would've been skewered by their long-range attacks."

Larek could only agree, and he resolved to look into another protective solution in the future. For now, though, exhaustion weighed him down from the middle-of-the-night wakeup, difficult fight, and healing he'd had to do as a result of getting hurt. Moving away from the site of the battle after gathering up some of the quills, as they had likely alerted anything within a mile of their location with the falling of the trees, the group settled once again to sleep after eating a quick meal of their dwindling supply of Squirrel meat.

Before he fell asleep, he looked at his Status to see how much Aetheric Force he had accumulated from the Pukwudgies – and was astonished to see that he had absorbed *600 AF!* Since he had personally killed 3 of them, and was fairly certain he didn't receive any from the others, that meant each of the monsters had been worth 200 AF – a 10,000% increase over what he received from Dirt Golems, which was just astonishing. Given how tough the creatures were, and the fact that they only survived because of the overpowered nature of Larek's Fusions, he thought that it was probably justified.

Resolving to look at his Skills in the morning to see where he wanted to apply his new bounty of Aetheric Force, the Logger-turned-Fusionist collapsed into sleep with ease, his exhaustion finally catching up with him.

Chapter 30

Crouching down as he crept up the sparsely vegetated hill, Larek got down on his hands and knees before crawling the rest of the distance up to the apex where he could look over to what was beyond. His robe was already dirty and blood-stained from the last week of travel, though it didn't have any tears or damage at all; unfortunately, the *Multi-Resistance Cloth* Fusion on it didn't repel dirt or stains, which was something he might have to address in the future when he improved it. What it did prevent was any of the dirt and blood from passing *through* the cloth, so if he were to turn it inside-out it would be as pristine as it was when he first put it on.

The last few days had been relatively quiet as far as encountering monsters went, as after the Pukwudgies they only encountered a smattering of monster groups as they passed through miles of farm fields. The first was a pride of **Savannah Lions**, though that pride numbered nearly 100 of the 7-foot-long cats; the monsters' quick, ambushing attacks were no match for Larek's *Repelling Barriers*, and they were quickly put down through the combined might of the group. Again, though, if it hadn't been for the protective Fusion, the abrupt attack from hiding places around the farm fields – where the monsters were difficult to see – would've resulted in some of them being hurt or killed, so he was doubly glad that he had them.

A day after the Lion ambush, they were traveling over what appeared to be a potato field – with no Farmers in sight at that point, nor at any point in their travels – when they were attacked by a horde of 800 **Walking Skeletons**, the same ones he had seen back in Barrowford. This time, the defenders were fewer but better equipped to handle the number of undead that attacked them, as they were relatively slow and cumbersome, practically falling over themselves as the Martials and Larek swept through them like a tornado, sending bone fragments flying everywhere. Kimble also showed off his pyromantic prowess by using a *Flame Wave* spell that was among the strongest in his repertoire; the result was a wave of flames 12 feet wide that coursed through the horde, burning over 50 Skeletons to ash in seconds. It was a spell that required approximately half of his Mana to cast, which normally would've wiped him out for a while; but thanks to the boost Fusions on his robe, he still had plenty of Mana after that to continue the fight.

Following the Skeletons, they went an entire day without encountering any monsters, but their dry spell ran out when a circling flock of electrified **Lightning Buzzards** flew in from the north and arrived before they could try and find cover to hide. The birds, which had a wingspan of over 8 feet, weren't all that more dangerous compared to a normal bird of the same size, but it was the arcs of electricity that surrounded them that made them a hassle to fight. They were able to launch bolts of lightning out of their wingtips, reaching targets up to 50 feet away – and the *Repelling Barriers* did absolutely nothing to stop them. Since they were more of an energy than something physical that could be blown into the ground, the protective Fusions were useless, though their robes provided them a measure of security as the physical aspect of being electrocuted by a bolt of lightning was diminished significantly.

Burns and being temporarily paralyzed upon being struck by the bolts were bad enough, however, and the only time the Buzzards got close enough to the ground to attack at close range was when they had struck someone and paralyzed them. It made their ranged damage-dealers extremely important to take out the 300 or so flying monsters that harassed them from the sky, raining down lightning bolts constantly, and it was a bit of a nightmare to survive through the entire experience. Fortunately, no one was in any major danger of dying, as the Buzzards couldn't get close enough in their dive-bombing runs upon paralyzed individuals because of the *Repelling Barriers* – which worked just fine in sending the birds crashing into the ground when they approached at speed.

When they were attacked by a massive group of **Fire Sprites** the next day, the foot-tall floating flame entities numbering nearly 2,000, Larek couldn't help but think that this wasn't normal. From what he knew of Scissions based on his observations and from his Academy classes, it was unusual for there to be so many of one kind of monster released simultaneously, though there was mention that much-higher Classifications were unpredictable that way. 100 or 200 of some weaker monsters was perhaps possible, but not all that common; 500 of a monster was extremely rare.

Or, at least, that was how it had been before. Starting with the Jumping Squirrels, which amounted to over 1,000, everything they had encountered had been far more than there should've been if they were part of a Scission between Category 1 and 5, perhaps even Category 6. With 2,000 Fire Sprites added to that number, an amount that was almost unheard of coming from a Scission, it seemed that more than just the location of the Scission openings had changed.

"No, this is very *not* normal, Larek," Nedira had insisted when he mentioned it, with Verne and Norde backing that up. They had been getting ready to sleep the night after they annihilated the Fire Sprites – which were slow to move around, and whose close-range attacks consisted of flaring out a whip-like line of flames at their target – when Larek had decided to broach the subject. "Not only are these monsters completely unrelated to each other, something I wouldn't have thought to see, but their numbers and behavior are concerning."

Their variety was something else that he had noticed. Scissions typically had a theme to them, such as undead, flying monsters, or oversized bugs, and there were multiple waves of increasingly more dangerous examples of that theme as the Scission expelled its monsters. Either dozens of different Scissions had opened across the area and each wave went their separate ways, traveling far away from the others, or something altogether different was happening. When they added in the fact that the different monsters they encountered seemed to be stationary, establishing their own territory rather than wandering around – the Lightning Buzzards being an exception, though it could be that their territory was larger than they had known – it just made the entire situation even more worrisome.

When he unlocked access to Aetheric Force, Larek's notification had mentioned that the Corruption was attempting to widen the breach into its world by either destroying all of the "Guardians" or eliminating all sapient life. Neither of those seemed to be what the monsters were doing anymore, as they were establishing their own domains rather than deliberately seeking to kill everyone they could find. When those domains crossed over the widely traveled roads, villages, and farms, then they would attack those that intruded; but what was the end goal? Why the sudden change? Was it because of The Culmination that Ricardo had mentioned? Or was it something else entirely?

No one had any answers to these questions, however, and they were left simply trying to stay alive. They continued making their way east toward Whittleton, only encountering one other group of monsters, 400-strong. The **Tusked Boars** gave them no trouble, as despite their 5-foot-tall frames, their charges were stymied by *Repelling Barriers*; but they did raise another question when it was found that the monsters had been digging into the side of a large hill, getting far enough into it to create a long tunnel which ended with a decent-sized cave made of hard-packed dirt and stone. It wasn't a natural occurrence, either, as it was clear that it was recently excavated and there were signs of tusk marks along the walls. That, and there were large piles of dirt and stones scattered around the area outside of the tunnel and cave.

"Odd behavior. It makes no sense," Norde said when they explored the excavation, shaking his head in confusion. Larek could only agree.

"Whatever it is, we aren't going to solve it now, so let's get a move on. We should be getting close to Whittleton," Penelope informed them.

Thankful to have another source of food after the Squirrel meat ran out the day before, and with the Buzzards having a tough, stringy meat on them that tasted charred no matter how it was cooked, they butchered a few of the large Tusked Boars after they were killed and cooked them up before they left the area. With bags filled to the brim with meat, they didn't encounter anything else the rest of the day or through the night; it was only the next afternoon when Penelope thought they were only 10 miles or so out from the town they were headed for when Vivienne came back from scouting to report that something was happening up ahead.

Which was why Larek was now crawling up a hill, cautioned to avoid being detected. At first, he thought it might be because the Ranger had found something as dangerous as (or perhaps worse than) the Pukwudgies, and he welcomed the fight; he had accumulated over 2,000 AF over the last few days, including what he had received from those teleporting monsters, and it had greatly improved his Mage Skills.

Larek Holsten
Fusionist
Healer
Level 21
Advancement Points (AP) : 9/18
Available AP to Distribute: 2
Available Aetheric Force (AF): 34

Mage Skills:
Multi-effect Fusion Focus Level 10/10 (100 AF)
Pattern Recognition Level 20/20 (200 AF)
Magical Detection Level 20/20 (200 AF)
Spellcasting Focus Level 20/20 (200 AF)
Focused Division Level 31/31 (310 AF)
Mana Control Level 32/32 (320 AF)
Fusion Level 33/33 (330 AF)
Pattern Formation Level 33/33 (330 AF)

Using his AF, he had increased his maximum *Fusion*, *Pattern Formation*, and *Mana Control* Skills twice, and his *Focused Division* Skill a single time, using 2,170 AF in the process. With a little bit of effort on his part when they stopped for the night, he was able to raise his Skills to his new maximums, but as of yet there was no tangible benefit. He remembered Grandmaster Fusionist Shinpai mentioning that most people needed to be around Level 40 in their *Fusion* Skill to be able to consistently understand Advanced Fusions, so he expected something to occur soon that would let him apply what he had learned at the Academy but hadn't been able to apply. Regardless, he had made more advancement in his stagnant Skills in the last week than he had in the previous 6 months, and he was eager to absorb more Aetheric Force from the monsters he killed.

When Larek finally reached the apex of the hill and peeked over, joined by his other groupmates as they spread along the top, he wasn't sure what he was seeing at first. Naturally, he realized he was looking at what could only be monsters that came from a Scission. The 10-foot-tall, shaggy brown-haired humanoid figures had arms that stretched down to the ground and were practically dragging their knuckles along the dirt, and their legs looked like tree trunks attached to a gigantic barrel. That was the extent of their likeness to a person, however, as their oversized heads were on flexible necks that extended at least 3 feet above their shoulders; those heads were in the vague shape of a horse or mule, with a long jawline and large nostrils. Unlike a horse, their teeth were all 3 inches long while being sharp and pointed, and a long black tongue extended out of it like a snake's, flicking back and forth as if searching for a particular scent. Lastly, their knuckle-dragging, 7-fingered paws were tipped with 2-inch claws that looked sharp from a distance.

A whisper by his side from Verne let him know what it was, because it wasn't something that he recognized for class.

"They're **Dechonabras**. They look scarier than they are dangerous," he said. "At least to *us*," he quickly added. What was funny to Larek was how much the entire group had begun seeing monsters in a different light than they had when they first set out; something like a Dechonabra, if first seen right after leaving Thanchet, would've probably had them running away, or at least being more cautious than they had been lately when fighting monsters along their route. It was probably a bad habit to rely on his Fusions so much when there were flaws in them that could lead to their deaths, but that was something they could address in the future. With half of their group starting out relatively untrained in fighting monsters, as well as Larek and his roommates being unable to actually cast a spell, they didn't have any other choice but to rely on Fusions to keep them safe.

So, it wasn't the Dechonabras that were leaving Larek confused at what he was looking at. Rather, it was the fact that they were all congregating toward a point further away from where he and his group were lying along the ridgeline of the hill, stomping toward something he couldn't see. That confusion only lasted a few seconds, however, as he saw and heard a large explosion of flames coming from somewhere ahead, which lit up one of the Dechonabras as its hair ignited like a torch, and its scream as it burned alive was ear-piercing in its volume and pitch.

"Are those people from the SIC?" he asked, a little louder than what was probably necessary, but the obvious fight going on ahead was noisy enough to drown him out.

"I only caught a glimpse of them before they started to become surrounded, but I believe so," Vivienne confirmed.

Bartholomew started to stand up. "We have to help them," he stated, before he was pulled back down by Penelope.

"What if they are looking for Larek?" she hissed.

"Be that as it may, we can't let them die. They're going to be overrun any minute." The younger Martial trainee pointed past the massive group of over 200 Dechonabras that were trying to approach where Larek thought this group of people was fighting for their lives; in the distance, past where he thought they were slowly retreating toward, was another equal-sized group of the large, shaggy-haired monsters coming up behind them. The Fusionist immediately knew that if they didn't do something to help, Bartholomew was correct; they would be overrun within minutes. The Dechonabras were relatively slow when compared to some of the monsters they'd fought lately, but it looked impossible that those people would be able to escape.

A scream of pain rang out a second later, and this time it was recognizable as coming from a person rather than one of the monsters. It was that which made the decision for the entire group, because as much as he didn't want to risk being located by his father, he couldn't in good conscience let these people die. Even if they *were* sent to find him, he was fairly confident that it wasn't their fault; even an order coming from a higher-up that was being controlled by the Gergasi still meant that any searchers were being influenced by the powerful slavers – in a roundabout way, at least.

They'd deal with that if it came to that, but Larek hoped that he wouldn't be forced to kill them all so soon after saving their lives. Just the thought of needing to do that curdled his stomach, but he knew he would do it if it was necessary to ensure the safety of himself and his friends.

"We're helping," he announced, before he slid his bag off his back. Reaching inside one of the interior pockets, he pulled out a ring and slipped it on one of his left-hand fingers. While he couldn't sense the ring doing anything in particular, his experiments with the *Perceptive Misdirection* Fusion that Shinpai had placed on it proved that anyone seeing him would think he was about a foot shorter than he really was. It was still tall, but not "freakishly" tall like he normally was, and the Fusion even slightly altered where it sounded like his voice was coming from, so that it didn't sound like his words were coming from above his head. As his Professor had warned, it wouldn't hold up to any physical contact, and to those who knew how tall he really was, the results were a bit less than stellar – as if they could force their minds to see the real Larek. Regardless of those limitations, it was time to see if it worked for real when facing strangers, which was something he hadn't been able to test yet. It would be good to know if it worked so that he could go into a town or city without being singled out immediately because of his height.

"Let's go."

With his axe in his right hand and his staff in his left, Larek charged over top of the hill and got ready to go fight yet another horde of monsters. The altruistic goal of saving the SIC members about to be overrun was only slightly tainted by his anticipation of gaining more AF in the process of rescuing them.

However, what worried him a little more than that was the excitement he felt when getting ready to face the monsters ahead of him, something that he had previously vowed to himself to avoid whenever possible. Was this change in his attitude toward fighting and monsters a good thing... or a sign that his Gergasi blood was altering him in ways he couldn't anticipate?

No matter what it was, it wasn't something he wanted to think about right now. All he wanted to focus on was crashing the party down below and introducing his best friend to some new victims.

Chapter 31

Karley stumbled backwards as she was pushed out of the way, the Smasher that had saved her life raising the haft of the oversized warhammer in front of him to block the strike. Even with Barlin's prodigious strength, he was pushed back a step, and his weapon looked to have been bent slightly out of shape where it had been hit – despite the *Strengthen Steel +2* Fusion she had placed on it the day before. Even her best work with Fusions hadn't been enough to make it completely invulnerable to the strength of the Dechonabras, unfortunately.

"We've got to run! They're too strong!"

The Elementalist turned her head toward their Combat Healer, who flung out yet another spell when his Mana regenerated, the *Air Blade* cutting through half of one the large, hairy monster's legs nearby. While it stumbled and fell to a knee, it wasn't out of the fight yet, as it simply crawled forward and used its long arms to reach out toward Deivin; thankfully, the Healer was able to move out of range easily enough, but they were running out of room.

Quickly checking a portion of her Status, Karley saw that she also had regenerated enough Mana for another *Pyroblast*.

Karley Pastare

Elementalist
Healer
Level 25
Advancement Points (AP) : 4/20
Available AP to Distribute: 0

Mana: 152/1650

Intellect: 150 [165]
Acuity: 120 [144]
Pneuma: 50
Pattern Cohesion: 50/50

Mage Skills:
Fusion Level 15
Pattern Formation Level 60
Pattern Recognition Level 60

Magical Detection Level 60
Spellcasting Focus Level 61
Mana Control Level 62

*I'm glad I took the time to create that **Acuity Boost +2** Fusion on my staff last week; Fusions were never my expertise, and the additional Mana regeneration is the only thing keeping us alive. If we manage to survive these things, I'm going to see if there are any Fusionists back in Whittleton who can make +3 **Boosts** for me. It would be worth the extra cost—*

"They're closing in from behind! How are there so many of them?"

Even as she began preparing the spell pattern for another *Pyroblast*, which would consume 150 of her Mana once she cast it – and that was with the bonuses to Mana Cost that came with her Elementalist Specialization after it merged her Pyromancer, Aquamancer, Geomancer, and Aeromancer Specializations – Karley glanced behind her to see what Rhylla was talking about. The Silent Blade had better vision than she did, thanks to one of her Battle Arts that focused on improving her visual and auditory senses, but the line of Dechonabras enclosing them in was visible even to the Elementalist.

Crap.

It was at that moment that she knew they wouldn't make it out alive. Or, at least, everyone but Rhylla wouldn't make it because they were all exhausted, but the Silent Blade was fast and agile enough despite her exhaustion that she would easily be able to flee. As for Karley, Barlin, Deivin, and Zorey, their Defender, even if they had the strength and endurance to see it through, they wouldn't be able to escape before they were surrounded.

I knew this was a bad idea, but no, Zorey had to save the other SIC group in trouble. Now look where we are; those from the other group are dead, and we're just about to join them.

It should've been an easy patrol through the main road leading west out of Whittleton, but Rhylla reported that she'd heard fighting off to the south and away from their path. It went against their orders to stray too far from the road, as they didn't have nearly enough people to clear every acre of land around the town's exterior, but Zorey was one of those Nobles that took his position seriously and considered everyone's safety to be *his* responsibility. As a result, his role as leader of their group had them venture off the road and investigate this fighting that was nearby.

It turned out to be Swanek's group who had stumbled across a horde of **Harvest Voles**, the 2-foot-long, mouse-like monsters that were more of a nuisance than a threat when seen in a Scission. Of course, they became more than a nuisance when they appeared in their *thousands*, which was soon proven to be too much for Swanek and his group of SIC personnel. When Karley and her group arrived, their fellows had been in the process of falling back to the road, but they were cut off by the sudden movements of the Vole horde.

Only Swanek and one of his groupmates were still up by that time, the others having been taken down at some point. It was a losing battle, but Zorey was nothing but altruistic in his zeal for protecting his people, even if Swanek was a bit of an oaf with manners fit for a pig. Which was why one of his quiet nicknames in the SIC barracks had been "Swine-ek", because his piggishness was well known to everyone.

Regardless, they pushed ahead with their rescue, and the abrupt arrival of a fresh team of Mages and Martials was exactly what was needed. Within minutes, they had whittled down the Harvest Voles to under 100, though Swanek's last groupmate had fallen, and he was barely able to stand on his own feet by that point. Deivin was able to heal him up once they finally finished off the rest of the monsters, but that was, unfortunately, when disaster struck. Or more precisely, that was when the Dechonabras appeared out of seemingly nowhere and attacked them.

Swanek, for all that he was a pig, valiantly stood his ground while Karley and her group were able to retreat into a better position, allowing their Mana and Stama to regenerate. They *should've* run at that point, but Zorey couldn't abide allowing Swanek's sacrifice to be in vain and had them hold the line. His reasoning was that they were out patrolling to eliminate monsters and keep the roads safe, so they might as well ensure that the Dechonabras didn't endanger the local population.

It was a stupid reason, in her opinion, but she couldn't deny that it needed to be done. Preferably with a larger group than just the 5 of them, however.

The problem was immediately obvious when the Dechonabras were proven to be tougher than any of them had imagined. Karley recognized them from her Academy days more than a decade and a half before, as Thanchet had been attacked by a Scission at one point and they were one of the monsters, but they had fallen quickly and weren't much of a threat. Granted, that was probably because they were killed from the safety of the walls and were bombarded by dozens if not a hundred different spells simultaneously, but her memory of that time made them out to be weak.

The reality was that they were anything but weak. Their attacks were powerful, both their long-limbed strikes and in-close bites, and their hairy skin was slightly resistant to elemental magic and weapons; fire worked well enough, as had been proven by her *Pyroblasts*, as well as some air-based spells, but anything in her repertoire from water and earth was less effective. Barlin's warhammer could break bones whenever he struck, but the monsters were resilient enough that even a few broken bones couldn't keep them from advancing. Zorey's sword was able to cut through the hair and into the flesh beneath, but where he was typically strong enough to lop off limbs with a simple strike, the same feat required an application of Stama to accomplish the same effect, and the Defender was as limited in his Stama expenditure as Karley was.

Rhylla was the only one able to move freely around the relatively slow Dechonabras without fear, but her knives were limited in the damage they could do, even when empowered by a Battle Art. Nevertheless, her strikes were able to hamstring dozens of the monsters, allowing them to maintain a slow retreat as they defended themselves, but that appeared to be coming to an end with more of the Dechonabras coming up behind them.

"Zorey! Rhylla needs to escape and let the others know about this threat!" Karley shouted at the Defender as he blocked another attack with his shield. Unlike Barlin, who had taken a step back upon his block, the powerful Martial was able to deflect the blow with ease without moving; nevertheless, she could tell that it affected him by the way he was moving slower every minute, as even his high Strength and Body stats weren't enough to keep him upright forever.

"No! I'm not going to leave you," the Silent Blade said, even as she zipped ahead of Karley and hamstrung yet another Dechonabra that was encroaching upon her side. The monster stumbled and struck out wildly, its long arms undulating unpredictably. An outflung fist suddenly struck Rhylla as she backed up, clipping her on the side of her right leg, sending her flying. Karley heard the tell-tale snap of a broken bone as soon as the impact happened, and she knew the Silent Blade would have some issues fleeing now that she likely had a broken leg.

"Give me a few minutes for my Mana to regenerate, and I can heal that!" Deivin said, having seen and heard the same thing as the Elementalist, and he crouched by where the Silent Blade had landed in a heap, groaning in pain.

We're not going to have a few minutes at this rate.

With one of their group members down, a second looking after her, and with Kayley nearly out of Mana once she finished her *Pyroblast*, which happened a second later and luckily killed 5 of the nearby monsters and lit another half-dozen on fire, their defense was down to a Defender and a Smasher. While both of them were strong and resilient, neither of them was very fast; it was only a matter of time before a few of the Dechonabras made it through their defense and attacked those behind. She thought that her regeneration would allow her to cast a few more significant spells before the end, but it wouldn't be nearly enough.

Despair was beginning to set in as she watched her groupmates kill or injure another two-dozen of the monsters that got close to them, but there were seemingly countless more right behind them. Looking back, she estimated that they had another minute or so before those coming from behind completely encircled them, and by that point it would be all over.

Damn you, Zorey, and your need to be a hero.

She knew it wasn't fair to blame him like that, as she could've objected and the others would've listened, given that she had seniority in the group, but she hadn't. It was only because the others were Nobles that she didn't take on the role of a leader, as she had never become entirely comfortable ordering them around, even if the SIC professed not to regard things like Noble rank all that much, but in practice this was far from the truth. Thankfully, she never got too involved with Corps politics and kept her head down most of the time, so it hadn't really affected her... until now.

Karley was about to start casting a swath of low-Mana Cost spells, such as dozens of simple *Fireballs*, as a last resort – even though she knew they weren't terribly effective against the Dechonabras – but after she formed the spell pattern for the first one, filled it with Mana, and then sent it flying into the head of one of the monsters, she paused. It wasn't because the Dechonabra she was targeting somehow dodged most of the spell at the last moment by moving its head, which left scorch marks on its neck but not much else, but because she felt something she wasn't expecting.

Someone was using magic nearby. Despite her *Magical Detection* Skill stuck at 60, a common bottleneck that she had barely broken through with her *Spellcasting Focus* and *Mana Control* Skills, it was still powerful enough to detect Mana being used within 360 feet. Looking at Deivin, she could tell that it hadn't come from him as he protectively hovered over the broken-legged Rhylla; instead, she had a strange sense that it was coming from *behind* the Dechonabras that were attacking them from the front.

"Someone is here!" she shouted, her words temporarily startling the others. Fortunately, they were stalwart enough in their defense that they didn't falter for a moment. "They're casting spells from the southwest," she explained.

"I don't feel anything," Deivin said, but he didn't naysay her. He knew that she was a higher Level than any of the others, and that came with higher-Level Skills, such as *Magical Detection*.

"We just need to hold on a little bit longer!" she added, before casting yet more spells as her Mana gradually regenerated.

That was, of course, easier said than done, considering that they were soon to be entirely surrounded, but something miraculous happened. The front line of tall, hairy monsters approaching them from the front suddenly stopped and turned around, their momentum completely canceled as it looked like they were retreating.

"What? What's going on?" Barlin asked in confusion, as the Dechonabras that were so intent on killing them all seemingly abandoned their pursuit of the group. "Are they running away?"

Karley immediately knew that this wasn't the case. They weren't fleeing, nor were they walking away randomly; instead, based on their positioning, they appeared to be heading in a single direction.

Right to where she sensed the magic being used.

Looking behind her, the monsters that were coming up to enclose them from all sides were only 50 feet away by that point. As she stared at them, they seemed to open in the middle of their line, aiming to move to either side of Karley and her group. It was almost like they were a rock in the middle of a stream, and the monstrous water was parting around them in order to reach their destination.

What is going on?

Running her left hand through her sweat-soaked, shoulder-length brown hair to move it out of her face where it had fallen forward, the Elementalist looked on with shock as their impending doom was somehow waylaid, leaving them alive despite the odds that weren't in their favor. *How is this possible?*

She'd never seen or heard of anything like this before, though venturing out from the defensive walls of a town or city to hunt down roaming monsters was still new to most in the SIC. For all she knew, this was normal... but she didn't believe that to be the case. Either way, she was determined to find out what this was all about – as long as their saviors didn't fall into the same trap that *they* had by trying to save them.

"Rest up, regenerate, and heal," Zorey said to the group as he stood in front of them, his sword and shield at the ready in case the monsters changed their minds and turned around to attack. "When we're at half our maximum, we'll lend what aid we can to those who came to help us."

As much as a part of Karley wanted to flee while they had the chance, she agreed with their leader in this case. It wasn't so much that she wanted to help those who had come to rescue her group; it was that she wanted to know *how* they had done so. *Is it some sort of area-wide taunting Martial ability? A spell designed to catch the attention of any monsters within a certain area?* She didn't know, exactly, but she was determined to find out.

Chapter 32

It took a few minutes for Karley and the rest of the group to regenerate enough of their Mana and Stama to be ready to go, or at least for most of them.

"This is going to take a bit longer than I thought," Deivin explained, looking down at the mess that was Rhylla's leg. "Her Body Regeneration has already stabilized her, but there's more damage to her limb than just a broken bone."

"Hey, I'm right here! Stop talking about me as if I can't hear you," the Silent Blade snarled, the pain causing her to lash out. Thankfully, it was only a verbal lashing and not one with her knives, which would've been a bit more serious to the Combat Healer.

Deivin ignored her. "Regardless, it's going to take at least 15 minutes or longer to get her to the point where she can be moved without making things worse, and that's if I devote all my regenerating Mana into her healing."

As a Combat Healer Specialization, Karley knew that he had split his focus between offensive spells and healing spells, which meant that he wasn't the best at either of them. Most of the time, that didn't matter, because having the versatility to swap between roles was more beneficial than having a dedicated healer, but it was times like this that she wished he had picked one or the other. In this case, being a full Healer Specialization of some kind would've been better, but that also would've made Deivin less useful when fighting for their lives a short time ago.

"Stay here and work on her, then; we're moving ahead to see what we can do to help," Zorey announced. "If you see them coming back... *run*. Leave her if you can't carry her, but don't stop until you're back at Whittleton."

The Combat Healer nodded along with the Silent Blade, who agreed with the assessment. If she had been dedicated to staying before, even when it seemed like it was the end for everyone else, that resolve had only deepened when their only healer was staying behind to help her. Granted, Karley could use a few simple healing spells, the three that were necessary to gain the Healer Specialization, but that was only really useful for minor wounds and lesser injuries. Healing spells had never been her focus, and she only knew them because they were required to graduate from Copperleaf.

Returning her attention to the matter at hand, Karley looked at the field of dead Dechonabras that she and her group had left behind when they were slowly retreating from the horde of tall, furry monsters, but past them were at least a hundred more congregating around something in the distance. She could still feel the use of magic coming from where they were heading toward, and she could only assume that they were still alive; for how long, though, she wasn't sure. Unless they had a full assault group of 20, a standard that had come about due to the changing situation with the Scissions to deal with the threat of larger or more dangerous monster hordes, they were done for.

She couldn't help but wonder who they were, though, because she wasn't aware of any other patrols out this way other than Swanek that day, and a town like Whittleton didn't boast more than 60 SIC members in the first place. They had one dedicated assault group that was stationed in town and was able to respond to any of the larger threats nearby, while the other 8 patrolling groups of 5 were sent out on a rotational schedule to keep the roads clear. As a result, no one should be out here... unless they somehow got word of her group's plight and came to help, but then they likely wouldn't have been coming from the southwest.

Whoever it was seemed to be holding their own as Karley, along with Zorey and Barlin, rushed ahead to help thin out the numbers attacking their saviors. As soon as she was close enough, the Elementalist cast a *Pyroblast* that killed 5 of the monsters and set another half-dozen on fire; she was lucky that they were bunched up together as they worked against each other to reach their target ahead, and she capitalized on their impatience. The two Martials braced themselves for the anticipated counterattack from her spell, as causing that amount of death – along with those actively burning – was more than enough to force their attention onto the one that was death-dealing.

The two armored SIC members of her group stood there awkwardly when the monsters completely ignored the source of the devastating attack.

"What the—?" Barlin said, scratching his head at the sight.

"I've got no idea," her group leader said, before calling back to her. "Hit 'em again!"

She wasn't going to argue, especially since they didn't seem to be reacting to her spellcasting. Another *Pyroblast* exploded along the edge of the horde, tearing through another 4 of the Dechonabras and lighting another 5 on fire. Those that were on fire from her current and previous spell wouldn't necessarily die straight-out from the burning flames, but they would be injured severely and potentially crippled as their hair was burnt off – making them easy targets for the Martials to finish off.

Which was exactly what Zorey and Barlin did as soon as they saw that her spell garnered absolutely nothing as far as retaliation went. Cautiously, they approached the back line of monsters and attacked those that were still burning. It was only when they were within striking distance that their victims turned around and attempted to attack the two Martials, but they were already injured and were completely unsupported by any of the other monsters nearby. It was as if they were blinded by something more important to them than Karley and her group, and only when their group became extremely bothersome and in the monsters' faces did they react to it.

It was both exhilarating to be able to attack with impunity and oddly hurtful to be dismissed so thoroughly. As if they weren't worthy of any attention from blood-thirsty Scission monsters, like a new puppy that lavishes all their loving cuteness on a stranger while they were in her own house.

For the next minute or so, Karley lavishly spent her Mana, only keeping a small reserve just in case it was needed. After that minute, she went ahead and went all out as she realized that there was no need to hold anything back, because there were fewer than 30 of the Dechonabras alive – and they were being massacred by whoever had come to help them.

She caught her first glimpse of their saviors through the mass of bodies, and they were barely able to be seen over the mounds of corpses that had built up like a wall of fur, flesh, and blood that made their previous fight against the monsters seem like a friendly bout between enemies. Karley had seen a lot of death over the years, but the amount of carnage concentrated in one place sickened and confused her a little. The reason for that?

Because it was created by a group of what appeared to be 8 individuals, all of them young enough to still be at an Academy or Fort, with not just one, but *three* wearing the grey robes that marked them as early-year students who hadn't chosen a Specialization yet. As the numbers of monsters thinned out even further, she began to get a better look at them when she stopped casting her own spells in fear that she might hit one of them, and even Zorey and Barlin backed off when it was obvious they weren't needed.

Along the back line of the team that had saved Karley and her group appeared to be a Pyromancer from the Kingdom in his tell-tale red robe, young enough that she thought he might be a fifth- or possibly sixth-year student. Next to him was a young woman with reddish-gold hair that he recognized as being from Tyrendel, a land to the east of the Kingdom. *Or was it west?* She hadn't seen one from that land in a long time, as they were rare in the SIC, and she couldn't recall the exact details from her days at the Academy. What was even stranger was that there were *two* of these individuals from Tyrendel, as there was a young boy in a grey student robe standing next to the woman in a green Naturalist robe, and they looked enough alike that Karley suspected they were siblings.

Further adding to the strangeness of the group was another young boy in student grey, but this one was from... *the Dyran Hearthwood?* She thought that was what his appearance indicated, as he looked like a young tree come to life – and not one of the deadly Treedins that spawned from a Scission, either. She'd never met anyone from the Hearthwood before, but she at least remembered the description from her Academy days.

On the opposite side of the back line from the Pyromancer was a Martial woman in dark leathers, holding a bow that was delivering death to the Dechonabras by the second. From the Kingdom by her appearance, she and the Pyromancer were probably the most "normal" of the bunch, though the other Martial on the front line was similar. Younger than she would expect of someone fighting against monsters outside of a training stint on the walls of a Fort city, the shield and spear-wielding Martial was somehow holding his own against the much larger monsters, and he didn't even seem to be injured despite taking multiple hits on his shield – though those hits just seemed to slide off half the time rather than impact its wood and steel construction. She'd have to ask Zorey later if that was some sort of Battle Art she hadn't heard of, because it was highly unusual.

Opposite the young man with the shield and spear was a woman with blue hair and dark skin – and she had no idea where she was from. Never having seen anyone with that hair and skin coloring before, she suspected the woman was from a southern land, but couldn't exactly be sure; if she had learned about her homeland at the Academy, it had slipped out of her mind at some point. Regardless, the woman was wielding her oversized sword like it weighed nothing and was purely an extension of her body, as it cut through the approaching Dechonabras with an ease that was hard to believe.

But the *strangest* person of all was the one that caught her attention immediately. It wasn't his height, even though 6 feet was certainly tall, or his large, intimidating frame that made even Barlin look like an adolescent. No, it was none of that, even if it was unusual.

It was the fact that the large man was wearing a grey Academy robe and was dual-wielding a Mage's staff and what appeared to be some sort of woodcutting axe.

Her mind screeched to a halt at the purest form of discrepancy she had ever seen, especially when she saw him tearing through the monsters ahead of him with a swipe or chop of his axe, taking off limbs like he was trimming the branches off a fallen tree, only to back up a step and launch what appeared to be an overcharged *Stone Fist* spell at another Dechonabra without any sign of him forming a spell pattern. In fact, it wasn't just him that was casting spells that quickly, but the four Mages in the back were also doing the same, launching *Fireballs* or *Ice Spikes* that were larger than they should be, and she thought she even saw a *Water Jet* a few times. That was *in addition* to some larger spells being used, such as a *Flame Wall* blocking off the edge of the approaching line, or what she suspected were *Binding Roots* temporarily halting the advance of a few others.

It might have been the exhaustion of the day kicking in, but at one point she swore she even saw the young Martial with the shield flip his spear around and launch an *Ice Spike* from the end, before flipping it back around and stabbing his target with the spearhead. *Impossible. I must be hallucinating.*

When it seemed things couldn't get any stranger, the Dechonabras all seemed to be striving to reach the large student Mage wielding a staff and a woodcutter's axe, though she could only tell that because the piles of corpses were thicker around him. She couldn't understand why they were so engrossed in reaching the strange grey-robed Mage, though she thought that he was perhaps using a new spell that drew their attention to him? But why would he do something like that as a Mage?

Being able to defend oneself when out of Mana wasn't a new concept, and Karley had met a few that had taken a fancy to lugging around a sword or even a spear in replacement to a Mage's staff, though they were never quite as good with the weapons as even a second-year Fort trainee. They just didn't have the training and stats to pull off what was needed to wield them effectively, though she had to admit that being able to defend herself with something other than what was effectively a large stick sounded better than dying soon after she ran out of Mana. That was proven just a short time ago when it appeared as though their entire group was going to die and she was virtually defenseless.

But actually being strong enough to stand on the front lines as a Mage? It wasn't just unlikely, it was suicidal. Yet, somehow, this man had done it – and she was intrigued to find out how and *why*.

As the last Dechonabra fell with a barrage of spell projectiles through its face, the silence that fell over the corpse-filled and blood-soaked battlefield as the two groups stared at each other was heavy, especially when she realized that the three front-line members of the other group didn't appear to be injured in the slightest or even exhausted from the fight. Naturally, their breathing was a little hard because they had just fought hundreds of the powerful Dechonabras, but there was no visible sign other than splatters of blood over their robes and armor that seemed less than it should've been, considering the complete carnage around them.

"Hello!" the large, robed man suddenly spoke, his loud, deep voice startling Karley and her groupmates. "We thought you might need some help, and seeing that we were just passing through, it was easy enough to step in. I hope that was alright?" he asked, seemingly unsure of himself. "If not, then we apologize."

Karley was at a loss for words; the pure fighting aura that the tall man had practically exuded during the battle against the Dechonabras was gone, replaced by an expression that she could only place as shy and containing a clear lack of confidence.

Thankfully, she wasn't the leader and didn't need to respond, so Zorey took the initiative. "Well met! We certainly did need your help, I won't deny, as we were in danger of being overrun," the Defender said, before slumping slightly in place as the exhaustion of the last hour caught up with him. "If you hadn't arrived, I'm not sure that we would've survived; it was fortuitous that you arrived when you did. Though, like us, you were a little late to save Swanek's patrol, though we valiantly attempted to extricate them from their predicament. Were you sent by Major Proach out of Whittleton?"

Karley nearly said something, but held her tongue. There was no Major Proach or anyone by that name in Whittleton, so she suspected that Zorey was playing one of his stupid "Noble" games with these people. She was tempted to tell her group leader to leave them alone, as they had just saved their lives, but didn't want to get on his bad side. *Keep your head down and just do your job*, she thought to herself.

It wasn't the man that answered this time, but the young Martial wielding the sword and spear. Stepping forward, he put the butt of the spear on the ground and leaned against it casually. "No, we're coming from Dracefell via a stopover in Thanchet. We were forced to flee so that we could finish our *mission* when a Scission opened up in the middle of the Fort there – have you heard about that yet?"

What? A Scission opened in the middle of Copperleaf and Pinevalley?

"Seriously? The way things are going, it wouldn't surprise me if these things started opening up in the capital any day now. Thankfully, that's where the *greatest* of us are located, so there shouldn't be any problem, right? I just wish things would settle down and we could go back to how it used to be."

The Elementalist was now thoroughly lost, as it seemed as if Zorey was talking nonsense now. He should be freaking out – like she was – over the news that a Scission opened in the middle of a city like Thanchet, as it was one of the largest cities in the southern part of the Kingdom and was responsible for holding things together throughout the increasingly more dangerous countryside.

"I agree, but we can only do as we're *told*, right? Anyway, are any of you injured? We could definitely use an escort to Whittleton so that we can resupply, after having to leave Thanchet more quickly than expected, and we want to move quickly. We can quickly heal anyone that needs it."

Karley's group leader nodded. "Yes, one of our number suffered a nasty break, though our healer should hopefully be finishing up within a few minutes."

The tall man suddenly reached into the bag that she just realized was on his back the entire time he had been fighting, and after a second, he withdrew something that was swallowed up by his huge hand. A second later, he tossed something toward Karley and she instinctively moved to grab it, seeing that it appeared to be some sort of wooden bracelet. "That has one of those new healing Fusions on it that are designed for Martials. That will fix your injured group mate quickly once it is activated, but don't let it stay active for—"

"—too long, I understand. This is... thank you," the Elementalist said, before running back to Rhylla and Deivin. Having to dodge around the furry mounds on her way back to them, she couldn't help but look down at the open circle of wood in her hand, her awe at actually holding one of the powerful Fusions she'd only heard about nearly making her trip when she wasn't watching where she was going.

It was only a few months ago that she had heard about a new healing Fusion that some insanely powerful Fusionist had come up with, but she never thought she would see one. A high-Level group of SIC members had passed through the month before, boasting about possessing not only one of these Fusions, but also an impossibly strong stat Boost Fusion on their weapon; but they were gone before she'd gotten a chance to see either of them. From all the reports she heard, they were extremely difficult to get because not only were they in short supply, but they also cost hundreds of gold apiece. Even after saving her pay for years, that kind of thing was too expensive for someone like her.

Before she knew it, she was approaching the wounded Rhylla and their Combat Healer, who had made some progress on the Silent Blade, but Karley could tell he would need at least another 10 minutes. It appeared as though the unfortunate Martial's leg bone had shattered and she'd torn up her upper thigh as the bone shards pierced through it upon impact with the ground, which was a bit more serious than just a broken bone.

"You can stop, Deivin," she said, kneeling down next to the panting Martial. Deivin was forgoing any type of pain relief as he worked as quickly as he could to get her healed and up so she could move, so she was having to endure the additional pain that his healing generated as she was put back together.

"What? Why?" he asked, letting his spell go.

Instead of answering, she gave the wooden circle with the Fusion on it to Rhylla and told her to activate it. Instead of arguing, the Silent Blade did as instructed as the Elementalist and Combat Healer looked on.

"Is that—?"

"Yes."

That was all that needed to be said as they saw the effect from the Fusion in action. Within seconds, her leg had finished up sealing all of the external signs of damage, and as the Silent Blade cried out at the intense spike of pain that ripped through her as her leg bone rearranged itself and fused back together, Karley could also see the smile on the woman's face. In less than 15 seconds, she was as good as new, if it wasn't for the blood still painting her upper thigh and the ripped leather of her armor.

Deactivating the Fusion a few seconds later, the Silent Blade sat up and swayed a little, but offered up the wooden bracelet back to Karley. Before she could take it, Deivin snatched it up and stared at it with awe on his face. She couldn't blame him, because she felt the same way. It was one thing to hear about something like this; it was entirely different seeing it herself.

It wasn't long until she heard noises from behind them, and as she turned around she saw the rest of her group and the newcomers heading her way. Getting to her feet, she was going to help Rhylla up, but the Martial got to her feet just fine – if a little wobbly. Healing can take a lot out of a person, even if it was from a Fusion, she noted.

"Is she good? Alright, let's head out," Zorey announced, and she fell in behind the group, bringing up the rear with Rhylla and Deivin by her side. As she watched the others move ahead of them, she couldn't help but look closer at them, and found that her earlier assessment was fairly accurate. In other words, they were *young*; a few of them looked like they might be recent graduates, but the others should still be at an Academy or a Fort. She knew that she wasn't the only one looking at them, as her groupmates were also checking them out as they walked behind, but Zorey acted as if everything was normal with them.

Is it just because he is grateful for their help and doesn't care how strange their group is? Or is it something else?

The mystery was eating her up inside, and she nearly started asking questions, but again, she held her tongue. She figured they would find out more once they got back to Whittleton, and after the day they had, she was more than looking forward to getting behind the town's walls, where she could feel a measure of safety that had been absent over the last few hours.

Chapter 33

Larek wasn't sure what game Bartholomew was playing, but a subtle wink aimed at him calmed the Fusionist down a little after he heard the Noble's words to the strangers. As the others were playing along with the explanation of their presence, something they probably should've talked about before this point, he did the same – but he was still worried that the Martial trainee had revealed too much.

It wasn't until he got close to the shield-wielding stranger in his full suit of plate armor that he realized that the man was also a Noble; it was at that point that some things started to click together in his mind. The two of them were saying things that seemed just a little off to Larek, but now he could only assume that they were meaning more than they actually said. He was reminded of his time at Crystalview and the reasoning he was given that led to his participation in the Skirmish; while it had ultimately been so that the Dean could officially announce his abilities to everyone, the excuses he had been told were that the Nobles and their intrigue would eventually figure out that he had secrets that he wanted to hide, and that he was getting preferential treatment because of that. At the time, it sounded a bit contrived, but now he couldn't help but think there was some truth to it.

Regardless, he tried to stay calm as he walked amongst his group, which was now surrounded by the strangers as they walked over a series of hills, before coming to a road. The sight of the dirt path nearly made him miss a step as they, as a group, had been avoiding it since they left Thanchet, but now they were deliberately traveling along it. It would be impossible to hide their presence now, especially after they had saved these people, and he could only hope that they didn't recognize him.

Fortunately, their surprise at hearing about Thanchet and what happened there seemed genuine, and other than some overly curious glances his way, the illusion on his ring seemed to be working properly. That made him feel a little bit better about the situation they found themselves in, but he was still on his guard.

As soon as they set foot on the road and were able to travel a little faster over the cleared path, he finally looked at his notifications and his Status to see what he had gained from the last fight.

Axe Handling *has reached Level 83!*

Dodge *has reached Level 10!*

  Not too much in the way of Skills, but he did end up receiving 882 AF to put toward increasing his maximum Skill Levels. As far as he could tell, he obtained 9 AF per kill, and he had apparently killed 98 of the Dechonabras; he would've liked to have killed more, but the entire group had participated in the fight so that they would be able to save the people that were on the verge of being overrun.

  Of course, their sudden attack on the rear flank of the monster horde had worked better than anyone had expected, as it caused every single Dechonabra to turn toward him – and completely ignore those they were trying to kill just seconds before. Their hatred for one of his "kind" served a purpose, even if it was unintentional.

  No one but Bartholomew and the Noble SIC member spoke on their way back to the town of Whittleton at first, but what they were saying just sounded like inane small talk to Larek. Feeling a gaze on him from behind, he glanced back to see one of the Mages they had rescued from the Dechonabras staring at him. She was obviously from the Kingdom based on her appearance, but she looked older than the others in her group; if he had to guess, she might be around age 30 while the others were likely in their early 20s, though he could be wrong. He wasn't the best judge of a person's age, but that was the impression he got – and her robe indicated that she was relatively powerful as it was one that he'd only seen once or twice.

  Thinking about his Specializations class, he looked at her dark blue robe and asked, "Elementalist?"

  His voice seemed to startle her, and she nearly fell flat on her face, but the Martial walking next to her caught the woman before she could faceplant. He began to apologize, but he was interrupted before he could even open his mouth as she snatched his *Healing Surge* Anklet from the healer on her other side, who had been staring at the Fusion on it with apparent fascination.

  "Hey! I was looking at—"

  "Here!" the Mage said, holding the anklet out to him. "Thank you for letting us borrow this; it worked remarkably well."

  "And *I* was studying it to see how it worked—"

  "Ignore him, he doesn't know what he's talking about. Here," she said again, practically shoving it at him.

  He just shrugged and said, "Keep it." It didn't really matter to him if they kept it, since he already had the same Fusion on his robe. He'd only kept it just in case something happened that prevented their clothing-based Fusions from working, but he could always make another on something else. It sounded like they needed it, especially if they continued to encounter hordes of monsters like they had that day.

"What? No, we couldn't possibly afford—"

Next to him, Nedira walked backwards as she chuckled and smiled at the protesting woman. "Don't worry, we won't need it, and I think the one who made it would prefer it be used by those who do. What's your name?"

"Karley."

"Well then, Karley, treat it well and don't sell it, because it could save your lives one day. It will technically work for you, too, but if you're heavily injured, it will send you into a coma for a few days until your body recovers. It's made for Martials, but let me see if I can *find* you one that will work for anyone once we get to town," she said.

When Nedira stressed the word "find," she tapped Larek on the shoulder. He immediately understood what she meant by that. He nodded imperceptibly as he thought about what he could use to put some *Graduated Parahealing* Fusions on once they got to town. He hoped they had something he could purchase, because the best he could do right now was use a rock or a stick. *I suppose a gold or platinum coin would work, but I would think those would be better serving as their original purpose.*

Why she wanted him to make Fusions for the woman was something that it took the rest of the walk to the town for him to figure out, but he quickly discovered that Nedira was doing the same thing that Bartholomew was doing: Becoming friendly with the local SIC population so that they wouldn't be too suspicious of their presence in the town. When Verne and Norde joined in on the conversation Norde's sister was having not only with the Elementalist – if that was, indeed, her Specialization – but the healer and the Martial who had been injured with the broken leg, he could see the strangers becoming more comfortable around his group. Even Penelope and Vivienne were joking along with the Martial with the big warhammer slung across his shoulders, though their laughter was subdued for some reason.

Larek suddenly remembered the mention of another group of SIC members having been killed just before they arrived and figured that was it. He thought it was actually insensitive for them to have left their bodies behind, but no one mentioned it on their entire journey.

Not that he had anyone to ask, because no one was talking with him as they moved along the road. He somewhat envied the ease with which the others seemed to be able to speak with complete strangers about seemingly nothing at all. Social interactions were something that he'd gotten better at over the last year, but he was still a little uncomfortable speaking with complete strangers. Halfway to the town, at least according to their temporary traveling companions, he realized that he didn't feel as awkward as he usually did around people he didn't know as he began to interject small tidbits into the conversation behind him – and for one giant reason.

Or, more accurately, *not so giant* reason: None of them were looking at him like he was a tall freak. The normal reserve that plagued him whenever meeting anyone new, causing him to keep his defenses up, had nearly dissolved when not a single one of them looked at him with anything other than curiosity, with not even a hint of disgust or anger – especially those from the Kingdom. Even with most of the Kingdom's veteran SIC members he'd met, who had better than average reactions to the sight of him, there was always at least *some* negative reaction, even if they dismissed it soon after; but with these people, there was nothing.

It was… refreshing. Liberating, even. Sure, it was probably because he was wearing a veritable "mask" disguising his most prominent feature, but he suddenly felt freer than he had in a long, long time.

"What was that spell you used to blow up the Dechonabras?" he asked during a lull in the conversation.

"Spell? Oh, you mean my *Pyroblast*? It's an expensive effect for the Mana Cost, but it was one of the only things that seemed to work against large numbers of those monsters," the Elementalist, Karley, replied. "Though, I have to say, it didn't look like you needed any help," she continued, looking Larek up and down. "Does that have anything to do with the fact that there are, at least what I believe to be, incredibly powerful Fusions on your robe? My *Pattern Recognition* Skill is pretty high, but even I am having difficulty making out exactly what they are. Probably because I suck at creating Fusions, but I'm usually able to recognize them fairly well."

Larek's mind froze for a moment as he debated his response. They had already discussed keeping his ability with Fusions a secret, as it would inevitably lead anyone looking for him right to his location; his notoriety at Copperleaf and the reason his father was alerted to his presence in the first place made revealing his prowess with Fusions a bad idea. But they could still hide the fact that *he* was making Fusions if they were creative about it; besides, from what the Elementalist had mentioned, it was going to be difficult to hide what he had already created.

He saw Nedira just about to answer for him when he hesitated, but he forged ahead and took the initiative. "Yes, they are what we're all using to enhance our capabilities. The Fusionist who made them wanted to ensure that we would succeed in our journey and provided an abundance of Fusions for us. As Nedira mentioned earlier, there might be a few things that we can spare to make your task easier around here, but we should really get to Whittleton before looking into such things."

There. He thought that should be a good enough explanation of why they had the Fusions, and it meshed with a little bit of what Bartholomew had told the other Noble about their need to get to Whittleton.

However, the curiosity of all their new traveling companions was piqued at the mention of Fusions, as Larek hadn't necessarily been keeping his voice low in his explanation. As a result, the Martials began pestering Penelope, Vivienne, and Bartholomew about what Fusions they possessed, while Karley and the healer were left speechless as Nedira described – in detail – the different Fusions she had on her robe and staff.

"…and apart from those powerful *Boosts*, we also have one that increases the resistance of the robe's cloth."

"Resistance to what, exactly?"

Nedira hesitated slightly before she answered. "Most things? Cutting, primarily, but it also provides nominal resistance against elemental effects, such as fire and earth-based attacks. The biggest drawback is that it cannot currently prevent impact damage, so getting punched by one of those Dechonabras, for instance, can still pulverize your bones. Luckily, we have other protections, such as a barrier that helps to deflect some of those powerful attacks, as well as a built-in healing Fusion that is made so that anyone can use them."

"That's incredible! That must have taken weeks for each robe to be created," the healer, Deivin, conjectured.

"Oh, well, something like that," Nedira said quickly.

"But how were these young students able to cast so many spells as quickly as they did?" Karley asked.

"That's easy! Fusions!" Verne answered enthusiastically. Now that Larek had set up a viable excuse to explain where the Fusions came from, his roommate was eager to show off. "Watch!" he continued, before rotating the staff he was using as a walking stick and aiming it at a tree they were passing. The next moment, an *Icy Spike* flew out from just ahead of the staff's tip, flying quickly through the air to impale itself into the trunk of the tree.

"Wait, what? How is that possible?" the two stranger Mages asked simultaneously, incredulous at the display.

"I have no idea, but here; try it out." Verne handed the staff to the Elementalist, before pointing to either end. "That one is essentially a *Fireball*, while the other is the *Ice Spike*-based one you just saw. All you have to do is aim the tip and mentally activate the Fusion on that end, and it will emerge. Just don't use it more than once every 5 seconds or so, or you'll degrade the Fusion at a faster rate."

Karley took the staff in trembling fingers and did as instructed, and everyone had stopped their march along the road at that point to watch. The Elementalist held up the staff and attempted to aim it, but was shaking too much to be very accurate; to top it off, she had also chosen to use the *Flaming Ball* Fusion, so when she activated it, the ball of flames shot out at an angle, completely missing the tree and ascending into the air above its branches, before harmlessly dissipating after reaching a certain distance. The sudden eruption of a fireball out the end of the staff caused her to squeak in surprise and drop the wooden stick, and she began to apologize profusely.

"I'm so sorry, I just wasn't expecting—"

Verne just chuckled as he quickly bent over and picked up the staff. "Don't worry about it; it also has a strong *Strengthening* Fusion on it, so it won't get damaged easily."

"How long can you use it? When will it start to become non-functional?" the healer suddenly asked, his eyes stuck to the staff like they were glued to it. Larek got the impression that he was looking at it not as if he was planning on stealing it, but more out of curiosity and the need for knowledge, just as he had been looking at the *Healing Surge* Anklet earlier.

Larek answered this time. "For years, as long as it isn't abused by too-frequent activations, as Verne warned about. The strong containment barriers and the Mana Overflow Bypass installed into their construction are enough to maintain the integrity of their formations for a long time."

"Are you a Fusionist, as well?" Karley asked, looking at him suspiciously.

He shrugged. "I dabble a little bit here and there," he answered non-committedly.

"I see. This is a bit overwhelming, if I'm being honest."

It was at that point that the Noble that had been walking with Bartholomew turned to the boy and asked, a bit too snootily for Larek's taste, "If *they* have such wonders, what do *you* possess?"

Larek was immediately angry at how quickly he and the others were dismissed, but a look at the other strangers' faces at the question made him realize that *they* weren't happy with it either. Nedira's hand on his arm prevented him from saying something he might regret, and he immediately tightened his grip on his anger as he saw the brief flash of disgust on the young Martial trainee's face as well. He consoled himself that Bartholomew was just playing a part right now, and that there wasn't a good reason to get on the other Noble's bad side. If they wanted to get in and out of Whittleton without causing a ruckus, then he would put up with the indignity for a little while.

"Not as much as I would've liked, but I also received all of the *Boosts* and protective measures as the others. In addition, my spear is unnaturally sharp and strong, and when I do this—" he answered, flipping his weapon around so that the butt of it was pointing at the same tree Verne had hit earlier, before an icy projectile from the Fusion on it shot out at the tree trunk, "I now have a powerful ranged attack."

To see a non-Mage essentially "casting" a spell, even if it was through a Fusion, was enough to leave the strangers speechless… for a few seconds, at least.

"I need to get me one of those," the other Noble said a bit breathlessly. "How do I contact this Fusionist?"

"You… can't, unfortunately," Bartholomew said with what sounded like deep regret in his voice. "After Copperleaf was attacked by the Scission, the Fusionist was carried off to the capital, as far as I know. I don't think I need to explain further than that."

The Noble sighed, disappointment written all over his face. "No, you do not."

"But cheer up! As already discussed, we may have some things that we can spare to make life easier for you here. We could really use a nice place to stay for the night and the ability to load up on some supplies, but I'm sure we can scrounge up a few Fusions for you."

A regular bed – even if it was undersized – sounded like heaven to Larek, and he wasn't the only one who hurried their steps as they continued their trek to Whittleton. In less time than he expected, the incognito Fusionist saw the walls of the town ahead, and relief that they had finally arrived spread throughout his entire body as he grinned at Nedira walking next to him. His smile was apparently infectious, because she returned one just as wide as his own, and he had to admit that – despite all the hardships of the last week – their travels to this point had been worth it.

But a hot meal that didn't consist of only meat from slaughtered monsters and a safe place to sleep was even better.

Chapter 34

Moving through the gates of the town, Larek could see that the stone façade of the walls wasn't very thick, as it was simply reinforced with wood behind it that created a walkway where defenders could stand. At only 12 feet high, it was one of the shorter defensive barriers that he'd seen in a town, though he had to admit that he hadn't seen very many. Those that he had seen had been in passing as he had traveled to one Academy or another, and they weren't exactly something he had paid attention to; now that he had the opportunity, he couldn't help but notice that the defenses were, for lack of a better word, scrawny.

It wasn't that he didn't think they were enough to hold off a small Scission or two, but more that they had a less permanent-looking structure than even the wall around Barrowford. Like it was half-finished and any construction after a certain point was stopped, as if it was suddenly decided that no more was needed.

Then again, he thought, *they don't really need anything stronger than this right now, do they?* With how the Scissions around the Kingdom seemed to be in a bit of flux, towns and cities were relatively safe from attack at the moment. It was only those moving around the countryside that risked running into monsters.

"How many live here at Whittleton?" Larek asked their escorts as they finished passing through the open gates, only to be bombarded by the sheer amount of noise coming from the people inside. The walled town was on top of a short hill, so it was impossible for him to see much of what was actually inside, though from outside from the spread of the walls he suspected it was a good size; now that he saw all the people, he wasn't sure what to think.

"Just under 30,000," Karley replied loudly with a sigh, shouting to be heard. "It's expanded heavily over the last few months as things started to become chaotic throughout the Kingdom, and we've had to expand the walls *twice* to accommodate the expansion. That's why things look a little unfinished around here."

"And how many SIC are stationed here?" Penelope practically had to yell the question as their progress was temporarily impeded by the press of people moving around behind the walls. From the outside, the area outside of the town looked relatively deserted to Larek, with only a few people moving around, but inside the walls was a different story altogether. Hundreds or thousands of people were moving around, pushing carts, shouting and trying to sell their wares, or even constructing one of a dozen different buildings he could see from their position. It was just as overwhelming as his experience when he arrived at Peratin on his way to Crystalview Academy; in a way, it was worse, because Peratin had room for all the people inside the city, whereas Whittleton seemed to be bursting at the seams.

"There are 60 of us—er, I suppose 55 of us, now," the Noble, whom Larek learned was named Zorey, interjected into the conversation as he took over the explanation. Thankfully, while the man had more than a little of the confidence and sense of entitlement he saw in many Nobles, he didn't have the same condescending tone when he talked to Larek and the others in his group. "Which reminds me, I need to go report Swanek and his group's unfortunate demise. Karley, if you would, please show our new friends around and find someplace for them to stay. Good luck with that," he said, murmuring that last bit under his breath as he shook his head, which Larek was just barely able to hear over the sheer cacophony of noise coming from the crowd.

As the Noble took off into the crowd, the healer and the two Martials begged off from showing the newcomers around, though that was understandable for at least two of them. The healer, Deivin, hadn't really taken his eyes off the *Healing Surge* Anklet that Larek had let them keep, and the Fusionist had the impression that the man wanted to go somewhere to be alone with it and not be disturbed. The Martial who'd had her leg mangled was still looking quite peckish and exhausted from her healing, and Larek could tell that she just wanted to eat a whole bunch of food and then pass out somewhere comfortable. As for the warhammer-wielding Martial, he just looked like he had hit his limit with socialization for the day and didn't want to be saddled with the newcomers, so was more than happy to be able to escape that kind of responsibility.

"I guess that leaves just me, then," the Elementalist said with a shrug. "Come on, let me show you around."

It took approximately 10 minutes to get through the crowd of people, 99% of them from the Kingdom with only a bare handful having the appearance of someone from a different land, until they were moving through cramped alleyways where the noise wasn't nearly as bad as it was near the entrance. Penelope spoke with their guide as they moved through the busy town.

"You only have 55 SIC members here to protect the *entire* town? How is that possible?"

The woman shook her head. "Well, it used to be 80 of us, but then again there used to only be 5,000 people living in Whittleton," she explained, hopping over a pile of unrecognizable refuse on the ground inside the alley they were passing through. "But with the expansion and the craziness of the Scissions nearby, we've lost over a quarter of our forces, and replacements are hard to come by. That, and communication feels almost nonexistent, so we don't even know when we'll be reinforced. Thankfully, trade is still coming through as we keep the roads clear, but most of the food around here is starting to shift to coming from other lands outside of the Kingdom. None of the locals want to work the land with the threat of a monster horde appearing to wipe them and their entire family out – and I can't say that I blame them."

Larek couldn't help but think that was the reason they hadn't seen anyone on the farms they passed on their way to Whittleton. It appeared as though their fields had been planted in the spring, but with fall fast approaching, there was no one available to harvest any of the crops that had been growing. He remembered hearing that the SIC had been doing everything in their power to ensure that the farms continued to operate normally, but that didn't seem to be the case everywhere. Overall, it wasn't a good situation, but it also didn't seem that this farm abandonment was happening all over the Kingdom – or else everyone was going to be in a heap of trouble. Larek was inclined to worry about it, as it might also affect his family if their regular allotment of food was disrupted, but there wasn't much he could do about it.

At least, not at the moment.

"But enough of *our* problems; here's the tour that was promised to you," the Elementalist switched her tone, affecting a more cheerful attitude. "As you saw when you arrived, the west gate is the most populous and in a constant state of construction it seems, as it was the final area after the last expansion that was to be filled. The fact is that, even when those buildings you saw being constructed are finished, we'll still be short on housing for our recent influx of people. I fear that we'll have to expand once again—but anyway, we've finally come to our Central Square! It used to be a lot more humble than this, but you can still see some of its old charm under the new construction."

Larek and his group emerged from the alleyway into a large, open area that he judged to be around 500 feet wide in a squarish configuration. There were only two main roads leading to this open area, one from the west and a second opposite of it to the east, and along the perimeter of the square were tall, 2-to-3-story buildings with a few possessing signs out front, advertising what they held within. He recognized one as an Inn, another as a General Store, one as a

Blacksmith, and the last one with a sign as the SIC Headquarters for Whittleton. Based on its size, he didn't think it was large enough to house all of the SIC members, even at their diminished capacity, so some of them must have had other accommodations in the town.

Other than these main buildings, which he assumed had been the heart of the settlement for years until the expansion happened, the rest of them he assumed were residences of some sort; all of them with clearly new construction added to what was likely previously only a single story. In the center of the Central Square was a small garden area with a few visible whitewashed wooden benches and a splashing fountain with a wide basin that looked out of place with the hordes of people wandering around, ranging from those who looked a little more well-to-do than a normal citizen of the town – reminding him angrily of the young women back at the village of Rushwood – to those who were wearing nothing but rags and had haunted expressions on their faces. No one seemed to be starving yet, at least, but there was certainly a disparity in their financial outlook.

Looking at the road that led off to the western gate where they had arrived, he wondered why they hadn't taken it instead of navigating their way through alleyways. His curiosity was sated immediately after seeing that the entire thoroughfare was full of even more people hawking their wares than were near the gate, and the crowds were equally as thick. Getting through the mass of people would be difficult to do as a group, and he was glad that they had been led around it.

"The main roads leading from either gate are filled with refugees, who have turned them into two giant marketplaces. At first, they were told to disperse as they were clogging the pathways to the gates, but after a while they refused to listen to the SIC and stayed where they were despite the threat of punishment," Karley explained, waving toward both thoroughfares. "It turned out alright, however, as we are now considered one of the premier trading hubs in the southeast, all thanks to the refugee population, which makes trade much safer for the caravans that stop here, as they can unload most of their product without having to travel toward some of the harder-to-get-to towns and cities out this way. Of course, with the reduction of our forces here, we're going to have a harder time clearing the roads out on patrol, but there's not much we can do about that until we get reinforcements."

She led them forward, heading for the inn across the Central Square. The number of people moving about was overwhelming to Larek, who hadn't seen this many people all together in a relatively small space before. Gauging how large the town actually was turned out to be a little easier from the open area of the Square, and he estimated that it was approximately a quarter of the size of the Academy and Fort back in Thanchet. If that was the case, then it had just as many people inside its walls as Copperleaf and Pinevalley, all living pretty much on top of each other.

Their guide was stopped halfway across the Square by the arrival of another SIC member who zipped through the crowd with ease and an obviously high Agility stat. From the direction of his arrival, Larek assumed that the younger Martial had come from the SIC building across the way.

"Karley! The boss wants to see you immediately," he told the Elementalist as soon as he was close enough to be heard.

"Tell her to wait; I'm showing our guests to the Waterbury," she replied, gesturing toward the Inn.

"Who? Uh... oh. Sorry, I don't know anything about them. She seemed insistent that you hurry, though."

Sighing, Karley turned to Bartholomew and then Larek, as if unsure who the leader was. "Sorry about this, but I'm going to have to leave you here." She pointed toward the Inn. "That's the Waterbury Inn, the only place that *might* have a vacancy, if only because it's expensive and most of the refugees can't afford it. As you can imagine, prices have shot up for just about everything in the town, lodging most of all. I'll try and visit at some point to see if you have what you need, but until I figure out what Mariel wants, I'm not sure when that will be." She hesitated for a moment, before adding, "Thank you again for your assistance back there against the Dechonabras. I honestly didn't think we were going to make it back alive."

"It was our pleasure," Bartholomew said, giving her a short bow before she blushed and took off toward the SIC building.

The group looked at each other before Larek shrugged, unsure what to do now. He'd never been responsible for finding lodgings, as most of his experiences with Inns had been cases when his stay was planned and paid for ahead of time.

"I've got this," Vivienne said after a few seconds, pushing ahead of the others. "I grew up helping my parents with their Inn, so I'm probably the one best suited for this." That was something that he had not known about their Ranger, which wasn't surprising since the woman didn't really speak all that much or talk about her past.

It didn't take much longer to move through the crowd toward the Inn, and while they drew the attention of many they passed, he was thankful that it still didn't seem to be because of his height; instead, it was because they were a highly unusual mix of people who were travel-stained and exhausted from their journey, and they stood out against the prevalent majority of Kingdom-born people nearby.

Ducking to avoid hitting his head on the entrance, his first sight of the inside of the Inn revealed a relatively empty common room, which wasn't what he was expecting from the crowds outside. Looking around, he noticed that the tables and chairs that comprised the majority of the furniture he saw were very well-made and polished until they gleamed, and the lighting was surprisingly bright with natural light streaming down from dozens of windows dotting the walls. There were a few private-looking booths along the left-hand wall and a long, wooden and brass-decorated bar that lined the back of the room, a couple of patrons sitting at its shiny surface as they sipped at amber-colored drinks.

Behind the bar was a large, stern-faced woman who was polishing the bartop with a greyish rag that had seen better days but was likely still clean. As soon as they entered and stood at the threshold, her polishing stopped and she pointed at them. "I told you, if you can't pay my prices, then you don't belong in *my* Inn! Get out! Get out before I call the SIC and you'll regret ever messing with me!"

The shout caused the couple of people at the bar to turn around and stare at them, and he noticed that the patrons were well-dressed and potentially Nobles of some sort based on that criteria; unfortunately, he was too far away from them to know for certain. Regardless, the attention and the angry shout made Larek shrink back and nearly turn around and leave, but Vivienne stepped forward up to the bar and slammed a gold coin down on its surface. The instant the glint of gold was visible to the woman behind the bar, her demeanor instantly changed.

"Welcome to the Waterbury Inn, travelers! Or should I say members of the SIC? Either way, what can Grenda do for you today?" The abrupt change was a bit shocking, as was the welcoming smile that transformed her face from one of a stern disciplinarian to a doting mother figure. Larek felt like his emotions went through a whiplash at differences he observed in the woman.

"We need three rooms for the night," the Ranger immediately responded.

"You're in luck! We just so happen to have exactly three rooms vacant at the moment, which is a rarity considering how full the town is at the moment. You can have them for the night for 15 gold—"

"15 gold?" Vivienne asked, shaking her head. "Does it come with personal massages and beds that feel like we're floating on clouds?

No; 1 gold for the three rooms and you'll throw in three meals and baths for everyone."

The woman, Grenda, held her hand to her chest like she'd just been wounded. "A single gold? Why don't you simply ask to stay for free while you're at it? I've got an Inn to run here, not a charity. Since you seem like nice people and you have a few younglings with you, I'll knock off a little. 12 gold and I'll throw in the meals and baths."

Vivienne stood her ground without budging. "It might not be a charity, but you're slowly going to run out of clientele because the refugees aren't going to be staying here anytime soon. You need our business, and I'm inclined to be generous to such a fine establishment. 2 gold with everything included."

The two went back and forth, arguing about the price, but all Larek could do was stare at the Ranger. This was the most he'd heard her speak at one time, even counting the time when she had pretended to assassinate him in the baths, and he was amazed at her ability to bargain with the Innkeeper. Just watching the two go at it, he thought he might end up getting an extra Level in his own *Bargaining* Skill as a result, but he didn't have much luck.

"...alright, you have a deal. 4 gold and a total of 10 of these *Illuminate* Fusions that you say you can provide; if you can't produce them, then you'll owe an additional 6 gold."

Wait... what did I miss? He could've sworn he just heard that they were trading some Fusions for their rooms.

"Not a problem," Vivienne said, before turning to Larek and beckoning him forward. "You're the expert here, what do you need to know to create those Fusions?" she asked.

He looked at the Ranger and silently conveyed to her, *Is this a good idea?* with a look.

An almost imperceptible nod made him mentally shrug. If she thought it was acceptable, being one of his bodyguards, then he supposed he didn't have any reason to worry about it. Turning to the Innkeeper, who looked at him strangely, he asked, "What would you like them on? Also, would you prefer a single illumination level or the ability to change their brightness with a touch?"

"You can do that?" the woman asked, shock clearly written all over her face and tinting her words.

"Sure. It's a relatively simple Fusion, so it won't take too long."

"Then I would want the ability to change their brightness, if I get a choice. And... can you place it on anything?"

He wavered a little bit on what to answer. "Well, not anything, but close to it."

"Can you place it on the glass chimneys on my oil lamps? They're already perfectly placed, and not worrying about changing them out would be ideal."

Larek looked around the room and saw what she was talking about. There were exactly 10 oil lamp wall sconces around the room in strategic places, providing a fairly decent amount of light to the room, but he was also used to magical lighting, so it was dimmer than he preferred. *Illumination* Fusions would probably be perfect for the space, though the entire ambience would change as the light would be steadier and constant as opposed to the burning oil that was used at the moment.

As for the glass chimneys? He'd never created a Fusion on glass before, but he didn't see why it wouldn't work. The problem with the material was that glass was, obviously, fragile and prone to breaking; he couldn't even imagine what might happen were one of them to fall off the sconce and accidentally shatter on the floor. If he was to make an adjustable illumination level Fusion, then there would probably be enough Mana inside that the shattering of the lamp chimney, and therefore the Fusion formation, would likely cause an explosion large enough to affect all the other glass in the place, setting off a chain reaction that might blow up the entire Inn.

Only one way to avoid that, I suppose. I'll just have to **Strengthen** *the glass at the same time.*

He was already planning out how to do it when he moved his attention back to the Innkeeper. "Not a problem. I'll have to take the chimneys up to our rooms to get the work done, but there really shouldn't be an issue."

"Excellent! Well then, upon payment of the gold, I have your keys ready to go; I can also have my daughter direct you to your rooms and locate the bathing rooms for you. You're welcome to come down anytime within the next 2 hours for a late lunch; otherwise, we serve dinner at 6pm." Vivienne somehow conjured the 4 gold pieces that the rooms were costing them and placed them on the bar, where they were snatched up quickly by the Innkeeper, only to be replaced by three keys, each of them with a round metal tag with a stamped number on it.

There was suddenly a young woman at their side, appearing as if from nowhere, and he could instantly tell that she looked like a much younger version of the Innkeeper, all the way to the scrunched-looking nose and slightly curved eyes. She, like her mother, was likely from the Kingdom, but they also had a slightly different set of features that made them unusual to his eyes.

"If you'll follow me, I'll show you to your rooms," the young woman said softly, in complete contrast to the loud, impactful voice of the Innkeeper, before turning on her heel and quickly treading toward a staircase around the back of the bar.

"I'll be back down for the chimneys later," Larek told the woman behind the bar, before wasting no time in joining his friends as they followed their guide. It didn't take long before they were shown to rooms 3, 4, and 5 on the second floor of the Inn.

"These are your rooms, and if you follow this hallway down to the end, you'll find a divided bathing room. There are only two bathing tubs per gender, so you'll have to take turns, but there shouldn't be any other guests using them at this time. If you have any questions or other concerns, please let myself or my mother know, and we'll be sure to help with anything you might need." The speech she gave seemed rehearsed, and she didn't even wait to see if they had any questions or concerns at that moment, as she immediately fled back downstairs, leaving the group looking at each other.

Rather than breaking apart immediately into the different rooms, Vivienne unlocked Room 3 and everyone quickly walked inside, closing the door behind the last to enter.

Nedira immediately rounded on the Ranger. "Are you crazy? What was all that about?"

That's what I would like to know.

Chapter 35

The Martial trainee simply crossed her arms and looked completely unperturbed after being practically yelled at. Nedira had kept her voice down, as they didn't need anyone listening in to their conversation, but the intent was there.

"I told you that I would handle getting us some rooms, and I did just that," Vivienne said calmly in response. "The cost in gold, by the way, is a complete rip-off and virtually on the level of highway robbery, but I knew that walking into the place. I've met Innkeepers like this before who believe their establishment should be exclusive to those with money or those who are important enough that having them stay for even a night would be a large boost to their reputation. The moment she said 15 gold for the three rooms, which is almost enough to buy this Inn in most small towns, I had a feeling she would refuse us lodging even if we paid the entire amount. I had to bargain her down to four, which was a feat in itself."

"I don't care about the gold, as we have more than enough to pay the full amount she wanted; it's the Fusions that I don't get!" Nedira complained. "Didn't you get that we're trying to downplay our connection to the Fusions that have already been seen? But now you've gone and put Larek in danger!"

Larek couldn't help but agree with Nedira, but he assumed that the Ranger had some reason for having him go along with it. He was proven right a few seconds later as Vivienne explained.

"We don't have anything to worry about. Innkeepers are greedy by nature, and anything that would give them a leg up on their competition they keep close to their chest. There is absolutely no way that she will tell *anyone* where the Fusions came from, as that would be revealing the source of something that is exclusive to her own establishment. Unless a Gergasi shows up and compels her to talk, of course, but that isn't likely. Not even a Noble could pressure her enough to fess up, even with a bribe or threat of physical violence. The Inn game can be more cutthroat than you could probably imagine, but there are a few things such as this that are fairly universal and can be relied upon if you know how the game works."

Everyone was silent for a few seconds before Nedira, a little more subdued, asked, "What about those two at the bar? Won't they blab to anyone who asks? They certainly heard our conversation."

"Those two? Naw, they were her employees. Good enough outfits that I almost didn't place them at first, but their boots gave them away. They won't say anything and risk the cushy job they have here, so we're safe from them."

Impressed by her knowledge and answer for everything, Larek finally took a look around the room they had entered. His first impression of it was that it certainly appeared as though it was worth the expense they had paid, given that it was at least twice as large as the room he shared with Verne and Norde back at Copperleaf – but it was much more richly decorated. Draping wall coverings in deep red and purple gave the space an elegant feel, which was only enhanced by the beautifully carved furniture, including the two beds sitting across from each other that were larger than any that he'd ever seen before. Their size was large enough that he didn't think he'd have any problem with his feet sticking over the end, and they were wide enough that they could sleep at least 5 or 6 people comfortably.

The large window at the end of the room looked out onto the bustling Central Square, but had gauzy curtains that could be pulled to prevent most of the people outside from seeing within, as well as some thicker ones that looked opaque enough to fully block out the light. There was a pair of stained-wood wardrobes standing in opposite corners, and what looked to be nightstands near each side of the two beds, all crafted with intricate carvings that looked like they took a long time to create. All of this was enhanced by a giant, fluffy red-and-purple rug that covered at least two-thirds of the polished hardwood floor, giving the room a comfortable feel.

"I still don't think it's a good idea, given that anyone from the SIC can simply walk inside and see those Fusions."

Vivienne shook her head. "Unlikely. Based on the pay structure of the SIC, it is unlikely that any of them would frequent this Inn, as there are likely a dozen others throughout the entire town by this point which would be much cheaper and friendlier. Even if they do, by the time they discover who created the Fusions, we'll be long gone. Besides, you've already promised to give them some of our 'extra' Fusions, so they are less likely to look into the lamps at that point."

Vivienne seemed to have an answer for everything, but by that point Larek didn't really care all that much. What he wanted to do was get clean, rest and relax, and eat before he tackled the *Illuminate* Fusions for the lamps – and not necessarily in that order. Before he could claim one of the beds, the interrogation turned to Bartholomew.

"What was that all about, Barty? Some sort of 'Noble' thing?"

The young Martial trainee rubbed the back of his neck, looking embarrassed. "Yes, basically. There's a... I'm not sure how to say it, but there is a *connection* of sorts among those of us that have a stronger slave bond to the Great Ones, and we can recognize it immediately upon meeting others. By subtly acknowledging the bond, and that we were on a special mission, I deflected any questions about why we fled Thanchet after the Scission appeared. Otherwise, he would've questioned why we didn't stay and help fight the monsters that emerged from it, as is expected of those of the peerage and the SIC. It also got us an escort to Whittleton and will hopefully help keep whoever is in charge of the forces here from interfering with us. Otherwise, I have a feeling they would try and requisition us to bolster their numbers. It's rare that such a thing occurs, but it's been known to happen, especially between different Noble houses."

That also made sense to Larek, so while everyone else continued to argue about how precarious their position was in the town, as well as plans about how quickly they could get all the supplies they needed for the rest of their journey, Larek walked over to the nearest bed, plopped his bag and staff down on it, and announced, "I'm taking a bath."

That, thankfully, was enough for the others to leave off their conversation as they realized they were also tired, dirty, and hungry. Larek didn't take too long in the bath, as he knew the others wanted to bathe as well, and with Bartholomew nonchalantly watching the bathing room for threats while he got his business done, he was in and out within 10 minutes. Once he was clean, including a quick scrub of his robe to get most of the stains out, Larek lounged on his bed for a few minutes in his damp clothing, waiting for the others to finish.

It took nearly an hour for everyone to get the baths they wanted, which gave Larek more than enough time to create an *Extreme Heat* Fusion on a gold piece from his bag. With it activated on the floor of his room, the ambient temperature rose significantly for a short time, which was more than enough to dry off his robe and the clothing of everyone else who had washed their outerwear in their baths. It was slightly uncomfortable because of the heat, which made Larek think about a way he might be able to make a Fusion in the future that would be ideal for removing the moisture out of clothing without having to practically cook the person inside.

But he had more important things to do, such as stuffing his face full of delicious food. The late lunch they received vindicated the expense of their stay at the Inn, as whoever had cooked it had to have had a high *Cooking* skill, as all the roast meats, freshly baked rolls, and even the salad of mixed greens had something *extra* to it that made him salivate even as he ate it. If he was being honest, it was the most delicious meal he'd ever had in his life – and it was only basic lunch foods. He couldn't wait to see what dinner had to offer later that night.

After they were all done, stuffed to the point where Larek thought everyone would have to roll themselves up the stairs, he went over to the bar where Grenda was still polishing the bartop with the same rag she had been using before. "I'm going to take the lamp chimneys now, if that's alright with you?"

"Absolutely. However, if you cannot finish them by 5pm when dinner starts, I'd rather you do it after or in the morning. The lamps look tacky and unfinished without the chimneys, and we can't have that."

He nodded in understanding. "Shouldn't be a problem." Enlisting the aid of the others, as it would be extremely difficult to carry up all 10 glass lamp chimneys himself, they brought them up to Larek's room and laid them on the bed where he indicated, before he moved onto the mattress as well. Now that he had bathed, eaten, and even relaxed a little bit, he was able to fully appreciate the softness of the bed as he sat comfortably on it; it was so soft that he thought he might have trouble sleeping, but he put that worry off for later.

"Larek?" Penelope asked, interrupting him before he could start working. "Viv, Kimble, and I are heading out to the marketplace to look for supplies. Is there anything specific you need?"

That left Nedira, Bartholomew, and his two roommates to stay inside the Inn with him, so he nodded. They were also going to stay in his room for the moment while the others were gone, he noted, instead of going to their own. Just as it was at Copperleaf, Verne and Norde were staying in his room and sharing the other bed, but the sleeping arrangements were a little different for the others. In one of the other rooms, Nedira would have a bed all to herself while Penelope and Vivienne were to share the other; in the third room, Kimble and Bartholomew would have their own beds. All Larek cared about was that he didn't have to share his large bed with anyone, leaving him all the room he could possibly want while he slept.

"The only thing I need is another set or two of clothes that will fit me, which might mean they have to be custom-made," he answered after some thought. "The same goes for Norde and Verne, as along with my own robe, their student robes make them stick out too much. I can easily place Fusions on whatever you get, so there won't be any loss of coverage – though see if you can find long-sleeved shirts, as those will make coordinating areas of ambience easier."

"We'll see what we can find. Anything else?"

Larek thought about it for a moment. "Simple necklaces with some sort of medallion on them? Possibly some other accessories that I can place Fusions on? If I'm going to make some stuff for the SIC members here, I need something to put them on – because I'm not about to go and add Fusions to all of their robes and armor."

The three that were about to leave looked at each other before turning back to him. "Yeah, I think we can do that."

He couldn't really think of anything else for himself, and they would likely know better than him what they were going to need on their journey across the Kingdom, so he left it at that. As soon as they left, with Bartholomew locking the door behind them, Larek settled down to work on his project. He had already been planning it out after he received the "commission", but now that he had a chance to devote the rest of his attention to it, he finished up his design of the final formation.

What he wanted to accomplish with this Fusion was two-fold, but fortunately both of the Effects were something he'd already done before – even though the material was largely new to him. The first Effect was simple enough, as it was just to strengthen the glass so that it would be very difficult to break. The second was the *Illuminate* Effect, which was also straightforward – except that he wanted for it to be adjustable based on whatever the person adjusting it wanted.

The problem with that was conforming an Effect to mental commands was something that was available in Advanced Fusions, which was something he couldn't do yet. Granted, mental commands were easily able to turn a Fusion on or off, but having it change the Effect based on the thoughts of the one interacting with it? Not something he was capable of. Therefore, he needed some other way to ensure whoever was using it could select the correct *Illuminate* Magnitude they wanted.

At first, he had been stumped about what to do, other than trying to fit on a number of different smaller Fusions, all with different Magnitudes which could be turned on individually. This seemed like a waste, however, and could become confusing, especially since non-Mages couldn't actually see the Fusions to know which one they were activating, though they could "feel" them a little when they were there.

He *knew* he could make it work in a single Fusion, so he worked on how he could allow for the change of light levels without a mental command aspect to it. In the end, the solution made him believe he was trying to make it too complicated, as it didn't need to be fancy; it just needed to work.

The answer? Taps.

With a 4-by-4 grid formation, he placed the *Illuminate* Effect in the upper lefthand corner of the grid, followed by Magnitude 1, Magnitude 2, and Magnitude 3 sections along the top row. The next row contained an Input that would measure the number of finger taps against the glass in a 2-second timeframe; next to the Input were 3 Variables, all corresponding to the different Magnitudes. So, if someone tapped twice upon the glass within 2 seconds, it would activate the Magnitude 2 *Illuminate* Effect.

Underneath that row was a fourth Variable, which would react to 4 taps on the glass chimney, which would deactivate the Reactive Activation Method next to it, which was also tied into the Inputs, Variables, and the *Illuminate* Effect above it. With just a Mana Cost section to tie it all together, he was fairly certain that the Fusion would work as intended. He still had to test it, of course, but he was fairly confident in the design.

The last 5 sections of the lower right-hand corner of the grid formation were relatively simple in comparison. There was a Splitter between the *Illuminate* Mana Cost and the Mana Cost for the *Strengthen Glass* portion of the Fusion, and then all it took was a Permanent Activation Method, the *Strengthen* Effect, and a Magnitude of 9 to ensure that it was durable enough to prevent it from shattering easily.

After firming up his design in his head, he was about to start when he remembered that he still had to allocate his recent influx of Aetheric Force toward his Skills. With a total of 916 AF to spend, he did a little math and decided to finally raise his *Multi-effect Fusion Focus* Skill up to 17 from 10, spending a total of 910 AF, leaving him with only 6 AF remaining. Since he was creating a Fusion with multiple Effects, he figured he would get more out of this than any of his other Skills at the moment, as he would only be able to increase the maximum Skill Level for 2 of his Level 30+ Skills with what he had.

When that was done, he took a deep breath and started forming the grid formation he had planned out. He was only making a single one at the moment instead of attempting to divide it up 10 times to add Fusions to all the lamp chimneys simultaneously, as he wanted to ensure it worked – and was unsure how much it would actually cost in terms of Pattern Cohesion yet. He had an impressive pool of 7,580 Pattern Cohesion due to his +10 Pneuma Boost, but draining a large chunk of it all at once was always excessively draining and he didn't want to push it.

The creation of the new Fusion was easy enough, especially as it wasn't too complicated, and even the strengthening of the unfamiliar glass materials went smoothly. In no more than a minute, after triple-checking to ensure he got it right without any errors or inconsistencies, he finished the formation and started to pump it full of Mana. With his rotating funnel, the process was done in just over 2 minutes as it filled up completely. As Larek snapped it into place on the lamp chimney, there was a tone that rang out from the chimney that reminded him of someone flicking their finger against glass, but it faded a moment afterwards.

Picking up the clear glass chimney, he tapped it once and smiled when he saw it turn on. The light it gave out was only Magnitude 1, so it wasn't terribly bright, and so he could look at it without blinding himself; he was amazed to see how incredibly even and vibrant the light was as it passed through the material. What was even more interesting was the way it reflected *inside* the chimney, as it almost appeared as though the light was being broken up into different-colored beams that eventually blended all into each other. *I wonder if I can create different-colored **Illumination** Fusions? Like one of them being red, another blue, and so on?*

New Fusion Learned!
Graduated Illuminated Strong Glass +9
Activation Method(s): Reactive, Permanent
Effect 1: Strengthens glass to make it more resistant to breaking
Effect 2: Illuminates an area
Magnitude 1: Strengthens glass by 900%
Magnitude 2: Illumination level 1, 2, 3
Input: Finger taps
Variable(s): 1, 2, 3, or 4 taps within 2 seconds
Mana Cost: 67,500
Pattern Cohesion: 850
Fusion Time: 112 hours

Multi-effect Fusion Focus has reached Level 11!

Dismissing the notifications detailing his newly created Fusion and his Skill Level-ups, he looked up to see everyone staring at him and the lamp chimney in his hand. "Here, check it out," he said abruptly, tossing the glass with its new Fusion on it across the room toward Verne. The boy cried out as he dove to grab it, but the smooth outside of the chimney slipped through his fingers. As it hit the ground, his roommate cringed in worry as he expected it to break, but Larek just grinned as it bounced off the portion of hardwood floor that wasn't covered by the enormous rug.

"What? It didn't break?"

Larek shook his head. "No, I made it stronger. Tell me what you think; one tap is the lowest light setting, two is the next, and three taps is the brightest. If you want to turn it off, tap it *four* times within two seconds."

As he watched Verne and Norde play with the light, temporarily blinding themselves as they stared directly at the lamp chimney at its brightest setting, he turned back to the other chimneys. With the success of the first one, and a Pattern Cohesion cost that was high but wasn't too bad, Larek reformed the pattern he had just created but made it much thicker. Once it was filled with Mana once again, he used his *Focused Division* Skill to split it up; based on the fact this was classified as a Major Intermediate Fusion, as it didn't have anything *too* complicated in its formation to cause it to become a Supreme, he was only able to make 6 equal copies at once, so he added the Fusion to an additional 6 of the glass chimneys. He had to wait another 10 minutes while his Pattern Cohesion regenerated, but as soon as he was basically full again, he finished off the last trio of them. After he was done, he had increased his *Multi-effect Fusion Focus* Skill by a total of 4 Levels; it wasn't enough to hit his maximum, but he had a feeling it wouldn't take much more than what he'd already done to get there.

Satisfied with his work, he sat back and relaxed for a few minutes as he watched both Nedira and Bartholomew look at the one he had given his roommate earlier. While it was still relatively early, he knew he had to deliver these back to the common room before dinner, but he was in no hurry at the moment since the process had been much faster than he expected.

The creation of a new Fusion only emphasized his love of the craft, as it made him feel more alive than ever. He could feel his understanding of Fusions become deeper the more he increased his maximum Levels, and it only pushed him to want to do more. That required killing more monsters, of course, so that was exactly what he was going to do. It was why they were in Whittleton in the first place, to get the supplies they would need to do just that.

After a good 30 minutes of relaxation, just simply lying on his too comfortable bed, he looked at the others and asked, "Ready to help me bring these down?"

At their affirmations, they gathered up the altered glass lamp chimneys and headed out the door.

Chapter 36

"And... that should do it." Larek stepped back and saw that all of the glass lamp chimneys had been reinstalled into their sconces. Since the daylight had done a fairly good job of lighting up the common room of the inn, the oil flames hadn't been burning, but the sun was already shifting enough in the sky that it was starting to become darker inside the room.

"They don't really look any different. How do they work?" Grenda asked, coming up behind him. Out of the corner of his eye, he saw Bartholomew twitch toward him as if he wanted to protect Larek from some sort of assassination attempt by the woman, but the Innkeeper was simply curious about the new additions to her Inn.

"Like this," the Fusionist said, tapping the glass once, and two seconds later, the entire glass chimney started to give off a subtle glow. It wasn't as impactful as it would be if it was darker inside the room, but it was visible. He then went on to demonstrate how to change the light levels and how to turn them off, and then he mentioned that they had a *Strengthening* Fusion on them to prevent them from being damaged. "It won't make them *impossible* to break, but they won't shatter if they accidentally hit the floor."

"Simply amazing," Grenda said a little breathlessly, before playing with the *Illuminate* Fusion for herself. She picked up how it worked quickly and was soon moving all over the room with swift feet, turning them all on to the Magnitude 2 setting. Soon enough, she was back to Larek, looking at him with a calculating look in her eyes. "How long will these last?"

He honestly didn't know, because even the very first Fusions he'd made were still working perfectly well, with formations that appeared just as strong as they were when he created them. "At least a year, but I can't tell you how much longer than that." That was the truth, after all.

"A year? I thought Fusions only lasted a few months at most."

Shuffling his feet nervously as he tried to think of an excuse, Verne came to Larek's rescue. "It's a new technique taught by that new Fusionist that was at Copperleaf. You've heard about that?"

She nodded. "Yes, I think just about *everyone* has heard of this Fusionist fellow, but I don't believe any of the SIC forces here were able to acquire anything that he made. And you say you learned from him? Are there many that have learned these new 'techniques'?"

"No, uh, not many," Larek answered. "And although I've learned as much as I could, there's just so much more that isn't possible for me." *At least, not yet.*

Again, that was the truth as he was talking about himself. Thankfully, it seemed as though that satisfied the Innkeeper, as she grinned widely, as if she had just achieved a huge victory. "To think, I've got the *only* Fusions made from someone who studied under this fabled Fusionist! There's no one who can match something like this!"

Larek was going to mention that he was planning on gifting some Fusions to the SIC, but he decided not to at the last moment. She could believe what she liked, he mused, even if it was only going to be true for a short time.

"If you don't mind, I think we'd love to get some more rest before dinner later," he said politely, wanting to get away from the overbearing smile that the woman was presenting as she lovingly rubbed one of the glass chimneys.

"Uh huh. Yes. Rest. Dinner."

Leaving the Innkeeper to whatever fun she was having with her new Fusions, the group went back up to his and his roommates' room, where they all lounged on the enormous beds, except for Bartholomew, who stood relaxed near the doorway after it was closed and locked.

"Should we go exploring through the town?" Verne asked after a few minutes of relaxation. Larek should've known the boy would be bored, despite all the action they'd seen over the last week.

"Probably not a good idea," Nedira said, shutting down Verne and her brother's hopes to explore. "I know it might be fun for you, but there are too many dangers out there, and until we get you changed into something less conspicuous than your student robes, it's probably safer if we all stay here."

Larek agreed, but he also didn't want to have to go out into the town if he could avoid it altogether. There were just too many people and he still wasn't the most comfortable in crowds; more than that, his ring that held the *Perceptive Misdirection* Fusion on it wouldn't work if someone touched him physically, and there were so many people out there that it was inevitable that someone would run into him. It was almost a miracle that it hadn't happened already.

"Ah, you're no fun at all," Verne complained. A second later, he turned to Larek. "I know! Are there any fun Fusions you can create?"

"Fun? What do you mean by that?" Larek wouldn't really describe his Fusions as being "fun". Useful? Absolutely. Deadly? Some of them, sure. But fun? Not necessarily.

"You know, something that we could make into a game. Or simply something to play with that won't tear a hole through the walls or hurt one of us."

Looking through his list of available Fusions, he quickly dismissed every single one, as none were suitable to be used in a game or to play with. The Fusions were either used to enhance a material, heal someone, protect them from being hurt, or to hurt something in return.

It wasn't until he saw the Fusion that he had just created on the list that he remembered being curious about whether he could change the color of the light that was emitted from an *Illuminate* Fusion. The longer he considered it, the more he thought it could be done, as it should simply be an alteration of the Effect to display a certain color.

From that simple, curious thought, Larek designed something "fun" for Verne and Norde to pass the time. At least, he hoped it would be.

Getting down on the floor and instructing the others to move the giant rug covering the hardwood, the Fusionist designed a Lesser Intermediate Fusion that he was able to use his *Focused Division* Skill to create at least 9 at the same time. In a square, grid-like 7-by-7 pattern, he arranged these new Fusions all over the floor for a total of 49 of them, each of them separated approximately a foot from each other.

New Fusion Learned!
Red and White Illuminate Wood +2
Activation Method: Reactive
Effect(s): Creates either a red or white illumination in a fixed location
Magnitude: Illumination level 2 in a 1-foot square of wood
Input: Physical pressure
Variable 1: If no pressure is detected, deactivates after 2 seconds
Variable 2: Upon initial activation, emits a white illumination
Variable 3: If previous activation emitted a white illumination, it now emits a red illumination
Variable 4: If previous activation emitted a red illumination, it now emits a white illumination
Mana Cost: 140
Pattern Cohesion: 15
Fusion Time: 55 minutes

Multi-effect Fusion Focus has reached Level 15!

Larek wasn't absolutely sure if the coloring of the different illuminations would actually work, but all it took was some extra focus on the Effect that he wanted. Since it was simply a slight change in the output of the Effect and nothing significantly different, he felt the changes would work perfectly for his idea. He thought that once he was eventually able to create Advanced Fusions, the number of different colors in the same Fusion would increase as he would be able to focus on more at the same time; but for now, all he needed was red and white.

Taking the idea of using the number of finger taps to change the brightness on the lamp chimneys and changing it slightly, he used simple physical pressure to activate these Fusions. From there, though, instead of waiting 2 seconds to register the Inputs, it would activate immediately and then deactivate once 2 seconds passed. Then, using his Variables to dictate what color the illumination would be depending on what color it was last time, it was easy enough to put it all together. All it took was a single Mana Cost that powered two different Effects (white and red illumination), a single Input, four Variables, and a Magnitude of 2 inside a 3-by-3 grid formation. It didn't need to be too bright, but he wanted to ensure it was visible even in a brightly lit room.

Because it only required an initial Mana Cost of 140 Mana, as well as 15 Pattern Cohesion, Larek was able to get the entire grid of 49 done in a few minutes. It actually took him longer to design the grid formation than to ultimately create them, and when he was done, the others just looked at him in confusion.

"What did you do here, Larek? I see the Fusions, but I don't understand what they do," Nedira asked.

"I don't even see that much," Bartholomew complained.

Larek looked at his handiwork and frowned, as a flaw in his design emerged. While Mages could see the Fusions easily enough, even if they might be a little blurry because they weren't adept at making them out, no Martials or normal people would know they were there other than perhaps by sensing their presence. It meant that the latter group of people would find it harder to play the game he designed, so he would have to figure out a way to designate where they actually were for those who couldn't see the Fusions themselves.

Shrugging, he debated changing the Fusion to see if he could make them at least visible with some sort of indicator to everyone, but he decided not to. He had created this for the boys to play with, after all, and everyone would at least see the results.

"I made a grid of Fusions that will illuminate a square of the wooden floor when you step on them, and will disappear after 2 seconds when you step off. My thought was that one of you could step through it and make whatever pattern you want, and the other would have to match it. The first steps through it will be white, while a second step will turn it red; if it doesn't all turn red when the second person matches the pattern, then they've made a mistake and will lose."

It was a simple enough game, but it allowed him to apply a lot of the things he'd learned to create something entirely new. He could also feel that customizing his Fusions was becoming easier than it used to be; whether it was just from practice or because his Skills were slowly improving when he accumulated enough Aetheric Force, he wasn't sure.

Verne and Norde immediately scrambled down from the bed where they had been watching Larek work on the floor, and the tree-like boy tentatively stuck his foot on the Fusion closest to the edge where he was located. As soon as his foot made contact, a square of white light glowed on the wood beneath his appendage, a pure white that was a bit different than the illumination given off by his recent creations downstairs, which was an off-white that was bordering on yellow. Verne giggled as he picked his foot up, waited a pair of seconds for the glow to dissipate, and then placed it down again. This time, a vibrant red glow shone up from the wood, bathing his foot with an eerie radiance before he removed it again. Another test had it light up white again, and then Verne moved across the entire grid of Fusions, making a simple path that only took a single step out of line as he made his way across the 7-by-7 grid.

Once all the Fusions deactivated, Norde easily made his way over the same path, making the lights glow red as he accurately achieved a perfect placement of his feet as he moved across. As Larek stood up, sat on his bed, and watched the two explore the new "game" he had made, Nedira smiled at him and said, "Thanks."

"Hmm? For what?"

She waved at the Fusions on the floor. "For that. With all that we've been through, I sometimes forget that my brother is only 11 years old; the same with Verne. They've had to endure so much more than they should by their age, and sometimes it's good for them to just be a kid and *play* every once in a while." Her smile faltered slightly as she added, "At least until we go back out there and start killing monsters again."

He nodded as he pulled her close, feeling comfortable with her pressed up against his side with his arm around her as he watched the two boys experiment with more elaborate pathing through the grid. He began to see some flaws in his design after a little bit, such as when one of them made a mistake, they would have to try and reset it by jumping from the edge and stepping on whatever had been wrong, before hopping away while avoiding touching any other Fusion, but it wasn't really something he needed to worry about at the moment. If he ever redesigned it, he had some ideas for improvements, but for now, it was enough of a diversion that it suited their needs; it wasn't important for it to be perfect.

As the light began to dim even further outside, Larek realized that it was getting late, and dinner would start to be served soon. Their other groupmates hadn't returned quite yet, so they held off on heading down to eat until they arrived, but fortunately Verne and Norde hadn't tired of their game yet; in fact, they had even designed a few other ways to utilize the lights other than his "follow the path" one he had envisioned, and it was interesting to see their creativity.

A gentle murmur was eventually heard somewhere below them, which only rose in volume as the sun continued to set, making Larek realize he was hearing dinner being served in the common room below. It was a bit surprising given the fact that every other time he'd been down there it had been essentially empty.

"The Innkeeper probably heavily discounts her normal prices for dinner to drive business," Nedira mused after he questioned how busy it sounded. "With her normal rates, she'd never make any money if no one could afford to stay *or* eat here. She can then be picky in who she allows to rent rooms."

That sounded entirely plausible, since Vivienne had mentioned that the rate for their rooms for a single night was outrageous, but the food was spectacular enough that the Innkeeper could probably still charge higher-than-normal prices without pricing everyone out. The customers from the dinners she served were probably the majority of her business at that point, and the rooms she rented out were just a bonus, of sorts.

Just when Larek was beginning to worry about Kimble, Vivienne, and Penelope, he heard a commotion outside the door. There was a knock, followed by Penelope's voice saying, "We're back. Open up."

"Use the correct phrase, please," the Martial trainee near the door called out with a smile on his face.

There was a pause, before Larek heard a petulant-sounding Penelope say, "Bartholomew is the greatest."

The next moment, Bartholomew opened the door to smile at the three people outside, before waving them in. All three of the new arrivals were overloaded with packs stuffed with supplies, and while the two Martials appeared unaffected by the weight of the things they were carrying, Kimble looked like he was about to pass out. Larek jumped up and started to help unload everything from the Pyromancer's arms, placing them either on the floor or his bed, while the blue-haired Martial and the Ranger were able to handle their unload themselves.

Meanwhile, Verne and Norde had stopped their play for a moment upon their friends' arrival, but had resumed after it was obvious they weren't needed to help. Kimble, after recovering from his trek with packs full of heavy supplies, raised his eyebrows in surprise when he saw what the two students were doing, and he looked at Larek with a questioning gaze. The Fusionist just shrugged, not wanting to explain what he had done.

He had more important things he wanted to discover, such as whether Penelope and the rest had been able to get everything they needed.

"Long story short, we got *most* of what we needed," the blue-haired Martial said immediately upon unloading her burden. "I'll explain more later, but for now, let's get some food – I'm starving!"

While Larek wasn't starving, he could certainly go for some more of the delicious food if it was anything like earlier. Given that they weren't going to be visiting any other towns or cities along the way to Silverledge Academy and Fort Ironwall, he'd rather get as much of it in as possible before they were forced to eat the supplies they were going to bring with them.

"Might as well go now, then," Larek said. "You can see my handiwork down there, too, unless you saw it when you came in?"

Penelope and the others shook their heads. "No, it was too busy and we had our hands full, as you saw. I'm eager to see them once I can actually pay attention."

As soon as Verne and Norde finished whatever they were doing, they joined the rest of the group as they made their way back downstairs, ready to fill their bellies after all the activities of the afternoon.

Chapter 37

"No! This is the stupidest idea I've ever heard!"

Karley slapped her fist down on the Major's desk, emphasizing her point. She didn't know where this kind of asinine idea her boss had come up with had originated, but it was ignorant and short-sighted – not to mention *dangerous.*

"I don't care what you think of my orders, but I *will not* have you blatantly flaunting your insubordination for everyone to hear. Keep your voice down, or I'll be forced to take drastic measures to ensure your voice is never heard again."

The threat coming from Major Kuama's mouth was enough for Karley to snap her jaws shut on the next thing she was about to say. She highly doubted that she would be *permanently* silenced, as they needed every single member of the SIC in or around Whittleton alive in order to maintain the safety of the roads, but that didn't mean her boss couldn't make her life a living hell in the process.

With a more even and quieter tone, the Elementalist said, "I apologize for my outburst. I'm just seeking to understand what could possibly possess you to think this was a smart idea."

"That's better. I respect your opinion, but I can't have you acting like this when other people can hear." The older woman leaned her elbows on her desk and rubbed at her temples, and for the first time Karley saw the deep exhaustion that lined the Major's face. While they weren't exactly friends, the Major had been in charge of Whittleton's SIC forces since the Elementalist had arrived a few years ago, and Karley had a healthy respect for the powerful Martial. From what she understood, the common-born Impaler was only a year or so away from retirement age, though she suspected that the spear-wielding woman would continue to serve in the SIC until the day she could no longer hold up a weapon. It wasn't that rare for those who've served decades in the SIC to continue along that path after their required duty was done, as it was the only thing that many of them knew; returning to "normal" life afterward was sometimes scarier than facing down a horde of monsters.

Major Kuama waved her toward a chair, and only after she reluctantly sat down on the edge of its seat, did her boss speak. "We have no choice, Karley. We need something to even the odds against these monster hordes out there, and I've gotten no response from the higher-ups on when we might expect to see any reinforcements. You *know* this better than anyone other than me, because there's not much you miss around here." There was a small smile that quickly vanished as the Major looked at her. "As much as I'd like to say that things are going well, they aren't. I know that Swanek was a pain in the butt, but he was helping to keep the roads safe for travel, just as all of the other patrol groups we sent out. With him and his group dead, it's slowly becoming obvious that it's only a matter of time before everyone else from the SIC is whittled down until there are no defenders left.

"That's why we need to act now before it's too late."

Karley shook her head, though she didn't voice her disagreement. That was because she didn't really disagree that things currently weren't looking good, and the eventual demise of everyone in the SIC inside Whittleton was inevitable if things didn't change soon. But that didn't mean her boss' current idea showed anything approaching intelligence.

"And so your solution to that is to abandon everyone in Whittleton to the monster hordes? How does that, in any way, make sense?" *It's the stupidest idea I've ever heard*, she thought again.

"We're not going to abandon them *forever*," the older woman retorted. "We're just going to take all our forces to Thanchet and link up with them. From there, we'll be able to branch out with the combined forces and cover more of the southern portion of the Kingdom. If anyone is going to have reinforcements, it'll be one of the cities where a Fort and an Academy are located; it will be in their best interests to take on more responsibility for the surrounding area, which would include the roads around Whittleton. I've already heard about a few other towns sending their forces to join up with the regional headquarters down in Thanchet, and it is the best idea to consolidate our numbers to combat this ever-changing situation."

"What about the people of Whittleton?"

"What about them?" the Major asked. "The town hasn't been attacked in months, nor have any of the monsters roaming around even approached the walls. We aren't trained to handle this kind of situation, Karley, and the only way we're going to get help is if we go out and seek it."

"But you're talking about abandoning your duty here!"

The powerful Martial shook her head. "No, our duty is to protect the people of the Kingdom from the threat of the Scissions, but we can't do that as we are. Another year or two as it is right now and we won't have anyone left to send out to clear the roads. Something about the way the SIC responds to these threats needs to change, and this is just the start of making those changes. It might not be what you want to hear, but it's what needs to happen."

Karley slumped back in her chair, unable to think of another protest that the Major wouldn't just shut down immediately.

"We're beginning our trek to Thanchet tomorrow afternoon."

Tomorrow? So soon?

"Oh, and Zorey mentioned something about these individuals who helped to fight off the Dechonabras. We'll be taking these Fusions they somehow possess before we leave."

"What? No, we can't do that!"

"We *can*, and we *will*. From their descriptions, they sound like deserters from Copperleaf Academy and Fort Pinevalley. I personally don't care that they're cowards, because I'd rather not have them in the SIC if they're going to run at the first opportunity, but we need those stolen Fusions they somehow got their hands on. They will better serve in our possession than in that of those *children*; I'm sure all it will take is a promise not to turn them in for desertion and they'll hand them right over. Of course, that will be the first thing I report when we get to Thanchet, but they'll at least have a head start."

Karley couldn't believe what she was hearing.

"I don't think you understand what you're suggesting, nor do you understand the danger into which you'll be putting whoever intends to force those people to give up their Fusions. You didn't see them fight, and—"

"That really doesn't matter, and it isn't your decision to make, anyway. We're already putting plans in place to confront them in the morning, as we have logistical issues that we have to take care of before we can leave tomorrow afternoon." The Major stopped and stared Karley in the eyes with a penetrating gaze. "I need you on board with this. You're the most senior and most respected member of the SIC in Whittleton, even if Nobles like Zorey think they're better than us common folk just because of an accident of birth."

The Elementalist couldn't meet her boss' gaze after a moment, because she was absolutely not on board with any of this, especially taking the Fusions away from the group that had given them aid. She could follow along like an obedient member of the SIC when they left Whittleton, even if such a decision was the height of stupidity in her own opinion, but to deliberately steal what had to be at least a few Platinums'-worth of Fusions from the young Mages and Martials that had *saved her life* would be almost criminal.

Despite her abject reservations that they were doing the wrong thing, she eventually nodded. *This is stupid. They don't deserve this. There's got to be something I can do.* Even as she thought that, the old fear of sticking her neck out too far crashed over her. *No, just keep your* head down and don't make waves. This isn't your responsibility. Besides, what if the Major is right? What if they are deserters and stole all of those Fusions? It makes sense when I think about it; they're too young to be entrusted with any sort of mission, after all.

Still, even though she resolved to stay out of it, especially after voicing her concerns only to have them disregarded, Karley couldn't help but think that this was all *wrong*. Nothing about it seemed smart, but there really wasn't anything she could do about the entire situation.

Or was there?

"That is all then, Karley. Get with Zorey, and he'll direct you to where you can help in our evacuation preparations." With that clear dismissal, the Elementalist got up from her chair with trembling legs, completely floored by what she had just been told; her mind refused to accept it. It was only when she was closing the door to the Major's office behind her that she realized she wasn't trembling from fear; no, she was trembling with anger.

*No, boss, I'm **not** on board with this. That secondary plan of yours is foolish and ungrateful, and I aim to put a stop to it.*

Squaring up her shoulders, she resolutely started to look for Zorey, knowing that she had to play along with the situation at first before she could make her move. Once she had the opportunity, she was going to ensure that her saviors were able to escape from the machinations of the Major, deserters and thieves be damned. Karley owed them at least that much, and she always paid her debts.

* * *

The common room was crowded by the time they emerged from the stairs, and their appearance caused a minor disturbance as they were noticed. Again, it was thankfully not because of his height, but because of their appearance; they looked foreign and of Mage and Martial origins, especially since Larek and his roommates were still wearing their grey student robes.

As for the clientele eating dinner, it was clear to see that many of them were dressed better than the majority of the people he had seen in the streets earlier in the day, though only a few gave him the sense that they were Nobility. The rest were just well-off financially, it seemed. Though, on a second look, there were some that had decent enough clothing but it wasn't what Larek recognized as being too fine, so it was possible that dinner in the Waterbury Inn was expensive, but not completely unaffordable.

What surprised him was that there weren't any members of the SIC present, at least not at first and second glance. It was possible that they were wearing something other than robes and armor, but he didn't see any sign that that was the case.

There was only one table left empty in the back corner, and while it was small and only had four chairs around it, there were a few empty chairs around that he thought they could snag and bring to the smaller table.

They did just that. Although there were a few looks by the other patrons that said they didn't appreciate the acquisition of the empty chairs, no one said anything. As soon as they sat down, the same young woman who had shown them up to their room appeared as if from nowhere yet again. "Dinner for everyone?"

As everyone nodded, Verne spoke up. "Just a large salad for me, if at all possible."

"Done. Should be out in a few minutes. Drinks?"

Everyone just ordered water, which caused the Innkeeper's daughter to make a face, but she left without another word.

"Not very personable, is she?" Bartholomew said, adjusting his armor as he got comfortable in his seat.

"No, but I don't care as long as the food is as good as it was earlier," Penelope added.

Larek looked around to see Grenda behind the bar, serving drinks to those around her, but he could see a huge grin on her face that seemed not to have faded from when he saw her earlier. The reason for that was the lamps along the walls, which had at least a dozen people up close to them, checking them out from only a few feet away. They were currently at the Magnitude 2 light setting, which wasn't too bright but Larek thought it was probably a lot brighter than the oil lamps would've been. Most of the conversations around the room seemed to be centered around the new Fusions, as heads were turned toward them every once in a while by the people eating at the tables or drinking by the bar.

"Grenda! *Hic* Where'd you get these things?"

The Fusionist looked toward the right of the bar to see a much older man swaying unsteadily, a cup clutched in his hand as he stared at one of the lamps. He seemed to be inordinately fascinated by it, like a moth fixated on a flame, and even when he stumbled slightly to the side and sloshed a part of his drink on the floor, his eyes never left the light created by the Fusion.

"I got it from Nunya!"

"What? Who?"

"Nunya business, you ol' fool!" The Innkeeper cackled at her own joke, before she sobered up and the grin slipped off her face. "You better not be spilling any more ale on my floor, or I'll be cleaning it up later with your face."

"*Hic* Leave off it, Grenda," the man said, before he mumbled something that Larek couldn't hear due to the chatter of the other patrons in the room. "No, seriously, who did your Fusions? *Hic* I've never seen anything like this before."

Their conversation was beginning to draw the attention of dozens of other people inside the common room, and Larek began to worry for a moment. *He can see the Fusions? Is he a retired Mage, perhaps?*

"What do you mean?"

The man was silent as he continued to stare at the lamp, before he jerked his entire body. "Huh? Who? What does *what* mean?" He stumbled a few steps back to the bar before he sat down heavily in one of the stools there, before laying his head down and passing out.

At least 3 or 4 others asked Grenda the same question, but she always deflected it, refusing to name the one who created the Fusions. Larek glanced briefly at Vivienne and she nodded at him, as if to say, "See? I was right."

His relief was interrupted when their meal was delivered, the plates of which barely fit on the small table, but none of them cared as they dug into it. Larek closed his eyes as he savored the whole chicken on his plate along with roasted potatoes and vegetables, as well as the still-steaming bread rolls that went with it. No one spoke as they all practically cleaned their plates, and it was only after they sat back in satisfaction that Kimble gestured toward one of the lamp chimneys that Larek had altered earlier.

"Those are amazing. I know they might seem a little mundane to those who go to an Academy, as Fusion-powered illumination is the norm, but the work is so well done that it's impressive, nonetheless. And the glass adds another element to the light that makes a huge difference. Were those colors inside the chimney what gave you the idea for those lights I saw on the floor of your room?"

The Fusionist nodded, smiling at how much the Pyromancer appreciated his work. "Yes!—"

"You should try it, Kimble! The Light Grid Game is actually pretty fun!" Verne said excitedly. Larek could tell that his roommates wanted to go back up and play with it some more, but he was more interested in what supplies the group had obtained.

"Later, Verne," Larek said, before turning to Penelope. "So, tell me, what were you able to find?"

The blue-haired Martial leaned forward and the others did the same, making their conversation a little more private as she spoke in lower tones. "Food, camping supplies, stuff for your work; all that was fairly easy. We were also able to find some simple clothing for Verne and Norde, as well as second outfits for the rest of us if we ever need to change for any reason." She paused for a moment, before pointing at Larek. "The problem, as you can imagine, is you and your incredibly large frame. There were, as you can imagine, no clothes that were readily available to purchase for you, and there is apparently only a single Tailor in the entire town. Unfortunately, it's an older woman set in her ways, who wouldn't take any extra monetary incentive to let us jump the line of her standing orders, which puts us about a week out until she can get to it."

"Monetary incentive?"

Nedira put her hand on his arm. "She means bribe."

"Exactly," Penelope confirmed. "I'm sure there are more people in the town that have at least a few Skills that would help in the creation of an outfit, but finding them and convincing them to do the work was proving to be extraordinarily difficult, so we came back before it got too dark. Half of the stalls were closing up at that point, and no one wanted to point us in the right direction."

"What does that mean, exactly? No other clothing for me?"

Penelope, Vivienne, and Kimble shook their heads.

"We'll have to take a chance in another town or city where we might be able to slip in and purchase something that can be altered for you a lot easier than in this place," Kimble proposed. "The problem with this place is it is overloaded and used to be a only very small town, so there aren't as many professional businesses set up to handle the influx of people, which makes getting things like custom tailoring orders done quickly almost impossible."

That was disappointing, but he supposed he'd have to live with it for now. Regardless, it sounded like they got everything else they needed – including supplies that Larek could use to make some additional Fusions for the SIC that night.

"Alright, let's head back up. I've got work to do and—" As the Fusionist began to stand up from his chair, something in his peripheral vision caught his eye, and he looked over at the entrance to see a familiar face. He immediately thought he saw her eyeing the lamps, as if she had been told of their existence and came to investigate. That thought was proven wrong when her gaze skipped right over them and

searched for something else. As soon as they alighted on Larek, who had paused as he went to get up, she rushed through the now-boisterous patrons with a frightened look on her face.
Uh, oh; what now?

Chapter 38

"You need to leave. Tonight. Don't tell anyone where you're going, and run as fast as you can."

Larek immediately froze in the seat he had sat back in at the Elementalist's approach, when she whispered her order as soon as she was close enough to not be overheard. *They found us*, was his first thought. *How?* They had only been in the town for approximately 6 hours, which couldn't have been enough time for them to communicate with whoever was heading up the search for Larek and his group. Unless, of course, he was severely underestimating how much effort the Gergasi was putting into tracking him down. They could have means of tracking him that he wasn't even aware of.

A quick glance around the table showed that everyone else was also frozen where they sat, as the warning they were given registered in their minds. There was a hint of both fear and disappointment in their faces, which he shared; he really didn't want to be found by his father, but he was also looking forward to sleeping in a real bed again.

"Why?" Penelope asked after a few seconds of silence around the table. The rest of the common room was still as lively as ever, but their immediate area was like a void of noise.

Larek didn't think it was necessary to ask questions; he was ready to jump up, run upstairs to grab their stuff, and then flee as fast as possible without looking back. Still, he had to acknowledge that it would be beneficial to have confirmation as to whether the Gergasi and those they enslaved were on their trail.

The woman leaned over their table, whispering again to the point where Larek had to concentrate to pick her voice out from the conversations happening around them.

"My boss has decided to clear out of Whittleton and join up with the larger SIC groups near Thanchet. She seems to think that having our forces centralized where we can coordinate the defense of the roads with better efficiency is the way we should approach protecting the people of the Kingdom, especially with our diminishing numbers here. I can't say I agree, but I can see some twisted logic in it, despite the fact that it feels like we're going to abandon everyone here to the monsters outside."

"That's... actually not a bad idea, though pulling *every* SIC member out of the town seems a bit unsafe," Penelope cautiously noted. "But what does that have to do with us?"

"She's making plans to take all your Fusions in the morning before we leave, and then to tell the forces back in Thanchet that you're all deserters and thieves. Her idea is that what Fusions you have would be better utilized by her people rather than a bunch of kids."

Larek immediately relaxed his tense muscles when he heard the reason the woman, Karley, wanted them to flee. Granted, it wasn't exactly *good* news, given that the local SIC wanted to steal the Fusions he'd created and then alert those from Thanchet about their location, but it was still better than the alternative.

"Why did you all just relax in relief when I told you that? Is there something else that you're running from?" the Elementalist said, looking suspiciously at them all.

"No, we're on a special mission to—"

"Don't give me that bull you spouted to Zorey," the woman said, standing up straight with the fear completely gone from her face. "I can tell there's something bigger going on here, especially as the prospect of facing our entire SIC branch doesn't seem to worry you."

"Do they just want the Fusions, or are they planning on killing us?" Larek asked instead of explaining anything. His thoughts were more on how they could get through the next 24 hours without dying or alerting the Gergasi of their location rather than fleeing for their lives once again. Even if they were to try and sneak out that night, there was no guarantee they wouldn't be tracked and ambushed by the SIC – all for the Fusions they carried with them.

"She just wants the Fusions; there's no plan to kill a bunch of what appears to be students and trainees. In all honesty, she couldn't care less that you fled from a dangerous situation, but she's covering herself in case someone's actually looking for you."

"Easy enough, then. We'll just give her some Fusions and they can let us go on our way." It sounded like a simple solution.

The Elementalist shook her head. "I can't let you do that. If you go out there without them, you'll die; you don't have the experience or training to survive crossing through the Kingdom, even if you primarily stick to the roads."

At her words, Larek really looked at the woman for the very first time, reaching out with every sense he possessed. As his hyper-focused state kicked in, there were a few things that he could tell about the Elementalist immediately. The first was that she was indeed from the Kingdom, but she wasn't in any shape or form a Noble of any kind. The second was that the Fusions on her staff were decently made, if weak, as well as being only a month or so away from fading. Lastly, by digging down and evaluating any connections to her that might be out there, he couldn't feel even a trace of Dominion Magic around her.

He hated the power with a passion, but over the last week he had also learned how to detect it in others. It wasn't something that he set out to do, but being in close proximity with his groupmates without anyone else around made it almost natural, based on his understanding of Dominion Magic.

Which was basically nothing, all things considered, but it at least gave him a starting point. What Larek discovered was that he could feel a very faint connection with everyone in the group that felt familiar to him, as if there was a tiny bit of *him* around them. He couldn't see it, manipulate it, or even focus on it to do anything with it, but it was there. The other thing he discovered was that there was something similar, but *much* stronger, surrounding Bartholomew, and it didn't feel familiar at all. He could only assume, based on what he knew about the Martial trainee, was that because he was one of the Nobles that had a direct slave bond with the Gergasi, that was what Larek was detecting. Again, he couldn't do anything with it and was just barely able to sense it; to whatever controlled his Dominion Magic, it was simply present to his perceptions.

Utilizing the same type of senses as he stared at the Elementalist, he attempted to see if this woman was similarly affected by Dominion Magic, either directly or possibly through proximity to one who was. At first, he couldn't detect anything, but as he concentrated on the sensations he received from his companions, he felt *something*. If he had to describe it, he would say it was more like an echo than anything, a bare shadow or wisp of Dominion Magic; he could only guess that it was so faint because she had been close to someone who was affected by Dominion Magic, but wasn't targeted directly. At least, that was what his intuition was telling him.

Instead of directly responding to the woman warning them of the danger, he glanced at Bartholomew and asked, "Was that individual you were talking to on our way here, uh, like you?" It was as subtle as he could get without blurting out that he was asking if the Noble had a slave bond.

"Huh? Oh... yes, certainly."

That was all he needed to know. Turning back to the confused-looking Elementalist, Larek waved toward the stairs. "Come up to our rooms and we can discuss this further."

"What? No, I can't do that. They're going to miss me if I'm away for too long."

"It won't take much time, and it will help both of us," he responded, before getting to his feet.

Nedira tried to drag him back down by pulling on his arm. "What are you doing? We can't—"

"It's too late for that; either way, our presence as we passed through here will be remarked upon, but this way, no one gets hurt."

"Fine, then let's hurry. If we're going to get out of here before—"

He gently cut her off by placing his hand over hers, which was still on his arm. "We're not leaving. At least, not yet."

She stared up at him for a few seconds in silence, before huffing dramatically. "You better have something good planned, or I'm dragging you out of here by your ear."

He smirked down at her. "As if you could even reach it," he joked, which elicited a round of chuckles from the others as they got to their feet. All but the Elementalist, who still looked confused and now angry.

Despite that, she followed them upstairs without a word, though Larek noticed that she jerked back in shock after passing one of the new lamp chimneys to which he had added a Fusion earlier. Even that only caused her to pause for a moment as she stared at the Fusion formation before shaking her head and hurrying to catch up with the rest.

As they had done earlier, everyone piled into the room Larek was sharing with his younger roommates, but instead of going straight to his bed to sit down, he stood next to it, turned toward the others who had gathered. He launched right into his plan without preamble.

"First, we're not going to give your boss any of the Fusions that we're using right now, because they are necessary to us if we're going to travel across the Kingdom. As much as I dislike the thought of SIC members essentially *stealing* from others, I can also understand where it is coming from; they want to protect themselves, and thereby, protect the people. They aren't doing it to make themselves wealthy or simply powerful, except in the pursuit of saving lives. But while I might understand the thought, that doesn't mean I can condone them simply taking items from us when we're using them.

"Instead, I'd like to give your boss and the other members of the SIC here a gift of other Fusions that aren't what we're currently using, but which, nevertheless, would be useful. After we give these Fusions to them, do you believe they will leave us alone? Better yet, would it be enough to convince her not to mention us to anyone in

Thanchet? We're truly not deserters, nor are we thieves; it's a bit more complicated than that, but that's all I can tell you."

Creating Fusions for the SIC members in Whittleton was in line with what he was already planning on doing, if a bit more than he had originally planned. The creation of additional Fusions would take a little longer than it would normally, especially with this little wrinkle in the situation, but if it would delay the search for them, it would be worth it.

Skeptical, Karley folded her arms over her chest and stared at him for a few seconds before answering with slow, measured words. "If you can provide the same kinds of Fusions that were demonstrated to my group, as Zorey has already reported what he saw to her, I believe Major Kuama would be willing to let you go and not mention your passage through this town. She only wants them to help protect her people and allow them to do the duty they are obligated to do without as much fear as they currently have when going out on patrol. As I said before, she doesn't really care who you are and only wants what's best for the people under her responsibility."

"Good. Then I—"

"But that's impossible. There are 55 of us stationed here in Whittleton, so unless your bags were filled with Fusions – which is highly doubtful – then there's no way she would be satisfied with just a few spares that you might have brought with you."

Larek sighed, annoyed that she cut him off, but didn't let that get to him. "We didn't bring any 'spares' with us; what we've been using were created by—"

"What are you doing?" Penelope asked him quickly before he could say any more, marking the second time in the last minute he was cut off.

"Look, I already checked and she isn't under the influence of… anyone. She came here to give us this warning, and if that isn't enough proof that she's on our side, at least nominally, then I'm not sure what it would take to convince us. We're going to need her help if this is going to succeed, as she'll have to be the one to negotiate for us."

The Elementalist held out her hands as if begging him to stop. "Whoa, wait, I never agreed to that!"

"Too late, you're already involved," Nedira said as she moved over to Verne and Norde's shared bed and sat down with an annoyed expression on her face. Crossing her arms, matching what Karley had done earlier, she added, "He's too stubborn to let it go now, so you might as well play along."

Me? Stubborn? Well… I guess she has a point.

"I'm sorry, I'm confused; what are you all talking about?" the woman asked, practically screeching as he could see her starting to drift into the realm of the hysterical.

"It's what I've been trying to tell you, but I keep getting cut off," Larek said, exasperated. "I'll make those Fusions for you, but I need to know what exactly I'm going to need so that everyone is covered."

"I don't know what game you're playing—"

He shook his head. "No game. Now, how many Mages and how many Martials are here in Whittleton as part of your forces?"

The Elementalist looked around at the other people in the room, as if searching for an explanation of the joke being played on her, but everyone just looked back at her with stony expressions on their faces – even Verne and Norde, which was something he didn't see from the normally exuberant boys very often.

"But this is imposs—"

"People keep saying that, but I've proven that to be a lie on at least a few occasions," Larek said wryly, happy to be cutting *her* off in mid-sentence for a change. "Now. Mages and Martials? How many of each?"

She stared at him for a few seconds with her mouth hanging open, before she blurted out, "25 Mages and 30 Martials. But—"

"Can I see your staff? And is there any way you can scrounge up enough Mage staves for the rest of the Mages here in Whittleton? I don't have any extras here, as they're kind of bulky."

She mutely handed over her staff after looking at everyone else watching her actions, and she audibly gulped. "Here." As soon as he took it and began to starve the mediocre Fusions on the wooden staff in order to eliminate them, he looked up into the woman's eyes to see astonishment radiating out of them. And what he thought might be a spark of hope.

"Fire, stone, water, or ice?" he asked. "Pick 2 for all the staves, because that will make the process much faster."

"Uh… fire and stone, I guess?"

He just nodded, before moving to his bed so that he could sit down. He inadvertently walked over the grid of lights he had created earlier and activated a few of the squares, but he ignored them as he finished up the Fusion elimination process. Fortunately, it was fairly simple and fast with the Fusions he was getting rid of, because of their almost temporary nature and Magnitude, so it didn't take that long.

As he quickly created the formation for a *Flaming Ball +7* Fusion and then began to fill it with Mana, he could hear the intake of breath as Karley watched him work. He didn't let his focus waver for a split-second, however, though he allowed himself to gently smile at her reaction.

It didn't take too long for the formation to fill up with his Mana, and when it was done, he snapped it into place along one tip of the staff. Looking up, he saw the woman was staring in astonishment at him and the staff, but she quickly shook herself. "I-I'll go get the staves."

"Barty, Viv – go with her," Penelope ordered.

Larek largely ignored them as they left, knowing that it was probably the best idea to have two individuals from the Kingdom move through the town and even the SIC building rather than someone from a different land, such as Penelope or Nedira. It wasn't because they would be less trusted, but the others would fit in better because almost everyone in town was from the Kingdom and they wouldn't stick out.

As soon as the door closed, he checked his Pattern Cohesion and made sure it wasn't too low – a precaution he'd taken back at Copperleaf to ensure he didn't run out when making so many Fusions for the Dean and Shinpai – and got back to work.

Chapter 39

Nearly tripping over her own feet, Karley rushed toward the SIC headquarters building inside of Whittleton with no thoughts to her own safety. Her hands shook as she carried the bundle of staves in her hand as she realized she could've dropped them if she had accidentally fallen, which was much more of a concern to her than anything else. Considering what she witnessed over the last hour, she knew she didn't want to be on the bad side of the individual that scared her more than a little bit with the extreme power he wielded, even though it wasn't directed at her.

Behind her was Vivienne, one of the Martials who was part of the group she received the staves from; she was carrying another bundle of staves and a bag that held additional items that had Fusions added to them, each of them by themselves worth more than she thought she would ever earn in the SIC over her lifetime, even if she lived to be 200 years old. Together, what the two of them held was enough to buy a significant portion of the Kingdom, if they were sold to people rather than being kept. Of course, selling them was stupid when one considered how powerful they were, because anyone who possessed them would see a significant jump in their abilities.

First were the staves she was holding, each of them holding three Fusions each. All of them were so strong and complicated that Karley was barely able to make out a portion of them. Two of the Fusions would propel what was essentially a strong spell projectile, one of which was essentially a *Fireball* and the other a *Stone Fist*, two very basic spells that were useful to beginning Mages, but were overshadowed by stronger spells once a Mage learned more and had progressed their Level to a certain degree. These projectiles, however, were *strong*; having seen them demonstrated on the journey back to Whittleton, she would equate them to having at least 6 to 7 times the amount of Mana that a normal *Fireball* or equivalent spell would require injected into the spell pattern – which made them significantly stronger.

While any Mage could inject more Mana into a spell to make it stronger or enhance the effects, the amount of Mana injected was typically capped at 2 to 2 and a half times the original cost; this limiting factor wasn't because of the expenditure, but because the spell patterns that were created during the normal process typically couldn't handle much more than that. That wasn't to say it couldn't be done in an emergency or through some deliberate experimentation, but that could sometimes become disastrous as the pattern ruptured before it was cast, resulting in an explosive decompression of Mana in the area as it was released from where it was being held.

Apparently, each of these projectile-based Fusions could be used *every 5 seconds*, which was incredible, as any faster would begin to degrade the Fusions' formations. Even with that restriction, Karley was told that the Fusions would last for at least a year, if not longer, as long as they weren't damaged through rapid usage.

The same could be said for all of the Fusions, including the other Fusion on the staff that strengthened the wood to the point that it was virtually as strong as a steel bar. It also meant that they wouldn't be harmed if she was to accidentally drop them, but she didn't want to do it anyway because it almost seemed like sacrilege to treat something so precious like that.

Apart from the staves, there were enough leather-strung necklaces holding simple copper medallions in a variety of styles, each of them a healing Fusion of one of two types. The first was designed to heal Martials and tapped into their *Body Regeneration* Skill, while the other was appropriate for Mages or any of the normal, common people of the Kingdom and beyond. It wasn't as powerful and took a little longer to heal than the one designed for Martials, but that only made sense when it was typically Martials that took the brunt of the damage during a fight against monsters.

Last but certainly not least, on some decorative steel bracelets for the Mages and steel anklets for the Martials were *Boost* Fusions – but not just any *Boosts*. These were all Magnitude 10, something she didn't even think was possible, and each of them provided a 100% increase to the Intellect, Acuity, and Pneuma stats for Mages and Strength, Body, and Agility stats for the Martials. To effectively *double* the capabilities of each member of the SIC stationed in Whittleton was incredible, and if it was just those stat-boosting Fusions, that would've been amazing by themselves. When she took in everything else that the powerful young man had created before her very eyes, it was a bounty that was almost unbelievable.

And he was giving them all to her and the SIC *for free*, requesting only the promise not to try and take anything more from them, nor mention them to anyone in Thanchet. Even if they were deserters or thieves – the latter of which she wholeheartedly dismissed after seeing the Fusion process for herself – their contribution to the safety of her and the SIC in Whittleton couldn't be overstated. There was just one thing that complicated matters.

Larek. That was the Fusionist's name, which coincided with what she had learned about the prodigy Fusionist that was apparently attending Copperleaf Academy. If this was indeed the same person, and she had no doubts about that at the moment, then his presence outside of the Academy could only mean two things. The first, and what had seemed likely after first learning his name, was that he had run away with his friends – which would brand him a deserter. It only took her a few seconds to conclude *why* he probably deserted, and it was for the same reason she imagined anyone would want to run away when they had something other people wanted. More than likely, someone – or even the entire Academy – was treating him like some sort of Fusion production line, forcing him to create Fusions for the benefit of the SIC. While Fusionists ultimately did this when joining the SIC after graduation, it wasn't *all* they did, and she knew that dozens of those with that Specialization made Fusions on the side for those who were willing to pay for them. With Larek reportedly still a first or second-year student – she couldn't remember exactly, but it fit with his robe color – he shouldn't be subjected to that kind of exploitation, so she could well imagine that might be a reason to run away.

The other thing his presence outside of the Academy might mean was that he was being transferred somewhere else, potentially the capital, where his talent could be put to better use and nurtured in a way that was inaccessible even to Copperleaf. It was this latter premise that had the most credence, as she had heard mention that they had an objective and a mission to complete, though that could've been a fabrication of some kind for all she knew. Regardless of the reason, if there was a reason he didn't want to be found by anyone from Thanchet or the Academy there, then she would do her darnedest to respect that; not only had he and his group saved her life and the lives of her own team, but they had also given them Fusions that would help propel them to new heights of power and safety. It was more than a fair trade, in her opinion.

Karley stepped through the open front doors of the SIC headquarters building to find that the bustling commotion of a large group of people intent on leaving the next day was still in effect. The Elementalist had managed to sneak away earlier from any packing duties as she made up an excuse to evaluate the walls and relieve those on watch so she could warn Larek and his group about the plot to steal from them in the morning; she felt slightly guilty about the entire thing, especially pitting herself against the orders of her boss concerning the group, but in the end she believed that it had been the right move. Especially with how it turned out.

Vivienne neatly dropped and stacked the staves just inside the doorway before dropping a pack with all of the other Fusions in it next to the stack. Eyeing both, she realized she was going to have to distribute them soon or they would begin to start degrading as the different Fusions fought over ambient Mana in their proximity, but she was told she had an hour or two before any serious damage to the Fusion formations occurred. She thought she'd have plenty of time to get that done, especially when she announced at large what she brought with her.

"Thank y—" she turned to say to the young woman, but the Martial from Larek's group was already gone. Mentally shrugging, she delicately put her own bundle of staves next to the one on the floor, before looking for her boss.

Thankfully, it didn't take long. "Major! I have some good news!"

Her boss, who had been racing through the hallway ahead of her for one reason or another, stopped when Karley called her name. Scowling at the interruption, Major Kuama looked over at the Elementalist standing next to the pile of staves on the floor. "What?" she snapped. "I don't have time for your games."

"No games, boss. I've got a surprise for you and everyone here."

That caught the attention of a few other members of the SIC forces walking by, as they stopped what they were doing and looked curiously at Karley. One of them was Deivin, the Combat Healer from her group, and all it took was one look at the pile behind her for him to rush over with a very unmanly scream of joy. "Karley, you beautiful goddess – what did you do?!"

Blushing and shaking her head, she warned Deivin to be careful. "Those are real, so don't be knocking holes in the building." Waving to the Major, who was now looking at the Combat Healer in confusion at his enthusiasm, especially when he picked up one of the staves, began rubbing it lovingly, and then whispered to it like a long-lost love, she quickly explained. "I was able to negotiate a deal with the group staying over at the Waterbury Inn, so there's no need to—"

"You did what?! No one gave you the authority to—wait." The next second, the Major was right in front of her face. "You told them, didn't you?"

Karley hesitated for a moment, but she eventually nodded. "Yes, but—"

"Why in the world would you go and pull a stunt like that? Your insubordination—"

"Boss? Boss? Major Kuama!"

Deivin was quickly joined by the Martial he had been walking with, Brant, and they had opened the bag full of powerful Fusions. When they looked inside, the burly Striker immediately tried to get the Major's attention. Karley sighed in relief as the Major's intense stare switched targets as it homed in on the Martial. "What! Can't you see—"

"Boss, you're going to want to see this," Brant said, tossing a pair of steel anklets toward the Major, who deftly caught them in the air.

"Why are you—oh. Ohhhh, wow." Her boss' vision went unfocused for a moment as she undoubtedly looked at her Status, and her mouth dropped open in shock. Karley could well understand that reaction, as she had felt it only a short time before when she put the two bracelets around her wrists. "How? This *doubles all my stats!*" Her exclamation was so loud that it wasn't a surprise when there was a sudden stomping throughout the entire building as nearly everyone heard her, despite there being walls and floors between them.

"Like I was trying to tell you," Karley explained again, "I negotiated the gift of these items for *everyone* here, on the condition that you don't try and steal anything from them, nor mention their presence to anyone in Thanchet." The other stipulation was that she not reveal that it was Larek that had made them all, though that was a bit of a stretch with all the staves. When she mentioned that to him, he just shrugged and told her to figure out a good explanation. For what these Fusions did, she would be willing to make up any story he wanted.

"They had all of this with them?" the Major asked, her shock wearing off when she heard Karley's words. "Why? And why do they not want us to mention them to anyone in Thanchet? Are these all stolen?"

"Yes, they had them all with them, or at least nearby," she answered as smoothly as possible. "As for why? They're on a mission to do something, but they wouldn't answer what it was or where they were going. They said it's Academy business, but that's all. I also do not believe they stole anything, either."

Her boss snorted. "Yeah, right. Who else would have this stuff, otherwise?" Looking at the crowd that was now snatching up the items with powerful Fusions on them, the Major added, "There's no way they have them legitimately; no one would trust a bunch of kids to transport it all. Not only that, but their desire for anonymity is suspicious. I've a mind to capture them and bring them to Thanchet when we leave tomorrow."

"No!" she practically shouted, holding out her hands pleadingly. When the Major looked at her with a shocked and then ticked-off expression on her face, she realized she had just yelled out an order at her boss. "I'm sorry, I didn't mean it like that," she backtracked. "I just meant that there is no reason to do that, because we already got this much from them, and they aren't hurting anybody. Just let them go on their way, and we get all of this for free."

"Nothing's for free, Karley. Is this a bribe? What did you promise them?" the Major asked. As everyone got their staves and other Fusion items, without any extras left over, her boss added, "How did they know how many of us there are? Did they just happen to have the perfect amount to account for all of us?"

"Well, I told them how many Mages and Martials were—"

"So they gave you exactly what you asked for, huh? That likely means that they have even more that they're hiding. We're going to take it all and distribute as much as we can get our hands on in Thanchet. Hoarding these Fusions with the current situation concerning the Scissions and monster hordes running around is criminal, and I intend to bring them all back to face punishment."

"But you can't do that—"

"I can't *what?* It seems to me that you've forgotten who you're talking to."

Now getting increasingly more nervous as the Major took on a threatening tone, Karley tried another tactic. "I really would suggest leaving them alone; I don't want anyone to get hurt."

"We're not going to hurt them, unless they force us to. We'll leave the punishment to those in authority back in Thanchet."

She shook her head. "I wasn't talking about *them* getting hurt."

The Major stepped back in surprise, before chuckling. "Ha! That's funny. If you think a couple of kids can hurt the veteran members of this force, then you must have hit your head. Do you need to see a Healer? Or better yet, use one of these healing Fusions I see we have now?"

Karley just shook her head again. "I'm serious. They could be more dangerous than anything you've encountered before." She couldn't explain how or why she knew that at least the Fusionist was particularly powerful, but she tried to convey that it would be a bad idea to try and take their stuff or capture them.

The Major looked at her and then glanced around at the happy celebrations and exclamations of shock that were still emerging as the SIC forces obtained their new gifts. She was silent for a few moments before she turned back to Karley and slowly nodded. "Fine. There's something you're obviously not telling me, but I've known you long enough to understand that you're looking out for all of us." She sighed before continuing. "And thank you for negotiating all of this," she said, waving at the now-crowded front room of Whittleton's SIC headquarters.

Karley released the breath she had been holding in relief, and practically sagged in place. She was hoping that she would get through to the Major if she simply worked all the different angles, and that thankfully proved to be accurate.

"Your welcome, boss. Believe me, this is the best outcome we could get from all of this."

Turning away, the Major nodded. "I'm sure it was."

Snatching her own staff away from someone who was trying to nab it from where she had left it, Karley began to instruct everyone on the restrictions of the new weapons and healing Fusions. She had to switch some that were made for Mages or Martials because the recipients didn't know their properties as well as she and Deivin had learned. The boosts were self-explanatory, though she saw more than a few Martials become a little unsteady as they got used to having double the stats they used to have just a short time ago.

Overall, it had been a success, and Larek and his group would leave tomorrow unmolested and free to do whatever mission they were on. Karley and the SIC in Whittleton would also depart, heading toward Thanchet and whatever plan the Major had to join up with the forces there.

To think, in less than 12 hours she had gone from nearly dying to being more than twice as powerful as before, and it was all thanks to an oddly powerful stranger. She wished him the best of luck, and as much as it would be nice to obtain more Fusions from him, she also hoped that he was able to fulfill whatever mission he had – or that he escaped the obligations that his talent imposed upon him.

Chapter 40

"I still don't think that was a smart idea."

Larek nodded at Nedira's words, before looking at the scattered accessories around his bed. In order to get all of the new Fusions done in a timely manner, his friends dumped out quite a few of the purchases that Penelope, Vivienne, and Kimble had made earlier so that he could pick through them. Most of it ended up being copper or even leather bracelets or bands, but there were enough steel accessories that he had been able to make them all into Fusions for the SIC. He wasn't able to add a *Strengthen* Fusion to them as well as the boosts, but the material was sturdy enough normally that he hoped they wouldn't be likely to be damaged enough to release the Mana inside the Fusions. He had at least used the technique that made the formations a bit more "malleable," such as what he used on cloth and leather, so even if they were deformed slightly, they would still be fine.

"Maybe. Maybe not," he replied, shrugging. "It was the best solution I could come up with that would actually benefit people without violence, and based on what we've learned about what is going on out there in the Kingdom, it sounded like they needed it."

"But they were going to steal from us! It makes no sense to help them after that threat!"

Larek understood where she was coming from, so he explained the motivations he had developed while they were still downstairs in the common room. He was fairly sure that she didn't really share the same thought process as he did, but she fortunately didn't say anything after that. He could tell that she was just worried about him and his safety, and with everything that had happened over the last week, he couldn't blame her.

Vivienne slipped through the door a short time later, back from helping the Elementalist deliver all of the new Fusions to the SIC.

"Done. They're extremely happy. Deal delivered and accepted."

He was about to say, "Good," but she continued.

"At least *on the surface*. Most likely an ambush outside of town tomorrow when we leave."

That took him by surprise. "Really? What makes you say that?"

"The Major in charge agreed too quickly. Mage girl accidentally hinted that you have more than this, likely hidden in a cache somewhere."

Larek sighed in exasperation. He had thought that all this would be enough to get them away from this town without any problems, but that seemed to have backfired. The Fusionist wanted to blame Karley, but he realized that most of the blame should probably be on himself, if he was being honest. If he hadn't wanted to essentially "bribe" the SIC into looking the other way from their presence, then they might have been able to get away from Whittleton through some other avenue. He was also the one who wanted to help save Karley and her group from dying to those Dechonabras, and while that was technically his fault because it was his decision, he still didn't regret it.

"So... solutions?" he finally asked after a few seconds of silence in the room. "My idea obviously failed, and I'm willing to admit when I'm wrong and out of my depth." Even worse, with the SIC planning on ambushing them tomorrow, they would all be utilizing the Fusions he had created. *Well, that's not actually a **bad** thing, especially with the precautions I put in place.*

While he hadn't *known* something like this would happen, he had thought it might be a distinct possibility. As such, during the Fusion creation process, he had added a very tiny flaw in every single formation in the Mana Overflow Bypass; it wasn't enough to compromise the Fusion, or even normally affect it at all, fortunately. But with Larek's sense of Fusions and formations, especially ones that *he* made, he was fairly certain that he could reach out with his Pattern Cohesion and subtly widen the flaw to the point where the formation would break. It was like leaving a back door unlocked; it was technically still closed, but with a little application of the door handle via his Pattern Cohesion, he could open it up.

He would normally never do anything like that, and attempting to alter an existing Fusion was highly dangerous, as it could explode – which was exactly why he added the flaw. If the SIC wanted to ambush him and his friends, they would find in store a rude awakening.

He wasn't sure how far away he could be to still affect the formations, but as he already had practice manipulating his Pattern Cohesion a bit away from his body when he was applying it toward *Focused Division*, he thought he could probably reach at least 15 feet or so before he would have issues. Since it was technically only a tiny little wedge that he needed to shove into the flaw to bust it open, he thought he might be able to reach out perhaps twice that distance or more at a stretch.

Larek didn't mention any of that to the others, however. He didn't want them worried about him doing something to their own

Fusions; he had only added the flaws this time because he didn't trust the SIC here at Whittleton.

They wanted to steal all their stuff, after all.

His musings were interrupted when Nedira spoke. "We should leave now. As much as I want to stay in a real bed tonight, we can't afford to be ambushed tomorrow."

Vivienne had walked across the room at some point and was looking through a slit in the window coverings. She shook her head at Nedira's suggestion. "No. There are people watching."

"Then we all can use the *Camouflage Sphere* Fusions, right? They won't be able to see us leave then?" Nedira asked, looking to Larek for help.

He thought about it for a moment. "Moving slowly enough, it might work?"

Vivienne shot that idea down, too. "Too easy to spot."

Larek and Nedira didn't argue the point, as they both knew from experience that the Fusion was easier to see while in motion. *Camouflage Sphere* really just excelled when it came to small movements or standing still, as the distortion it caused in the covered area was otherwise too visible – especially for people looking for any evidence that someone was moving around. Two or three of them *might* be able to pass by the watchers if they moved at a virtual crawl, but *all* of them? Not likely.

"Stay another day?" Verne ventured, and Larek had to admit that the idea had promise. If they were going to ambush them outside, then staying inside the Inn would prevent that possibility.

But that also risked someone getting hurt if the SIC force in Whittleton decided to change their plan when they didn't emerge tomorrow morning. If they came into the Inn after them and a fight broke out, the collateral damage and the potential for the people of Whittleton to be hurt by the battle would be high. And there *would* be a battle, as Larek doubted that the Major from the SIC would simply settle for the Fusions they currently had on them; it was highly likely that they would try and capture the entire group so as to find out where the "rest of the Fusions" were stored. Becoming a prisoner again was the last thing Larek wanted; once was more than enough for the Fusionist.

It wasn't just Larek who shook his head at his suggestion, as even his roommate realized that it probably wouldn't work a few seconds after he said it.

"I'm not sure there's much that we can do, other than breaking out of any ambush set up for us," Penelope said after almost a minute of them looking at each other in silence.

Larek briefly thought about some elaborate plans involving misdirection, illusionary images, and even some additional defensive Fusions in case they were discovered escaping Whittleton, but he wasn't sure if it would do much good. The problem was that as soon as it became known that they were no longer in the Inn, the SIC could easily search for them in whatever direction they went, as they knew the area much better than Larek or those with him. With around 30 Martials that were part of the SIC in Whittleton, each of them could utilize the new Fusions they were just given to track and easily chase them down with their higher Agility stats. His own group couldn't move nearly as fast as would be required to flee from them successfully, and he didn't think it would be worth it to even try.

But breaking out of an ambush by the SIC had its own dangers. Not only could one of his friends or bodyguards become seriously hurt in a confrontation like that, but it was possible that one of them could die. He was fairly confident they would win in a situation like that, especially if he was able to surprise them all by exploding their new Fusions, but that didn't lessen the risk to his group. These were veteran members of the SIC, after all, and while they might not be the most powerful members around – such as those who had defended the walls of Peratin and Thanchet – they were likely more than a match for any of his bodyguards individually.

Even if he was able to surprise them with exploding Fusions, was that what he wanted to do? He had created the flaw in the formations just in case he was forced to utilize it for his own protection, but he had really hoped that it would never be necessary. Killing them would only hurt the people of Whittleton and the surrounding area, and while he still wasn't exactly enamored of the common people due to their instinctual prejudice against someone of his height, that didn't mean he necessarily wanted them all to die when they no longer had a force of defenders to help them. Their town might not necessarily be attacked right away, but without anyone to patrol the roads, travel would become even more dangerous than it was right now, leading to less trade, fewer shipments of food, and eventually starvation because of lack of food.

He might not like the majority of people, but he wasn't a heartless monster that wanted them all to die.

The Gergasi already fulfill that role quite well, he thought to himself.

Besides, as much as he hated what the SIC were willing to do to get their hands on more of his Fusions, they were technically on the same side. They were going about things completely *wrong*, of course, but the intent to protect themselves and others by making themselves stronger was a worthy endeavor – even with their misguided and misinformed tactics.

One solution that stood out was to negotiate personally with this Major in charge of the local SIC forces, perhaps even explaining who he was and what he was doing. Unfortunately, given how most of the leadership he'd seen in his travels thus far through the Kingdom were Nobles or were enslaved by the Gergasi in some way, it was entirely possible that this Major that Karley told him about was the same. Even if the local leader wasn't enslaved, there was at least one Noble *that was*, and the likelihood of Larek's location and heading being exposed was high at that point. Unless every single Noble was killed to slow the spread of information, of course, but that wouldn't necessarily endear him to the local SIC, either. At best, they would still simply come after Larek's group and capture them; at worst, they would attempt to slaughter his group when they caught up to them.

It really wasn't looking like there was a good solution there that didn't result in tragedy for one group or another. Either Larek and his own group would suffer, the local SIC would suffer, or the entire town of tens of thousands of people would suffer – it was seemingly a lose-lose situation that the Fusionist didn't know how to solve.

"Killing any of the SIC forces here, even in self-defense, would probably be the worst thing we could do," Bartholomew responded to Penelope's statement about breaking out of the ambush – which likely meant killing some of the ambushers. "If anything, that would simply turn the entire Corps as a whole against us, leading to a Kingdom-wide manhunt to track us down."

"Even with the situation with the Scissions and monsters as it is?" Penelope asked incredulously.

The Noble Martial nodded. "Absolutely. There's nothing like the murder of one of their own to bring the SIC together, and even with restricted travel and the dangerous countryside, we would have swarms of people looking for us." He paused for a moment, before reluctantly adding, "Unless we killed them all, of course, but then we'd be dooming a good portion of the people near this region unnecessarily."

That tracked with what Larek was thinking, and he couldn't in good conscience do that to either the SIC or the common people of Whittleton. "That won't be happening," he quickly interjected. "In fact,

I don't want to kill *anyone* if we don't have to, unless they force the issue. No, we need to think of something else."

Not sure where to go from there, he looked around the room at his companions, before settling his gaze on the floor in an effort to think. He let his vision go unfocused for a minute or so, before something caught his eye. Looking at the light-based game he had created for Verne and Norde to play with earlier, an idea began to form in the back of his mind. When Penelope began to speak again, he held up his hand for silence as more and more of his idea crystallized into one cohesive whole.

When Larek finally felt it snap into place in his head, he did some mental calculations while he checked his Status to confirm he still had over 7,500 Pattern Cohesion. What he had planned was going to take a lot of preparation and a huge chunk of his Cohesion all at once, but he thought it would work.

Looking up at Vivienne, he asked, "Do you think you would be able to get outside of the town tonight for a short while without being seen?"

The Ranger looked back at him as if she had just heard the dumbest question ever asked. "Of course," she answered. "Why?"

"I have a plan," he said, nodding, even as he pulled a leather band over to himself from the pile of accessories on his bed. He needed to design and test the Fusion he had in mind first, but if it worked like he thought it would, he would need a few things that weren't likely to be found easily inside the town. "I need approximately 100 small rocks of different sizes, all varied enough that they wouldn't look out of place if you were to drop them on the ground. They need to be at least as big as my thumb and no bigger than your fist. Do you think you can do that?"

She only thought about it for a second before nodding.

"Excellent. While you're out doing that, I'll let the rest of you know what I'm planning and then I need a test subject...." He smirked at the way his friends flinched when he said that. "Don't worry, there shouldn't be any *permanent* harm."

That didn't seem to reassure them one bit.

Chapter 41

The morning sun seemed particularly bright when they left the following morning, each of them with stuffed packs strapped to their backs and pockets bulging with supplies. Vivienne had finagled some extra food out of the Innkeeper early in the morning for their departure, since they theoretically wouldn't be visiting another town or city anytime soon, as it turned out to be too dangerous for them right now. While Larek had been working on his Fusions the night before, everyone else had also started to divide up all the supplies, ensuring that everyone had some of the food purchased the day before, a quantity of coins, and their letters of transfer that would allow them to integrate themselves into Silverledge and Ironwall.

Strangely enough, it was actually the first time that the Fusionist had looked at the letter, but it was essentially what Shinpai had described to him before they left Copperleaf Academy. It basically noted that due to some unforeseen circumstances revolving around Copperleaf Academy and Fort Pinevalley, Larek was to be transferred immediately to Fort Ironwall; it was not only signed by the Dean but also the head of Pinevalley, Vice General Whittaker. Whether that was his real signature, Larek didn't know, but he supposed it didn't matter at this point.

It further noted that Larek was discovered to have the potential in him to become a Martial at a very late age, and due to this difference in the normal assimilation into the Fort, they decided it would be best for the "experts" at Fort Ironwall to handle his education. It was couched in flowery language that Larek immediately understood was designed to flatter the people in charge of Ironwall, making it seem as though sending Larek there was because of their greater ability to train Martials and other such praise. He figured that would either blind them to his real abilities... or make them suspicious and look into him a bit more than he was comfortable with. He didn't necessarily want to go back to hiding what he could do, especially with Fusions, but in order to unlock his *Stama Subjugation* Skill, learn how to fight monsters with a technique that extended beyond "pretending he was cutting down a tree", and learn the secret of creating and activating Battle Arts, he felt that it would be worth it.

As they passed through the town, their presence drew a little more attention than the day before, as they had been transformed from dirty, exhausted newcomers to travelers appearing to be heading out on a lengthy journey with their full packs and staves camouflaged as normal walking sticks – but the extra scrutiny didn't feel too abnormal to Larek. All he knew was that there was no sign of any SIC people watching them depart, though Vivienne noted that they were out there in the crowds.

It wasn't until they reached the eastern gate of the town, after navigating their way through all the people and new construction that seemed to be everywhere, that they saw a familiar face.

Karley the Elementalist stood near the gate, nervously shifting from foot to foot with her new staff held upright with a tight grip. When she saw them and looked at Larek, he intuitively knew the nervousness wasn't because she was part of an ambush that was going to be set up for them, but because she was at least a bit fearful of the power he had shown making the Fusions the night before.

"There you are!" she said, relief written all over her features when she saw them. Trotting up to them with a smile as she looked at everyone but Larek, she said in a rush, "I wanted to catch you before you left and say thank you for everything you provided to us here. In addition, I spoke with Major Kuama and she agreed not to mention anything to anyone in Thanchet about your presence here, nor will she try to steal anything from you."

Bargaining *has reached Level 6!*
Bargaining *has reached Level 7!*

Larek dismissed the notifications and thought it was strange that his *Bargaining* Skill had only increased in Level now, instead of when he had negotiated with her the night before. He supposed it was because she was negotiating for the Major instead of for herself, and now that he had confirmation that it had been "successful", the Skill increased. Not just once, though, but twice; he could only assume it was because the negotiation had been a life-or-death situation with huge stakes that could be lost if it fell through.

Of course, it didn't take into account the fact that the Major had likely lied to her about trying to capture them and steal their stuff. But as far as the woman was concerned, the negotiation was successful – and Larek could tell from the way she sounded that she really believed that.

"Thank you, Karley. I appreciate your help and hope you can get some use out of those Fusions," Larek replied, which caused the Elementalist to look at him again. As her eyes went to his, or at least where she perceived his eyes were because of the *Perceptive*

Misdirection Fusion on his ring, he could see that she was nervous. Swallowing audibly, all she could do was nod.

I'm starting to wonder if it is better to be feared because of my height rather than my power; the one I can't do anything about, while the other is what makes me the way I actually am. Then again, both are technically because of my Gergasi ancestry, so I guess that it's a wash.

"Take care, Karley," Penelope said as they walked by, the blue-haired Martial trailing her fingers over the sleeve of the Elementalist as she passed. The woman froze in confusion at the touch, but before she could respond, Larek and his group had already exited Whittleton.

When they were approximately a quarter-mile from the gate as they traveled down the road, their walk so far being relatively silent, he heard Penelope and Vivienne giggling. When they saw his questioning glance, Penelope explained. "That girl has no idea what is going on, so I decided to muddy the waters a little more. She's going to be so confused and thinking about things that she'll likely avoid being roped into the ambush being prepared for us."

Now it was Larek's turn to become confused, but he restrained himself from asking questions. Whatever it was that Penelope had done was irrelevant, though he hoped it had been beneficial. If it kept the Elementalist out of what was to come, that was all for the better; she seemed like a generally good person, and he didn't want her to get caught up in everything.

Another mile down the road, Vivienne glanced back at him surreptitiously, letting him know that they were being followed. The Ranger then ran ahead of the group and acted the part of a scout, as would be expected, with the others giving no sign that anything was amiss. Larek nervously fiddled with the stones in his robe pockets as they walked before he forced his hands to stillness after a while.

It was approximately 30 minutes later that Vivienne came back, supposedly to simply just check back in with them, but the Ranger actually had information for them. As she spoke, she flashed a few hand signals they had developed the night before that Larek interpreted as "5 minutes" and "Hidden", but any more than that was too fast for him to understand. He knew his part just as everyone else did, however, so that was all that mattered.

"Looks all clear for the next few miles," Vivienne announced loudly, which easily reached the ears of their pursuing ambushers. Instead of disappearing into the distance to scout more afterward, the Ranger only moved a hundred feet or so ahead, as if she was confident that everything was safe ahead and wanted to stay near the group.

So far, so good.

Keeping an eye on the road ahead, it soon became blatantly obvious where the ambush was going to be – even to one untrained in looking for such things. The dirt pathway had been generally straight as it cut through a relatively level landscape, with short grassland bracketing the road and the sight of a forest off to the south being the only major landmark in sight. Once they passed over a slight hill that was just barely able to conceal the pathway ahead, he could see that the road turned more to the northeast as it made its way through a short mountain of what appeared to be a mixture of stone and dirt that looked entirely out of place, as well as a small pond next to it. It almost looked like some sort of giant had thrown a huge, dirt-filled stone ball that smashed into the ground, leaving a divot for water to collect in, before bouncing up and cracking apart to make the small mountain.

It was honestly more of a hill than a mountain, but with the relatively level terrain, the 40-foot-tall and 80-foot-wide dirt and stone pile was as mountainous as it was going to get in the area.

Needless to say, if they were going to be ambushed anywhere along the road, this was certainly the place to do it. The SIC could easily hide behind the mountain and attack them either by going around or over top of the stone pile, and with those coming up behind them, they would be trapped between an outcropping of rock and the might of the forces arrayed against them.

It made his plan a little harder, considering they didn't know the terrain, but he thought it would still work.

Judging the distance to be about right, Larek reached into his pocket, grabbed one of the stones that Vivienne managed to scrounge up the night before, and dropped it on the road after activating it. It rolled to a stop next to some others just like it, blending into the pathway with ease. His dropping the stone prompted Verne and Norde to bend down and pick up some other stones as they walked, before chucking them into the nearby grass; to an outsider, they looked like just a pair of kids alleviating their boredom. Of course, every few stones they threw to the sides were replaced with ones in their pockets, but it wasn't very obvious, even to those looking for the exchange. Meanwhile, Larek continued to drop another stone every 10 feet or so along the road, ensuring an even coverage over its length.

Playing into the "young and bored" theme, Bartholomew started to do the same, only his were thrown ahead more than to the side, and he used his greater Strength stat to launch the rocks at the mountain, where they impacted and sunk into the dirt portions. Larek repressed a wince as one of them ricocheted off of the stone portion of the mountain and flew far enough to plunk down in the small pond nearby. He hadn't put any *Strengthen* Fusions on the stones so he was worried it might crack, but it stayed intact at least long enough to settle onto the bottom of the pond without a trace.

As they got closer to the mountain, Vivienne turned around from where she had already passed the front edge of it and bent down to pick up her own stones. "Hey!" she shouted, emphasizing her shout as she threw her own projectiles off to the sides. "Does this look or sound like you're making my job any easier?" she complained, while continuing to throw out some of her stones. "Each impact or rustle in the land makes me think there's a monster nearby."

"Oh, come on, we're just having a little fun," Norde complained with a very convincing whine.

"Well, I hope you're having fun when some monster I wasn't able to hear eats you," the Ranger scoffed, throwing out another handful of stones in the process in disgust.

"Fine, fine – just one more." Norde and Verne threw one more stone each, followed by Bartholomew with a smile at his fellow Martial. By that time, they were essentially right in front of the mountain, and as Vivienne joined them, she held her hand in front of her leathers and started counting down from 5. When she closed her fist, Larek activated his *Repelling Barrier* along with everyone else.

When nothing happened for a few seconds as they slowed their walk, he thought for a moment that Vivienne was mistaken and there was actually no ambush waiting for them. The Ranger also looked disappointed that she hadn't timed it accurately, but a hint of a smile touched on her lips as she looked behind the rest of the group.

Larek didn't see them, but he could only assume that the ones that were trailing them had finally decided to show themselves. *His* attention was on what was ahead of them, which was the appearance of dozens of Martials and Mages streaming around the mountain, along with a few cresting the top of the large hill.

"Halt!" A woman, whom he took to be Major Kuama by Vivienne's description of the powerful Martial, appeared at the head of the pack down below and started shouting. "By the authority granted by the Scission Interception Corps, I hereby demand that you put down your weapons and surrender. In addition, you will lead us to whatever Fusions you have stolen so that they can either be returned or distributed to those who can use them. You have 5 seconds to comply."

"You dare to interrupt our mission of importance?" Bartholomew indignantly shouted in response. "I don't believe you understand the *great* task that this *one* is undertaking!"

It was their last ploy to avoid the confrontation from getting out of hand. They were banking on the Major being enslaved to the Gergasi, or Great Ones, and the Noble bodyguard was attempting to imply that they were traveling because of specific orders.

Unfortunately, while there was a reaction from a few of the SIC members as they arranged themselves in a large cordon a significant distance away from the group, the Major showed no reaction to Bartholomew stressing "great" and "one" in his shout.

"If you're truly on a mission, we'll determine the veracity of that claim back in Thanchet. Now, no more talking. This is your last warning. You now have 3 seconds to surrender. Don't throw your lives away. Two... Give up now and you won't be harmed. One... I'm sorry, but the SIC needs those Fusions. Zero... Go!"

At "Go," the ambushing SIC members shot forward, Martials and Mages alike, to close the distance. While the Mages didn't necessarily need to be too close in order to attack, if they needed to help restrain and break through any magical defenses, they would have to be close to counteract them.

Unfortunately for the entire SIC force, they hadn't banked on Larek and his group being prepared for this. After they passed over a certain distance, there were flares of light that sprung up out of seemingly nowhere, highlighting a 20-square-foot section around some innocuous-looking stones. Anyone who passed through the light suddenly tumbled forward, their body collapsing as if they had suddenly lost control of it.

Larek looked around, seeing that not a single one of the ambushers was still on their feet. A movement out of the corner of his eye, however, belied that initial estimation, as he saw the Major struggling to her feet, a glow around her that signified to him that she was using her Stama in some sort of Battle Art.

*Well, it was **mostly** a success. She must be inordinately strong for this not to have worked on her.*

Sighing, he joined the others as they watched the powerful Martial struggle her way through the light that had suddenly paralyzed the rest of her forces, a grimace of anger on her face that said they were going to pay for whatever it was they did.

Or was it fear?

He couldn't tell, but he thought he was soon going to find out.

Chapter 42

"What did you do to my people?!" the Major managed to growl out even while pushing herself toward Larek and his group.

"They're paralyzed," Larek said. "Like you should be, too, but I guess you're too strong for that."

The woman struggled to pull herself forward after a while, using her deadly-looking spear as a means to hold herself up. "I won't fall for these tricks, criminal!"

"Criminal? Why do you say that?" he asked, actually curious what her justification was for that label.

"You stole all of these Fusions—"

"We did no such thing. None of these Fusions were stolen or taken or acquired in any way that would be considered criminal activity." As easy as it would be to simply say that *he* had made them, he wasn't sure he could trust the Major with that information. The fact that she didn't react when Bartholomew mentioned being on a mission from a "Great One" made her a little more trustworthy, but her pushing for his group's capture was something that generated a lot of bias against the local SIC leader. "In fact, what you are doing now would be considered criminal, so *I* should be the one bringing *you* back to Thanchet. Setting an ambush on the road like a common bandit trying to pillage a caravan looks a lot more guilty than whatever it is you think you know about us."

Throwing the criminal accusation back at her had the opposite reaction to what he was expecting. Instead of growing angrier and raging at him, the Major's fury seemed to drain out of her, along with the bright glow that surrounded her entire body. He wasn't sure what kind of Battle Art she was using, but it seemed as though she had stressed it enough that she collapsed to one knee, and Larek could tell that it was only the minimal usage of that Art and the spear in her hand that were keeping her upright by that point.

She had been so close to breaking out of the *Paralytic Light +10* Fusion, too. The idea for it had come from the light game he had created for his roommates and the *Paralytic Touch* Fusion he had added to Penelope's sword; he thought he might be able to combine the two, and it seemed to have worked. Essentially, stepping on the area around the Fusion caused a light to emerge, and wherever it touched was immediately paralyzed as long as the light was touching it. He was able to exclude paralyzing internal organs and blood flow, thankfully, which was why he needed to have test subjects the night before to ensure it worked, because he didn't want the SIC members to actually die when their heart or brain stopped working. The effect only lasted for 6 hours before deactivating, as he didn't want them to be paralyzed on the ground forever.

But it likely wouldn't stay effective that long, as they had learned the night before, because it seemed as though both Mages and Martials could slowly become accustomed to the paralyzing effect after about 10 minutes and their bodies would start to fight through it. It wasn't nearly as fast as what the Major had done with her Battle Art, but it would still allow them to drag themselves outside of the range of the Fusion after a while. It also wouldn't affect anyone that was completely covered from head to toe, as it needed to touch at least the tiniest bit of bare skin to function properly; likewise, with monsters that didn't have biological bodies, or were furry enough that the light was blocked from actually touching the skin underneath, the paralyzing effect would be much less effective, if not useless.

"Who... are... you?" the Major finally struggled to ask.

Larek shook his head. "I'm no one, and you didn't see any of us. We have no quarrel with you, and we honestly do have a mission of importance to complete." While that was bending the truth a little, he *was* told by the Dean to go to Fort Ironwall. He had a letter of transfer and everything.

"Why? Where... are you... going?"

"That, I can't tell you, unfortunately. Suffice it to say that it is a secret, and sharing our destination and mission would compromise that secret." All of that was true, technically. He glanced at Penelope and the blue-haired Martial took it from there.

"We need you to swear on your authority as an officer in the Scission Interception Corps that you will not follow or harass us after we leave here today, nor will you mention our presence to anyone else. Doing so will net you nothing and could potentially cost you your lives. This is your one and only warning to leave us alone to complete our mission. We don't want to have to hurt you, which is why all of you will live after this; just as easily, we could've killed you all before you even knew what was happening. Please don't make the mistake of coming after us, or that will be the last one you'll ever make. Do you so swear?"

There was a slight hesitation before she answered. Looking at the Major in her kneeling position, he could see that her body was starting to resist the paralyzing effect already, but it was still a bit away from giving her the freedom of movement she so desired. Finally, after what felt like hours, she reluctantly spoke. "I swear on my authority in the Scission Interception Corps that neither I, nor anyone under my command, will pursue or harass anyone in your group after you leave here today. In addition, I, as well as anyone under my command, will not mention seeing you or knowing of your presence to anyone else, short of a direct order from the King."

"Thank you," Larek said sincerely. While swearing on her authority didn't really mean much if she decided to pursue Larek anyway, he still felt better after hearing that. And if it just so happened that she received a direct order from the King to reveal his whereabouts, who was essentially an extension of the Gergasi's enslavement, then there wasn't much he could do about that no matter how much the Major wanted to uphold her sworn vow.

Regardless, it seemed as though they had managed to get out of the ambush without anyone dying *and* securing a promise not to pursue them in the future. His late night of effort placing the powerful *Paralytic Light* Fusions on nearly 100 stones had paid off, resulting in as good of an outcome as was possible. He had also increased his *Multi-effect Fusion Focus* Skill to Level 17 through the entire process, so it was beneficial in more ways than one.

Now they just needed to get out of there before nearly 60 angry SIC members shook off the paralyzing effect of those same Fusions and took out their frustration at feeling so helpless on some readily available targets. He didn't trust all of them to follow the Major's swearing on her authority right away, mostly because some of them might not have been able to hear the entire conversation.

Thankfully, his group had deliberately left a narrow path through the stones that would allow them to pass through the field of light without being affected themselves. "We'll be on our way, then. The paralyzing effect will start to fade after a short while, so you should be able to remove yourselves from the light field soon enough. Take good care of those Fusions you received; they might just save your life one day."

The Major just grunted as the last of the glow around her faded and she collapsed to the ground. She was already starting to twitch a little as she struggled to move, a clear sign that her body was adjusting to the Fusion's effects. The others saw this as well and they hurried to move through the strip of clear space between the light fields they had left. At one point, Norde accidentally stepped too close to one and fell halfway into one of the Fusions, but Larek was able to drag his paralyzed body out by his exposed legs and get him moving, though the boy stumbled a little as he got used to moving again after being fully paralyzed.

All of them broke into a jog as soon as they were past the entire field of *Paralytic Light* Fusions that blanketed the area, leaving the road in order to head in a more northeasternly direction. However, they only traveled a few hundred feet through the short grass before something made them freeze in place as if they too had been paralyzed like the SIC force back at the ambush spot.

A Scission.

Larek slowly turned with the rest of his group toward the north, expecting to see what felt like an extremely powerful Scission appear nearby, but they didn't notice a single thing despite being able to see for at least a mile or two into the distance. Despite the changes in Scissions that had happened over the last year or so, he was fairly certain that the detectable distance from one of the monster-spewing openings was still less than 2 or 3 miles, even if they were a powerfully high Category. Not only that, but the further away you were, the weaker it would feel, so when he felt a Scission stronger than anything he'd felt before, he expected for it to be well within sight.

"What—? What's going on?" Verne asked, looking around for the Scission but not finding it – just like the others.

"I don't know, but this feels bad," Nedira responded, clutching tighter to her staff.

No one moved, as if even shifting their weight would somehow cause the Scission to appear in front of them. Each of them simply stared at where they could feel the emanating power coming from, but they were unable to view anything that would indicate what it was they were feeling.

Suddenly, as he looked toward the forest to the north, a very familiar dark haze with streaks of grey seemed to billow out over the trees, hiding them from his field of vision.

"Do you see that?" Larek asked, pointing toward the trees.

"See what? I don't see anything." Nedira visibly tried to track where he was pointing, but she just shook her head. The others tried looking toward the trees, as well, but they didn't see anything, either.

If they can't see it, then that likely means it's Corrupted Aetheric Force. Why is it there? Better yet, where did it come from? Do Scissions release it normally into the world?

"There's what I believe to be a cloud of Corrupted Aetheric Force surrounding the forest in the distance," he explained.

"Did it come from the Scission?"

Larek began to nod at Penelope's question, because it seemed like the most obvious answer, but stopped himself. The more he looked at the dark cloud, the more he began to think that it didn't come from a

Scission. In fact, he didn't think there was a Scission at all, as it felt... *different*. He wouldn't be able to explain it to anyone else if they asked about it, but something seemed to have changed inside of Larek when he unlocked the ability to absorb Corrupted Aetheric Force and purify it into something he could use. There was an instinctual connection he had with it that told him that this wasn't a Scission.

It was something different.

"No. There isn't a Scission."

The others tore their gazes away from staring to the north to look at Larek. "I'm pretty sure I know what a Scission feels like, Larek," Penelope said. "But you're usually right about these types of things, I've found, so I'll bite. If it isn't a Scission, what is it?"

Slowly shaking his head, he said, "I don't know. But I think we need to find out."

"What?! Are you crazy?" Nedira shouted at him, before regulating her voice. "That's the last thing we should do, especially with how powerful it feels. Let's get as far away from it as possible."

That was the logical choice, as Larek never really wanted to get close to a Scission and the monsters they spewed out – even with his newfound need to kill them in order to advance his Skills. Especially if that meant going toward something that felt more powerful than any other Scission he'd felt before.

But he was leaning toward a very illogical and dangerous choice, as something instinctual was pulling him to investigate what was happening.

"No, we need to go see what this is. I can't explain why, but..." He didn't have the words to try to convince them, so he just shrugged.

He almost changed his mind when there was a sudden spike in the power levels coming from the disturbance in the distance, and the others looked at him with incredulous expressions on their faces. After almost a minute of silence, during which he could feel each of his companions wanting to argue against such an action, but holding their tongue for some reason, Nedira sighed heavily and said, "This is stupid, you know that, right?"

"I feel like you think a lot of things that I've been doing lately are stupid," he gently accused her, to which she flinched back a little.

"I—" She stopped and started again. "I just don't want you to get hurt, Larek."

"I know that, but I'm also following some new instincts of mine that I can't explain; simultaneously, it feels like the first time that I get the sense that I know that what I'm doing is actually correct." It was strange to say something like that, but as soon as it crossed his lips, he realized that it was true. He really did feel like this was the right thing to do, as much as he wasn't sure *what* it was he was doing.

"That doesn't make any sense, but... I trust you," Nedira said after a few seconds of thought. "I think I've always trusted you, which makes me feel weird, especially when I can't determine if it's your Dominion Magic working on me or not." She took a deep breath. "But I can't honestly say that you're wrong to investigate whatever this is, especially when you say it's not a Scission."

Larek knew that there were some issues between them that they still needed to address, but that wasn't something he could worry about at the moment. Instead, he took her acceptance of his explanation as confirmation that she would follow him toward the forest covered in the dark fog. And where she went with him, the others would follow.

After glancing at each of his companions, receiving resigned nods in return, he started walking toward the source of whatever it was they were feeling. After a few steps, Vivienne took the lead again, scouting for them as usual. They didn't hurry, as none of them actually *wanted* to see what was happening in the forest, and *running* into danger was probably not the best of plans.

They were probably a mile away from their destination when there was another spike of power coming from ahead, before it seemed to diminish at a steady pace afterwards. Looking ahead, Larek saw the Corrupted Aetheric Force – which, as he got closer to it, he could confirm was exactly what he thought it was – start to recede, as if it were being sucked into the middle of the forest.

For the first time, the others could finally see something happening, as the trees that had been covered by the black fog (at least to Larek's perspective) began to change at a rapid pace. Along one strip of the tree line, all of the leaves on the trees seemed to rapidly become covered in frost, turning them white within seconds. The whiteness of the leaves spread to the branches and finally to the trunks of the trees, terminating in a very thin layer of what appeared to be fresh snow upon the ground. The entire section gave an impression of coldness that was completely at odds with the already-warm early fall day.

That wasn't even the strangest of the changes, as next to the section of ice and snow-laden trees was a clear delineation of the forest. Instead of being covered in white, the trees had seemingly petrified, turning to stone and creating a hazard of sharp leaves that decorated the trees, as well as blanketed the ground with those that had fallen. It was even more impossible-looking than the section that was apparently frozen in the middle of winter next to it, but somehow the next area of the forest was even worse.

It was on fire.

Flames flickered from the now-burnt trees, which were free of any sign of leaves, and only the blackened trunks and branches were left. The flames seemed to be restricted to the branches, however, as the trunks and ground were free of the fire that burned like a torch – but there was no smoke. At all. Neither did the flames seem to be consuming more of the trees, contrary to what Larek would've expected to happen. Instead, the fire raged without any source of fuel, burning without smoke or even the crackling noise that should be accompanying such a blaze, and he suspected that it might even be an illusion of some sort. It looked real enough from far away, however, so he wasn't planning on testing that theory by touching it anytime soon.

"What is happening to the trees?" Verne asked, his voice shaking; it was difficult to tell if it was from fear or fury. The tree-like boy, having grown up in what was essentially a forest (as Larek had learned at one point), was a pragmatist and understood that felling trees was just something that was done in the Kingdom, so that didn't bother him. What did obviously bother him was the complete transformation of what appeared to be a good chunk of the forest they were looking at, at least little by little. The dark fog was still visibly being sucked into a deeper portion of the forest, leaving behind the dramatic transformation in its wake.

"I—"

Larek was cut off in his response when he heard someone else speak from just behind his group.

"Is this *your* doing?"

Whipping his head around, he saw that Major Kuama was standing there with her spear planted butt-first in the short grass... along with 50+ angry-looking SIC members spread out on either side of her.

Uh, oh. Looks like they managed to break free faster than I thought.

Chapter 43

Larek started to take an involuntary step back at the appearance of the SIC so close to him, but Penelope stopped him with a firm hand on his back. He understood immediately what she was doing, as they needed to present a strong front toward these people, and moving backwards as if trying to run would run counter to that impression.

At least, that was what logic was telling him, but being so close to the furious-looking SIC members nevertheless made him want to run.

"No. This is not of our making," Penelope stated fearlessly to the Major. "We were coming to assess the threat that we felt here. That is all."

There were a few mumbled mutterings that Larek wasn't able to make out completely, but no one suddenly attacked them either. After about 10 seconds, the Major finally looked past them and at the forest that was still transforming. "What is happening? I've never seen anything like this before."

With a mental sigh of relief, as it seemed as though at least the Major was prepared to honor her sworn vow for the moment, Larek glanced back at the radically changed trees and shook his head. "We've never seen anything like this before, either, but it feels extraordinarily dangerous."

That was patently obvious, he thought, but it didn't hurt to emphasize that there was something worse afoot than their own disagreements. That seemed to do the trick for the Major, as she nodded at his words. "It's a stronger Scission than anything I've felt before, but I can't actually see it, which is worrying."

Larek spoke without thinking. "It isn't a Scission. It's something else."

"What are you talking about? Of course it's a Scission! I know what a Scission feels like, *boy*."

Nedira came to his defense. "Oh, yeah? And does a Scission normally do *this?*" she asked, waving toward the trees.

"Obviously not, but—"

"Now isn't the time to argue," Larek interrupted the local SIC leader before their discussion could blow up into a full-blown fight. "I could be wrong, though I don't believe so; regardless, I think this is a threat that needs to be assessed and stopped immediately, don't you think?"

He could see Major Kuama's lips pressed firmly against each other, as if she was physically fighting with herself so as not to say something she would regret. After a few seconds, she gave a very short nod and said, "Yes. But if this is something like a Category 6 or above, then we're screwed."

"Well, then it's about time you put those new Fusions to the test, don't you think?" Penelope retorted with a bit of snark.

"Please don't antagonize the powerful people looking for an excuse to get back at us for what we did to them," Larek told the blue-haired Martial in a quiet voice. The way she opened her mouth right after he said that told him that she was going to deny doing just that, but she shut it just as quickly without saying anything. She didn't indicate that she heard and would do as he asked, but he got the impression that she would.

As the one in charge of overseeing the safety of the local area, Major Kuama was put into a situation where she couldn't easily back away from the threat represented by the powerful feeling coming from the forest. That didn't mean she had to like being backed into a corner by Larek and his group, but she immediately took charge of the situation as if she had been investigating strange, transforming forests her entire life.

"Despite your poor attitude, *girl*, you have a point," she said. "This land is *my* responsibility, however, and I won't put up with you endangering my people on this operation. You might be powerful, but you aren't a part of the SIC just yet, if you ever will be; as a result, I want you to stay back and out of the way while *we* investigate this threat. *Do not* engage with whatever we find inside here unless I specifically ask for your help, though at that point I would imagine everything will have gone to hell already."

It wasn't exactly ideal being pushed to an observer role, but Larek had to admit that it was probably a lot safer for his group. He agreed quickly after hearing the stipulations of their quasi-joint cooperation. "Fair enough. You lead and we'll follow."

Thankfully, none of his companions disagreed with this, especially as they didn't want to be so close to the powerful threat they could feel anyway.

The individual members of the SIC gave them murderous looks as they passed by, but none of them made any move to attack Larek or anyone with him. They had all obviously been informed of the Major's sworn vow not to attack them, which extended to anyone under her command. It was either that, or it was just a temporary truce while they dealt with more pressing issues, such as whatever was found inside of this forest.

The SIC entered through the white, snow-laden section of the trees, given that the petrified forest, with all of its sharp-edged leaves, appeared dangerous and the other section was aflame, but Larek couldn't say that it was much better. The moment he stepped foot over the line that seemed to differentiate the forest from the grassland, the environment plummeted to freezing or near-freezing temperatures, which caused the Fusionist to shiver slightly as his clothing wasn't necessarily appropriate for the weather. He found that his body naturally adjusted to the cold after a few seconds, as his Martial stat was proving to do more than just providing him with an extra-durable frame.

Unfortunately, that didn't help the Mages, not only in his own group but the ones that were part of the SIC, as he could see a few of them shivering slightly as they moved through the stillness of the snow-carpeted forest. Larek resolved to create some more of his *Temperature Regulator* Fusions at some point, which would help alleviate some of the discomfort that being in a cold environment brought with it.

Instead of rushing ahead, which would undoubtedly be stupid when venturing into an unknown situation, the Major sent a few Martials to scout the way ahead, and they advanced at a relatively even, if slow, pace. Despite the delay in investigating, as well as their current walking speed, they had only traveled about a half-mile before Larek could see the dark fog ahead of them still moving toward what seemed to be a central point somewhere in the forest.

It was at about that point that they found the body of one of the Martials sent out to scout. He was surrounded by two other scouts, who were looking down at his body in confusion and anger; Larek recognized one of them as Rhylla, the Silent Blade Martial they had saved from the Dechonabras the day before.

"What happened?"

The two scouts looked up at the Major before Rhylla answered. "Doran attempted to push past that strange haze to see what might lay beyond it," she said, waving toward where Larek saw the dark fog. Larek could only assume that because they couldn't see it like he could, they instead saw this "strange haze". "He passed through it and completely disappeared from my sight. A few seconds later, we found him like this on the ground after the haze retreated further ahead."

It killed him? Considering that he had been absorbing the Corrupted Aetheric Force for about a week, Larek suddenly worried that it was actually harming him.

The Major cursed up a storm, though she kept her volume low so as not to alert whatever else was in the forest. "Leave him for now; we'll pick up his body on the way back," she eventually said, before looking toward the retreating dark, or in her case, the strange haze. "And don't get near that stuff; we'll follow along and destroy whatever we find that we can actually fight."

So, that was exactly what they did. For the next 30 minutes, they made their way forward, staying well out of range of the strange haze that seemed to be the catalyst for the changes in the forest. After quietly asking Nedira what she could see of this haze, she said that it was like a visual distortion in a flat plane that was at least higher than the treetops; she could see the vague outlines of normal trees through it, but as soon as this distortion moved past them, they were transformed into the white, snow and ice-laden winterized forest everyone was moving through. It made absolutely no sense to him or anyone else, but Larek could also sense that the power was slowly increasing the more they walked; it might not make sense now, but they were quickly going to arrive at the epicenter of whatever it was that they were feeling.

Shortly after the half-hour mark, looking off to their right revealed that the petrified section was getting closer to them for some reason; either they were moving off-course, or the width of the sections was getting smaller. The latter was likely proven correct when they saw that off to their left was a section of burning trees that was slowly encroaching on the narrowing, frozen section of the forest. He didn't know what was happening at first, but then he began to see a distinct curving of the dark fog as he looked to the right and left. An epiphany spread through his mind and he blurted out, "It's a condensing circle of alternating sections."

"That would be my guess, as well," Nedira said, nodding.

That was proven to be correct, as within another 5 minutes the section of frozen trees narrowed dramatically until it was only 20 feet wide, and they could see at least a dozen other alternating sections to their left and right. By the time the section became only 5 feet wide, the reality of the environment became obvious to everyone as the transformed forest looked like the spokes of a wheel. Unfortunately, the spokes of that wheel led to a central hub, which turned out to be a relatively large, circular clearing approximately 150 feet across which was free of trees. None of them could see inside the clearing, as even through the haze it appeared empty, but that didn't last long as they stopped right on the edge of the clearing and waited for the fog/haze to retract even further.

Strangely enough, while the forest had been dramatically altered, what was slowly revealed inside the clearing appeared entirely unchanged, with a short grass that grew to about shin-height on Larek. There were even a few wildflowers that grew in small clumps here and there, but other than that, it seemed relatively normal.

That was the case until the first of the monsters appeared.

Standing approximately 6 feet tall, the 12-foot-long lizards had thick, darkly iridescent scales all over their bodies that shone in the mid-morning sun. Each of their four feet had large claws that appeared as though they could rend someone from head to toe with just a swipe, and their long, thick tails had a set of spikes along a round protrusion found on its tip, which Larek could imagine would be strong enough to punch through un-*Strengthen*ed steel with ease.

That all seemed normal enough, coming from Scission monsters, but when he considered that they had three heads on long necks, that made them even more dangerous.

"**Greater Trizards**," Verne whispered as soon as they were spotted.

The name sparked a memory of learning about these particular monsters back at Copperleaf Academy, and what he remembered wasn't good. Each of the three heads wasn't just able to bite a victim with significant biting force, but could actually expel a breath-like attack that was elementarily charged. In other words, one of the heads could breathe fire, another had the ability to petrify parts of a victim with its breath, and the third was able to freeze or slow a target with a blast of ice-infused cold air.

The environment they passed through was starting to make a little more sense, though *why* they were like that was still in question.

None of the Trizards reacted to the arrival of the SIC and Larek's group, as they were all facing toward the middle of the clearing. Larek expected the Major to order an attack while they were distracted, but she kept them back as the foggy haze was still too close for comfort. That changed after another minute when the dark fog contracted even further, revealing dozens more of the Trizards, until they numbered even more than every single SIC member and Larek's group combined.

The last few feet of the fog's condensing revealed something new located in the middle of the clearing. At first, it appeared as though it was a Scission, but it was smaller than any that Larek had seen before – even smaller than the Category 1 Scissions that had attacked

Crystalview Academy. It was only when he realized that it was round like a sphere, instead of a large circle on a flat plane like a normal Scission, that it became obvious this was something completely new, something no one had seen before. At least, no one other than the Gergasi, who might have seen something like this before, but it was unlikely that any of the SIC knew what this was.

The sphere itself was dark like the Corrupted Aetheric Force that was sucked into it at a rapid pace now, though it also seemed to glow with a weak aura around its shape. When he concentrated on what he felt from it, his senses were unable to determine exactly what it was, though he could tell that it was related to a Scission... and yet was completely different.

With a sound that reminded Larek of cracking wood, the dark fog was completely sucked into the sphere, followed by a visible pulsing of the darkly glowing object as it expanded from its previous 4-foot diameter to one that was at least 8 feet wide. An ominous feeling was projected outward with the transformation, prompting everyone to grip their weapons or staves harder for a few seconds, but nothing jumped out at them.

At that point, the Greater Trizards finally moved – though not at the SIC or Larek's group. Instead, they sped along the ground toward the larger sphere, moving much faster than the Fusionist expected. As the first one touched the round object, it seemed to explode into the dark fog that Larek recognized as being Corrupted Aetheric Force; it only stuck around for less than a second before it was seemingly absorbed by the sphere, just like Larek did to the Corrupted Aetheric Force he gained from killing monsters.

It was feeding on them. And if that meant what he thought it meant, then the sphere was getting stronger somehow.

"We need to stop them!" Larek shouted, pointing toward the Trizards, most of which were nearing the sphere already. Unfortunately, his plea went unanswered as the Major largely ignored him.

"Why? They're killing themselves."

He shook his head, worried about what was going to happen next. "No, they're *sacrificing* themselves," he clarified. *That* got the Major's attention, finally, but it was already too late.

Before any of them could move to stop the monsters, the last Trizard disappeared in a flash of dark fog and was swallowed up by the sphere, which then sent out a shockwave of dark force that passed through every single person nearby, knocking a few of the more unsteady off their feet. The physical impact wasn't that significant and didn't really hurt anyone, thankfully, but the result of the shockwave certainly would if it was left unchecked.

No more than a second after the last Greater Trizard was absorbed by the sphere, a new one seemed to slide out of the middle of the darkly glowing object before fully manifesting and dropping to the ground.

This one wasn't blind to the presence of the SIC and immediately moved toward the group, its three heads already dripping what appeared to be drops of fire, dirt, and frost.

Whatever this sphere was, it wasn't a Scission – but it did seem similar. The biggest difference that Larek found when he looked at it with whatever senses that he had at his disposal was that, while both the Scission and the sphere spawned monsters and spit them out into the world, the former was only temporary and would stop after a while. The latter, the sphere, felt more *permanent* – which was a frightening proposition.

A Scission-like opening that constantly releases monsters out into the world? What else could possibly go wrong on a day like this?

With an inward wince, Larek remembered that he shouldn't think things like that, or so Verne had mentioned when they were journeying from Crystalview to Copperleaf. It was bad luck or something like that, but at least he hadn't said it out loud. That had to count for something, right?

As he gripped his axe tighter and prepared himself for a fight while the Major directed her SIC forces to attack, he certainly hoped so.

Chapter 44

For the first time, Larek got to see what happens when experienced members of the SIC applied his powerful Fusions in combat against deadly monsters. Granted, he'd seen what his bodyguards could do with a 100% increase to their stats, but they technically weren't even graduates yet. They had gotten a bit of practice fighting monsters over the last week or so, but that couldn't really compare to those with higher Skill levels, higher stats, and actual experience fighting against all the monsters coming out of a Scission as part of a decently sized SIC force.

The difference was obvious from the first seconds of the fight, and he was immediately glad that they hadn't been forced to actually fight these people – because he was fairly certain they would've lost. He wasn't talking about losing after a prolonged battle, but within *seconds* of the fight starting, despite having the *Repelling Barrier* Fusion to help fend off attacks. They were just that good at what they did, and considering that they were stationed in what was a relatively small town before it ballooned up in size lately, there was a likelihood that they weren't the best around.

But that certainly wasn't obvious when he saw them in action.

As if they had practiced such a maneuver before, three heavily armored Corpsmen raced to the front of the first Greater Trizard with their large shields held out in front of them. As they moved into position close to the dangerous monster, all three of the Trizard's heads audibly inhaled a second before they breathed out a combination of flames, brown gas, and a white fog that slammed into the shields presented to them. Just before they hit, there was a glow that surrounded each of the shields that Larek recognized as some sort of defensive Battle Art due to the Stama usage. While he didn't know exactly what it did, he could see that the elemental breaths of the Trizard had absolutely no effect upon the shields as they seemed to splash off without harm.

Seeing that it had done no damage via its breath attacks, which cut off after 5 seconds, the Trizard seemed to ready itself to pounce upon its victims, but a battleaxe seemed to come out of nowhere as another of the SIC fighters in chainmail appeared by its side, slamming the weapon into one of its long necks and decapitating the frozen-breathed head with ease. The shearing sound of the attack as the battleaxe cut through its hard scales was certainly audible to everyone, and Larek looked at the weapon the individual was wielding afterwards, only to see that its edge and handle had been bent out of shape from the blow.

What that meant to Larek was that the battleaxe-wielding Corpsman's Strength stat was apparently so high that it didn't matter that its weapon wasn't technically sharp enough to cut through the scales of the Trizard; he simply forced it through with his prodigious strength, regardless of his weapon's non-ability to cut. It was similar to how Larek used his axe to cut down trees back when he was a Logger with his family. The only reason the axe survived his greater strength was because of the Fusions – but this man had a Strength stat that far outstripped what the Fusionist used to wield back then. His battleaxe might have been sturdy enough for his previous Strength, but when that Strength literally doubled? The steel that went into the axe had the physical characteristics of copper by that point.

The decapitations didn't stop there, however, as a glowing arrow slammed into the eye of the petrification head, before it exploded from the inside of its brain. The last head, the one that breathed flames, was suddenly impacted by a barrage of sharp stone slivers and blades of ice that didn't do too much individually, but the sudden onslaught battered and then broke through the hard scales and then punctured its neck in multiple places. While it wasn't exactly a clean decapitation, its head was essentially only attached to the rest of its body by a few strands of skin and muscle.

Regardless, it was quite dead.

Those quick and effective attacks were just the start of the combat prowess he was witnessing, especially as the clearing began to fill up with more and more of the Greater Trizards. They only emerged one at a time from the sphere, but with an additional monster appearing every second or two, there was more than enough to go around for the SIC members to unleash their physical and magical attacks against them.

Explosions blew off heads in ones or twos as the Mages tore into their advance, while at the same time, large boulders flew through the air and shattered upon contact with the Trizards, shredding scales and embedding shrapnel into their tough hides. Fist-thick beams of water sheared through the defenses of the three-headed lizards, cutting through their bodies if the spell was concentrated enough in a particular area for long enough. Projectiles made of pure light slammed into the faces of the Trizards, doing some damage but also blinding the monsters and preventing them from being able to dodge future unseen attacks.

Larek saw other large lizards struggling to break free from their bodies being encased in thick ice, while others were slowly torn apart by tornados of whirling blades of air, their scales sheared off by the dozens and exposing the more vulnerable hide and flesh beneath. There was one Illusionist who used illusions to distract a pair of Trizards and eventually had them assaulting each other with their breath attacks, though that didn't last long when they realized what had happened to them.

By that time, however, one of them seemingly had the shadow underneath it reach up and grab hold of its legs before ripping them off with a spell Larek had never even heard of before. It came from a Mage who had a black robe, which made him immediately think of his Professors back in Copperleaf, but it was somehow different – almost darker than the ones his instructors wore.

The other Trizard that had been caught in the illusion fared just as poorly, as the legs that had been ripped off the other one with shadows were somehow levitated up and used as bludgeoning projectiles. They flew through the air with such speed that they practically whistled, and when they smashed into the other Trizard's head, two of them were obliterated immediately, while the third managed to dodge the initial attack. Its reprieve was short-lived as the legs stopped in mid-flight before moving back toward its head, surrounding it on four sides, and then its head was smashed like a ripe melon as the legs all came together in the blink of an eye.

There was even a Naturalist among the Mages that entangled the legs of a half-dozen Trizards as roots emerged from the ground, before turning into pincushions as those roots extended thousands of sharp thorns that dug even into the hard scales of the lizard monsters. One of the Trizards was killed when a huge cloud of green fog was inhaled by the monster in anticipation of a breath attack; the breath attack was immediately stopped as the green fog started to eat away at the Trizard's insides, and it flailed around in helplessness as it slowly perished because of the nasty spell.

Each of the Mages' attacks were *strong*, much stronger than Larek had ever seen before. While there weren't any large-scale spells that covered half the clearing, which he was sure they could cast if it was necessary, the ones they did cast were enhanced by their additional Intellect granted to them because of Larek's Fusions. When he added in the staccato barrage of staff-created projectiles also fueled by his Fusions, it was a symphony of elemental destruction that was only complemented by the efforts of the Martials.

Battle Arts were on display by the now-powerful individuals wielding their melee weapons and bows, as exploding arrows, piercing stabs, enhanced chops, and incredibly quick movements allowed the

Martials to get their attacks in with deadly efficiency and power before removing themselves from retaliatory attacks by dodging or simply moving fast enough that they couldn't be hit. They largely acted defensively by corralling the new arrivals into attempting to attack their shield-bearing members, who were able to withstand their best efforts to breathe their deadly breath all over them, while at the same time doing something to gain and hold their attention rather than letting them go after the more vulnerable members of their group.

The Mages might have had flashier spells, resulting in more monsters' deaths, but the Martials were the ones who took the brunt of the attacks and ensured that the spellcasting group was allowed to attack freely. That didn't mean there weren't any injuries, of course, because with dozens of the Greater Trizards swarming around the clearing, avoiding every attack became impossible. He saw who he thought was Rhylla fly across the clearing when she was slammed in the back by a tail whip by one of the Trizards, her leather outfit pierced by the spikes on the tip of the monster's tail. The impact was so strong that she was almost bent backwards as her spine was partially shattered, and it couldn't have felt good when she impacted a tree at the end of her flight.

No more than 2 minutes later, however, she was up and throwing herself back into the fight, having used her *Healing Surge* Fusion that Larek had provided to all the Martials, though with that amount of internal healing, she was already looking exhausted and in need of a large meal to replace whatever bodily reserves had been consumed by the healing process.

There were other injuries as time went on, including those who were hit by a breath attack they weren't expecting, or practically eviscerated by a claw strike, but each and every one of them was able to heal and get back into the fight within a minute or less. Whenever this happened to one of the SIC Martials, the Major was the one who rushed in from place to place, pulling the wounded out while they healed themselves, while using her spear in a blur of attacks that impaled more than a few of the Trizards through their durable scales like they didn't exist. She was a force of nature all by herself, killing dozens of the Trizards within the first few minutes, and she didn't look like she was planning on stopping anytime soon.

The same couldn't be said for the rest of the SIC force. After 10 minutes of non-stop fighting, the flow of Trizards didn't seem destined to slacken, and the bodies of the slain were starting to fill up the clearing, making maneuvering around the area quite dangerous, while also presenting inadvertent walls to help protect the emerging monsters coming from the sphere. The flow of the battle had been easily in the SIC's favor up to that point, as everything was quickly killed shortly after emerging, but it slowly shifted until they were forced to fight more and more defensively as the Trizards inadvertently gained a foothold by using nearby corpses as shields to block many of the long-range attacks sent their way.

On top of that, despite double the stats they used to have, the rapid expenditure of Mana and Stama was taking a toll on the fighters' reserves. The inexhaustible staff projectiles helped to alleviate that a little, especially as they allowed the Mages' Mana to regenerate while they used the staves' Fusions, but the Martials had no such reprieve. Low on Stama, the first of the Martials to get seriously hurt by the Trizards when they couldn't use a Battle Art to dodge in time was evidence that they were fighting a losing battle; while they were able to be healed, the process was so intensive that the individual could barely stand up because of their body's exhaustion, let alone fight.

Larek was startled when Major Kuama appeared next to him, the strange blue blood of the Trizards liberally dripping off the spearhead of her weapon. "It's not closing. What kind of Scission is this?"

Again, Larek said, "It's not a Scission. It's something else."

"Well then, *how do we stop whatever this is?* We can't keep going like this forever."

The Fusionist didn't know why *he* was being asked, but he eventually concluded that it was due to him being adamant that this wasn't a Scission. It was obvious that it wasn't the same, but apparently the Major thought he knew something different about it than he actually did. In that respect, the local SIC leader was partially correct; Larek had an idea, but wasn't sure if it would work.

"Attack the sphere," he said. "It's possible that it can be destabilized and therefore prevent any more of these Greater Trizards from being pushed out."

The Major shook her head. "Scissions are invulnerable. We've tried to do that in the past—" she said, before pausing. "But this isn't a Scission, is it? So, it might work." She paused for another few seconds before looking straight at Larek. "Would you be able to lend your help to attack the sphere? We're already overextended as it is."

Larek nodded as he glanced at his group. "Absolutely."

The next moment, the Major was gone and back into the thick of the fighting. "We're attacking from a distance," Larek said, looking straight at Penelope. As the only one who didn't have a long-range attack, she was the most vulnerable if she tried to aid the SIC by moving ahead into the larger battle. "Something tells me that they aren't going to like this, so I need you here to protect us."

She just nodded as Larek, Kimble, Nedira, Verne, and Norde lifted their staves and aimed at the sphere, while Bartholomew rotated his spear so that the butt of it was facing forward, and Vivienne readied her bow. As if they had practiced it, each of them released an attack near-simultaneously, and as balls of flames, icy spikes, stone fragments, and a Stama-infused arrow shot across the space toward the sphere, he could see Nedira and Kimble already casting additional spells to add to the damage. With a deft rotation of their staves, all five of the Mages fired another projectile from the other end just as the first of their attacks landed on their target – only for them to be sucked into it with no apparent damage.

While there was no visible damage to it, there *was* a very imperceptible change in the dark glow around it. If Larek hadn't been looking for it, he probably wouldn't have noticed it; as it was, there was *just enough* of a difference that it registered to his sight. "It's working! It'll probably take a lot more than that, but—"

As if the sphere had some sort of awareness, Larek felt its attention lock onto him even as he released another projectile from his staff. Out of the corner of his eye, he could tell that the others felt it, too.

"What is that? What is it doing?" Verne asked, his voice shaking slightly.

Larek didn't have to answer that, because a second later it became obvious. Whereas previously the Greater Trizards had essentially been spreading out randomly to attack whoever was closest to them, there was a visible shift in their direction as they emerged from the sphere.

They were heading straight toward Larek and his group.

Chapter 45

"This isn't working!"

Larek couldn't help but agree with Nedira. The first minute or so saw the dark glow around the sphere begin to dim more and more as their long-range attacks hit it, but they seemed to hit a wall beyond which it wouldn't dim any further. To the others, it appeared as though it was regenerating its glow randomly, but Larek could see exactly why it was happening.

The stream of Greater Trizards flowed toward his group as soon as they emerged from the sphere, and the abrupt change wasn't lost on the SIC members killing them. If anything, the monsters' obvious target was actually a boon to them, because they could concentrate their spells and defense in one place rather than the seeming randomness that it had been before. Walls made of earth or ice were used to funnel the attacking Trizards into a killing zone of wide-area spells that absolutely devastated the monsters as they passed through; if they didn't die right away, they were severely wounded and were easily cut down by the Martials waiting for them to arrive at their defensive line.

But for each one that died, Larek saw the tell-tale dark haze of Corrupted Aetheric Force emerge from their corpses and then be almost immediately sucked up into the sphere. When it was absorbed, the dimming glow was rejuvenated, creating a constant cycle of death outside and subsequent renewal inside the sphere, and it didn't appear as though that was going to change anytime soon. Larek debated asking the Major to have the Mages turn their attention to attacking the source of the Greater Trizards as well so as to get ahead of the constant regeneration, but he immediately knew that wasn't going to happen.

After constantly fighting and casting spells for nearly 15 minutes, he could see that the SIC Mages were starting to run empty on Mana. Fewer and fewer devastating spells were cast upon the emerging Trizards as they had to turn to their staves to supply the majority of the damage, though as soon as they had enough Mana they would cast another spell to help slow down the tide of monsters. The Martials looked a little better, as their Strength and Body stats were helping them weather the assault more effectively, but Larek was also seeing less use of their Stama in Battle Arts as time went on.

If they were called off the defenses to attack the sphere, it was entirely possible that the Trizards would break through and reach Larek and his group. While everyone was prepared for that eventuality, that would also likely spell the beginning of the end, and the only hope they had for surviving would be to run.

We need to do a lot more damage to it, but how? Nedira and Kimble were already adding their own spells to the mix of projectiles from the staves, but that was just barely keeping the pace of damage where it was. It was possible that they might have some luck whittling the sphere down even further if they used the Fusions on the staves faster instead of waiting 5 seconds, but he had severe doubts that even that would be enough. Instead, they needed to do a large amount of burst damage all at once, which just wasn't possible with what they had.

Looking at the SIC, he thought about asking them to toss their new Fusions toward the sphere, where he could use his Pattern Cohesion to break one and make it explode, which would then cause a chain reaction that would destroy *all* of them – but he doubted they would be willing to do that. For one, they had just received the powerful Fusions and wouldn't want to give them up without a fight. Secondly, those Fusions were the only reason everyone was still alive; if they lost them, the Trizards would undoubtedly overrun their positions as every Martial would lose half their strength, every Mage's spells would be weaker, and their Mana would regenerate slower. Lastly, the Major would probably think Larek was trying to pull some kind of trick to get them all killed if he asked her to do such a thing, and he wouldn't blame her – because it sounded suicidal to give up their advantages.

*What about cracking open **our** Fusions?*

It was a good thought, but none of the Fusions he'd made for his group had a flaw he could exploit to cause them to explode. It would be next to impossible to break one of them without time and focus, and that difficulty would be exacerbated if he attempted to do it at a distance. Besides, throwing all their Fusions at the sphere would entail stripping off their clothes and armor and giving up their weapons, which would leave them completely vulnerable if the worst were to happen and they were forced to run.

Even as he continued to batter the sphere with his staff, Larek ran through a multitude of Fusions in his mind that he could create that might work to help do some more damage, or even help in their current defense, but there wasn't anything that he could think of – at least not any that were already created. If they had more of the *Paralytic Light* stones they had used against the SIC, they might come in handy to delay the onslaught of monsters long enough to destroy the sphere. Unfortunately, they had thrown out every stone that had the paralyzing Fusions on them already, and running back to see about gathering one up was both risky and would take too long. Larek had a feeling that unless they figured something out within the next 5 minutes or so, they would either have to flee or be overrun.

Trying to create another Fusion in the middle of a battle, with everything going on around him, would be next to impossible. While he had adopted a method of hyper-focused attention to his Fusions that blocked out most distractions, doing such a thing with all of the screams of pain, sounds of a variety of spells being cast all over the battlefield, and the incessant thuds and strikes against hard Trizard scales was entirely too much for him to block out. Besides, he wasn't even sure he could create a Fusion successfully under such stress, which meant he was equally as likely to accidentally lose control of it during the process as complete it – which would be disastrous and potentially deadly.

All of that meant that their options were extremely limited. Kimble and Nedira were the only ones in his group that had the ability to cast stronger spells if necessary, but whatever they tried thus far over the last minute and a half hadn't been much more effective than a normal *Fireball*. Even with their higher Mana regeneration thanks to their *Boost* Fusions, they couldn't keep up the more-powerful spells for long, either, just like what was happening to the Mages in the SIC.

Vivienne was already shooting what arrows she had left by that point toward the sphere, and there wasn't much else that she could do at a distance. It was possible that if she, along with Bartholomew and Penelope, went close to the sphere and attacked it at close range, they might be able to do enough to reduce its glow down even further, but that also ran the risk of being close to the sphere and becoming the target of every single Greater Trizard that emerged into the world. If that happened, Larek doubted that the SIC would be able to stop them all from reaching his bodyguards, so getting that close wasn't a good idea.

Unfortunately, Verne and Norde were only able to contribute through their use of the staves they both possessed, which left Larek to do something. With additional Fusions out of the picture, and it being unlikely that any of those he had created before would be used as a type of Fusion bomb, there was only one other thing he could think of that *might* make a difference. If he left his companions to continue attacking the sphere, would his attacks against the rampaging Trizards provide him with Aetheric Force? Would he be able to siphon some of the Corrupted Aetheric Force that was regenerating the sphere?

There was only one way to find out.

"I have an idea," he told his companions, before explaining what he saw and his potential solution to the problem to the others. There were a few minor protests, but without any other options, none of them stopped him from moving up, with Penelope by his side to help defend. As soon as he reached the line of Mages firing their spells and staves into the bunched-up Trizards trying to break through the Martial line, Larek used his own staff to add to the carnage. It took about 30 seconds before his attacks finally helped to finish off an already wounded Trizard, and he watched as the dark haze of Corrupted Aetheric Force appeared over its corpse.

Almost immediately, approximately 10% of the dark haze broke off from the rest and hovered in the air, and he could sense that it was waiting for something to come claim it. Based on his experiences against a variety of monsters, he usually only absorbed any Corrupted Aetheric Force at the end of a fight, so he had to assume that this was something similar.

Unfortunately for him, this fight looked like it was going to last for a *long* time, unless they were able to destroy the sphere. In addition, his contribution toward the death of the Trizard was relatively miniscule, considering that it had already been heavily wounded by the SIC forces, and the other 90% of the Force was sucked back into the sphere.

"Did it work?" Penelope asked, after seeing his success in taking down one of the monsters.

He nodded at first, but then shook his head. "Yes, but not enough. I'm either going to have to kill all of these Trizards myself, or at least find a way to do a whole lot more damage than I'm currently doing." If they were some of the weaker monsters they had fought over the last week, he could see this being not too difficult; unfortunately, the Greater Trizards were tough to kill for someone of his limited means, and while his projectile Fusions were powerful, only multiple attacks in the same place were able to break through the monsters' protective scales.

If he had some other way to do damage without throwing himself into melee combat with the Trizards, then he might have a chance. However, even with his axe being able to cut through the scales of the three-headed lizards, it was too dangerous to get that close. His *Repelling Barrier* was unlikely to prevent all of the breath attacks that the Trizards could use on him up close, and without that protection, he was basically defenseless against them.

If only he could cast some spells to supplement his Fusions, then he might have a chance to do more damage, especially considering that he essentially had unlimited Mana that he didn't have to worry about running out of. Of course, Larek couldn't actually cast any spells—

Well, that's not technically true.

What he *should* have said was that he couldn't cast a spell *successfully*.

At least, he thought that was still the case, despite not trying since his first failed attempt back at Crystalview Academy. He hadn't tried to cast another spell since then because it was too dangerous, especially if he were to try it at Copperleaf, and even his *Advanced Fusions* Professor warned him not to try it again.

But he was running out of options at this point, and even if they were prepared to run away right now, that didn't guarantee they would be out of danger. Despite their large size, the Greater Trizards were actually quite fast; while the Martial trainees and Larek were able to run quickly because of their high Agility stats, the Mages in his group had no such advantages. They could carry them, of course, but if they had to fight their way out, that would be cumbersome, not to mention attempting to flee through ice and snow of the transformed forest.

Therefore, they *might* have been able to escape, but it was likely that many of the Mages from the SIC wouldn't. And though he didn't really care for many of them, given their desire to ambush and steal from him earlier, he also didn't want their deaths to lead to a reduction in the safety of the local area. Given the fact that the sphere was literally pumping out monsters by the second, Larek had the feeling they were going to need all the defenses they could get in the coming days.

Unless he was able to destroy it here and now, of course.

"I'm going to do something stupid, and you're going to need to carry me," he abruptly said to Penelope.

The blue-haired Martial whipped around and said, "What? No, don't do whatever you're thinking. If *you* think it's a stupid idea, then it's got to be catastrophically moronic."

"Too late. Get ready to grab me and run."

Mimicking what he had done a little over a year ago back at Crystalview, Larek used his Pattern Cohesion to create the relatively simple spell pattern for *Stone Fist*. As soon as it started to form, he was pleased to see that his *Focused Division* Skill really did work for spell patterns as well as it did for Fusion formations, as it was thick enough to split it into 4 equal spell patterns for his plan to work.

He could immediately feel that the patterns he made were even sturdier than what he used in his Fusions for some reason, now that he was able to compare the two. Regardless of the reason behind the difference, what it meant to him was that it was unlikely that he would ever be able to cast a spell without some extreme practice, and even then, he wasn't confident of his chances of it actually ever happening.

Using the ability he had honed while practicing *Focused Division*, he mentally moved the entire spell pattern out toward the sphere in the distance, which became harder to do once it passed about 10 feet away from him, but he was hyper-focused on what he was doing, so he pushed through any difficulty in his way. At 20 feet, he felt a slight strain on his mind but ignored it as he pushed it further. At 40 feet, there was a painful spike through his entire body that nearly kicked him out of his hyper-focused state... but he was so close.

Just a little more.

Finally, at 50 feet, which was where the sphere was located, he nearly passed out as the spell pattern arrived right in front of his target. Once it was in position, the strain of keeping it there was strangely negligible, as it appeared as though the difficulty lay in the act of moving it that distance rather than keeping it intact. That was probably because the pattern was strong, and even if his focus wavered a little bit, it wouldn't dissipate like a normal Mage's would.

"Boy! What are you doing?"

His action hadn't gone unnoticed by the Mages in the SIC, and he took the time to look at the young man who asked him the question, even as the Corpsman cast another spell that killed another of the Trizards. The 20-something-year-old Pyromancer was from the Kingdom and felt like a Noble, but there was a strange difference there that he recognized in Kimble; while he was technically a Noble, he probably wasn't very highly placed. At least, that was his assumption from the feeling he got.

Raising his voice, as he wanted everyone to hear him – including the Major – Larek announced, "I'm about to detonate my spell pattern next to the sphere! Get ready to retreat!"

"What are you on about—whoa! No! You're going to kill yourself!" The Pyromancer looked on in horror as Larek filled his *Stone Fist* spell pattern from a distance, which didn't take more than a second. After it was filled, it should've dissipated and cast the spell, but *his* pattern was too strong for that; instead, it pulsed once but then started to pull more Mana from him while sucking out additional Pattern Cohesion simultaneously. With a flex of his *Focused Division* Skill, which was insanely difficult at that distance, he forced the charging spell pattern to split into 4 equal patterns and then strained to move each of them nearer to the sphere.

Relinquishing his control of them, Larek slumped to his knees and looked at Penelope. "Tell everyone to run and help me out of here, if you would."

The blue-haired Martial immediately shouted for everyone to start running while she moved to Larek and threw his massive frame over her shoulder. Despite her high Strength stat, she grunted as he felt himself picked up and manhandled like a corpse, which was how he was feeling at the moment. Having strained himself moving the spell patterns, he felt weak, but that weakness was only exaggerated by the fact that both Mana and Pattern Cohesion were being pulled out of him at an incredible rate.

Every time his Mana regenerated, more of it was pulled out to feed the spell patterns even at a distance, and his Pattern Cohesion dropped 1,000 points within seconds. It hit 2,000 a few seconds later even as he bounced up and down over Penelope's shoulder as she ran, and then another 1,000 joined it shortly thereafter. Dragging his head to look up at the sphere and his spell patterns in the distance, he saw them beginning to shine with an almost blinding light in the middle of the forest clearing, while a flood of Greater Trizards followed after the retreating SIC forces after they started to flee. Larek was thankful that they realized the danger of staying too near the upcoming explosion and resolved to flee for their lives rather than stay.

He felt the weakness in his whole body increase yet again as the Pattern Cohesion that streamed out of his body topped 4,000 and kept going. If what he suspected was true, based on his experiments with Fusions, each additional spell created with *Focused Division* would take an additional 20% Pattern Cohesion from him, meaning that they would likely end up siphoning 6,400 Pattern Cohesion from him in the end.

That was the most he'd ever lost at one time, and he wasn't sure if he would survive it. But he felt like he had to try.

He nearly lost consciousness when the amount of Cohesion lost topped 5,500, but he held on to the end. Pushing through the darkness encroaching upon him, he looked up as he felt the last bits of required Pattern Cohesion being imbued into the spell patterns and was instantly blinded as all four of them detonated simultaneously, the light from the explosion it created so powerful and bright that he lost his eyesight. Less than a second after he found himself blind, the shockwave of the explosion slammed into him and Penelope, sending her stumbling forward, and he flew off her shoulder into the air.

Because he couldn't see where he was going, he was unable to brace for the impact with a frozen tree, where his head smacked against the trunk with enough force to send him into the unconsciousness he had been fighting up until that point.

Chapter 46

Waking up with a groan, Larek opened his eyes and was briefly surprised that he could actually see the sky above him. The last thing he remembered was being blinded by the explosion of his spell patterns, but everything after that was just gone.

What happened? Where am I? More importantly, did it work?

"Please be fine, please be fine—Larek! You're awake!"

The sight of Nedira leaning over him brought a smile to his face, as it proved that she had been able to get away from the explosion. Out of the corner of his left eye, he saw Verne and Norde sitting in some short grass, which was also great to see, and it also helped him locate where he was. Since there wasn't any snow or frozen trees around, he could only assume that he had been brought out of the transformed forest and was lying down in the grass outside. In addition, based on the angle of the sun in the sky, he was fairly certain that only a short time had passed since his spell patterns exploded, so he must not have been out for very long.

Before he said anything to Nedira, Larek did a mental check through his body to see if he was hurt anywhere, but it didn't take long for him to determine that he felt physically fine. Quite hungry, though, which meant that he'd likely had some extensive healing done on him in addition to his eyes, but whatever it had been was gone.

He frowned when he looked at his body in a different way, however. When he concentrated on his Pattern Cohesion, it was in shambles; thin in places, ragged in others, and even slightly torn in parts that worried him a little. Overall, it was bad, but he didn't think it was *bad* bad: he was fairly certain that with some rest and not using his Pattern Cohesion in any way for at least a week or two, he'd be fine. His Pattern was fairly resilient, he'd found, but he had pushed it quite a bit with what he just did.

"What? What is it?"

Nedira must have seen the frown on his face, because she looked worried at his expression. He hurried to reassure her. "I'm alright. I overextended my Pattern Cohesion a bit, so I need to lay off the Fusions for a week or two."

The fifth-year Naturalist's expression turned from concern to relief and then to anger in a matter of a few seconds. She punched his shoulder, which didn't hurt but surprised him. "What was that, you idiot?! You almost killed yourself and all of us with that little stunt!"

"Ahh, well, yes, about that," he said a little sheepishly as he looked away from her, seeing that all of his companions were gathered around and everyone was thankfully alive. "I'm sorry I didn't warn you, but we were running out of time and I had to do *something*."

"Moron. Why do you think you need to be the one that does everything? We might have come up with a solution if you told us what you were thinking, but no, you had to go and nearly kill yourself."

He was slightly hurt at the way she was talking to him, but he tried to look at it from her perspective. He *had* nearly killed himself, after all, and she was worried about him. He could only imagine that he would feel the same way if any of his friends threw themselves into a dangerous situation like he had.

Reaching out to cover her hand with his own, he looked her in the eyes and said, sincerely, "I'm sorry. I... wasn't thinking clearly, and I shouldn't have put myself and all of you in danger."

Some of the anger softened in her face, but he could tell she was still a bit mad at him.

Before she could say anything else, he asked, "So... did it work? Was the sphere destroyed?"

Larek heard footsteps heading in his direction and he turned his head from where he was lying to see Major Kuama heading toward him. He stiffened in preparation for a betrayal of her sworn vow, but the worried look on her face strangely made him relax. If she was worried about something, then it meant she likely wasn't planning on trying to hurt him or his companions.

"I couldn't help but overhear your question," she said when she had his attention. "We sent some scouts to check it out, and I'm not exactly sure of the answer.

"First, there is no sign of any Greater Trizards other than the remnants of some corpses, and the trees around the area of the blast – which was damn stupid of you, even if it seemed to work – have been flattened in a circle that reaches a little more than 400 feet from the explosion's epicenter. As for the dark sphere, it's still there, but it's comparatively tiny at about the size of my closed fist here. The scouts attempted to damage it further, but their attacks all passed through it as if it didn't exist at all, but it is obviously still there because of its visibility.

"When we couple that with the transformed forest still looking as it did when we entered, I'm not sure what to think. I believe the threat is over for now, but whether it will return? There's no way to know."

That was at least a little bit of good news, though it was worrying that the sphere was still there – if seemingly inert instead of constantly spewing out monsters.

I guess we can say that the task was failed successfully.

"Regardless, this is something we have to report to those higher up in the chain of command, so when we travel to—"

Whatever else the Major was saying was lost to Larek as a notification suddenly slammed into his mind.

Welcome to The Culmination, Guardian!

Congratulations! You have located and temporarily closed the first Aperture to appear in this world!

*While Scissions are **temporary** portals into the world of the Corruption, Apertures are **permanent** connections between the two worlds. These permanent connections are established when the Corrupted Aetheric Force present in their physical manifestations (that the sapients of this world refer to as monsters) infuse a particular density of Corruption inside their chosen territory. When an Aperture is first established, the environment in their chosen territory can and will transform to better accommodate the physical manifestations of Corruption, making these areas particularly dangerous for mundane sapients without access to Aetheric Force. In addition, during this process, all physical manifestations that will populate the Aperture and surrounding environs are absorbed for their Corrupted Aetheric Force and used as fuel for the establishment of the permanent connection.*

After the Aperture is opened, the Corruption will then seed the transformed territory with the same physical manifestations that were used in its creation, evenly disbursing them around the area to defend its territory until a threshold has been reached. This seeding process is the absolute worst time to try and temporarily close an Aperture, because there is no limit to the number of physical manifestations that will emerge from its opening as it attempts to populate its territory. It is best to wait for the seeding process to finish before temporarily closing the Aperture, as it will take much less time and effort.

As this is your first temporary Aperture closing, keep in mind that the Aperture will reopen once the Corruption on the other side of the opening reaches a critical level, which all depends on the strength of the physical manifestations. For weaker physical manifestations, the closure can be measured in days or hours; for the truly powerful manifestations, closures can last for up to a year.

Warning! Do not allow the Apertures to remain open for too long; otherwise, they will begin to spread their Corruption beyond the bounds of the original territory. As their territory expands, more physical manifestations are added to seed the expansion, and it can even begin to develop stronger versions of the manifestations as time goes on. Temporarily closing an Aperture will revert the territory to its original dimensions, so keep this in mind when evaluating which Apertures take priority so as to reduce the loss of nearby mundane sapients.

In addition, Apertures left unchecked for long enough and allowed to expand will gradually raise the ambient Corruption in this world, increasing the frequency of Scissions and the potential for additional Apertures and therefore more chances for spreading the Corruption. Too much ambient Corruption can lead to a widening of the main breach into the other world, which will increase the risk to Guardians and all sapient life.

Good luck and good hunting!

Larek was glad that he was still lying down, because the sudden information overload was not only jarring, but overwhelming after all that had happened. When he read through the notification, he groaned again while wanting to close his eyes and fade back into unconsciousness.

This can't be happening. Can it?

"What is it? What's wrong?" Nedira said, hearing him groan. Larek was about to explain to her and the rest of his group what the notification told him about Apertures, but then he realized that the Major was still nearby looking at him. *How do I explain all this?* He immediately knew that he had to tell the woman something, given that this Aperture would open again at some point and he would have to venture back into the forest to close it; otherwise, they ran the risk of it expanding and threatening Whittleton. It was only a few miles away, after all.

Overwhelmed by all the information and with the Kingdom—no, *the entire world*—at stake if this knowledge wasn't immediately shared with the SIC, he mentally shrugged and displayed the notification above him large enough that everyone could see it. He debated censoring the parts about Guardians, but decided not to after giving it a brief thought;

it was unlikely that anyone would know that term, as those who knew about the Gergasi thought of them as Great Ones instead of Guardians. It was still a risk to share it all, especially when there would inevitably be questions about how he received this information, but he thought it was too important not to.

The soft murmur of the voices that Larek just then realized were coming from the local SIC force gathered at the edge of the transformed forest faded away as they all turned to the displayed notification hovering above Larek. That silence continued even as they finished reading it, and the Fusionist could see shock clearly written across those faces he could see from his position. That shock only lasted long enough for the quickest of them to register what they just read in their minds, before the floodgates were loosened.

"This can't be real, can it?"

"Apertures?"

"*Permanent* connections? To what world are they talking about?"

"Who or what are Guardians?"

"I don't understand, what is the Corruption, and what is this Aetheric Force stuff?"

"Who is this guy and how did he get this? Is this an illusion?"

The cacophony of questions was too much for Larek to handle, so he began to ignore it. The most important response wasn't from the rest of the SIC, but the Major. When Larek looked at her, she was frozen in place, her hand on her spear with its butt on the ground, staring at the notification. After a few seconds of Larek watching her, the local SIC leader looked down at him with conflicting emotions spread over her face. "If this is true, then we have no time to waste disseminating this information. Are there others like you who will be able to spread this knowledge?"

Larek shrugged, which wasn't as impactful lying on the ground, but it got his point across. He didn't really have an answer for her, because he didn't know.

"And this is just the first? Can we expect more of these... *Apertures* to open all over the Kingdom?" she asked.

"I would assume so, but I really don't know. I only found out about them moments before I displayed the notification, so your guess is as good as mine."

While the whole situation with Apertures and Corruption mattered to the Kingdom and the SIC as a whole, Larek didn't think it really applied to his own situation all that much. Sure, he needed to kill monsters in order to improve his Skills via the Aetheric Force he would receive from their deaths, but he was in no position to go around and help close Apertures right now. He needed to get stronger in his ability to make Fusions, as well as attend Fort Ironwall to learn how to fight.

The reason for that wasn't even because he wanted to fulfill Dean Lorraine's hope that he would close this "breach" mentioned in the notification, but simply because he wanted to survive. From the first days after leaving Rushwood, he was finding that the world was a much more dangerous place than he ever imagined, and it just seemed to be getting more dangerous as time went on. If he didn't learn how to defend himself, his friends, and his family from all the threats lurking out there, up to and including the Gergasi working behind the scenes, then he would become just another victim of unfortunate circumstances. Helping to save the Kingdom and perhaps even the entire world was of secondary importance to him. That, of course, didn't mean he wanted to watch the world burn around him, because that would mean there was no safe place for the people he cared about to live.

He'd help where he could, which was why he originally wanted to provide the duplicitous SIC force in Whittleton with Fusions, as well as sharing the notification with the Major. But he still had no plans to go out of his way to challenge the Gergasi and close this aforementioned breach into another world.

Finally standing up, as he felt better – if quite hungry – by that point, Larek remembered helping to kill one of the Greater Trizards back near the Aperture and wondered if he actually received any Aetheric Force from it.

Larek Holsten
Fusionist
Healer
Level 21
Advancement Points (AP) : 17/18
Available AP to Distribute: 2
Available Aetheric Force (AF): 5,424

To say that Larek was shocked at the current total of 5,424 AF available in his Status would be an understatement. For a moment, he wondered where it had come from, because he doubted that he had received over 5,000 AF from just a portion of that Trizard he had killed. It was only when he thought about all of the monsters that had been alive outside of the Aperture when his spells detonated that he remembered that he had likely killed at least two dozen or more of them in the explosion. *So, I got all of their Aetheric Force, too?* It was the only thing that made sense, but he wasn't going to argue whether he earned it or not; the current state of his Pattern Cohesion was proof enough that he more than paid the price for it.

He was in the process of figuring out where he wanted to allocate his bounty of Aetheric Force when he was interrupted by the Major.

"I don't know where you came from or where you're going, but I have to thank you for your help," she said begrudgingly. "I feel a bit ashamed of how I acted earlier. I was desperate and grasping at an opportunity that presented itself, but that is no excuse for my actions as an officer in the SIC. I'll see to it that your wishes about your anonymity are upheld, even if I have to beat in a few heads to get the message across with all these meatheads."

The Corpsmen that heard her didn't seem to take offense at the Major calling her subordinates meatheads; instead, it seemed to break the tension in the crowd as Larek heard a few chuckles. While they weren't suddenly friendly toward Larek and his group, their hostility took a back seat to the entire situation with the discovery of the Aperture and future danger of even more appearing nearby.

The Fusionist could tell that the Major wanted to get back to her job, so he reached out and shook the hand that she offered. "Thank you. We need to be on our way, as well, so—"

Larek stopped as his whole body stiffened in response to something. The Major dropped his hand and whipped around with her spear at the ready, as an overwhelming *presence* could be felt coming closer to their location.

Oh, no. Not this again.

Chapter 47

As if a weight settled upon the members of the SIC gathered on the grass in front of the transformed forest, none of them moved when the oppressive feeling of a presence approaching their location spread amidst them all. Even Major Kuama wasn't immune to this pressure and was only able to move her head after a few seconds, following the source of the presence up into the air and above the trees to the north.

As for Larek and his companions, they weren't restricted by the pressure and began to run to the east as fast as they could, with Larek and the Martials picking up the slower members of the group and carrying them.

But it was already too late. They managed to move perhaps 500 feet before a figure streaked out of the sky and slammed down in front of them, the shockwave of the impact sending them tumbling backwards. Unhurt, other than a few scrapes along his skin, Larek got to his feet and picked up Nedira, Verne, and Norde, who had fallen next to him when they were sent flying. He was about to flee with them when he heard a strong, feminine voice behind him commanding him to "STOP".

The Fusionist immediately froze, nearly upending himself with the suddenness of his stopping, but he pushed through the command that he instinctively recognized as Dominion Magic being used on him and started running yet again. Unfortunately, he only made it a dozen feet before the figure that had crashed into the ground with such force was in front of him, pointing, straight at his face, an incredibly thin, glowing sword that was made out of some material he'd never seen before. It almost looked like glass or crystal but gave an impression of extreme durability that was unmistakable to someone who utilized Fusions to strengthen material – but there wasn't a single Fusion on the blade.

Looking up from the point that would have impaled him through the eye if he hadn't stopped himself, he saw what he immediately recognized as a Gergasi, but instead of the imposing figure of his father – whom he had expected to be the one to track him down – this was clearly a woman wearing a flowing, diaphanous white and cream belted dress that cut off just below her knees, some sort of flat sandals that were attached to her feet via cords that wrapped around her calves, and a pair of golden-colored bracers on her forearms that were practically flush with her skin. On top of her head she had long, silvery hair with golden stripes interlaced throughout, which was tied back in a ponytail that stuck up at an angle on the rear of her head. The angry expression on her face was the only thing that reminded Larek of when he saw his father back at Copperleaf, though the burning-red color of the irises in her eyes was new – or at least he thought so, as he hadn't been close enough to the Gergasi at the Academy to know for sure.

She was also 9 feet tall, which made the normally giant Fusionist feel positively tiny due to the 2-foot difference in their heights, which was more impactful than he thought it would be. He'd fought taller monsters lately, but there was something about the sheer power that this dangerous figure gave out that made an enormous difference.

White wings, spreading out 6 feet to either side of her back, folded in upon themselves and disappeared as the woman spoke again, though with only a fraction of the command he felt earlier. "Who are you to disobey the command of your superiors? How did you—?"

The Gergasi abruptly put her sword away in the blink of an eye, sliding the weapon into a sheath he hadn't even noticed on her belt and hidden in the folds of her dress. "Ah. I see. Vilnesh's spawn. How fortuitous to find you here."

For the first time, Larek noticed her voice was light and melodic, almost hypnotizing in its cadence as she spoke – which was quite different from what he remembered hearing from his father. There was a subtle hint of Dominion Magic under her words, however, which he immediately shook off as it attempted to bury itself into his mind.

"Stronger than I expected. You know, your father was quite annoyed that he lost you back at the Academy. He spent a good two days rampaging against the manifestations streaming from the breach in his anger, which was quite entertaining to watch, I must admit. There's not much that gets to that insufferable pain in the butt, so I must applaud your feat of escaping his clutches so handily." She chuckled lightly with a smile that seemed to shine brighter than the sun, and he felt a smile tugging at his own lips.

Clamping down on the subtle Dominion Magic trying to worm its way in, Larek couldn't help but notice out of the corner of his eye Nedira and his roommates smiling as if they had just met a new friend, and he could hear a short chuckle coming from Verne and Norde. Their eyes, on the other hand, appeared terrified despite their otherwise outwardly relaxed stances. His own influence upon them was just barely keeping them from fully obeying the Gergasi woman, though he wasn't sure how long that would last.

The Fusionist found his voice somehow. "That's good to hear and I'm glad I could provide some amusement for you. That being said, we should really be on our way."

The smile upon her face didn't change, but Larek could feel the pressure pushing at him a bit more forcefully all of a sudden, which made him flinch and grit his teeth as he resisted it. "Amazing. You're so much stronger than even Vilnesh suspected, and I'm looking forward to seeing what other surprises you have in store for us. Alas, that won't come about with you running free, because we need to study you back at the Enclave and see what makes you different from our other failures. It'll be interesting to see what makes you tick, though it will be a shame that our experiments will probably leave you broken and useless once we're done with you. So, as much as it might annoy your father to let you go, I'm going to have to take you back with me."

Pushing back the pressure until it faded to a distant presence, Larek asked in confusion, "He didn't send you here?"

"Send me? No, of course not. You're *his* mess to have to deal with, and I don't jump at his beck and call, for all that he'd wish otherwise." She briefly turned her head to look at the transformed forest, and when she looked back at Larek, the burning red in her eyes had cooled to a dull orange. "I'm here because of *that*. We sensed it forming all the way inside the Enclave and I was dispatched to investigate; it wasn't until I was nearly here when I got the notification that this 'Aperture' had been discovered and then subsequently closed. What happened?"

Larek kept his mouth shut, not wanting to give her any more details about what he could do while he tried to find a way to escape. There was no way he was going to the Enclave where his father was without a fight, though he was also fairly certain that he had absolutely no chance against this woman if it came down to that. Unfortunately, that also meant that he was looking into ways to make some of the Fusions on his robe rupture and explode, killing him in the process; he would rather not have to kill himself, but from the impression he got from the woman, she wasn't planning on bringing him back for a simple family reunion, but to run experiments on him in order to see what made him different.

Torture for who knew how long or a quick death at his own hands? He knew what choice he'd make if it came down to it.

His silence didn't affect the outcome of the question the woman asked, because at that point the SIC had quickly made their way over to the group. The Major was close enough to overhear her speaking and had no resistance to the Dominion Magic the Gergasi was using, and she immediately began to recount all that had happened after they investigated the feeling of what they thought was a powerful Scission, only to find that the forest was transformed and a large, dark sphere was pumping out Greater Trizards every second. She didn't leave anything out, including Larek's part in the explosion that eventually closed the Aperture, though she didn't mention anything before the forest's transformation – so there was nothing about the *Paralytic Light* Fusions or the ambush that Larek and his group had thwarted.

"You're more and more surprising, the more I learn about you. What was your name again? Calling you 'Vilnesh's spawn' is just too bothersome."

Larek didn't say anything as he kept his mouth shut. The pressure of the Dominion Magic attempting to command his obedience was getting easier to repel, but the same couldn't be said for his companions. His protection only extended so far for them, and soon enough Nedira and his roommates were giving up his secrets.

"His name is Larek Holsten."

"Larek."

"Larek is an awesome Fusionist."

She smiled at them, which seemed to send a thrill through his friends, for giving up his name and ability as a Fusionist; each of them shook in what looked like a combination of fear and pleasure, and it sickened him to see Dominion Magic being used so flagrantly in his presence.

"Thank you." Turning to him, she attempted the same smile on him, but he was able to completely ignore the pressure that came with it. "Larek, huh? I'm Lady Chinli, though since you're *technically* family, I suppose I can let you call me Chinli if you wish." Her smile vanished as quickly as it arrived. "I need to investigate this Aperture for myself; only then will we be going back to the Enclave. STAY HERE AND DON'T MOVE." The sudden command delivered via Dominion Magic made him stagger with a blinding headache, which made him realize that he wasn't as immune to it as he thought. "That was for *their* benefit, because if you try to run… I will kill everyone here."

A second later, Chinli was gone, having launched herself into the sky as white-feathered wings sprouted from her back once again. As he rubbed his temples in an effort to ease the pain of the Gergasi's command, Larek looked at his friends – only to see them frozen in place, unable to move even a muscle that wasn't required to keep them standing upright. There was a look in their eyes that told him that they were trying to fight the command, but were unable to make much progress. A glance at the members of the SIC revealed that they were in the same boat, though their eyes were glassy and almost dead to the world; he supposed it was because they didn't have the benefit of being slightly resistant to the Dominion Magic the woman was using that his friends had due to their closeness with Larek.

When he could think again, he moved to Nedira and held her head in his large hands as he tried to *will* his own Dominion Magic to break the command she was under, but nothing seemed to happen. He had no control over it, after all, though the more he tried to reach for something and push it toward her, the more he felt like he was getting somewhere.

He wasn't going to leave without his friends, so he put everything that he could into breaking them free. Just as he felt like he was on the cusp of finding whatever it was that controlled his Dominion Magic, a subtle feeling at the edge of his awareness, he felt the presence of Chinli appear behind him again.

"Nice try, but you don't have even an ounce of control, do you? We can teach you how to use it, of course, though you probably won't be able to utilize it for long before you're too far gone to understand what it is," the powerful Gergasi said, sounding slightly regretful. He didn't believe her for a moment.

Sighing and letting Nedira's head go, he turned toward the woman. "I'm not going with you. I won't be subjected to whatever 'experiments' you have planned—"

"You can and *you will*, even if I have to use force. This isn't a debate."

"I'll kill myself before I'll allow you to take me alive."

She seemed taken aback by that. "You wouldn't dare. You're too important to us and finding a solution to our problems."

"Oh, I can and *I will* kill myself if you try and force me," he snapped back. He was tired of feeling helpless against this purely evil being, and it felt vindicating to have the power to resist her.

Chinli was silent as she stared at him, and he felt additional pressure pushing into his mind, but his own Dominion Magic – as weak as it was – proved to be more than enough to protect him, though with some mental pain in the process. "I have to take you back with me, no matter what. If you kill yourself, all our efforts over the last 1,000 years will be lost—"

"I don't care about that or any of you, for that matter."

The burning red in her eyes was back. "You *will not* kill yourself. Because, if you do, then I'm going to kill everyone here. I was going to let them go and wipe their memories of you and this meeting, because we can't have that kind of knowledge floating around, but your death would mean that I'll have to kill them. Furthermore, now that I know your name, it'll be that much easier to hunt down whatever family you have and kill them, too. In fact, I may just have to look for your friends' families, as well, and end their lives – and they won't even know why. Is that what you want? If so, why don't you just kill yourself right here and save me some time."

Larek's mind blanked at the threat the woman just delivered. He knew going into his own threat of killing himself that he was likely putting his friends in danger, but he didn't realize the Gergasi would go that far in revenge. As much as he wanted Nedira, Verne, Norde, and even his bodyguards to live through this, if she was going to go after his family, as well as his friends' families, then it wasn't just their own lives on the line anymore. If he killed himself, he would essentially be killing dozens or potentially *hundreds* of people – all to save himself from the torturous experiments that awaited him.

He knew right away that he couldn't do it. Larek couldn't let his choice directly end with the deaths of so many people, including his own family. He was going to have to leave with her, no matter if it was going to lead to a hellish existence or not, because that was just who he was. Trying to make the selfish choice for once, as beneficial to him personally as it would be, wasn't something he was anywhere near comfortable with doing.

"Fine. You win. I'll come with you and not fight to escape."

She smiled at him again, though there was a cruel smirk to it. "As if you could fight against me in the first place. This just makes it easier on the both of us."

Chinli then looked away from him and closed her eyes, before a wave of invisible, intangible Dominion Magic pulsed away from the Gergasi and slammed into each and every person nearby. While Larek was only slightly affected with another spike of pain drilling into his mind, everyone else suddenly collapsed as if their bones suddenly turned to mush.

"What did you do!? You said you weren't going to hurt them!" Larek shouted in a panic, dropping by Nedira's side and putting his hand on the side of her throat, looking for a pulse. He exhaled in relief when he felt it, though it was clear that she was unconscious along with the rest of them.

"They'll be fine," Chinli assured him, a hint of impatience in her voice. "In an hour, they'll wake up and not remember meeting you or I, which means they can go on their way," she explained dismissively. "Now, it's time for you to uphold your end of the bargain and not try and run away from me, or I'll ensure they never wake up from this."

Staring down at Nedira and then Verne, Norde, Bartholomew, Kimble, Vivienne, and finally, Penelope, he whispered a quick goodbye, hoping that they would still remember him if he ever saw them again. He thought there might be a chance that some portion of their memories would be safeguarded because of his influence and Dominion Magic, but he couldn't say for sure. Of course, that wouldn't really matter if he couldn't find a way to see them again, which meant that he'd have to find a way to escape his fate in the Enclave. For the moment, he needed to play along and not fight the woman, because she was likely to be on her guard for any escape attempts.

"Let's go," he said simply, turning away from his unconscious friends. The next moment, he felt an odd weight around his waist and he looked down, only to find a strange magical loop made of glowing yellow light surrounding his body like a belt. There was a flexible tether that led off of it and attached to a similar loop on Chinli's belt, linking them together.

"Don't scream. It's always so bothersome when they scream."

"What do you—?"

Larek didn't get a chance to finish his question before he was lifted off the ground and shot into the air, dragged behind the Gergasi woman as she flew straight up and then a bit to the northwest. The wind whipped his robe into a frenzy as the speed of the air tried to rip the breath out of his lungs, but he managed to stabilize the panic that set in as he squinted through the blowing air to see that he was at least 2,000 feet above the surface. He immediately felt a bit queasy and light-headed, so he forced himself to close his eyes.

Don't look down. Got it. This will all be over soon, so don't scream or panic, as much as you want to.

Of course, even though the terrible experience of being flown through the air would end eventually, he couldn't help the dread that crept into his mind at the thought of their destination... and the waking nightmare that would come with it.

Chapter 48

The absence of wind blasting into his face at full speed finally prompted Larek to open his eyes, only to find that the tears that had involuntarily leaked from them because of the constant pressure of the air had dried and acted as a sort of glue, keeping them closed. Reaching up with wind-burned and slightly numb fingers, he forced them open to see that they had stopped in the middle of the air, still a few thousand feet above the surface.

It was only at the point that he opened his eyes that Larek realized there was something pressing on his senses – and it wasn't the overbearing presence of Chinli nearby. Looking up from the ground far below, he spotted a Scission ahead of them... in the middle of the air. He hadn't even known that it was possible for Scissions to appear that far from the ground, and there had been no mention of this phenomenon in any of his classes at either Academy.

"Hold on, Larek; don't try to move," the winged Gergasi said to him, her tone clearly annoyed. He had an irrational fear that she was somehow annoyed at *him*, brought on by the fact that he was suspended at least a half-mile above the surface, and he couldn't imagine being dropped from that height if she was angry with him. The Fusions on his robe couldn't save him from a drop of that magnitude, and healing would likely be of no use if he ended up dying on impact with the hard ground.

The yellow light around his waist suddenly disappeared and he dropped; his stomach was in his throat as he felt himself falling, but he was caught by something else before he moved more than a few feet. Still hyperventilating from the near-death drop, he watched as a semi-transparent yellow light surrounded him completely in an ovoid shape like an egg, and he could feel himself buoyed up like a log on the river. While there was no rush of air around him, Larek sensed that the yellow egg-like shield around him was based on some sort of Air spell, though so advanced that he couldn't even begin to work it out.

Now secured against falling, but stuck where he was because he was afraid that trying to break out of the yellow shield would cause him to plummet to his death, the secured Fusionist looked up at the Scission and the Gergasi facing it.

Appearing in the air, it was difficult for Larek to gauge the scale of the Scission as there weren't other objects near it to base its size on. The only thing he could utilize to determine its Category was the strength of the pressure coming off of it, and even that was mixed because of the proximity of Chinli; there was a strange similarity between the two that he'd noticed before, but that was made even more evident now as there wasn't much to distract him from the comparison. It wasn't necessarily that one of them was supposedly "Corrupted" while the other was the "Purified" form of Aetheric Force; while that was there, it was more of a resonance between the two that he could feel even within himself to a small degree. What that meant, he wasn't sure, but he didn't have time to analyze it further than that because the Scission was already changing color toward its threshold.

"Blasted Corruption! It's becoming bolder than I expected."

Larek didn't like the feel of the Scission, especially as it settled on a deep purple color and its pressure reached a crescendo that outstripped the feeling the Aperture imparted earlier that day. "Can't we go around?" he asked, unsure if the Gergasi could hear him through the yellow shield of air around him. The sense of danger he felt from the Scission only increased as it firmed up and made ready to start pushing out monsters; as much as he didn't want to be a prisoner of the Gergasi, he more didn't want to be ripped to shreds by a monster thousands of feet above the ground.

The giant woman snorted. "I could easily go around, of course. But the manifestations inside will follow me wherever I go, now that the Corruption has my scent. I can't risk it following me back to the Enclave. Better to kill it out here rather than—oh, *blast it!* **Warped Void Hunters**! This could get a bit nasty."

Out of the deep purple Scission flew a half-dozen slightly transparent, dark-purple-winged beasts that looked like a cross between a bat, a wolf, and a hawk. They had the furry bodies of wolves – though with 6 legs instead of 4 – with leathery wings like a bat stretching out to their sides that were at least twice their body's length in wingspan, while their tails were actually made of black feathers that appeared wildly incompatible with the rest of their forms, but somehow it still worked. Their head had the rounded shape of a hawk and a translucent, curved beak that had a point that appeared specially made for rending flesh. What shocked Larek the most about them was their eyes, which looked like nothing but a dark, starry void, as if he were looking up at the sky at night, but there was a deep vastness to them that felt like they were pulling him in as soon as his gaze met them.

As Chinli pulled out her crystal-clear sword and swooped in toward the emerging monsters, Larek finally got a better size perspective of both the Warped Void Hunters and the Scission itself. Based on her 9-foot-tall form, the Void Hunters were approximately 50 feet long with 100-foot wingspans, while the Scission was at least 200 feet wide, one of the biggest that Larek had ever seen. The Gergasi appeared tiny in comparison, but the power that she exuded outstripped the threat he sensed from the monsters, if only by a slight amount. He felt confident that she would win in a fight against them, though not necessarily easily.

That was good news for the current predicament, but it was also worrying for his plans to eventually escape from his captivity. If the Gergasi were able to defeat even these strong monsters, then what chance did he have of finding a way to extricate himself from all the torture and death they had planned for him?

Chinli flew with incredible speed at the lead Hunter approximately 500 feet away from Larek's location, which meant he was easily able to observe the way she created a crescent of light that sprang from the tip of her sword as she slashed it down with such a speed that he couldn't even see it move. The light arc sped away faster than she was flying to close the remaining distance from the winged Gergasi and to the monster, and it passed completely through the Hunter as if it wasn't even there.

That turned out to be more accurate than Larek expected. As soon as the crescent of light neared the monster, it faded from view, and the Fusionist recognized that it was actually some sort of illusion that the attack passed through. The "real" Warped Void Hunter appeared directly behind Chinli with an audible *pop*, and it struck out with its curved beak with blinding speed.

The Gergasi was obviously prepared for the attack as she had already whipped around and slashed her sword against the descending beak, causing the Hunter's head to snap backwards from the force of the attack. Fire erupted from Chinli and enveloped the monster before it could recover from its repelled strike, until Larek couldn't see anything that wasn't covered in flames but its wingtips. The Fusionist thought that was it for the monster, as the fire appeared extraordinarily hot; the next second, his assumption was proven wrong as the fire seemed to be sucked into the Hunter like it was being absorbed. It was only when the flames dissipated enough that Larek was able to see that it was actually the Hunter's eyes that seemed to pull in the magical flames, as if their bottomless voids were able to contain all the magic in the world without fear.

The winged Gergasi took advantage of her opponent eliminating her flames to strike out at it while it was distracted, as she flew over top of it, carving a deep, lengthwise furrow out its back with her sword. The Hunter painfully bellowed with a warbling screech that likely would've deafened Larek if he hadn't been at least slightly protected by the shield of air around him; as it was, the piercing pain was just shy of causing permanent damage, but his hearing was still muffled afterwards. Larek decided to wait to heal himself with his *Healing Surge* Fusion until later, because if the Hunters screeched another few times like that, he'd have to do it all over again.

A rain of icicles pounded on top of the Hunter as soon as Chinli finished her attack with her sword, with more than a few of them piercing through the wound she had inflicted, but they were quickly absorbed by the Hunter's void-filled eyes. That seemed to be the plan, however, as the Gergasi went in for another attack, diving down low and cutting off more than half of its tailfeathers and its entire left hind leg with a swift strike. She had to avoid a strike by the Hunter's massive wing as it counterattacked, another *louder* screech finally deafening Larek as it screamed in pain.

A mostly invisible barrage of wind blades attacked the Hunter from all directions the next moment as the Gergasi cast yet another spell. Because they were largely transparent, only showing up as distortions with the hint of air magic around them, he could see exactly what was happening with the Hunter this time. It was clear that the act of absorbing the magical attack through its eyes required most of its concentration, as it basically just hovered in place during the process, which made it extremely vulnerable to other attacks. Chinli took advantage of this, and he could see the Stama flowing through her body, through her arms, and into her sword, lighting it up like a beacon in the night. She flew next to the dangerous monster and struck out at the base of its left wing, her sword cutting through some heavy resistance to shear through the leathery skin, muscle, and bone of its appendage.

The absorption of the wind blades faltered from the attack, and dozens of them managed to make it through to open relatively large wounds all over its body – but none of it was as debilitating as losing one of its wings. The Warped Void Hunter began to lose altitude, but it disappeared after a second and reappeared with a *pop* 100 feet above the Gergasi as it attempted to recover from its freefall.

With that victim effectively taken out of the fight, Chinli turned her attention to the other 5 Hunters as Larek saw the Scission fade from existence. The fact that only 6 monsters emerged from the Scission made them all the more dangerous in his opinion, and it reminded him of the Pukwudgies that he had fought before and how strong they were. These Hunters, however, seemed to be many more levels of difficulty above them.

The monsters were also quite smart, as they halted their advance when they saw that one of their number was being absolutely dominated by the winged Gergasi. Rather than charge ahead and potentially share the same fate, they stayed back and out of easy range for her to reach. This confused Larek at first, as he expected them to need to get close in order to kill the giant, but they showed that they had something else up their sleeves.

Each of the non-injured Hunters opened their hooked beaks simultaneously, and a swirling vortex of black and purple formed a few inches in front of them. As one, the monsters launched these 9-foot-wide balls of whirling energy at the Gergasi, who immediately took evasive action. Dodging below the swirling orbs of what Larek could only assume was a powerful attack, the Fusionist was shocked to see the projectiles curve in their path and follow the winged woman as if they had minds of their own. A sudden wall of stone appeared in the path of one of the balls, and when the swirling black and purple orb hit the stone, he watched as the projectile reduced in size by about a third, while the stone that had touched it disappeared. It was only when he noticed something out of the corner of his eye that he realized that the stone had actually been teleported approximately 200 feet away to the east, though it was crumbled instead of solid, as if it had been smashed apart with a sledgehammer.

Repeated spells and even Battle Arts were used to slowly whittle the pursuing orbs of teleporting death down, all while Larek could see that the Gergasi was slowly attempting to work her way toward the otherwise stationary Hunters. Their relative inactivity gave the Fusionist a hint that *they* were still controlling their projectiles, rather than the orbs acting on their own, so he assumed that Chinli was going to punish them for being relatively defenseless.

He was right in his assumption, but was wrong about its effectiveness. As she went to attack the nearest one after destroying one of the projectiles completely, the spell she used showing up a few hundred feet below her, the Hunter disappeared and reappeared with a *pop* approximately 300 feet away. A second attack by a different monster resulted in the same thing happening as her victim teleported out of her reach.

"Aaargh! STOP MOVING!" Even though he was still deafened, Larek somehow heard Chinli's frustrated shout, followed by a wave of Dominion Magic that passed through him as it erupted from the Gergasi. If he hadn't already been stuck in place in the middle of the air, he would've frozen for a second or two; as it was, there wasn't much effect on him after the command wore off.

There was even less of an effect on the Warped Void Hunters, because although he saw their wing flaps stutter for a half-second, the use of her Dominion Magic didn't do much. He could see her getting angrier by the second, the flames in her eyes visible even a thousand feet away; this increased even as the Hunters whose projectiles had been completely destroyed formed another one and launched them before the woman could react. Before too long, there was another full complement of deadly orbs tracking her, and everything she did to get close to the teleporting monsters didn't seem to work. Despite her great speed, moving faster than he could fully track most times, the ability of the Warped Void Hunters to teleport was even faster.

Finally, he could see the Gergasi stop after she gained some distance from the pursuing orbs, the rage on her face evident as she moved her hands in a blur, creating an intricate spell pattern that was larger than she was. It took nearly 2 seconds for it to fully form, which he thought was likely the equivalent of a normal SIC Mage taking an hour or so, and just before the nearest of the projectiles reached her, Larek could see it had been completely filled with Mana. A split-second later, a pressure wave of flames, boulders, ice chunks, crackling lightning, and a hazy, green mist erupted from around the woman, pushing out so rapidly that the Hunters didn't have a chance to teleport away. The amount of magical power that flowed into them was more than they could absorb easily, and they were quickly overwhelmed. Larek couldn't see more than that as the wave passed over his little bubble of air, and he flinched as it parted around him without harm.

But the wave of magical destruction had another effect that Chinli hadn't expected, nor did he think she even saw the results of. Deflected away from her, the projectiles sent out by the Hunters were cut off from the control of the overwhelmed monsters, which sent them off with incredible speed in multiple directions. One of them, reduced to only a few feet wide, shot straight at Larek; it was moving so fast that he didn't have a chance to react other than to put his hands up ineffectually.

The swirling orb passed through his air shield as if it was wet paper, shredding it apart and shrinking minutely in the process. He only barely saw this as he began to fall, but he didn't move very far before the projectile was upon him. His *Repelling Barrier* didn't even activate as the orb apparently wasn't something physical, so it reached him without any problem whatsoever.

At least this means I don't have to worry about being tortured now—

Chapter 49

A darkness that surpassed anything he'd seen before enveloped Larek's perception, plunging him into an endless cold void. Expecting to feel himself being completely ripped apart from the impact of that swirling mass of black and purple energy, similar to how he had seen the spells that Chinli had thrown at them fall apart, the Fusionist instead felt... nothing.

Am I dead? Is this what happens after someone dies?

He'd never really thought about whether there was an afterlife before this, but now there wasn't much that he *could* think about. He couldn't move, couldn't speak, and didn't even know if he still had a body as he couldn't sense or feel anything; his thoughts were the only thing that seemed real anymore. With only his consciousness that seemed to exist in this perpetual darkness, he began to wonder if this was it. Would he be stuck here for eternity? Is there something more than this? What will happen to everyone he left behind? His new friends? His fami—

A sudden brightness blinded him after the sensory deprivation of the dark void, followed by the feeling of wind rushing past his ears that he thought he should be able to hear, except for the fact that he was still deafened by the screams of the Warped Void Hunters. Regardless, the abrupt change in his circumstances caused Larek's mind to lock up as he attempted to figure out what was happening.

It was the whipping cold air blasting across his face that finally seemed to restart his thinking processes. Opening his eyes against the incessant wind trying to rip his eyes out of their sockets, he discovered what was happening to him an instant before his half-mile drop into a lake slapped the side of his body as he fell into the water below him.

Pain reverberated throughout his entire frame as the force of his fall against the surface tension of the lake smashed the left side of his face, snapped his left wrist, lower *and* upper arm (which was outstretched and hit the water first), broke his left leg in a few places, and cracked at least three of his ribs. He didn't know this all at once, of course, because the shock of so much damage was of secondary importance compared to the fact that he had inadvertently sucked in a lungful of water soon after passing through the surface.

Drowning and under at least 20 feet of water once his descent into the lake ended, Larek panicked and attempted to suck in even more water in an attempt to breathe – but that, of course, didn't work out too well. With his body spasming from the abrupt lack of oxygen, the incredible damage his body had sustained finally hit him, and he knew he was going to die unless he did something about it.

Upon mentally activating his *Healing Surge* Fusion attached to his robe, he experienced the incredible pain of his body speeding up his normal *Body Regeneration* to fix everything that was broken; not even his *Pain Immunity* Skill could block it out. It was at this point that he felt every single broken or cracked bone in his body, and could even feel the way his face was reshaped in response to what had to have been incredible damage, to the point where he was surprised he was still conscious. If he hadn't already been drowning, the agony of his healing would've done it anyway as his mouth involuntarily opened in a silent scream.

The healing took so long that his body had floated to the surface by the time it was all done, and he broke free of the water – only to find that his lungs were still filled with it. A lethargy borne of both his recent healing and the healing he had undergone after suffering from his explosive spell patterns weighed his limbs down and made it almost impossible for him to move, but he forced himself to swim for the shore of the lake approximately 50 feet away. A few seconds of struggling through the water made him realize that he wasn't going to make it; he felt himself slowing down and his face fell into the water again, the effort of keeping it above the surface too much for him.

No! Keep moving!

Larek's mental objection and order directed toward his body caused an explosion inside his chest that felt like it was shredding his insides, but it also seemed to give him a surge of strength that allowed him to keep going. Every stroke of his arms through the water was accompanied by a pulse of alternating strength and weakness, but it was just enough to get him through.

His vision was starting to become spotty by the time he dragged himself onto the rocky beach, disregarding the rough stone under his hands and knees. He collapsed as roughly as he could on his front side, aiming for a rounded protruding rock, and the impact against his chest did exactly what he hoped would happen. The pressure on his chest was enough to force a little of the water up from his lungs, and once it started coming out he actively worked to cough the rest of it out. It felt like half the lake emerged from his lungs as he spent the next few minutes roughly expelling every trace of liquid inside of places it shouldn't be, and while his breathing was still a bit bubbly, the fact that he could breathe at all was a miracle in his eyes.

Unfortunately, the effort of pulling himself out of the water, along with the panicked removal of the fluid in his lungs and the healing he had undergone to fix his broken bones, all combined to overwhelm his mind and body to the point where he passed out, oblivious to the world.

* * *

"Whadja thin got 'em?"
"D'know. Coulda been justa bout anytang."
"Don see no marks 'o nothin. Musta drowed."
"Betta fo us. Dat robe seems fency-like. An dat reeng shood brang in a preety gol' or so. Chick dat bag fo' anytang—"

The sound of strange voices, their accent funny to his mind, along with an incessant tugging at the straps of the pack on his back, roused Larek from unconsciousness. A sudden jerk as one of the straps slid over his moving arm woke him up fully, and he reacted without conscious thought.

Even without opening his eyes, his fist lashed out and smacked the questing hand away, and he felt and heard a dull *crack* as his fist met soft flesh.

"AAAAHHHH! He ali'! Bro' me 'and, e di'!"

The accent seemed to get thicker to the point where Larek couldn't even understand it; or it could've been that it was screamed out rather than spoken regularly. Forcing himself to turn over, he finally got a look at those who were talking – though only their backsides, as the pair of short figures dressed in what looked like multicolored rags were hightailing it away from the prone Fusionist.

Larek tried to call out to them to apologize for hurting one of them, because it had been an accident stemming from a misunderstanding, as they obviously thought he was dead, but his voice only came out as a croak. It felt dry and raw, which only got worse as he hacked up yet another mouthful of water coming from his lungs. Groaning as he got to his hands and knees, he forced himself to cough for another few minutes to get as much of the liquid out of his body as he could. By the time he was done, his throat was extremely raw, but he thought he finally got rid of the rest, and he was able to breathe easier.

He nearly healed himself with his Fusion, but held off for the moment. A debilitating weakness weighed on his body to the point where he wasn't sure if he would even be able to get up and walk, and he didn't want to make it any worse.

After a few more minutes of recovering from his coughing fit, Larek finally stood up on wobbly legs that stabilized after a moment, before looking around. Based on the angle of the sun and how much his robe had dried, he figured he had been unconscious for a few hours, and while the sleep had helped to recover his strength a little bit, what he really needed was something to eat.

Moving off of the rock beach was a challenge, as he nearly fell over the uneven rocks multiple times, but his Agility stat seemed to help him stay upright – even if he wasn't graceful about it. Surrounding the lake behind him, which he saw was ovoid-shaped and stretched about 1,000 feet from one end to the other at its widest point, was a band of trees that blocked out any view of anything farther away. That was just fine with Larek, as he collapsed next to one of the odd-looking trees, which were all much shorter than he was used to seeing at about 25 feet tall. Their leaves were also *huge*, larger than both of his hands put together, and their branches were thin and springy, and he wondered how they bore the weight of multiple leaves.

He let that curiosity fade away as he sat down, before feeling something at his waist.

Bestie! You're still here!

Larek felt under his robe for the axe, pulling it out and laying it over his lap in case some monster attacked him – not that he had the strength to swing it at the moment. Still, it made him smile seeing that his best friend seemed to have survived everything he had gone through; it was his faithful companion and was sturdy enough to get him through just about anything.

After that, he struggled to get the pack off his back and swing it around so that he could access it. Untying the straps, he immediately saw that it had been waterlogged from his dip in the lake, and some water even leaked out as he pulled the opening up further. Over the next half-hour, he pulled out all the supplies that had been stored in the pack, finding that most of the food that had been in there was essentially ruined, though he put aside some jerked meats and hardtack that were surprisingly still fine thanks to an expert job with a sort of waxed linen wrapping. When he found any food that was still edible, he consumed it immediately without considering saving it for later in case he was unable to find more. His rationale was that he needed sustenance *now* to replace what the healing had consumed from his body, and it would surely be easier to find food once he could get up and move.

In the end, he ate every single thing in his pack that hadn't been ruined, which equated to a basic meal at the Academy. He could tell that he needed *a lot* more than that in order to fully recover, but he had a feeling when it finally digested he would at least be able to move around and fight with his axe if necessary.

Unfortunately, he had lost his staff all the way back near the Aperture when the Gergasi had landed, and he hadn't been able to grab it to take with him when Chinli took him away. He would have to recreate another one to use—except that he couldn't right now. His Pattern Cohesion, despite being full, was raw and ragged throughout his entire body from the strain he had put it through with directing his spell patterns to overload and explode. Closing his eyes and internally evaluating his current condition, he realized that it was even worse than he thought. He had a feeling that if he were to try and do *anything* with his Pattern Cohesion in the next few... days? Weeks, perhaps? Regardless, it was bad enough that he might kill himself if he tried to utilize his own Pattern Cohesion for anything, even the simplest of Fusions. It was worse than anything he'd felt before, and he was honestly surprised that he actually hadn't died from the damage.

Thinking about the Aperture and his missing staff inevitably led to thoughts of the events that led him to his current situation. First, he thought about his friends and how the Gergasi said something about erasing their memories of Larek and of herself, which he hadn't taken the time to fully consider before now. He had made a deal with Chinli to spare their lives and that had seemed the most important to him at the time, but if he *did* find his way back to them, would they even recognize him? Would they even care to get to know him, a stranger, again?

After considering it for a while, he realized that it might be for the best for everyone that they forgot about him – at least temporarily. Just knowing him had put all of them in extreme danger, and now they would be able to learn at Silverledge Academy and Fort Ironwall without having to look over their shoulders every few seconds. On a more personal, selfish note, their distance and ignorance of him would hopefully dispel whatever he had inadvertently influenced them with. When the time came to meet them again, preferably when he got a handle on his Dominion Magic, he could interact with them – and especially Nedira – without worrying that he *made* them like... or love him.

But that all depended on whether he could even live long enough to see them again. With no sign of Chinli swooping down and capturing him again, despite him being in one place for a while, he was hopeful that he had escaped her clutches. The first question that burned in his mind about that whole situation was, "Why isn't she coming after me?" – from which stemmed a number of other questions.

Was she killed by those Warped Void Hunters? He didn't think so, based on what he saw there at the end of their fight.

Does she think I'm dead? That was a distinct possibility, given he was hit by one of those orbs of whirling energy that seemed to destroy everything they touched.

How am I still alive? Again, that went back to those orbs of whirling energy hitting him, but he had no explanation for why he hadn't been torn apart.

But the most important question of all was: *Where am I?* He didn't remember seeing any lakes along the ground where Chinli and the Hunters had been fighting, so he could only conclude that he wasn't within a mile or two of that area. When he added in the strange accent of the would-be scavengers that he had scared away, he could only conclude that he was somewhere else in the Kingdom he was unfamiliar with. It was even possible that he wasn't even in the Kingdom anymore; if that was the case, then he needed to find out where he actually was so he could get back as soon as possible.

That thought made him pause for a moment, as he considered his motivation for returning. If what he suspected was true, then the people who knew him the most at the Academy were either dead or had their memories wiped of his existence. The Gergasi, Chinli, quite possibly thought he was dead after being impacted by that destructive energy orb created by the Hunters. That meant that, as far as he could tell, no one had knowledge of his whereabouts or even where he *should* be. In other words, he was free to do what he wanted, just like he wanted all along.

So, why was he immediately wanting to return? Initially, it was because of family and friends. Now that he wasn't constrained to the Academy, he could surreptitiously visit his family to ensure they were safe with all the craziness of the Scissions and Apertures going on. After that, he would consider visiting Silverledge Academy and Fort Ironwall to connect with his friends again, to determine if they were safe, and to see if Nedira would have the same feelings about him that she did before.

But there was another reason to go to Fort Ironwall, and that was to unlock his access to Stama and learn about fighting and Battle Arts – two subjects where he was sorely lacking in knowledge. After that, well, he supposed it depended on what his future plans looked like with the SIC, because he would have an obligation to join them because of all the instruction they had provided him in both the Academies he'd attended and the Fort he hoped to attend. It wasn't that he particularly *wanted* to join the SIC, given how he felt about the entire process and his reluctance to save the world as Dean Lorraine wanted, but he had to do *something*.

He'd seen the damage that Scissions could cause, and now with the new Apertures that were likely opening up everywhere throughout the Kingdom, the threat to everyone was only increasing. Even though he hoped to find his family and friends safe, if people like himself didn't step up to defend the Kingdom from the threats that the monsters posed to them, then they were all doomed. Especially considering that the so-called "Great Ones" were of no help.

From what little he knew of the Gergasi, who were powerful enough to combat the monsters, he was fairly certain that they were unable to leave their Enclave for long because the Corruption of Aetheric Force coming from the world they were connected to was attracted to them. Twice now, a Scission opened almost on top of the two Gergasi that he had personally seen, and he was convinced that it wasn't a coincidence. If that happened every time they left their Enclave, then it was no wonder that they were rarely ever seen outside – and therefore would be of limited help against the Apertures.

Shaking his head to clear it, Larek repacked his bag, which now contained about a dozen steel bracelets that he had planned on adding Fusions to at some point, 8 platinum coins, 30 gold coins, and his transfer letter signed by the Dean and Vice General from Copperleaf and Pinevalley, which miraculously wasn't ruined by water; and then he began to stand up to leave... toward somewhere. The only direction he could envision heading was where he had seen the two rag-wearing scavengers scamper off to, as it was possible there was a town or city nearby. From there, he would be able to determine where he was in relation to the Kingdom, and to formulate a plan for going forward.

Before he fully got up, an insistent reminder in the back of his mind prodded at him. *Notifications? What for?*

When he looked at them, he dropped back down on his backside, temporarily overcome by information that flooded into his mind.

Chapter 50

Apparently, Larek had accidentally made greater strides in his advancement than he thought was possible.

Body Regeneration *has reached Level 27!*
......
Body Regeneration *has reached Level 30!*

Not only had he increased his *Body Regeneration* Skill, thanks in no small part to all the damage that had been done to it via his destructive plummet into the lake, but he maxed it out at Level 30. The result of that increase in his skill actually boosted his overall Level to 22, which also had the benefit of giving him an extra 18 AP to distribute into his stats, for a total of 20 AP with what he had previously. Along with over 5,000 AF gained from killing all those Greater Trizards, he now had a lot of choices to make with how he wanted to distribute his resources.

But that wasn't the biggest surprise in his notifications, because he also achieved something that he hadn't thought was possible, and it changed his whole outlook on the future.

Congratulations!

Defying your fate in the face of imminent death has unlocked your full potential, Guardian!

Stama Subjugation *Skill has been unlocked!*
Stama Subjugation *has reached Level 1!*

New Skills have been added to improvement through allocation of Aetheric Force!

New—
ERROR DETECTED
Flaw in stat alignment present... correcting...
Unable to correct...
Incompatibilities normalized...
Adjusting stats...
Adjustment complete!

There was an awkward wrenching in his body and Pattern Cohesion when he read the notification; it was riding right on the edge of pain while he writhed on the ground, his blood feeling like it was burning him from the inside, but it thankfully faded after a few minutes of near-painless torture. He opened his Status and looked for anything that had recently changed.

Larek Holsten

Fusionist
Healer
Level 22
Advancement Points (AP) : 3/18
Available AP to Distribute: 20
Available Aetheric Force (AF): 5,424

Stama: 830/830
Mana: 1400/1400

Strength: 75 [83] (+)
Body: 75 [83] (+)
Agility: 75 [83] (+)
Intellect: 70 [140] (+)
Acuity: 104 [208] (+)
Pneuma: 747 [1,494]
Pattern Cohesion: 9,574/14,940

Martial Skills:
Stama Subjugation Level 1/20 (200 AF)
Blunt Weapon Expertise Level 1/20 (200 AF)
Bladed Weapon Expertise Level 2/20 (200 AF)
Throwing Level 5/20 (200 AF)
Dodge Level 10/20 (200 AF)
Pain Immunity Level 20/20 (N/A)
Body Regeneration Level 30/30 (300 AF)

The changes to his Status were subtle, but significant in spite of not being immediately obvious. As to the notification about an "ERROR" being detected in his stat alignment, he wasn't sure what that meant exactly, but from what he could tell, the relationship between his Body and his Pneuma stats was strengthened, and the 4 points that he had put into the Pneuma stat so long ago were now included in the multiplication by his Body stat – but it was more than that now.

Originally, he had thought that every point he put into Body *also* added 5 points to his Pneuma, which was highly beneficial, of course. But now that he looked at it closer, he realized that the relationship between the two stats was *broken*, for want of a better word. What it was *supposed* to do was multiply his Body by his original Pneuma stat, which he calculated to have only been 5, giving him a final Pneuma of 100 when he first unlocked his stats. When he added 4 to the stat later, it wasn't factored into the multiplication because there was something wrong with the connection between them. Now that it appeared to be fixed, he now technically had 9 Pneuma, which was then multiplied by his Body stat, which was 83 with the +1 *Body Boost* Fusion on his robe, giving him a total of 747 Pneuma, or 1,494 with his *+10 Pneuma Boost* Fusion.

At first, it seemed like it was entirely beneficial, but when he noticed that there was no longer a **(+)** next to Pneuma, meaning that he couldn't add any more AP to it, he began to worry. An attempt to add an AP to the stat did absolutely nothing – it was as if he suddenly ran into a wall. If he wasn't able to increase his Pneuma, how would he be able to increase his Pattern Cohesion in the future? Granted, he had a lot of it right now, nearly 15,000 in fact, but he knew that the stronger and more-complicated Fusions that he wanted to create once he was able to create Advanced Fusions would require more, so he would eventually hit his limit.

It wasn't until he did a little more searching through his stats that he had a sudden intuition that his Martial stats – Strength, Body, and Agility – weren't as limited as they were before. Based on what he looked at next, which was his new *Stama Subjugation* Skill, it felt like his Martial stats were also "unlocked" for him, despite already having access to them. He was confident that if he utilized a *Strength Boost +10*, *Agility Boost +10*, or – most importantly – a *Body Boost +10*, he would no longer suffer from the increase. That meant that if he was able to effectively double his Body, he could subsequently double his Pneuma and Pattern Cohesion at the same time. Not only that, but the restriction of keeping his Martial stats even so that he didn't feel wildly unbalanced seemed to be lifted, as he was confident he could add all 20 of his AP to Body and it would be just fine.

There were solutions to his problem after all.

With his stats now adjusted and more in balance than they ever were, Larek closed his eyes again and looked at his Pattern Cohesion, wanting to see how it had fared after all of the changes. Thankfully, the alteration of his stats didn't seem to have harmed his internal pattern any more than it already had been; if anything, the increase in his Pneuma seemed to have a soothing effect upon its ragged edges, like a healing balm that would help speed up its healing. Instead of weeks or perhaps months of recuperation, he thought it might only be at most a week before he could start making Fusions again, as long as he took it easy.

Finding himself better than he had been just an hour or so ago, the Fusionist turned his attention to his new Skill. Obtaining *Stama Subjugation*, the Skill required to handle his Stama, was a vast surprise, but he supposed his near-death experience with the fall into the lake, extreme injuries, and almost drowning contributed to a situation that "cracked it open", as Penelope had mentioned. When he delved his mind into his chest, he could feel the roiling energy that he identified as his Stama right where it had always been – but now he felt as if he could begin to interact with it. He didn't do much more than mentally touch it before pulling away, as he didn't have the energy to experiment at the moment, but he hoped to do a lot more when he was in a better position.

As for the Battle Art he had already unlocked, he could feel that he was right on the edge of understanding how to activate it at will, but he also sensed that he didn't exactly have enough control of his Stama to do it reliably. Resolving to wait until he had increased his new Skill at least a few Levels before trying it out, he last turned to his Martial Skills and found that they all now had a cost in Aetheric Force listed next to them where there had been simply (N/A) before. Though that wasn't entirely true, as *Pain Immunity* seemed to have that label still, as if it had already been increased to the maximum and couldn't increase any further no matter how much Aetheric Force was thrown at it. Given its name, though, he supposed that there wasn't anything better than "immunity" to pain, so it made sense.

With his Stama and Martial side of his abilities now "unlocked", Larek realized that there was now one less reason to go to Fort Ironwall. Granted, he only had a vague description of how to utilize his Stama and how to appropriately use it in Battle Arts, but he had a feeling he would eventually figure it out with enough practice. That still left finding his friends and learning how to fight, which was still greatly needed, but was it enough to risk going to the Fort? He wasn't in as much danger of his Stama getting out of control, now that he had the Skill to manage it, so the pressure to go was a lot less intense than it was a short time ago.

There was a risk in going, after all, as it would mean being in closer proximity to those who could reveal his nature to the Gergasi. He had narrowly managed to escape from a short life of torture before death and had no desire to end up back there if he could prevent that possibility. Finding his family, on the other hand, *was* something he would risk doing – if only to ensure they were safe. He still desired to help out the Kingdom somehow, as the threat of the Apertures and the monsters that came out of them was still there, but would he have to tie himself to the SIC to do that?

It was something to think on, but he didn't have to decide either way at the moment. Right now, the most important thing for Larek to do was to get up and moving to find some sort of civilization nearby. Not only did he need to find out where he ended up, but he could also use a mountain of food to help replenish the resources his body had used up. A place to sleep that wasn't in the middle of a potentially dangerous forest would be nice, as well. The night before – *has it only been half a day since we left Whittleton?* – inside the Waterbury Inn and the enormous bed spoiled him after roughing it for the previous week outside, and he wasn't ashamed to use the coinage he had in his bag to purchase another good night's sleep somewhere safe.

Picking himself up again from the ground with a slight groan, he made sure his pack was secured to his back while he held his axe in his right hand just under its head, ready to use it in case he was attacked. While he thought he *might* be outside of the Kingdom, he couldn't know for sure and wanted to be prepared if he was attacked by nearby monsters.

Moving further into the odd trees, he carefully picked his way through the foliage as he listened for any kind of movement around him. He'd learned a tiny bit of tracking and moving stealthily through the landscape after watching Vivienne do it so often, but he was by no means *good* at it; he still had a lot to learn about that kind of thing, which was another point in favor for visiting Fort Ironwall to gain that kind of knowledge.

Angling his direction to the northeast, which was the direction he saw the two scavengers scamper in earlier, he only traveled for less than an hour before the trees began to thin considerably. A few minutes later, they disappeared entirely, exposing the landscape in front of him – which was certainly not what he was expecting.

Larek had come out of the last of the trees on a slight hill, giving him a view of what appeared to be a hot and humid, semi-flooded plain. Off to the southeast was an extremely wide river that he could barely see the other side of, and rivulets led off from the engorged waterway to spill out along the rest of the landscape. Strangely terraced fields of what he could only assume were a few harvestable plants were scattered all over the eastern and northern portions of his view, and he could see people working in these fields. He thought they were harvesting them, given that it was fall and that was when he heard it happened most often, but the more he observed their actions, it looked like they were planting things in the exposed soil instead.

Every single one of them was wearing something similar to the scavengers that had accosted him earlier, though these appeared in better condition and not as ragged. With a better look at them, he realized that all of them were quite pale of skin where it was largely covered by their loose clothing draped over them, while anything exposed to the sun beating down on them was slightly reddened as if sunburned. For some reason, he was surprised to see that they weren't tanned like most of those from where he came from, but that also gave credence to the theory that he wasn't in the Kingdom anymore.

With their hair cut short and in shades of dark red to light brown, their appearance was slightly odd to him, but he took that as a good sign. Without the prejudice of the Kingdom hounding him, even if he was still wearing Shinpai's ring, he felt more confident of making his way into the large town he saw to the northeast, which was nearly large enough to be considered a city, he thought. The strangest thing he noticed about it was that there was absolutely *no wall* surrounding any of the buildings, though he thought he saw some sort of stone-walled compound somewhere in the middle, but he couldn't be completely sure.

Seeing civilization ahead of him and the prospect of food and a bed to finish recuperating in, Larek started to walk toward the town in the distance. As soon as he walked down the slight hill from which he had been observing the landscape, he discovered that finding his way to town was easier said than done, as it was difficult to pick his way through the flooded portions of the terraced plain without stomping all over the fields in his way.

Still, the Fusionist persevered and eventually came to an elevated road of some sort he thought would lead to the town. While he was making his way there, he was cognizant of many of the people in the fields moving away from him and running toward the buildings in the distance, but his exhausted mind and body figured that it was just time for them to stop working for the day and go home. It wasn't exactly late yet, as the sun would still probably be up for a couple of hours, but he also didn't know when they started the day – so they could've been working for most of it already.

It wasn't until he was approximately a half-mile from the town that he saw a group of people heading his way from the direction of the town, but these people were different from the ones he saw in the fields before. Riding horses and wearing shiny armor that gleamed in the slowly descending sunlight, the contingent of approximately 20 figures was intimidating, to say the least, as each of them held a long spear rigidly upright, while one of their number had some sort of colored fabric attached to it that fluttered with the wind of their passing.

As they got closer, Larek stopped and moved to the side of the raised road, thinking that they were intending to pass him. While he stood there, he tried to see what they looked like a little better, as they looked like Martials of some sort, but he didn't see any sign of an SIC badge anywhere on their person or on their banner-like fabric attached to what appeared to be a wooden pole. With their full helmets hiding their faces, he couldn't even say if they looked like the same kind of people as those in the fields earlier – which he just noticed were completely empty. He knew he wasn't moving that fast along the road, as he was conserving his energy, but their rapid disappearance was a shock.

"HALT!" the armored rider in the front of the group shouted as soon as they were close enough for Larek to hear him. The Fusionist just looked around to see who they were talking to, given that he had already stopped walking a while ago, but he didn't see anyone. A second or so later, the entire company of riders stopped and surrounded Larek on the road in a semicircle, before leveling their spears directly at him.

I guess that means they were talking to me.

"You're wanted under suspicion of attacking an Ectorian earlier today." The lead rider spoke loudly but didn't shout, and Larek was slightly surprised to hear a feminine voice coming from inside the helmet. Not that he didn't think she looked like she should be commanding the contingent of armored individuals, but because the "HALT" from earlier sounded masculine and harsh. "You will come with us now or be killed immediately."

As he thought about protesting, one look at the speartips that were only a few feet away from his face made him think again. He thought that this might all just be a misunderstanding, as he could only assume that the person he had injured earlier had told someone what happened, so he thought it better to go along with them for now. He was in no condition to fight, and while he thought his Fusions would help protect him quite a bit if he was attacked, he didn't want to take the chance of getting injured again. Besides, he needed information, food, and supplies if he was going to leave this place sometime soon for the Kingdom, and that would be difficult if he ended up hurting some of their... guards? Protectors? Martials? He wasn't sure what they were called here, but he was fairly certain that none of them were able to wield Stama or Mana.

As he nodded and said, "Alright, I'm coming with you," he was immediately marched down the road inside a circle of horses that gave him no room to escape even if he had the strength for it. The buildings of the town ahead slowly got bigger as he saw them through the gaps of his escort, but he ignored how different they appeared compared to the ones in the Kingdom in favor of thinking about something quite inane.

If the scavengers and these people are from the same place, where's the accent?

Chapter 51

Instead of the stone and wood construction of the buildings he was used to, the first thing that Larek noticed when he was close enough to the town to understand what he was looking at was that none of them were constructed of anything he was familiar with. Instead of wood being the main component in the construction of their walls, it was a strange mixture of what appeared to be dirt or clay with long strands of plant fibers interlaced in an interesting overlaying pattern. It was only when he looked closer at the fibers that he realized they had likely come from the trees he had just left, though from their leaves and branches rather than their trunks.

The rooflines of the buildings he saw were angled like he was used to seeing, which helped to let rain fall off, but instead of tiles or even thatch comprising the material, they were created using the dried, leathery-like versions of the leaves from those same trees. They were layered so that they covered the entire roof without any holes or gaps, and they appeared easy enough to replace if they were damaged. Larek thought that it was an ingenious use of the local plant life, as it didn't seem as though they had a lot of wood available for some reason – despite the forest nearby.

In fact, the only construction he saw that used wood at all were the doors and window shutters he saw on the buildings, but from the look of them, he understood why it wasn't used in normal construction. Having seen plenty of lumber in his relatively short life, he could tell right away that the wood he saw was unsuitable for large construction projects, as it had a "rubbery" characteristic to it that was visible even at a distance; where it was attached to metal hinges, the doors he saw almost appeared to sag in place, though it wasn't enough to compromise the purpose of the doors. It was more that they were a bit more flexible than the former Logger would expect from any type of wood, and he briefly wondered what Verne would say about it. That inevitably made his thoughts wander toward his friends, but he pushed them aside.

He was truly on his own for the first time since he left home and he needed to keep his priorities straight in order to survive. Right now, those priorities didn't include thinking about friends that were an unknown distance away from him and who likely wouldn't even know him if he saw them again.

The buildings on the edge of the town seemed to be residences of some sort, and most of them were smaller in comparison to what he could see further in. After passing the first few orderly rows of these tiny houses, the road went from being dark-colored dirt to long planks of wood underneath his feet that covered the entire width of the avenue. His first few steps on the strange wooden walkway proved that he was correct in his observation of the wood as a building resource, as it was springy underneath his feet; whether it would bend freely or if it would break once it bent past a certain point was unknown, but it was obviously quite durable and lightweight despite its extreme flexibility.

Since he was still surrounded by the riders that had ordered him to accompany them, he wasn't able to see much other than the buildings very well, but he caught glimpses of the people the large group passed as they made their way toward what seemed like the center of the town. Scurrying groups of the same individuals he saw out in the fields were the most prominent at first, and from what he saw of them, they appeared curious and carefree at the same time as they saw the procession pass them.

Once past the smaller residences, which seemed to be largely inhabited by these people, the size of the buildings grew to two and three stories, using the same sort of construction as the others. Whatever the resource they used to build the structures appeared to be just as strong as wood and stone, or even more so, and toward the center of the town the largest buildings were four stories tall.

The type of people they passed changed along with the buildings. Soon enough, there weren't any of the pale-skinned, rag-wearing individuals from the fields outside, as they were replaced by a darker-skinned people that were all wearing thin, loose clothing in primarily light colors such as white and tan, and they wore wide-brimmed hats that appeared useful for blocking out the sun. Their skin was darker in color than those in the Kingdom, but not nearly as dark as Penelope; they were somewhere in between, though there were also various shades that got closer to one extreme or the other. The only other thing he noticed about them was the shape of their eyes, which were slightly larger than seemed normal to him, though not significantly; they weren't exactly *huge*, but even a 25% larger size than he was used to was noticeable.

Larek found their group approaching what was likely the largest building in the entire town, which was four stories tall and was large enough to house at least a few hundred students if it was back at the Academy. Once they got close enough, the group of riders stopped in front of the entrance and spread out around him in a semi-circle with him in the middle, facing toward the building; only the leader – or so he supposed, as she was the only one that spoke to him – was apart from them, as she swung down from her mount and approached him.

Pulling off her helmet exposed her full face for the first time, and he wasn't surprised to see that her darker skin and jet-black shoulder-length hair matched the second type of people he saw inside the town – though her piercing, violet-colored eyes were certainly different. He hadn't actually gotten a great look at eye-coloring as they walked through the town, so he supposed that everyone may have had the same or something similar.

"Come with me," she said roughly. "If you try to escape or harm anyone else, I will put you down faster than you can blink."

Having already put his axe away earlier so as to not present a greater threat to these people, his hands were free to put up in front of him placatingly. "I have no intention of doing anything until this misunderstanding is settled." She scoffed at his words but didn't respond any other way; instead, she just turned around and walked a few steps up to the entrance of the building, and for the first time Larek was able to get a better look at its construction.

Various openings along the bottom of the outside wall were strange to him, because it almost looked as if they had deliberately weakened the foundation. It was only when it appeared to be relatively hollow underneath the building that he took another look at the wooden walkways around town, seeing that they were actually slightly suspended above the ground, leaving approximately 4 or 5 inches of space underneath. Thinking about the river nearby and how the fields appeared partially flooded, he could only deduce that the town *also* flooded at some point, and these openings and the suspended walkways were essential to managing the water without it flooding their homes and being able to get around without having to wade through what could essentially be a small lake.

His deductions were dismissed from his mind as he had to duck his head in order to walk inside the building, which was only partially illuminated from the light of the windows, though it was bright enough to see that he had entered a relatively large room that held more of the armored individuals like the riders outside and his violet-eyed escort, though they appeared much more relaxed with their helmets off. When he entered, however, they stiffened their stances and eyed him warily as he passed them at their various tables where they were eating and drinking; Larek was reminded of the Inn he had just stayed at, as there was a bar set up along the rear of the room, with a few other armored guards sitting on stools right up against the long counter.

The leader of the riders led him to the right and through yet another doorway he had to duck slightly to get through, and Larek stopped immediately upon seeing the pair of scavengers that had found him near the lake. They were sitting in a pair of what appeared to be some sort of woven fabric chairs behind a large wooden table, and one of them was cradling his hand, wrist, and lower arm which had been wrapped in a cloth bandage with a splint, showing clearly where Larek had accidentally broken it as he lashed out.

"Sit." The order was given by his escort, who pointed toward another chair situated in front of him and on the opposite side of the table from where the scavengers were sitting. When he hesitated, the violet-eyed leader flipped her spear down until the speartip was pointed at his throat; even though it was a few feet away, he could sense the threat implied in the maneuver. Granted, if she attempted to stab him in the neck, his *Repelling Barrier* Fusion would kick in, but he didn't think it was time to test its efficacy.

So, he sat.

He wasn't in the chair – which bent alarmingly beneath him, as he realized that the frame was made of the same spongy wood he'd seen throughout town – for more than a few seconds before someone else walked into the smallish room from an adjacent doorway. Larek looked at the newcomer and was reminded of Inquisitor Carl back in Barrowford; while the other person wasn't a Mage, he wore a fancier set of clothing compared to those he saw about town, though in white and yellow. He also wore a thick chain of what appeared to be braided gold and silver around his neck, with a large medallion depicting some obscure symbol he couldn't immediately identify on it.

"Thank you for finding the alleged perpetrator of this crime so quickly, Protector Ashlynn," the man said quickly, even as he jumped up to sit on a tall stool that had him towering over everyone in the room. His short dark-brown hair was nearly black in coloring, though Larek could see signs of greying throughout its length; his darker skin was also slightly wrinkled, but the Fusionist couldn't tell if it was from age or from being exposed to the sun.

"Just doing my duty, sir."

Turning his attention to the others in the room, the man on the tall stool looked at the two scavengers first. "I want to confirm that this is the individual who allegedly harmed you. Would you be able to definitively say this person is the perpetrator?"

Both of the rag-wearing scavengers nodded with anger in their faces. "Ye', dis de wan dat don do et. 'e bro' me 'arm!" said the one with the splint.

"Thank you." Turning to Larek, the man had a stony face as he asked, "Do you refute that you were the one that harmed one of the Ectorian people?"

Larek thought about lying, but it was obvious that they already knew he was guilty. He wasn't exactly sure what was going on, though he equated the process to what had happened back in Rushwood village with the Headman's daughter. This, however, felt a bit more... fair, perhaps?

Still, he didn't know who these Ectorians were, nor why it seemed like such a big deal that he had hurt one of them. It was an accident, after all, and surely, they had someone that might be able to heal them?

Or... maybe they don't. If this isn't the Kingdom, it isn't likely that they have a Mage that can heal nearby.

Regardless, he was going to admit his guilt while defending his actions, while also volunteering to heal the individual so that there was no ultimate harm done.

"I don't refute it, but the whole thing was an accident," Larek said. "He was trying to steal my pack from me, and I inadvertently struck out and hit his arm, breaking it."

"Is this true?"

"Na, 'o course na! I neva ta' fro' nane, ya know dat!"

Larek was starting to understand the speech of the scavenger a little better the more he heard, but it was still difficult to parse through the meaning. Still, he thought he understood what the man meant.

"He probably thought I was a corpse," Larek interjected as an explanation. "It was an honest mistake, just like my own inadvertent attack. I'd be willing to—"

"Why would Gwest think you were a corpse?" the man on the stool asked, cutting Larek off before he could fully offer to heal the scavenger. *Or I suppose I should think of him as Gwest, as that is apparently his name.*

"Because I had to drag myself out of the lake and *I was* practically half-dead at the time," the Fusionist said by way of explanation.

"And why were you in the lake?"

Now Larek hesitated to answer, because he wasn't sure what he should say. Out of the corner of his eye, he saw the speartip that Protector Ashlynn was directing inch closer to his neck, which he realized was moving slow enough that his protective Fusion wouldn't even activate. Sweating slightly, he cleared his throat while he talked his way through an explanation.

"I, uh, suddenly appeared above the lake and fell inside. Before you ask, I'm not *entirely* sure how I ended up there, other than I was fighting a Warped Void Hunter and was hit by one of its attacks; that was the last thing I knew before I found myself falling into the lake." He paused for a second before going on. "In fact, I have no idea where I am in relation to the Kingdom of Androthe."

That last bit caused everyone in the room to inhale suddenly in surprise. Strangely enough, the spear threatening him from the side was withdrawn after a moment and the butt of it *thunked* against the floor, which was made of the same material as the rest of the building.

"Kingdom of Androthe? You're a... what do they call you? Soldier? Fighter?" the man wearing the chain asked after a few seconds of staring at Larek.

"Do you mean a Martial?" Assuming that was what the man meant, Larek began to shake his head, but then he realized that it might make more sense to these people than admitting that he was a Mage. If he couldn't cast spells, after all, then it would be difficult to prove; also without the ability to create any Fusions, at least for the time being, he was basically without any way to demonstrate his skills as a Mage. "Yes, I'm a Martial – though I'm still in training," he said, adding the last as an explanation if they chose to test him somehow. He had the strength to prove that he had the stats, at least, though if they asked about any fighting skills, he would just have to admit that he hadn't learned much yet. It was even technically the truth, given the transfer letter in his pack.

"Ah. That explains much. What is your name, Martial trainee from the Kingdom of Androthe?"

"My name is Larek," he answered immediately, before glancing at the injured Gwest. "I want to reiterate how sorry I am to have hurt you, as it was not my overall intention. To make up for that, I have something that can help heal your injury within seconds," he added, gesturing toward the would-be scavenger, "though I need to eat something beforehand to regain my strength and you'll need something to eat afterward." There was no way he was going to take his robe off in order to heal the man, so he would need more sustenance to recover from his weakened state before he did another healing. With the damage that was done to the man, he was fairly certain the *Healing Surge* Fusion would only cause Gwest to become extremely hungry rather than send him into a coma.

"Would that make amends for the damage done to you?" the important man on the stool asked.

Gwest thought about it for a moment, but after eyeing Larek for a few seconds, he nodded.

"Before I do that," the Fusionist added, looking at the man with the chain and medallion, "could you tell me where I am?"

The man smiled as he answered. "Right now, you're in the glorious town of Enderflow, situated at the western end of the Sealance Empire."

Sealance Empire... Sealance Empire... I don't remember that from my Geography of the SIC class. "Where, if you happen to know, is the Sealance Empire located in relation to the Kingdom of Androthe?"

"Ah, yes, now that is a good question," the man said, his smile becoming a bit wider for some reason. "Let's just say that you're a *very* long way from home."

That's... just great.

Epilogue

Chinli finished off the last of the Warped Void Hunters that had impeded her progress back to the Enclave with Vilnesh's wayward half-breed in tow. As she turned to pick him back up from where she had left him safely suspended in the air, she was momentarily shocked to see that her charge was gone.

"WHAT?! How did he escape?"

He must be more powerful than anyone thought. Well, I guess I'll just have to punish his companions for his daring to escape.

Determined to chase him down, the winged Great One quickly moved to where she had left the half-breed, immediately identifying the residue from the destroyed spells she had cast over him. Searching for her personal Mana that had practically saturated his entire body in the short time that she had been traveling with him, as it was much more powerful than anything he could raise in defense – not that he had tried after smartly agreeing to come with her – she was stymied when she couldn't see any trail leading off in any direction.

Impossible! Unless... no, there's no way he was strong enough to overcome my Mana. But I better find it quickly before it fades away.

As she looked at the magical residue again, searching for the answer to how he had escaped, she felt her blood turn to ice as she recognized the trace sections of void energy running all throughout it. "No... no, this can't be happening. It's got to be a mistake."

She was in complete control of that battle from the beginning, as the Warped Void Hunters were all focused on her and had completely ignored the half-breed the entire time. The Corruption had targeted *her*, after all, and the half-breed was essentially insignificant enough so as to be completely ignored. There was no way they would've targeted him; in fact, her protections should have made it so that they *couldn't* target him, as he would've been essentially invisible to their perception.

Did he have some sort of affinity with void energy, and that's what I'm sensing here? Chinli highly doubted it, as he hadn't seemed to be able to use anything like that when she first met him.

However, if the half-breed hadn't done this, then that meant he had been hit by one of the void orbs controlled by the Warped Void Hunters, as impossible as that seemed. Another check of the residue didn't reveal any other solution concerning his whereabouts, and she spent another 10 minutes looking around the ground underneath where the battle took place for some other evidence of his remains.

When she didn't find anything, she wasn't sure if that outcome was fortuitous or not. On the one hand, that could mean he was still alive and could be recaptured and brought back to the Enclave; on the other hand, there was also no evidence that Chinli had ever discovered Vilnesh's spawn in the first place. As the minutes passed by without any trace of where the half-breed had ended up, she mentally wrote him off as lost.

She couldn't spend any more time looking for him, and even if she could somehow parse out exactly what happened to him from the magical residue left in the air, it was already beginning to disperse. Without any other leads, and the feeling of Corruption beginning to target her once again, she resolved to head back toward the Enclave *without* the half-breed in tow.

It wasn't difficult for Chinli to decide not to even mention his presence with her, because while Vilnesh couldn't harm her directly, he could make her life quite exasperating if he learned that she had lost the only semi-viable half-breed spawn ever birthed. Besides, ignorance on everyone's behalf was probably for the best, because it would please her to no end if Vilnesh was further annoyed in his inability to find his spawn in the future.

Yes, I think that's the play here. No one will be the wiser, nor will they even question me about it. I've got more information about what dangers these Apertures will represent to us in the future, after all, and they'll be much more concerned with that for the time being.

With a disappointed glance at where the magical residue from her shredded protection spells was starting to fade, she shot back toward the Enclave and put the whole half-breed disappearance out of her mind.

* * *

Nedira's hands shot to her head as she struggled awake, a throbbing pain that felt like it was threatening to split her brain in half causing her to hold her skull together. Or at least it certainly felt that way.

The light of the fading day was still blinding as she forced her eyes to open, but all she saw was a blurry collection of what she could only assume were clouds in the sky. Closing her eyes and groaning as the pain inside her head slowly faded, she eventually rolled to her side so that she could start picking herself up, only to run into something lying next to her. The act of touching the other person caused them to stir, and she heard a moan of pain that was immediately familiar.

Norde!

Her eyes flew open once again and this time she pushed through the pain and blurriness to see her brother stirring, his own hands pressed up against his temples. Nedira could only commiserate with her sibling as he seemed to be struggling with the same thing she was, but if it was anything like her own pain, it would start to fade soon.

Looking past him, she saw Verne near her brother, and just past the three of them was a quartet of other people that were beginning to wake up, as well. Kimble appeared just as debilitated as she was, but Bartholomew, Vivienne, and Penelope seemed to be recovering faster. *Probably due to some sort of Martial Skill or whatnot.*

"What—?" her brother mumbled from where he was still lying in the short grass around them, his eyes still closed. He licked his lips, which seemed to be dry, before he spoke again. "What happened?"

That was an excellent question. A quick perusal of her mind as the last of the pain from her head faded into a dull ache revealed that her memory of the events that led them all to be asleep and in pain in a field... somewhere... was fragmented or just plain missing. "I don't know," she answered, shaking her head – which she stopped immediately as it only exacerbated the pain.

It wasn't until she looked behind her that she noticed that there were dozens of other people that were also waking up in pain, and suddenly her memories flowed back into her mind as she recognized Major Kuama and the local SIC members from the town of Whittleton. That naturally flowed into her memory of the Aperture and the dangerous three-headed lizards that had been spilling out of it incessantly.

Thankfully, they had managed to temporarily close it through the efforts of... it was closed by... something? An explosion, perhaps? The exact method escaped her, but she figured it was something that the SIC managed to pull off and was therefore successful.

Regardless of her ignorance about how it was closed, they fortunately had a while until it would open again and start spewing out more monsters. There were more important things to worry about, because while this Aperture was the first of its kind, it wasn't going to be the last. They had to warn the rest of the SIC about this development, because they were the only ones that knew about—

Wait. How is it I even know about Apertures and how they operate if this was the first one?

Flashes of some sort of notification she read somewhere filtered through her mind, which held the information she possessed, but whose notification it was remained blank in her memories. Nedira thought for a moment that it might have been her own, but she couldn't seem to pull up anything like that while searching through her Status, so she gave up after a short time of looking for it. In the end she supposed it didn't matter; what mattered was that she had the knowledge, even if she was unsure where it came from.

As unsatisfying as that lack of information was, it still helped to explain their location. Picking up the pack that had fallen to the ground while she helped her brother up, she knew that their group was currently traveling toward Silverledge Academy and Fort Ironwall to attend classes there, and this whole Aperture thing just happened to occur while they were nearby. The exact events surrounding their discovery of it were muddled in her mind, but the important thing was that they discovered it in time and managed to close it – all before it expanded far enough to end up hurting someone.

Though why the local SIC would need the help of a bunch of students and trainees to do something like that was lost on her. A glance at her own robe was enough of a reason, she supposed, because the Fusions on it were so powerful that she couldn't even see them clearly. With them helping to boost their stats, they were probably just as effective as an average Academy or Fort graduate, and at that point they were probably better than nothing.

Looking at the incredible Fusions once again, something about them tickled a memory of a figure creating them, but she couldn't quite grab onto it enough to make sense of it. All she could remember was that it was someone extremely tall and from the Kingdom... but that couldn't be right. No one from the Kingdom was over 6 feet tall, and even that height was a rarity.

Shaking her head at the incongruity of her memories, which fortunately didn't cause any more pain, she looked toward the Major and the rest of the SIC, who appeared just as confused as she was at their current situation. Walking over to the powerful Martial figure, she asked, "Do you happen to know how we ended up *here*?" She gestured to the grass, indicating what she meant.

Unfortunately, the rapidly recovering leader of the local SIC didn't have an answer for her. "Not a clue. Perhaps it's a side effect of the Aperture being closed? I'll be sure to report it once we pass on the information to the higher-ups."

That answer wasn't exactly satisfying, but she couldn't figure out exactly why it wasn't. After all, it sounded completely plausible that it was the Aperture that had caused them all to collapse and hurt their heads, especially as it was something new and they didn't know all that it could do to the local environment. Nevertheless, there was a nagging feeling in the back of her mind that she was missing something obvious.

Shrugging, she gathered with her group, who had largely recovered from whatever it was that had affected them, before saying goodbye to the Major.

"Thank you again for your help," the local SIC leader said, though there was a hint of a question in her statement. "I'd appreciate it if you helped to spread word of this as you journey wherever you're headed to next."

"That was our thought as well," Penelope said in response. When she spoke, Nedira had a sudden urge to punch the Martial in the face for some reason, though when she investigated her feelings over *why* she felt that way, she came up blank. *Did she do something to me?* The whole situation was becoming stranger by the second it felt like, but she wasn't even sure where to look for answers to why it was becoming so strange.

She missed whatever the Major and Penelope said to each other before the SIC took off at a run back toward Whittleton. As her own group turned to leave, heading toward the northeast once again on their journey to her new Academy, Bartholomew kicked at something in the grass.

"Hey, you forgot your staff."

Nedira looked at the staff in her hand before glancing at Norde, Verne, and Kimble. All of them seemed to have their staves, so she wondered who the Martial trainee was speaking to. "No, we've got them."

"Well then, whose is this?" the Noble asked, kicking the staff up with his foot before catching it in his left hand as his spear was occupying his right.

"One of the SIC's?" Penelope asked.

As she looked at the extra staff, Nedira could immediately tell that it wasn't one of the staves that the Mages with the local SIC had been using. For one, it had different Fusions on it, and while she couldn't make them out because they were too complicated, they had a different *feel* to them that she couldn't explain. Secondly, it was near *their* group, and it also matched the construction of her own staff, which was just slightly more natural than a normal Mage's staff she had used back at Copperleaf Academy.

That had to mean it belonged to someone in her own group, especially since the SIC hadn't claimed it before they left. But if every Mage already had a staff, who did it—

A picture of that figure she saw in her memories flashed through her mind, as well as a question that she wasn't sure why she hadn't thought of until that point. *Why did a bunch of students and trainees leave Copperleaf and Pinevalley to travel through the dangerous parts of the Kingdom without an escort of SIC members or access to the Transportation Network? What was it that prompted our departure?*

As much as she attempted to remember something, nothing came up. Only a few random flashes of a tall figure effortlessly producing powerful Fusions that nobody else in the world could create gave a hint as to why. In the end, through deduction and a deep-down feeling she couldn't rightly explain, the only explanation she could deduce was that – as impossible as it seemed – it belonged to someone in their group that was no longer there.

But if that was true, who was it?

The better question probably is: What happened to them?

Nedira didn't know, but she was determined to find out as a longing that surprised her in its intensity shot through her chest at the thought of the figure in her memories.

*I'll find out **who** you are and **where** you went if it's the last thing I do.*

The End

Final Stats

Larek Holsten

Fusionist
Healer
Level 22
Advancement Points (AP): 3/18
Available AP to Distribute: 20
Available Aetheric Force (AF): 5,424

Stama: 830/830
Mana: 1400/1400

Strength: 75 [83] (+)
Body: 75 [83] (+)
Agility: 75 [83] (+)
Intellect: 70 [140] (+)
Acuity: 104 [208] (+)
Pneuma: 747 [1,494]
Pattern Cohesion: 14,940/14,940

Mage Abilities:
Spell – Bark Skin
Spell – Binding Roots
Spell – Fireball
Spell – Furrow
Spell – Ice Spike
Spell – Lesser Restoration
Spell – Light Bending
Spell – Light Orb
Spell – Localized Anesthesia
Spell – Minor Mending
Spell – Rapid Plant Growth
Spell – Repelling Gust
Spell – Static Illusion
Spell – Stone Fist
Spell – Wall of Thorns
Spell – Water Jet
Spell – Wind Barrier
Fusion – Acuity Boost

Fusion – Agility Boost +7
Fusion – Area Chill
Fusion – Body Boost +5
Fusion – Camouflage Sphere +2
Fusion – Camouflage Sphere +5
Fusion – Camouflage Sphere +6
Fusion – Extreme Heat +5
Fusion – Flaming Ball +5
Fusion – Flaming Ball +7
Fusion – Flying Stone +5
Fusion – Flying Stone +7
Fusion – Graduated Illumination Strong Glass +9
Fusion – Graduated Parahealing +7
Fusion – Healing Surge +1
Fusion – Healing Surge +3
Fusion – Healing Surge +5
Fusion – Icy Spike +5
Fusion – Icy Spike +7
Fusion – Illuminate Iron
Fusion – Illuminate Steel
Fusion – Illuminate Stone
Fusion – Illuminate Wood
Fusion – Illusionary Image +3
Fusion – Intellect Boost
Fusion – Intellect and Acuity Boost +10
Fusion – Muffle Sound +3
Fusion – Muffling Air Deflection Barrier +6
Fusion – Multi-Resistance Cloth +9
Fusion – Multi-Resistance Leather +2
Fusion – Multi-Resistance Leather +5
Fusion – Multi-Resistance Leather +7
Fusion – Multi-Resistance Leather +8
Fusion – Multi-Resistance Wood +7
Fusion – Paralytic Light +10
Fusion – Paralytic Touch +10
Fusion – Personal Air Deflection Barrier +4
Fusion – Pneuma Boost
Fusion – Red and White Illuminate Wood +2
Fusion – Repelling Barrier +1
Fusion – Repelling Barrier +4
Fusion – Repelling Barrier +7
Fusion – Repelling Barrier +10

Fusion – Repelling Gust of Air +5
Fusion – Sharpen Iron Edge
Fusion – Sharpen Steel Edge
Fusion – Sharpen Stone Edge
Fusion – Sharpen Wood Edge
Fusion – Space Heater +2
Fusion – Spellcasting Focus Boost +4
Fusion – Strength Boost +1
Fusion – Strength Boost +5
Fusion – Strength and Body Boost +10
Fusion – Strengthen and Sharpen Steel Edge +1
Fusion – Strengthen and Sharpen Steel Edge +7
Fusion – Strengthen Iron
Fusion – Strengthen Leather +1
Fusion – Strengthen Steel
Fusion – Strengthen Steel and Wood +8
Fusion – Strengthen Stone
Fusion – Strengthen Wood
Fusion – Temperature Regulator +3
Fusion – Tree Skin +2
Fusion – Tree Skin +8
Fusion – Water Stream +5
Fusion – Water Stream +7

Martial Abilities:
Battle Art – Furious Rampage

Mage Skills:
Multi-effect Fusion Focus Level 17/17 (170 AF)
Pattern Recognition Level 20/20 (200 AF)
Magical Detection Level 20/20 (200 AF)
Spellcasting Focus Level 20/20 (200 AF)
Focused Division Level 31/31 (310 AF)
Mana Control Level 32/32 (320 AF)
Fusion Level 33/33 (330 AF)
Pattern Formation Level 33/33 (330 AF)

Martial Skills:
Stama Subjugation Level 1/20 (200 AF)
Blunt Weapon Expertise Level 1/20 (200 AF)
Bladed Weapon Expertise Level 2/20 (200 AF)
Throwing Level 5/20 (200 AF)

Dodge Level 10/20 (200 AF)
Pain Immunity Level 20/20 (N/A)
Body Regeneration Level 30/30 (300 AF)

General Skills:
Cooking Level 1
Bargaining Level 7
Beast Control Level 9
Leadership Level 11
Writing Level 11
Long-Distance Running Level 10
Saw Handling Level 15
Speaking Level 16
Reading Level 17
Listening Level 42
Axe Handling Level 83

Author's Note

Thank you for reading Aetheric InFusion!

I want to thank all of my readers for the absolutely awesome response that this series has received, and I'm more excited to write more of this story than just about any other work I've done to date! I'm excited for what Larek gets up to next!

There is a lot more of Larek's story to tell, so if you want to read more, you can visit the series page on Royal Road under **The Fusionist**, or subscribe to my Patreon and read advance chapters for as little as $2 a month!

Again, thank you for reading, and I implore you to consider leaving a review – I love 5-star ones! Reviews make it more likely that others will pick up a good book and read it!

If you enjoy dungeon core, dungeon corps, dungeon master, dungeon lord, dungeonlit, or any other type of dungeon-themed stories and content, check out the Dungeon Corps Facebook group, where you can find all sorts of dungeon content.

If you would like to learn more about the GameLit genre, please join the GameLit Society Facebook group.

LitRPG is a growing subgenre of GameLit – if you are fond of LitRPG, Fantasy, Space Opera, and the Cyberpunk styles of books, please join the LitRPG Books Facebook group.

For other great Facebook groups, visit LitRPG Rebels, LitRPG Forum, and LitRPG and GameLit Readers.

Also, on Amazon, check out the LitRPG storefront for a large selection of LitRPG, GameLit, and Dungeon Core books from the biggest authors in the genre!

If you would like to contact me with any questions, comments, or suggestions for future books you would like to see, you can reach me at jonathanbrooksauthor@gmail.com.

Visit my Patreon page at https://www.patreon.com/jonathanbrooksauthor and become a patron for as little as $2 a month! As a patron, you have access to my current Dungeon Core works-in-progress, as well as advance chapters of the stories I have running on Royal Road. So, if you can't wait to find out what happens next in one of my series, this is the place for you!

I will try to keep my blog updated with any new developments, which you can find on my Author Page on Amazon. In addition, you can check out and like my Facebook page at https://www.facebook.com/dungeoncorejonathanbrooks as well as these other social media sites:

TikTok: @dungeoncorebooks
Instagram: dungeoncorebooks
Reddit: r/dungeoncorebooks
Twitter/X: @DungeonCoreBook
Threads: dungeoncorebooks

To sign up for my mailing list, please visit:
http://eepurl.com/dl0bK5

To learn more about LitRPG, talk to authors including myself, and just have an awesome time, please join the LitRPG Group.

Books by Jonathan Brooks

Glendaria Awakens Trilogy
Dungeon Player (Audiobook available)
Dungeon Crisis (Audiobook available)
Dungeon Guild (Audiobook available)
Glendaria Awakens Trilogy Compilation w/bonus material (Audiobook available)

Uniworld Online Trilogy (2nd Edition)
The Song Maiden (Audiobook available)
The Song Mistress (Audiobook available)
The Song Matron (Audiobook available)
Uniworld Online Trilogy Compilation (Audiobook available)

Station Cores Series
The Station Core (Audiobook available)
The Quizard Mountains (Audiobook available)
The Guardian Guild (Audiobook available)
The Kingdom Rises (Audiobook available)
The Other Core (Audiobook available)
Station Cores Compilation Complete: Books 1-5 (Audiobook available)

Spirit Cores Series
Core of Fear (Audiobook available)
Children of Fear (Audiobook available)
Carnival of Fear (Audiobook available)
Community of Fear
Caverns of Fear
Spirit Core Complete Series: Books 1-5

Dungeon World Series
Dungeon World (Audiobook available)
Dungeon World 2 (Audiobook available)
Dungeon World 3 (Audiobook available)
Dungeon World 4 (Audiobook available)
Dungeon World 5 (Audiobook available)
Dungeon World Box Set: Books 1-5 (Audiobook available)

Dungeon Crafting Series
The Crafter's Dungeon (Audiobook available)
The Crafter's Defense (Audiobook available)
The Crafter's Dilemma (Audiobook available)
The Crafter's Darkness (Audiobook available)
The Crafter's Dominion (Audiobook available)
The Crafter's Dynasty (Audiobook available)
Dungeon Crafting Series: Books 1 – 3 (Audiobook available)
Dungeon Crafting Series: Books 4 – 6 (Audiobook available)

The Hapless Dungeon Fairy Series

The Dungeon Fairy (Audiobook available)
The Dungeon Fairy: Two Choices (Audiobook available)
The Dungeon Fairy: Three Lives (Audiobook available)
The Dungeon Fairy: Four Days (Audiobook available)
The Dungeon Fairy: Box Set Books 1-4 (Audiobook available)

Serious Probabilities Series
Dungeon of Chance: Even Odds (Audiobook available)
Dungeon of Chance: Double or Nothing (Audiobook available)
Dungeon of Chance: All-in (Audiobook available)
Dungeon of Chance Complete Series: Books 1-3 (Audiobook available)

The Body's Dungeon (with Jeffrey "Falcon" Logue)
Bio Dungeon: Symbiote (Audiobook available)
Bio Dungeon: Parasyte (Audiobook available)
Bio Dungeon: Hemostasis (Audiobook available)
Bio Dungeon Omnibus (Audiobook available)

Tales of Dungeons Anthology
Tales of Dungeons Vol. 2
Tales of Dungeons Vol. 3
Tales of Dungeons All Hallows 2020

Dimensional Dungeon Cores
Core Establishment (Audiobook available)
Core Construction (Audiobook available)
Core Convergence (Audiobook available)
Core Retribution (Audiobook available)
Core Domination (Audiobook available)
Dimensional Dungeon Cores Complete Series

Holiday Dungeon Core
Christmas Core (Audiobook available)
Valentine Core (Audiobook available)
Easter Core (Audiobook available)
Independence Core (Audiobook available)
Halloween Core (Audiobook available)
Holiday Dungeon Core Complete Series (Audiobook available)

Time Core
Frozen Time (Audiobook available)
Corrupted Time (Audiobook available)
Poisoned Time (Audiobook available)
Scorched Time (Audiobook available)
Time Core Collection Books 1-4

Magical Fusion
The Fusionist (Audiobook available)
Academic ConFusion (Audiobook available)
Aetheric InFusion (Audiobook coming soon)
Global DifFusion (March 20, 2024)

Made in United States
Troutdale, OR
05/10/2024